JUSTIN SCOTT

THE MAN WHO LOVED THE *NORMANDIE*

HarperCollins*Publishers*

HarperCollins*Publishers*
77–85 Fulham Palace Road,
Hammersmith, London W6 8JB

This paperback edition 1993
1 3 5 7 9 8 6 4 2

First published in paperback by Granada Publishing 1983

First published in Great Britain by
Granada Publishing 1982
US edition published under the title *Normandie* Triangle

Set in Meridien

Printed in Great Britain

Grateful acknowlegement is made to Ernest Benn Ltd for
permission to reprint from the poem 'Unforgotten' by Robert
Service, from *The Complete Poems of Robert Service*.

Justin Scott

Justin Scott is the author of *The Shipkiller*, *The Auction*, *A Pride of Kings*, *Rampage*, *The Cossack's Bride* and, most recently, *The Empty Eye of the Sea*. Born in New York City in 1944, he now lives in Connecticut with his actress wife, Gloria Hoye.

For Gloria Hoye

'And ah, it's strange . . .
   Between these two there rolls an ocean wide;
   Yet he is in the garden by her side
And she is in the garret there with him.'

– Robert Service

NORMANDIE

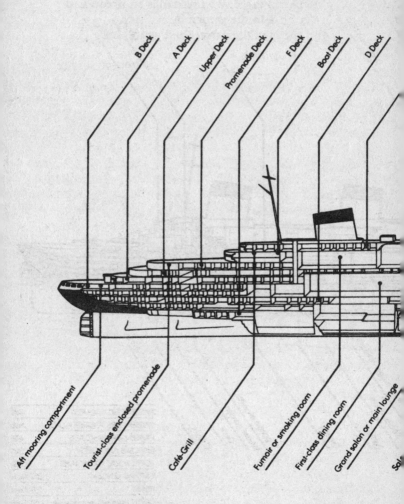

B Deck

A Deck

Upper Deck

Promenade Deck

F Deck

Boat Deck

D Deck

Aft mooring compartment

Tourist-class enclosed promenade

Café-Grill

Fumoir or smoking room

First-class dining room

Grand salon or main lounge

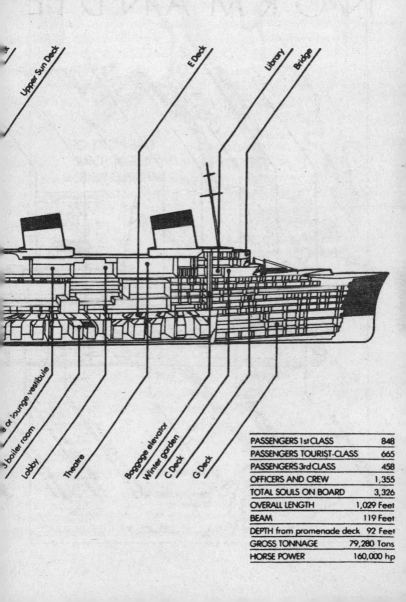

Upper Sun Deck

E Deck

Library

Bridge

...e or lounge vestibule

...3 boiler room

Lobby

Theatre

Baggage elevator

Winter garden

C Deck

G Deck

PASSENGERS 1st CLASS	848
PASSENGERS TOURIST-CLASS	665
PASSENGERS 3rd CLASS	458
OFFICERS AND CREW	1,355
TOTAL SOULS ON BOARD	3,326
OVERALL LENGTH	1,029 Feet
BEAM	119 Feet
DEPTH from promenade deck	92 Feet
GROSS TONNAGE	79,280 Tons
HORSE POWER	160,000 hp

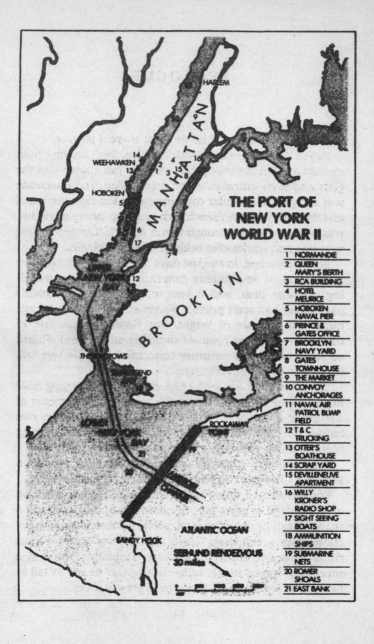

THE PORT OF
NEW YORK
WORLD WAR II

HARLEM

MANHATTAN

BROOKLYN

WEEHAWKEN

HOBOKEN

THE NARROWS

ROCKAWAY

SANDY HOOK

ATLANTIC OCEAN

SEEHUND RENDEZVOUS
30 miles

1 NORMANDIE
2 QUEEN
   MARY'S BERTH
3 RCA BUILDING
4 HOTEL
   MEURICE
5 HOBOKEN
   NAVAL PIER
6 PRINCE &
   GATES OFFICE
7 BROOKLYN
   NAVY YARD
8 GATES
   TOWNHOUSE
9 THE MARKET
10 CONVOY
   ANCHORAGES
11 NAVAL AIR
   PATROL BLIMP
   FIELD
12 T & C
   TRUCKING
13 OTTER'S
   BOATHOUSE
14 SCRAP YARD
15 DEVILLENEUVE
   APARTMENT
16 WILLY
   KRONER'S
   RADIO SHOP
17 SIGHT SEEING
   BOATS
18 AMMUNITION
   SHIPS
19 SUBMARINE
   NETS
20 ROVER
   SHOALS
21 EAST BANK

PROLOGUE

The Dutchman asked if he thought there'd be war.

Steven Gates answered with a blithe, 'No,' keeping both eyes on a girl in absinthe green who had just appeared in the glass and silver entrance to the grand salon. The *Normandie* was carrying her regular complement of the rich, the social and the celebrated. A French orchestra, top-heavy in violins, was swinging lushly through Glenn Miller's 'Careless', while stewards and scarlet-clad bellboys served cocktails.

Back in Europe, in the last days of August 1939, panicky tourists might be mobbing American embassies, demanding a rescue fleet, and it was true that the *Normandie*'s passengers had seen pursuit planes at Le Havre and huge mines off the Isle of Wight, but Gates saw no one in this vast two-storey room of glittering mirrors and vibrant colour who looked seriously concerned that the war talk was more than conversation.

The girl started across the first-class lounge, turning male heads as she weaved among the formal arrangements of Aubusson upholstered chairs. The table nearest Gates was empty, but he couldn't believe that a girl that good-looking was travelling alone.

'They were evacuating Paris,' the Dutchman protested to Kay and Charlie. 'You should have seen the rail stations.'

The girl veered towards the empty table and, so far, no one had risen to greet her. Her hair was auburn, too soft a shade to call her a redhead. A portrait painter would have chosen her green dress – lush spring grass and blossoms rising from the snow of her bare shoulders. She had a sure, long-legged stride. In heels, she was nearly as tall as he, and as leanly built. She'd be a great dancer.

'We've seen these scares before,' said Gates's uncle. Richard Prince was a grey-haired man, splendidly old-fashioned in white tie and tails.

Still alone, the girl stopped at the empty table and sat down, six feet from them. A steward appeared. *'Une fine à l'eau. S'il vous plaît.'* She had a contralto voice, rich and musical.

'Many say it's gone beyond diplomacy,' the Dutchman persisted gravely. Gates couldn't recall a crossing when Uncle Richard hadn't adopted an orphan. This van-Something-or-Other had cornered Uncle Richard in the *fumoir* last night, so of course the family had had to ask him for cocktails. He was a huge man, bigger than Charlie even, with golden hair and wide, handsome face usually split by a smile. When he didn't agree, or didn't understand, the smile would flicker for a second. An instant later, he would laugh.

Gates glanced over at the girl. She had a beautiful nose, fine cheeks, and a strong chin. He said, with another glance at her, 'The Polish crisis this summer will blow over just like the Czech crisis *last* summer, and the Austrian crisis, the Spanish crisis and the Ethiopian crisis the summers before. Not to mention the League of Nations crisis, which lurches into its second decade.'

Van-Something-or-Other's smile held . . . tightly? . . . and the girl seemed to prick up her ears at the mention of the League, so Gates enlarged his explanation. 'Summer's the crisis season in Europe. We get hurricanes. You get war scares.'

The girl looked him full in the face. She had improbably pale blue eyes and she was English. 'That's absurd.'

'I beg your pardon?' Gates replied.

'Unless you know something about Poland none of the rest of us do.' They all turned to look at her. 'I beg your pardon.' she said. 'I didn't mean to interrupt your party.'

'No, no, that's all right,' said Gates. 'I don't know about Poland, but if Nazi raiders were going to cut the sea lanes, I doubt that British bankers would have joined the combine my uncle and I formed to build a new liner. Bankers and shipbuilders have profited from European crises for centuries. If they say no war, I figure they're right.'

'They said the same thing in 1914. Then it was the Russian Steamroller; now it's the Maginot line.'

'Are you saying that the British government is really going to stick by its ultimatum if the Nazis invade Poland?'

'They haven't consulted me,' she said with a smile, 'but I do think there's a general feeling that we've got to stop totalitarianism *now*!'

The Dutchman interrupted. 'War is a terrible way to do it.'

She nodded agreement. 'I know. The World War mutilated my parents' generation. My mother lost her first husband and my father lost all his brothers.'

'But the German economy isn't geared up for a war,' Gates insisted. 'And their *Kriegsmarine* is five years from strength. That's a fact.'

Charlie Collins, Gates's brother-in-law, barked a harsh laugh. 'Spoken like a guy who's never sighted the Condor Legion down the wrong end of a gun barrel, Junior.'

The English girl turned to Charlie. Gates noticed she had a way of directly facing the person to whom she spoke; and if interrupting a table full of strangers bothered her, she didn't show it. 'Did you fight with the International Brigades in Spain?'

Charlie brushed at his thick black hair. 'Yeah.'

'He was wounded,' said Kay, Charlie's wife.

Charlie gave her a look, then: 'The French'll end up wishing they'd spent the sixty million bucks for this ship on an air force. It's going to be goodbye passenger liners, *American Glory* included. Sorry, Junior. You got to face facts. You and Uncle Richard are heading back to your drawing board all right, but it's going to be destroyers and aircraft carriers for a long time to come.'

Gates looked away, his attention caught by the English

girl who was watching something with a smile of delight. It was Jimmy Stewart, the young Hollywood actor, walking with a beautiful woman across the salon. As they passed the orchestra, they entwined as gracefully as two plumes of steam and danced a moment, silhouetted by a brilliant cascade of sculpted Lalique glass. The tableau was framed by the English girl's profile and Gates thought, this is too beautiful to end.

'Let's have champagne, Uncle Richard. I think the *American Glory* could use a toast. That's our ship,' he explained to the girl.

'Are you shipbuilders?'

'Designers. Naval architects.'

'Let me buy the bottle,' said van Slough, and signalled the steward over Richard Prince's protests. Prince stood up and said to the girl, 'Please join us. I'm Richard Prince.'

She rose and shook his hand and let him draw her into their circle. 'Thank you. I'm Cordelia Grey.'

'My niece, Kay Collins, and her husband Charlie,' he continued, moving over to make room between himself and Gates. 'And this is my nephew, Steven Gates.'

She shook hands firmly, but her fingers were delicate, finer than the bold walk suggested. Gates said hello. Her eyes held his for a heartbeat, then flickered towards the Dutchman, who had risen also.

'And this is our friend, Hendrick van Slough.'

Van Slough bowed his head with easy grace. 'Just Rik. Are you enjoying the voyage, Cordelia?'

'Actually, everyone calls me Cordi, please. I'm beginning to, but I felt awful until an hour ago. I'm a terrible sailor.'

'So far she's steady as a rock,' said Gates. 'Let's hope it stays calm. The *Normandie*'s a snappy roller. We were on her maiden eastbound voyage four years ago and she was smashing Lalique like it came from Woolworth's. What do you think of the *Normandie*?'

Cordi did not answer immediately. Instead, she glanced

down the long vista through the *fumoir* and up the broad stairs to the café-grill hundreds of feet astern. Her gaze returned to the grand salon with its gleaming columns and lighted cascades. The ceiling was high and uncluttered, the carpet a lavish blue. Nearby, a Lelen mural, gold leaf and paint on glass, held straining maidens, maddened horses, and doves and cupids in extravagant harmony.

'Will your *American Glory* look like this?' asked van Slough.

'No. She'll be as special. But different.'

Prince smiled. 'We only steal the best. Her hull is spectacular. She's got a very interesting electric drive – something Steven and I have had a chance to perfect on aircraft carrier engines. We'll do her a few knots better, I think.'

'Uncle Richard is being kind,' said Gates. 'Engines are his strong suit. I'm a hull man. He's an expert on high-pressure steam.'

'Will your ship be as fast as the *Queen Mary?*' asked Cordi.

'Now you've done it,' said Kay. 'In a sec they'll be talking about shaft horsepower.'

'The *Queen Mary* is much more conventional than the *Normandie* and our ship.'

'Oh, really? But she's faster.'

The two ships had been trading the Blue Riband since 1936.

'Marginally faster than the *Normandie*, with forty thousand extra horsepower,' replied Gates. He grinned and added, 'Technically speaking, the *American Glory* will eat the *Queen Mary* for breakfast.'

'Technically speaking, I gather she's still on the drawing board,' Cordi grinned back.

'Sure. We've just locked up our financing. We'll launch her at the end of '41.'

'Here's the champagne!' said van Slough. Three stewards arrived with a silver tray of fluted champagne glasses, a silver champagne bucket, and a bottle of Moët, which they presented to van Slough, then wrapped in white linen, opened with a discreet *pop*, and poured. Van Slough raised his glass.

'I shall make a toast for everyone. To the *Queen Mary* for Cordi. To the *Normandie*, for all of us tonight. And for the *American Glory*, in her time.'

They drank van Slough's toast and then he asked, 'Will you be staying in New York, Cordi?'

Gates found himself hoping she'd say yes. Their eyes brushed for a moment as she lowered her glass.

She said, 'That depends. I'm a radio correspondent. The BBC has assigned me to broadcast some programmes from the British pavilion at the World's Fair. I might stay if they like my work. Of course if there's war, I'll return home immediately. But we won't talk about that,' she added with a smile to Gates. Gates smiled back. Her work explained her magnificent voice.

'Do you live in New York?'

'We do,' said Kay, 'but I don't know about Rik.'

'I'm considering going into business there,' said Rik.

'You're emigrating from Holland?'

'No. I've never been to Holland. I'm from the Dutch East Indies, Djakarta. But I had business in France.' He glanced at the orchestra. Gates guessed what he was going to do and decided as quickly that he did not want that to happen tonight. He interrupted as van Slough asked Cordi if she'd like to dance with him, 'Cordi, we've got an empty place at our table. I'm sure Uncle Richard can fix it up with the *maître d'hôtel*. Would you like to join us?'

'Please do,' Uncle Richard said, with an expression that told Gates he'd noticed the byplay.

Van Slough's smile closed to a thin line as he watched the Prince and Gates family depart the grand salon with the English girl. Damned *touching* . . . not to mention inconvenient . . . the way the older man had interfered on his nephew Gates's behalf to stop her from dancing with him.

What did they think of him ... the Dutchman? Had he been too eager? He wished he had noted earlier the father-and-son aspect of the relationship between the naval architects. If he had, he would not have asked the girl to dance, not when it was obvious that Gates had been so taken with her. Should he look elsewhere, try some new names on his passenger list – ?

'Monsieur van Slough?'

One of the little bellboys in red was approaching with a silver tray. Remarkable how quickly they recognized individual passengers. Or was it because he was travelling as a guest of the French Line?

A radiogram lay on the tray. Van Slough opened it warily. Tagged with the indicator Urgent, the message itself was in cipher, but the boy, a thin twelve- or fourteen-year-old with an orphan's knowing eyes – victim of twentieth-century European chaos as he, too, had been – betrayed no surprise. Business information beamed by ship's radio was routinely enciphered.

Van Slough pulled a leather-bound notepad from his dinner jacket. 'Come back in five minutes for my reply.'

'No, monsieur. The radio room is closed.'

'What?'

'By the captain's order.'

Radio silence already. 'How did this get through?'

'It was the last, monsieur.'

'Tell the captain – '

An incredulous look scampered across the boy's face, followed by a smirk. Van Slough handed him ten francs.

'Tell the *purser* that Mr van Slough must see the captain immediately.'

The boy ran across the salon, empty now, the last passengers having gone down to the single seating of dinner. Van Slough knew he would miss his, even as he started to break down the short radiogram, because

17

at this stage any message at all had to convey trouble. The first word he deciphered – his code name – assuredly confirmed this.

The short message was far worse than he'd imagined or expected. Van Slough looked at the radiogram one last time and crumpled it in his hand. The one man in Germany who knew his code name – and the only man whom he had ever believed in – had lost his nerve: RETURN HOME ON THE *BREMEN*.

They had stopped at the head of the broad stairs that led down to the gigantic first-class dining room, which was so long that the distant reaches narrowed in perspective, the snowy tables diminishing endlessly. Three storeys high, three hundred feet long, with walls of decorated glass lined with lighted glass cascades like upended chandeliers and topped by a coffered gilt and mirror ceiling, the *Normandie*'s *salle à manger* dwarfed anything in New York or London.

'Good Lord,' said Cordi.

'They say it's longer than the Hall of Mirrors at Versailles,' Gates said.

'But it's floating.'

'Steaming,' said Prince, 'at thirty knots. We'll probably cover seventy sea miles before desert. Shall we go down?'

They descended as a group, with Cordi and Kay in the lead. Kay had let her blonde hair grow long this summer, and heads turned again as the two women came into view. Prince dealt with the *maître d'hôtel* and Gates said, 'Anyone against more champagne?'

Gates was happier than he'd been since the ship sailed. The girl had brought back the excitement he had hoped for – a celebration of hard-won summer victories in London for the *American Glory*, and the joy of the great *Normandie*. And she'd deflected the speculation about the war, sparking the moment, at least leaving room for hope. For all that, Gates was grateful.

They brought the champagne, and he proposed a toast of 'peace', and even Charlie couldn't break his mood with a sarcastic 'in our time' reference to Munich.

A group taking their seats at a round table for six near the stairs caught Cordi's eye. 'Isn't that George Raft and Sonja Henie?'

Prince glanced across the glittering room. 'Yes.'

George Raft waved and Prince waved back. Constance Bennett and Roland Young gestured for him to visit them. He held back until they started calling across tables. 'I guess I'm going to have to go over there and say hello. Excuse me.'

Cordi was delighted. 'How in the world does your uncle know such stars?'

'My father introduced him to some actresses back in the twenties. Uncle Richard has designed a fair number of the big yachts in Hollywood.'

'Why don't you go over and say hello, too? I'm all right here.'

'No thanks, they're really his friends.'

Cordi smiled. 'Don't you like beautiful actresses?'

'I don't design yachts.'

'Well, I must say I think your uncle's sweet, but I can't see him as a Lothario in hot pursuit of actresses.'

'My father was more the actress chaser.'

'Is your mother an actress?'

'No.' It was a subject he didn't like but somehow often got onto it.

'But – oh, I think I've stepped in it. Too much champers. Well, let's see . . . I was in the theatre for a while.'

'Really?' Yes, she had the combination of beauty and intense focus common to actresses he'd met.

'I played the West End. I was awful. Far too stiff. Then one day a man from the BBC came back and offered me a job. He said I had a perfect voice for the microphone.'

'*Radio?* I think my father at least used to suggest movies. Was he serious?'

'A bit of both. He was looking for a woman correspondent and I had a pretty good education to go with the voice, so here I am.'

'First job?'

'Oh, no. I did all sorts of trivial features in England and I read some radio plays. But lately I've been covering the League of Nations in Switzerland, with Alec – he's the man who gave me the first job.'

Gates saw no point in asking any more about Alec . . . he suspected she'd brought him up deliberately to define the limits of her availability.

Cordi filled the silence. 'Is your uncle married?'

'No. He's always been a bachelor, except he's . . . was sort of a father to Kay and me when my father left. Sort of inherited us after the Crash.'

After coffee Prince said, 'Why don't you two take a walk on deck? Ought to be warm enough.'

Gates walked Cordi to her cabin to get a wrap. In the elevator a red-faced American man was complaining to an icily reserved French woman that the *Normandie*'s radio room was closed. 'Radio's supposed to go twenty-four hours. I can't reach my broker. Wonder what's going on?'

Cordi's bare white shoulder kept brushing Gates's arm each time they passed other people in the long corridor. 'Everyone was worried about my going on a ship because of the war threat. My mother thought I should take the Pan American Clipper. But she worries about everything I do.'

'The Clipper would give her something to worry about.'

'Oh, I like flying. My cousin's a flight sergeant. He took me up in a Hurricane last summer. His wing commander had a fit – Here's my cabin, I'll just be a second.'

She was back quickly, wearing a short-sleeved brocaded Eton jacket and smelling faintly of new perfume. Something about her soft auburn hair had changed and her lipstick was darker, startlingly red on her pale, pale skin, and again he thought of flowers in the snow.

'Is something the matter?' she asked, the smooth skin around her eyes crinkling.

'No. Say, after a walk, would you like to go up to the grill and dance?'

The first officer and chief radio officer hovered impatiently as the *Normandie*'s radio operator laboriously tapped out the long string of letter blocks that composed van Slough's ciphered refusal to return to Germany. The first officer muttered in rapid French, 'Those idiots in Le Havre might not be so generous with our radio if they were aboard.'

Van Slough stepped into the light. In addition to his native German he spoke good Italian and Dutch, flawless English and enough French to get by. He said with a broad smile, '*I* am aboard.'

'Pardon, Monsieur van Slough.' The Frenchman coloured. 'I'm sorry, I — '

Van Slough laughed and clapped him on the back. 'Not at all. Don't worry about it. I sympathize, my friend. I don't like revealing the ship's position either, considering conditions, but your company would not have let me send if they didn't think my signal was important. If there's a war, the *Paris* will be even more in the way than it is now.' The French Line's *Paris* had burned and capsized beside her pier at Le Havre the year before.

'But why do you send to Hamburg?' asked the radio officer, encouraged by van Slough's friendliness.

'I have divers working under the River Elbe,' van Slough told him gravely, subtly putting the onus for the divers' safety on the Frenchman. 'I must get them out of Germany — before it is too late.'

'And is that why you send in cipher?'

'Of course. The Germans will intern Dutchmen, particularly skilled divers.' Van Slough looked at them both, then smiled abruptly, drawing them deeper into his camp. 'Fortunately your company has persuaded your government to help them cross the border. I'll return to France with the *Normandie* – if they get out safely – and we'll start salvage immediately. So you can see good reason to send this message. Le Havre must be cleared.'

'*Oui, monsieur.*'

Van Slough looked away. There were no divers, Dutch or otherwise.

The Abwehr received overseas transmissions in Hamburg.

And van Slough, a salvage expert from the Dutch East Indies, was, of course, dead, having had the misfortune to bear a strong resemblance in age, colouring and physique to the man whom Admiral Wilhelm Canaris, the chief of German military intelligence, had named the Otter.

'Must we wait for their reply?'

He toyed with them a moment, pretending he hadn't heard, as the radio operator tapped out the last of the letter blocks.

'Monsieur van Slough? May we shut down the radio?'

If he let them silence the radio, the Otter would, in effect, be punishing Uncle Willy's loss of nerve with a *fait accompli*. The reply the radio operator had sent was a new plan, but also a flat-out refusal to obey. And a message like that he had never sent – not from South America, Spain or Africa.

Though he looked thirty, he was twenty-four years old – born in 1915, in the middle of the World War – and he had been in Canaris's thrall since he was nineteen. For five years he had been his protégé and for five years he had obeyed. But Uncle Willy always said that Germany needed decisive men – bold soldiers – to implement the will of the nation and defend her in a hostile world. So he was sending Uncle Willy a plan. His own plan. Decisive.

But it was hard to go against Uncle Willy, despite the exhilaration of stepping out on his own, perhaps because it hurt to realize that the man he worshipped could also be crippled by his own indecision.

'Monsieur van Slough?' The anxious Frenchman cut into his thoughts before he'd regained control. His amiable face tightened and the officer almost recoiled in the instant it took the Otter to replace the murder in his eyes with another broad smile.

'No reply, thank you. You fellows have been great. Do you suppose the captain would object if I sent a bottle of Moët to your quarters? Yes? I'll send him one too. Then, of course, he can't.'

No reply. No debate. Uncle Willy had taught him too much to waste time in the eleventh hour. He knew how to set up business fronts with Abwehr money. And he knew how to recruit. Had Uncle Willy forgotten that the South Atlantic and Indian Oceans were ringed with secret supply dumps they had established together in foreign cities to support German raiding ships in the coming war against England? Had he forgotten that the Otter had learned by surviving behind Republican lines in the Spanish War how to assess which agent to trust, and which agent to kill?

Later, Uncle Willy could assign him to England, if he still insisted, if he hadn't regained his nerve. And later the Otter would go. When he was ready. When he had done what Uncle Willy had created him to do.

But not before – he realized with a sense of being born new, better, solitary – not before he had made a place in New York, had winnowed out the Abwehr contacts among the German-American Bundists and the Irish-American Sinn Feiners so anxious to help, so naive about what was needed in – intended for – the city destined to become the enemy's most vital harbour.

The brightly lighted café-grill was a large modern room high above the gracefully terraced stern decks. Steven led Cordi Grey past a beautiful curved bar opposite a huge half-circle of windows that overlooked the wake, which shone like cream in the moonlight. The furniture was tautly modern, in severe contrast to the rest of the ship, a concentration of polished steel and glass. In plain sight of the bar, and of the large crowd of people drinking at the tables, was the dance floor. The song the orchestra was playing was one of Cordi's favourites, 'Smoke Gets in Your Eyes'.

She followed him confidently. Their sides touched, shoulder to thigh through a promenade and joined tightly as they pivoted around their intertwined legs. A look passed between them before she turned her face.

'Very nice,' said Gates.

'It's so warm in here.'

'Let me help you,' said Gates. He slipped her Eton jacket off her shoulders and handed it to a steward without missing a beat.

Cordi had never moved like this in her life. When Alec had kissed her goodbye for the last time in Southampton he'd said, 'New world, new life, sorry for the corn, I'll miss you.'

'I'm coming back.'

Alec had shaken his greying head, for the first time admitting what they both knew wasn't necessarily true, admitting that this World's Fair assignment was Cordi's chance to break away on her own.

'But I will,' she'd insisted. And here she was two nights later blithely letting this happen – or *making* it happen – accelerating events. Alec had been right. But then he always was, the damned nuisance about an older man. Steven was smiling, his eyes full with her. He had a good mouth. Now when he held her his hand touched her bare back, where her jacket had been. They did another turn. She felt her breasts hard against his chest and their legs joined tighter.

Gates slowed their turns and held her firmly as they weaved a path through the traffic jam in front of the orchestra. She felt as if the whole dance floor was theirs, coupled to the liquid music and the throb of the *Normandie*'s propellers beating the sea under them. She felt . . . bonded to Gates, who seemed to feel it too, and whose legs linked to hers through every step.

'This is lovely,' she whispered, knowing that there was something different in her voice than the physical flirtation of dancing, and when the song ended and a fast one began she said, 'That's too fast,' and stopped on the edge of the dance floor. Their eyes met, turned away. Cordi tossed her head, colour rising in her cheeks. 'I'm awfully warm,' she said, fanning herself with her hand.

'Maybe we should take a walk, cool off?'

They looked at each other and the bond passed powerfully between them again, but electric now, not liquid, and flickering like a blue arc. Cordi looked down, then nodded her head. The smiling steward appeared magically with her jacket. Gates helped her into it on the way to the deck. She leaned back against him as they passed through the door and suddenly alone, she turned to face him, her eyes sure, her hair lifting in the wind, her lips parting.

The *Normandie* heeled suddenly, thrusting them back through the door. Glasses slid across tables and the entire café-grill assumed a steep slant. The dancers stopped in midstep, bracing themselves, and the orchestra faltered with a clatter of falling music stands.

'No,' Gates said.

Cordi steadied herself with a hand on his arm. 'What happened?'

Gates knew too well. An awful certainty spread through him. He felt very cold. While they were dancing the steward had drawn heavy curtains over the big windows. He saw his uncle at a table across the room – saw his sombre expression and the stunned, hurt look that he now realized had been there all evening, just behind Richard Prince's smile.

'What is it, Steven?'

The *Normandie* straightened up as abruptly as she'd heeled. The speeding ship had turned to port – Gates guessed about thirty degrees. He gazed around the hushed grill room, determined to hope that she had only manoeuvred to avoid another ship. But sensitive to the great liner's rhythms, he felt a new vibration begin to grow in her. Her engineers were pouring on the oil, sluicing more steam through her turbines, accelerating her dynamos as her huge four-bladed propellers chewed harder into the North Atlantic.

Gates met his uncle's eyes and shared a long, agonized look.

'It seems to have started,' said Prince, signalling for a steward.

Gates sank into a chair, ignoring the excited conversations springing up at the tables around him. Silent, he waited for the final confirmation. It was ten minutes coming.

The liner changed course again – violently, without warning – slamming thirty degrees back to starboard, and he couldn't deny it any longer.

The *Normandie* was zigzagging. Blacked out, and with her radios silent. *The war had begun.* The sea belonged to the raiders.

Book I

1

Two and a half years later, Steven Gates paused beneath the West Side Highway to behold the great liner. Thirty knots of cold wind from Jersey had stacked dirty ice between the *Normandie* and the dismal, unused Cunard Pier 90, two hundred feet north. The *Queen Mary* had gone, as had the new *Elizabeth*, trooping to the Empire. But the *Normandie* had stayed here at the foot of Forty-eighth street, lovingly maintained by a dwindling skeleton crew who had seen her through most of the two and a half years since her last voyage – the 'phony war', *blitzkreig*, the incredible collapse of France, the Battle of Britain, which Gates had tasted in London while coordinating British ship designs with American yard practices, and the German attack on Russia.

She had waited. And then, just two months earlier, the Japanese had attacked Pearl Harbor. The US Navy had commandeered her, and Gates had been among the marine architects hired to do a rough survey. On Christmas Eve the navy assigned scores of contracts to convert her into a troop ship, and two thousand workmen began swarming over the express liner, stripping her finery, reducing her to her basic capacity to carry human beings swiftly over water.

Now she was raising steam at last, and though a shroud of grey paint hid her colours and scaffolds clawed at her sides, the long war couldn't deny the majesty of her incomparable hull, nor the sleek and elegant lines that her diamond bows and mighty ovoid funnels etched from the sky above the Hudson. The navy had tacked the name *USS Lafayette* onto her after Pearl Harbor, but it was as crude a façade as the battle paint they slopped on her flanks, and all New York City still called her the *Normandie*.

Gates flashed his pass at a kid shivering in a brand new Coast Guard uniform outside Pier 88. He'd been in England again for sea trials of an Anglo-American escort boat and he wondered what sad things they'd done to the *Normandie* in the month he'd been gone.

Apprentice welders and electricians mobbed her gangways. It looked as if the painters had scraped the river mud from her waterline, but aboard she was desperately shabby. They'd emptied the first-class lobbies and broad stairways of furniture, stripped carpets, murals and decorative glass. Windows were painted out, walls holed where fittings had been ripped away, and ceilings ugly with naked wires dangling where Lalique had glowed. Workmen were assembling standee bunks – three-tiered beds of pipe and canvas – barracks for the troops.

The atmosphere was oddly festive. The war had channelled regular pay envelopes into neighbourhoods that hadn't seen steady work since the Crash. Shipyards were jammed up building convoy escorts, carriers, cruisers, and freighters. Gates had never seen so many apprentices on one job and he had an uncomfortable feeling that the last of the Depression's unemployed had found work on the *Normandie*.

Gates had come back to her this bitter-cold February afternoon in 1942 because his brother-in-law Charlie Collins, who was a welding foreman for one of the contractors, had said this morning at breakfast that the navy had lost control of the job. Uncle Richard had agreed that Gates should have a look, and if it was as bad as Charlie said, they'd jump channels to the Secretary of the Navy.

In the slip between Pier 88 and Pier 90 tugboats and barges were nuzzling up to the open cargo ports that breeched the thousand feet of her hull, loading foodstuffs and building materials. Steer and hog halves sprawled on a provisioning barge, carcasses frozen solid in the zero temperature. Far towards her stern, workmen on scaffolds, so distant as to appear as dots, were welding steel plates over her portholes for protection from machine-gun strafing. Below her waterline, deep in the bilges, longitudinal bulkheads would be fitted in Boston to increase her water-tightness in case of torpedo attack.

Window dressing, thought Gates. The last war had proved that liners had no business tangling with fighting ships. If the Germans ever got that close, she was a goner. Speed was her only defence. Further aft, beyond the winking lights of the electric arc-welding machines, painters were brushing on the last of the grey camouflage. Speed and stealth.

He went back inside, worked his way forward through the work gangs and hitched a ride with some navy boiler-maker mates on a baggage elevator down to the number one boiler room. As he'd expected, things were somewhat more normal on G deck, but even in the firerooms the litter of reconstruction was scattered everywhere. Uncle Richard had reminded him that the condition of the work spaces was as good a gauge as any of efficiency. A tightly run job had clean decks, unobstructed doors and empty corners, which indicated that the foremen had control of their gangs. This was not the case on the *Normandie*, Gates discovered as he walked aft through the four boiler rooms, through the turbine-alternator rooms and into the propulsion room that housed the four gigantic electric motors that drove the propeller shafts. Three times he had to stop to move planks blocking watertight doors on E deck alone. And as he continued his tour deck by deck up the ten levels from the boiler rooms to the open sundeck, he felt a deepening sense of alarm. Charlie hadn't exaggerated at all. In fact, he should have said something earlier.

Gates found disconnected fire hoses, inoperable fire extinguishers, electric wiring splayed from partially rewired switch panels, and junk in every corner and stair tower. The few fire patrols slouching along were a far cry from the French fire brigades he'd seen marching the corridors with military precision when the navy had asked him to survey her condition in the autumn of 1940. She was, as Charlie had said, a mess.

'We know,' admitted a harassed navy ensign Gates cornered in the commandant's office behind the bridge. He didn't know where the captain was. 'We're doing what we can. We have five hundred men we're trying to familiarize with the ship and we just now got new orders to get underway for Boston on the fourteenth.'

'*February* fourteenth? But that's only *five* days from now.'

'You're telling *me*? The contractor's still tearing up the carpet in the main lounge. No, you can't talk to the captain. He's got a full plate already. Who'd you say you are?'

'Steven Gates. Prince and Gates.'

'Naval architects, right? Why don't you go talk to the contractor, Mr Gates? We really got our hands full here.'

'Who's in charge of the fire watches?'

'Coast Guard.'

'Where are they?'

'I don't know. Try A deck.'

Gates went down four levels to A deck and walked aft five hundred feet until he found the main fire station. A single Coast Guard seaman manned the room and told Gates that the Coast Guard fire brigade headquarters had been shifted forward because the telephones were being rewired.

The yeoman on duty at the new headquarters was reading the *Mirror*. A Nazi U-boat had torpedoed a Swedish ore carrier off the Carolinas – the twentieth freighter they'd sunk in sight of the east coast in the two months since Pearl. And the Japs were rampaging down the Malay Peninsula, closing on Singapore.

'Nothing to worry about, sir,' he answered Gates. 'We got a fire watch and the contractor's got a fire watch and so has the navy. We're on top of it.'

'How's your pressure?'

'What?'

'Fire-hose water pressure.'

'Pretty good, sir. Who'd you say you were?'

Gates stalked away. When he found the contractor's office on an upper deck empty, he went looking for the naval inspector.

They'd ripped out the fireproof wall between the grand salon and the *fumoir*, over Uncle Richard's vehement protest, opening a single cavernous room eighty feet wide and nearly two hundred long. All the furniture was gone, as were the glass cascades of the four spectacular free-standing lighting fixtures. Rolls of fine blue carpet were heaped on the sides, still to be removed to warehouses with the rest of the French treasures that had adorned the *Normandie*. Brown bales were piled in the centre of the room.

An oily odour hung heavy in the cold air. Gates figured it came from the adhesive for the long, tight rolls of linoleum that would be laid in place of the carpets. Before he had time to think about the fact that none of the several dozen men in the room were laying linoleum, he spotted the uniformed navy inspector on the other side of the bales, arguing with a civilian contractor in an overcoat.

'You said you'd have this deck covered today.'

'That's before these got here,' the civilian replied blandly, patting one of the bales, which was wrapped in burlap. 'Do you expect my men to work under them?'

The navy inspector turned on a young ensign hovering at his elbow. 'Have a detail move these.'

'They're supposed to be stencilled before they go to the cabins, sir.'

'Then get somebody on that.'

'I'll be back tomorrow,' said the contractor, buttoning his coat over a loud checked suit. 'So long.'

'Can't you start at that end?'

'No glue.'

'*No glue?* What do you mean no glue?'

'My supplies ran out.' The contractor shrugged. 'I got to find some more. Anyway, it's getting late. I'll see you tomorrow.'

'Be ready to lay this deck first thing in the morning.'

'Soon as you clear them bales.'

The navy inspector watched angrily as he walked away with a jaunty stride. His gaze fell darkly on Gates. 'What do you want?'

'I'm Steven Gates. Prince and Gates.'

'I know who you are, Mr Gates. What do you want?'

Gates hesitated. Above the double-crossed sprigs of a civil engineer, the officer's shoulder bore the stripes of a full commander.

'We're consulting on the conversion – '

'*Were* consulting,' snapped the inspector. 'I saw your report. It was all right. Now what do you want?'

'I'm worried about your ship.'

'Not half as much as me, mister. My job isn't over yet.'

Put off by the man's truculence, Gates heard his own voice turn coldly precise. 'There are safety violations all over her.'

'No kidding, Mr Naval Architect. Three thousand men are running around this ship and half of them don't know the sharp end's the bow. What do you expect?'

'I expect the navy to protect her.'

'Well you're talking to the wrong guy. My job's to see the work gets done right. Yours is over. Why don't you go home?'

'I want to see your ship in service.'

The naval inspector had turned to watch a work crew wrap a heavy chain around the top of a three-legged steel stanchion that stood alone, twelve feet high, on the port side. He turned back to Gates with a sour smile. Behind him, a second crew wheeled in a burning outfit – two tanks, red for oxygen and green for acetylene.

'So does every other contractor in New York City. So long as they get their cut first. Look again, Mr Gates. This isn't a ship. This is a floating New Deal public works project. All these clowns are missing are shovels to lean on.'

'She's a fire trap,' Gates said coldly.

The inspector's blue eyes flared for an instant, then, to Gates's surprise, sunk deeper, tired and resigned, into the dark pouches that marked his exhausted face like dirty sunglasses.

'I'm doing the best I can,' he said wearily. 'I'm the only inspector aboard. She's got ten decks a thousand feet long and orders to sail in five days.' The confession sparked new anger. 'My job's checking workmanship, for chrissake. Why don't you go find the captain?'

Gates stared at him.

'What are you getting so hot under the collar for?'

Gates fumbled for an answer that would make more sense to a naval inspector than the feeling that they were violating a thing of beauty with their callous incompetence. 'The navy hired my firm to consult on the survey. That makes us partly liable for any foul-ups – '

'Don't worry about it. She'll be gone in a week.'

Gates kept staring. The inspector's expression changed from misunderstood to uncomfortable. He wet his lips and flipped open a writing pad.

'All right. Tell me what you saw and I'll see what I can do.'

He rested the pad on top of the fuzzy, burlap-covered bales and took notes while Gates read from his own notes. Far across the ravished salon the workmen tugged and pulled their chain. Gates had to raise his voice to be heard over their shouts until they'd bent the stanchion horizontal. The burner and his helpers who had cut two of its legs stepped over the burlap bales beside its twisted base to finish the job. He screwed the knob on his torch, honing the flame hard, bright blue, and tested the oxygen trigger.

There'd been four stanchions, Gates recalled, support for the four glittering light columns that had illuminated the grand salon. The burning crew was cutting the last. Gates wondered where they'd stored the fragile glass.

The inspector wrote diligently, grunting dismay when Gates reported that the new Coast Guard fire station had no telephones, and again for the missing hose fittings on A deck.

The men who'd bent the light stanchion ambled out of the door, dragging their chain. One of the burner's helpers climbed over the low wall of burlap bales with his asbestos spark shield. The burning foreman, who'd been watching the operation, tapped his shoulder and the two men trailed after the rattling chain, followed by another holding a fire extinguisher.

Gates's nose wrinkled. The oil stench . . .

'What's that smell?'

'Kapok.' The inspector tapped the bales he was leaning on. 'Life jackets. Eleven thousand of them wrapped in tar paper. That's probably what you smell. Some damned fool sent them over from Brooklyn two days early. The only thing early on this ship and we don't need – '

'Kapok?' shouted Gates. 'They're burning – '

'Oh, my God!'

Gates crossed the salon at a dead run, leaping over rolls of linoleum and torn-up rungs. Life jackets were stuffed with kapok because the cotton-silk plant fibres were impregnated with oil which repelled water and made them float. Tarpaper and burlap wrappings kept the kapok from drying out in storage. Any of the materials was lethally flammable.

Gates was twenty feet from the bent stanchion when everything but the burner and the last helper, a man with

36

hair as red as fire and bruises on his face, seemed to freeze as still as a silver moon in a cold black sky. The helper stepped out of the cramped work space they'd cleared in the bales, but the cutting job wasn't done.

The burner, his vision hampered by a dark cylindrical face mask, continued to wield his acetylene flame. The stanchion started to part. He touched his oxygen trigger. A high-pressure jet of flame blew the melting steel out of the cut before it could fuse.

The white sparks scattered from the flame and fell like hot snow on a bale of life-jackets. Gates, still running, felt suspended motionless above the deck. The fire – no bigger than the flame on a cigarette match – mounted the burlap.

The fire doubled in size, tripled, found a vertical line between two bales and rose like a burning elevator. Big and bright, it climbed on the top of the line, a knot of fire now, large as a basketball, shunted onto a horizontal line formed by the bale that crowned the bottom two; and highballed down that line in both directions, gaining speed.

Gates yelled, 'Fire!' and a dozen men took up the cry.

The foreman ran out of the door, crashing into a gawking labourer. The labourer went flying, arms pinwheeling, and fell over a linoleum roll. A fitter's helper scooped up two brimming fire pails and carried them across the salon at a dead run. He tripped over the labourer and sprawled flat. The water splashed to the deck five feet short of the flames.

The fire covered four bales. Instantly, eight.

The foreman crashed back through the door hauling a flat canvas hose. He aimed it at the burning bales and twisted the nozzle. The hose swelled and spewed water, and doused half the fire. The water stopped as suddenly as it had begun.

'Water!' the foreman yelled. 'Gimme pressure!'

Gates ran onto the promenade deck, searching for a fire extinguisher. Men were stumbling through a maze of standee bunks, barely able to see because the lights were dim and the windows had been painted out. He felt along the shadowy walls, found an extinguisher and yanked it off its mount.

Grappling with the unfamiliar French valves, Gates ran back to the salon past a pair of cursing workmen frantically spinning the valve on the standpipe that the foreman's hose was connected to. He yelled a path clear, and got the extinguisher operating just as he reached the flames beside the bent stanchion. The fire had retaken the area the foreman had doused and was spreading rapidly. Gates aimed at its base. A thin, liquid jet shredded the flames, knocked them down, undercut them. White smoke blanketed the bales.

'You got it, fella!'

'I got another one!' A shield man ran up with another extinguisher, fumbling with the mechanism.

Gates's fire extinguisher died. He shook it. Its contents sloshed about reassuringly, but when he triggered it again it spurted for a second, merely trickled and stopped for good. The fire spread up and sideways.

The man with the second extinguisher was still trying to puzzle out the mechanism. Gates grabbed it from him and trained it on the fire A rusty liquid spilled out of the hose and splashed at his feet. Gates shook it as hard as he could but it gave no more and in seconds the bales were burning fiercely again.

Half a dozen workmen leaped into the thick of the flames and beat them with their coats and hats and pieces of carpet and padding taken from the littered deck. Sparks showered away from the attack. The foreman grabbed a burning bale and yanked it out of the centre of the fire with his bare hands.

The burning bale landed beside another stack of life jackets. Gates tried to kick it away, but before he could the bale lighted the entire stack with a crackling roar. The men shouted for water and ran at the new fire and beat the flames that were suddenly leaping as high as the old. Both fires turned red and orange and hot.

A third stack exploded suddenly, as if burning from inside.

Gates saw thick, black smoke gathering in the high ceiling. The men began coughing. Holding their arms up against the growing heat, they went back into the fire and scattered the worst of the burning bales, separating them from those not yet ignited, but this second attempt to break up the fire only set off more bales and now the flames began to climb the walls.

Calls for water died on their lips and their eyes grew fearful at the unnerving sight of the flames climbing to the ceiling and licking hungrily at the thickening black smoke. The flames had grown tall, too tall, too broad, too hot, too bright to contain with bare hands and scraps of blue wool carpet. Of the sudden universal opinion that the fire was deadly, the workmen turned as a group and ran for their lives.

Gates and the foreman tried to stop them. Gates grabbed a flailing arm. The man pummelled at his head with his free hand. Gates held tight, trying to persuade him to fight the fire. The man struggled harder, and Gates realized that he was holding a terrified, skinny youth whose face was red in the flames and whose eyes were round with this new terror . . . this crazy man trying to drag him to his death.

He let go and the kid cartwheeled away. Losing his own balance, Gates lurched backwards, tripped over a linoleum roll and pitched towards the flames. The deck was hot where his hands skidded along it, painfully stinging skin already raw from throwing a burning bale. The end of the linoleum roll was burning. Fat, orange flames spewed dense, oily smoke. Gates scrambled to his feet, looking around for something to help put it out. There was nothing. The welding foreman was gone, his broad back disappearing through the door to the starboard promenade deck, the side of the ship next to the pier, and Gates was suddenly alone in the gigantic salon, alone with the flames.

He took one more look at the fire, accepted that they couldn't fight it without high-pressure water, and ran forward for help, leaping over linoleum rolls and carpet piles, vaulting a stack of life jackets, cracking his shins on an abandoned tool box. Behind him the fire found its throat and began to growl, like a dog that sensed something feared it.

Gates ran up the centre of the grand salon and through the *salon-galérie*, avoiding the enclosed promenades on either side because those passages, already narrowed by rows of standee bunks, would be jammed with frightened men making for the gangways. He reached the lobby just as an elevator slammed shut on a knot of men heading down. Alone again, he hesitated at the entrance to the theatre and looked back over his shoulder.

Two hundred feet aft the fire danced the breadth of his vision, and nothing but combustibles stood between it and the front of the ship.

The stairs to the bridge, two decks up, were somewhere ahead of the theatre, but Gates was afraid of getting lost in the backstage areas so he ran out of the lobby onto the port promenade. A frightened work gang, pursued by two more, were running up the cluttered passage, caroming off the bunk tiers, yelling out their fear and confusion.

Gates pointed across the lobby. 'Get off the ship!' Down the long, dark promenade, he saw more men running pell-mell, but no fire crews. He ran forward, found a crosspassage that separated the back of the theatre from the writing room and library and found, in that corridor, stairs. He went up them, his long legs taking three steps at once, past the boat deck and up another level to the sundeck. He ran through a maze of rooms and halls, through the chart room, dodging its high, thin-drawered tables and burst through a door.

The *Normandie*'s bridge was a vast, silent space of curving windows and polished brass, providing a startling view of everything ahead of the ship and isolation from all below. Gates was as shocked by the peaceful, silent beauty of the Manhattan skyline in bright sunlight as the officers on the bridge were by his explosive entrance.

They gaped at him. A telephone rang.

'Bridge — '

'Fire!' Gates yelled.

The telephone was slammed down. 'Fire in the main lounge — '

'Hit the alarm!'

The officer ordered ran the breadth of the seventy-foot-wide bridge, hesitated over an electric panel, then threw two switches. Nothing happened.

'It's a bad one,' Gates told them. 'You need help.'

Without waiting for orders, a sailor threw a switch on a New York City Fire Department alarm box.

'That's not connected,' another man said.

'Get down to the contractor's officer,' ordered an officer. 'Use the contractor's loudspeakers. And call the fire department — where do you think you're going?'

Gates was running past him and out onto the starboard bridge wing. The cold hit him like a wall. Men were working on the decks below and on the pier, trundling tools and material up the gangways, still unaware of the fire. Gates leaned far out, saw a cop and drew the sound up from the depths of his gut.

'Fire!'

Fifty feet below, the cop looked up, saw Gates waving, and shielded his eyes for a better look.

'Fire in the main salon, call the fire department.'

The cop ran into the pier building.

Gates sagged against the wing railing and tried to catch his breath. He heard shouts. Smoke eddied out of an open port on the promenade deck, a thin, harmless-looking plume. All else appeared normal. The ship thrust far out into the river towards Jersey, and nothing in the long, narrow slot between its hull and the pier seemed unusual. When Gates heard the sirens, they had the distant sound of strangers' problems.

2

The Otter's next step in his destruction of the troopship was to smoke the black gang out of her boiler room. They provided power – electricity, light, and water pressure. Without that power, the *Normandie* couldn't fight her own fire.

He shut a central fire-main valve he had concealed with a heap of filthy armchairs and hid there, watching until Larson had run off with the others, so that the red-headed Bundist who'd started the fire couldn't connect the German agent he knew as Herr Otter with the scrap dealer and general contractor the navy and many aboard the troopship knew as the big, genial Dutchman van Slough.

Then he fought his way across the promenade, through the rushing mob, yelling at them to go back with him, go back and fight the fire. A pair of terrified apprentices blocked his path. He pushed them out of the way and rammed through the doors of the burning grand salon.

The incendiaries that he and Larson had buried among the kapok bales had scattered Larson's starter fire like scarlet rain. It was one of the better tricks Uncle Willy's explosives instructor had taught the Bundists in their summer camp in Yaphank, Long Island.

A paper fuse, impregnated with flash powder, had ignited in the first rush of heat. It was one of several planted among the bales in the vicinity of the oxyacetylene, burning with the barest tip exposed. On ignition it had catapulted a minute ribbon of flame to the main incendiaries inside the kapok through a reed tube that provided air for the fuse, and would itself burn out of existence once the fire took hold. The only flaw in the arsonist's device was the

43

evidence of a partially blackened reed tube if the fire failed to catch. But in this case that was hardly a problem. The heat was already tremendous, the flames spooky-bright orange, rampaging over the life jackets, eating up the walls with malevolent gluttony, out of control.

He began to create a reverse chimney to the boiler room to exploit the smoke. Propping open every door he passed through, he went forward, around the ship's theatre and into a crosscorridor that divided the backstage area from the writing room and library at the front of the superstructure. A hundred yards and five walls now stood between him and the fire. It was quiet here, despite his trail of open doors, and he smelled no smoke yet.

The Otter took a fire axe from the bulkhead and opened another door which led to the baggage elevator that serve the forward first-class entrances. He worked the prong into the crack between the door and jamb, then levered the axe handle until the latches gave with a loud snap and the door slid open on a deep, black shaft. He pulled heavy leather and canvas welding gloves from his belt, pushed into them, and leaped at the centre of the elevator shaft.

The lift cables jumped into his hands, taut as steel bars and thin and greasy.

The elevator car was empty, its light out, its door open. The Otter dropped through the opening, stepped out of the car and looked about. The ship's hospital and mortuary surrounded the elevator shaft. The work on B deck was being done elsewhere, and he was still alone.

He found the elevator lights, closed the door, and threw the control wheel. The car descended quietly. Like all the *Normandie*'s machinery – her lifts, her winches, her pumps – it was virtually new and flawlessly maintained.

The baggage elevator touched bottom at F deck, just about at the waterline, and some thirty feet from ship's bottom. The Otter had been aboard since they had started the conversion to troop carrier, so he knew her well. Her bow was two hundred feet forward, and in that area were the three decks of stowage for baggage, automobiles and ship's stores, as well as tanks for fresh water and ballast. Aft of where the Otter stood were her four boiler rooms.

The Otter tore out the remaining elevator ceiling panels and extinguished the light. A hundred feet up the shaft he saw a glow where he had left the elevator doors open. The shaft was clear. He left the elevator and felt for his bearings in the darkened baggage sorting area. This deep in the ship, her decks slanted slightly as they rose to the bow. Following the downward cant, the Otter moved aft, stopping to loosen the overload fuses in the elevator machinery room, cutting the current, immobilizing the car.

A door opened on a stair that dropped sharply two levels to another door. Silently descending the steel treads, he removed one glove and touched his bare palm to the watertight steel door. It was cold. Propping the door wide open, he ran between the pairs of towering square watertube boilers to the next watertight door which led to number two boiler room. It too was cold, the room empty, the nine main boilers all cold. But when he pressed his bare hand to the next watertight door, the steel was warm, as though alive.

Number three boiler room lay beyond it. The midaft boiler room was the only one in service while the ship lay at dockside. Four cylindrical Scotch boilers were going full blast, supplying steam for the *Normandie*'s lights, her heat, electric machinery and fire pumps. He checked his watch. Four minutes since the fire began.

He visualized the *Normandie* as a vast oblong, honeycombed with hundreds of long horizontal passages and deep vertical shafts. He had bored deeply into her to open a line of shafts and passages and leave in his descending wake a clear channel from promenade deck to boiler room – a towering reverse chimney. This watertight door, pulsing warmly beneath his hand, was like a damper, the final barrier between the lethal smoke and the men who supplied the *Normandie*'s power.

'*Vent it!*' a civilian boilermaker shouted as black smoke billowed over the tops of the Scotch boilers in the number three boiler room. It was only 14.30, but the black gang had had one hell of a day already. Not that the Frenchies made bad boilers. He had served his twenty for the navy before this job, and had tended every sort of ship the navy had, from coal-fired World War I four-stack destroyers to the latest high-pressure, super-heated Prince turbines on fast, light cruisers, so he knew good boilers and these were the best.

Trouble was, not a piece of machinery aboard had a word of English on it. Valves that any fool would turn clockwise, didn't. Switches moved the wrong way. Levers sat in screwy places. Evaporators, saltwater heaters, pumps, feed tanks, even the Horowitz underwater sewage ejectors, you name it, were put where only a Frenchman would put them, so the simplest damned chore ended up a crazy game of hide and seek, with the black gang the steady losers.

'*Vent it!*' he bellowed again, adding his protest to the angry shouts sounding around the boiler room. Black clouds poured down from the ceiling. Wiping an oily hand over his stinging eyes, he headed forward to find the trouble with the Scotch boilers. Others followed, covering their faces, and swearing to settle the hash of whoever had moved the wrong switch.

The boilermaker listened intently. The Scotch boilers were roaring pretty loud, not the body-shaking sound of the mains but loud enough, and yet there seemed to be a sudden empty space in the walls of sound that ordinarily filled the boiler room. He thought he'd heard the ventilating fans shut down. Son of a bitch. Smoke was collecting in the high ceiling. Already the tops of the boilers that towered nearly three decks high looked soft and hazy in the harsh electric light.

A chief machinist's mate passed him at a dead run. They'd heard it too. The ventilators were off. Someone had fouled up again. Why else would smoke be filling the boiler room like black cotton candy?

The bridge telephone rang. It went unanswered while they crowded around the Scotch boilers looking for the trouble. When the smoke drove them back, an officer who'd run from the number four room picked up the bridge phone and listened briefly.

'They've got a fire on the promenade deck,' he announced.

A fireman reported that number two boiler room was dense with black smoke and presumably number one as well. The smoke began pouring into number three from the main intakes. The officer ordered the force-draught fans shut down, but it was too late. Smoke from the fire was probably being sucked into the boiler room air intakes in the centres of the two forward stacks. The boiler room crew stripped off their shirts, soaked them in water, and tied them over their faces.

Fire bells suddenly clanged, echoing in the steel chambers. A watertight door began to lower with a grinding rumble.

The Otter ducked through the diminishing opening, into a ventilator room. The deck shook from the Scotch boilers below. The powerful fan motors roared in their housings. Eighty feet aft was another steel watertight door blocked in a half-open position by a pile of wooden scaffolds.

Figuring that the foremost motors powered the forced-draught fans for the Scotch boilers, he traced their thick electric cables to switches and moved them, gambling that any change would worsen rather than clear the smoke in the boiler room.

The boards holding open the aft door were creaking and groaning under the tons of steel, threatening to splinter. The Otter slipped under and started up a ladder that was welded to the bulkhead and disappeared overhead in darkness. He climbed, playing his light up the rungs until he reached a ceiling. A mesh hatch swung up. He climbed through, not knowing where he was, but certain it was time to get out of the ship's dark belly.

When he had counted a hundred steps, he ran into another mesh hatch. Cold air poured down through it. He opened it and, craning his neck, saw daylight high overhead. The ladder stretched skyward, fifty feet or more. He started up apprehensively, the ice-cold rungs freezing his hands through the welding gloves. The ladder ran up a wall that curved away into darkness on either side. He was out of the narrow shaft. He climbed faster until, winded, he reached the top and saw what he had feared.

He was trapped in the top of the dummy aft funnel, the huge rear stack that ventilated the *Normandie*'s electric motor room instead of discharging boiler furnace smoke like her forward and midships funnels. Too tall to climb down the outside, the dummy's interior was perforated by ventilation ducts, many of which the Otter had already rendered useless by sabotaging the fans. Some of those ducts might be wide enough for him to tunnel below the fire, and not yet be blocked by smoke from the burning grand salon . . .

The *Normandie* lay an awesome distance below, black and grey smoke billowing from her waist and blowing over her bridge and bow, over the West Side Highway, and slithering ominously through the merlons and crenels of the midtown skyline. City fire engines were racing up Twelfth Avenue, sirens howling. On the ship, a mob of workmen was stumbling along the foredeck towards the bow. He looked south, over the roof of the French Line pier. A fireboat was charging up river, dodging ice floes and rail barges, heaving spray from her knife bow.

Trapped with two hundred men on the port side, blocked by fire and smoke from escaping down the gangways, Steven Gates stumbled down companionways, feeling his way forward in near darkness, dogged by the acrid smoke.

Around him men were falling, coughing and vomiting. Gates shuffled among them, shaken more by the cries of terror than the cutting smoke and dark.

An electrician fell down a stairway and broke his arm. Gates helped the man to his feet and threw his own coat around the man's shoulders as they struggled forward. Suddenly daylight poured into the smoky corridor. The man ahead had found a door to the foredeck. Gates broke out into the biting cold, still pursued by the billowing smoke. They ran as far as they could, ran to the tip of the bow where they huddled, flinching from the cold wind, coughing when it blew the thick smoke across their refuge.

Gates shivered near-uncontrollably. The temperature felt near zero, the wind stronger than it had blown all day. Moving to the port side to get out of the smoke, to see how bad the fire was, he saw an eerie sight – a man emerging from the top of the dummy aft funnel.

Some seven hundred feet separated him from the tiny figure atop the distant funnel. The easy way he popped his arms up the rim clearly spoke of calculation rather than fear. Yet if he didn't have a rope and the fire continued to spread, he was surely doomed, with no way down but a return to the pitch-black corridors thick with poisonous smoke. Even so, the man in the stack looked more like an observer than a frightened workman trying to find a way off the burning ship – like a seasoned fleet admiral assessing a battle action. The smoke billowed higher and Gates lost sight of him.

Deep in the ship's belly, many decks from daylight, the black gang in boiler room three waited for word from the bridge. The smell of fire was terrifying beneath the river surface, where there was steel above and steel below and steel on either flank. Twice they'd telephoned the bridge and twice they'd been told to keep steam up. The fire, they were assured, was nowhere near them. But the smoke was thickening, paint fumes gagged the throat, and no call came.

That the boilermaker had every civilian right to walk off the ship and read about it in the morning paper didn't figure in his thinking, so when the smoke got too thick to see, he joined the machinist's mates and firemen face down on the deck, where the air was cleaner. A new blast of smoke poured into the boiler room and hung thick as a bulkhead from deck to ceiling.

Finally, choking and coughing, the lieutenant ordered the Scotch boiler fires banked. The men groped forward the shut the oil feeds one by one. When the last fire in the last furnace was down, the lieutenant told them to abandon the boiler room. He stood at the foot of the stairs and counted heads as they trooped towards the long climb to safety.

'Round up all your flashlights.'

Good thinking. The boilermaker found two. The furnaces were cooling, steam pressure dropping, turbines and alternators slowing. It would not be too many minutes before the pumps and lights went out.

The Otter gripped the funnel. He had done it. Heavy oil smoke was gushing from the midships funnel, too thick to be the Scotch boilers' regular emission. The engineers had to be banking the boilers and vacating the firerooms.

He looked for a way out of the funnel and off the burning ship before the smoke ran wild. The front of the dummy stack was raked, but he'd need a line to survive the fifty-foot slide to the sundeck. He recalled that one of the ship's novelties was an air-conditioned first-class dining room. The cooling system vented through this stack. He might follow the air-conditioning ducts to the dining room, move forward through that room under the fire and exit nearer the bow.

With a final look, he started down the ladder, back into the ship. He found a horizontal shaft opening and was feeling his way into it, testing if his broad shoulders would fit, when acrid smoke came racing up the ladder, blinding, choking and dense.

Heeling sharply as she turned off the river at high speed, the New York City fireboat *James Duane* careened into the icy slip. She cut through the mush ice and shoved her padded nose tight against a provisions barge tied at one of the *Normandie*'s open cargo ports. Her crew, hooded and gloved against the biting cold, were already manning her five high-pressure turret nozzles. When she engaged her pumps, five thick, white streams rocketed over the *Normandie*'s towering hull. The water plumes struck between the midships and after funnels in the heart of the smoke.

The fireboat maintained power ahead to counteract the backward thrust of the gushing water guns while the men on the turret nozzles played them from side to side, seeking entry into the steel-encased fire. White steam clouds exploded where icy hose water met hot steel, bleaching the black smoke dirty grey. Then the water hit the painted-out promenade deck windows and the nearly molten glass disintegrated. Smoke gushed from the broken windows, followed by flame, seen for the first time, glowing a sullen red at the base of the smoke. The *James Duane* poured tons of water through the gaping holes she'd breached in the *Normandie*'s side.

'Get off the ship! Get off the ship!'

The warning thundered suddenly from emergency loudspeakers throughout the *Normandie*. No one had to be told on the promenade and sundecks, nor in the boiler rooms. The flames were driving the navy and Coast Guard firefighters towards the bow as their hoses grew soft in their hands with the dying water pressure. On the decks closest to the fire – the Upper and A immediately below the promenade – the alarm confirmed already anxious suspicions that the smell of smoke meant trouble. For most of the three thousand workmen and sailors below decks, however, the loudspeakers broadcast a warning of indiscernible danger, a drill or some damned thing.

'Get off the ship! Get off the ship!'

They crowded into the passageways and stairwells. The men near the gangways headed straight for them, but most, deep in the liner, tried to remember how they'd got where they were, even as smoke began billowing down the long corridors and the lights started to fade. *'Get off the ship! Get off the ship!'*

Outside, the voice echoed monotonously, unchanging over and over, echoing the length of the long, narrow space between the smoke-shrouded ship and the high walls of the French Line pier building. Fire engines drove into the building, their exhausts thundering into the cavernous space. The firemen uncoiled hoses, coupled to the pier hydrants, and humped the hoses towards the gangways just as solid walls of escaping workmen crowded down them. They ran out of the liner's ports by the hundreds, coughing, choking, panicked and bewildered.

The firemen fell back, blocked from the gangways until the first wave of workmen escaped. When the flow became a trickle of escapees from further below, the firemen advanced, plodding up the steep ramps in rubber coats, high boots and helmets. They dragged their long hoses to the fire with the deliberate and deceptively slow motion of men who knew from experience that speed was less important than a good set-up. When they sighted the flames beneath the blinding smoke, their high-pressure pumpers thundered into action on the pier and the flat canvas hoses they'd snaked aboard filled round and hard and throbbed with the thrust of tons of water.

'Get off the ship! Get off the ship!'

Gates stretched over the bulwark and looked down. Seventy feet below, the slip waters were pushing ice against the *Normandie*, which meant that the tide was going out. He looked to the land.

Fire engines were rumbling up Twelfth and across Forty-eighth, sirens howling, swinging under the highway and into the pier. It looked like the fire department had gone to three or four alarms. Ambulances, bells clanging, were pulling up to the foot of the ship. The police were pushing back gawpers who were gathering across Twelfth Avenue, despite the cold, and traffic had stopped dead on the West Side Highway. The overhead viaduct was so close to the *Normandie*'s bow that Gates could see the faces of the motorists who'd climbed out of their stalled cars for a better look. Behind the highway the smoke laid a dark pall over Manhattan, rendering indistinct the familiar outlines of the GE, Empire State and Chrysler buildings, and virtually obliterating the stately McGraw-Hill building in the foreground.

A long, articulated hook-and-ladder truck wormed through the square, boxy pumpers, parked on the quayside immediately in front of the *Normandie* and began slowly raising a slender extension ladder towards the rakish tip of her flaring bow. The ladder swung wildly, crashing into the hull, swaying from side to side before it finally dropped to the forepeak. The men swarmed to secure it, then started down in orderly procession, guiding and carrying the injured, while the rest waited silently for their turn.

The smoke grew thicker. It started to pour out of the dummy after-funnel, as if the great ship were steaming over the ocean instead of burning at her dock. Gates watched it. It meant that the fire was moving aft, as well as forward, aft despite the efforts of the two fireboats and the hose companies on the pier, aft in the teeth of the wind.

'Get off the ship! Get off the ship!'

Spewing gigantic jets of water, a third fireboat charged into the slip. Gates recognized the brand-new *Fire Fighter*, the biggest fireboat in the world with an awesome fifteen-thousand-gallon-per-minute water-throwing capacity. Her

53

high, thick white plumes crashed down on the smoke and for a moment it seemed to retreat, to flinch like a bloodied boxer. Then a powerful gust of wind fanned the fire back to full strength. The same gust blew hose spray across the foredeck, stinging Gates's face and freezing his suit stiff in seconds. Turning from a second gust, Gates saw the water running across the wooden deck to the port side. The rivulets froze quickly in place, pointing like arrows at the bulwark.

He felt a chill deeper than the wind would cut. The water was running downhill. The *Normandie*, pushed by the outflowing, ebbing tide, was already listing a hair to port and the fireboats and engine pumps were roaring full blast. His turn to descend from the burning ship had almost come.

Gates looked at the ladder, considered going to it, shivered with cold and fear, and ran back to the fire.

The Otter heard the remaining ventilation fans go silent all at once when the ship lost power, but he was trapped too deep to hear the loudspeaker order the workmen off. Choking, coughing, lost in a smoky horizontal shaft barely wide enough for his shoulders, he inched along on his belly by the dying glow of his flashlight. He was certain he would die – but he also knew triumph.

The silent fans confirmed that the smoke he'd channelled to the boiler rooms had driven out the black gang. The *Normandie* could no longer fight her own fire. He had done his job. The New York City Fire Department would do the rest by drowning her with hose water.

He saw nothing ahead in the duct, but he kept crawling, hoping. It was pitch black. The smoke blurred the flashlight beam. He was coughing continuously now. He felt claws in his throat and fire in his lungs.

An awful pain ripped deep in the back of his mouth, and the air he was trying to breath turned suddenly cold. A draught. The fire was pulling clean air through the duct.

He sucked it greedily, and as his mind cleared he saw he had crawled over a ceiling vent.

The Otter shone his flashlight down through the air vent's cross-hatching and saw a large room, apparently part of a first-class suite, with a bed directly beneath him, the bare mattress folded back, revealing metal springs. The grid swung up and open on hinges. He jammed his shoulders through the hole and fell to the bed, where he lay gratefully breathing the clear air. He stood up, felt his way in the darkness, found a door, opened it and stepped into a pitch-black corridor thick with hot, acrid fumes.

The fumes raced left to right on a powerful draught. The Otter hesitated, puzzling the draught's meaning, aware how poor his thinking had been in the air shaft, determined not to waste himself with another such mistake. He had more to do.

Steven Gates ran from the upper deck to the promenade deck, retracing his escape from the port side, splashing through water that was tumbling down the steps like a mountain brook. It was a foot deep on the promenade deck. His ankles went numb in seconds. He dipped his handkerchief and pressed it to his face. It was so cold it burned the skin, but anything was better than the throat-searing smoke, which was so thick and oily Gates could barely see the flames inside the salons.

The enclosed first-class promenade between the salons and the outboard windows flowed like a canal. The heat had shattered the windows. The fireboats were pouring water through them, but the openings were too high to let the harbour and hydrant water pour back off the *Normandie*.

Every thirty or forty feet a watertight door for boarding the lifeboats pierced the long line of windows. Gates waded aft, stopping to unscrew their stops and fling them open to let the water pour out. The fire had complete control of the interior – the lobby, the grand salon, the *fumoir* – but the wind, hard out of the northwest, blew the smoke and flames inboard, away from Gates. Occasionally it cleared brief paths in the smoke, down which Gates caught glimpses of hose-wielding city firemen circled by flame.

Gates continued aft, breathing through his handkerchief, wetting it again when sudden heat-blasts seared it dry, waiting for the wind to protect him, terrified he'd be trapped aft. He opened six doors and was struggling with the frozen screws on a seventh when the *Fire Fighter's* main turret fired a rock-hard water spout through the next window. It flung him eighteen feet across the promenade and slammed him into a hot steel bulkhead. He felt searing pain and collapsed into the freezing water.

The cold numbed his burned cheek and drove him out of the water and back to the watertight doors. He managed to open ten. The other two wouldn't budge. He sagged against an outer bulkhead, safe from the punishing fireboat water streams, and tried to remember where the other ports were on this side of the ship. He risked a quick look down at the slip and took a stinging faceful of fireboat water for his pains.

They had fifteen nozzles between them, all firing full blast, and several private tugs armed with fire nozzles had joined the effort to empty New York Harbour onto the fire. The water was cascading onto the promenade faster than it poured out of the doors Gates had opened. Counting what the fire department must have mustered on the pier side, he reckoned that the *Normandie* was receiving hundreds of thousands of gallons of water on her top decks and shedding only a portion.

He had to open other ports to release the hose water. Too much of it trapped could pull her down, just like the *Paris* in Le Havre in '39. But they couldn't know. The men hadn't been aboard long enough to understand her. How

56

many Americans knew enough about the big liners to even guess the danger? He felt a sudden anger. Where the hell was the navy?

The *Normandie* had a sophisticated trim-tank system to correct a list, but who beside her French crew — long-returned to France or dispersed among New York restaurants — could operate the trim system in her dark, powerless bowels? The anger burned anew that something so beautiful should be in such ignorant hands.

He started forward, ducking the fireboat streams. A rocket of flame shot out of the burning salon and sizzled against the bulkhead where he'd been standing. Gates ducked and ran, trying to remember where her ports were located ... they were scattered randomly, placed wherever needed to service the ship.

A deck. Two decks below. A tourist embarkation port aft and two first-class embarkation ports and a crew port forward. No. The crew port was on the starboard side. Then on B deck, a baggage port forward. On C deck, far forward, was the Plymouth embarkation port, the opening through which Plymouth passengers embarked from the lighter. At least three provisions ports serviced D deck. But they were too far down, too close to the water. If the ship listed too much they'd dip below the harbour surface. God ... he remembered, they were already open. That's where the barges were off-loading provisions. And a single man couldn't close them without electrical power. Nothing he could do about it. Besides, closing holes in the side of the ship was something the navy just might understand and do something about.

Gates ducked the fireboat spouts and ran faster. The tourist port was too far aft. He would concentrate on opening the forward doors on A, B and C decks to release the fire fighters' water before the *Normandie* listed too far. He ran down the same stairs he'd come up – an enclosed stairwell protected from the fire by the boiler room uptakes. The smoke was thick, and he dipped his handkerchief often in the water pouring down the steps.

The Otter stepped over a door sill into water. It was bitter cold and nearly as deep as the sill. He dipped his glove and brought it to his mouth. Salt. And sewage. Port side. The fireboats were pumping harbour water.

Shivering, coughing, he waded on. He felt doorways in the wall at regular intervals and guessed he was on an accommodation level. His feet were freezing. Which level, he had no way of knowing. He came to a T junction and turned again towards the smoke.

The fierce heat dried his wet hair in seconds. The paint on the walls was blistering from the burning ceiling. Dark rivulets were running down the wall like melted chocolate. The Otter knelt and lay prone in the water. Soaked head to toe, he took a deep breath and ran towards the flames. When he couldn't stand the pain he covered his face and ran blind. He felt his hair burning and flung himself into the cold water. The ceiling ahead was a sheet of flame but an open door lay fifteen feet beyond. He raced for it, leaped the sill and landed on a wooden deck, far aft, on the tourist-class enclosed promenade one level below the main promenade deck.

Spouts of fireboat water were climbing past the railing, arching over the next deck. He looked back into the burning ship. The same dark rivulets he'd noticed before were running down the walls of the corridor he'd escaped, hissing and steaming like volcanic lava as they dropped into the water. He stared at them, simultaneously trying to catch his breath and figure out what he was looking at. Then he understood, Lead sheathing on electric wire was melting in the heat. He traced one of the rivulets and saw that where it hit the cold water it had hardened and clogged a drain.

Good.

Already, the water in the corridor was lapping at the top of the door sill. In minutes the rising water would spill over the sill through the open door onto the deck and flow harmlessly down the side of the ship. The Otter heaved his weight against the watertight door and screwed it shut.

Steven Gates opened two barn-door ports on A deck and one on B, but the fire had breached C deck through the open space above the first-class dining room and by the time he tried to reach the C deck doors, the fire was moving forward. The fierce heat drove him out onto the foredeck. Twice he soaked his clothing, shielded his face with his jacket, and tried again, but it was hopeless. He retreated to the bow, where the last of the trapped workmen were descending the rescue ladder to Twelfth Avenue, and looked back.

The bridge was burning. Flames spewed out of its shattered windows. Smoke billowed from the boat and sundecks above it and blew across the foredeck. Fireboat water jets lined the port side, diminishing in the distance, and Gates wondered how much more water it would take to bring the fire under control.

He and a navy signalman were the last men on the bow. The signalman was perched on the bulwark beside the ladder, trading semaphore signals with a sailor on the quayside. He gestured at the ladder with his flags. Through a haze of numbing cold, pain and shock, Gates heard himself uttering nonsense.

'Get going, sailor. You've done your job.'

The sailor glared down at him and also uttered nonsense – although it was brave nonsense. 'I'm Signalman Second Class Corson, sir, and I think I'm the last navy man aboard, which puts me in command. Get off my ship.'

Gates shook his head, climbed over the bulwark and started down the spindly, bouncing ladder on a long, shallow angle. A great noise rose from the ground – the clatter of firefighting pumps, newly arriving vehicles, motorcycles, ambulance bells and prowl car sirens, and the shouts of police, firemen, and hundreds of civil defence volunteers in white helmets.

Two firemen helped Gates off at the bottom of the ladder.

'You better get those burns to a hospital, mister.'

'Where's the navy command post?'

'Beats me.'

They dragged a hose onto the ladder and started up the rungs at a fast rot. Gates lowered himself off the hook-and-ladder truck as more firemen followed the first two with a second hose. He looked for a way out of the maze of trucks and hoses, but before he found one, he was completely unnerved by the staggering appearance of the *Normandie*.

She was listing markedly to port. Her great knife bow tilted as if she were heeling into a crash turn, shifting suddenly onto the next leg of a secret zigzag pattern. She would lean further and further, Gates knew, as long as the fire department continued to drench the flames.

The fireboats were concentrating on her stern, probably, he guessed, because the land companies couldn't string hoses that far aft. Three provisions ports were open on D deck, low down on the black hull, near the waterline which was creeping up her side as she listed. Gates wondered how many interior automatic watertight doors had closed when the alarm sounded and were now trapping hose water. From where he stood, he could see only one of the ports he had opened. The navy had to shut those ports on D deck . . . they were too near the water.

Overhead, two small aeroplanes circled in the dull, smoke-darkened sky. Newspaper photographers, Gates assumed. Scores more were working among the fire-fighters, exploding flashbulbs at cops, ambulances, fire trucks, injured workmen and frantic navy personnel. A Movietone news crew was panning the chaos with a portable motion picture camera mounted on a light wooden tripod. One of the radio cars was from the British Broadcasting Corporation, and Cordi Grey flashed in his mind . . .

Traffic had stopped both ways on Twelfth Avenue, as he'd seen it up on the highway, and the police were having difficulty clearing ambulance lanes through the spectators. Onlookers and volunteer civil defence wardens were trading rumours at full voice. Much repeated was the fear that hundreds of workmen were still trapped inside the burning ship.

'Hey, buddy! What are you doing? You can't get out that way!'

The civilian boilermaker had somehow separated from the boiler room crew. Lost, he wandered empty, dark and smoke-filled corridors searching for the way off the burning ship. The decks were awash, and his feet were frozen. In a panicky moment he'd thought she was sinking before he realized it was hose water.

Then he got lucky and found a corridor he thought he recognized. He slogged forward, looking for a gangway onto the pier, and as he walked he played his flashlight down crosscorridors and into staterooms, in case somebody else was hurt or lost. Which was how he'd spotted the guy down the end of a crosscorridor who was about to step through an open port. It was a long way down to the drink.

He shouted again, but the man didn't hear. The boilermaker went after him before the poor guy fell out. Probably spooked by the smoke. Jesus, now he was pulling the damn door shut. It was a swinging barn-door type. As the boilermaker neared, the guy got one half shut. Powerful bastard. He'd pulled it shut against the water pouring out. Nutty as a fruitcake – and now he was screwing down the stops . . .?

For a second the boilermaker asked himself seriously what he was doing here. Not only would he have to calm the poor crazy bastard down, they'd have to take the time as the fire and smoke closed in to open the door again to let the water out. She was listing already, listing badly.

'Hold it, buddy, knock it off!'

That got him. He whirled around and jumped to his feet, bigger than he'd looked crouching there.

'Calm down, buddy. I got a way out of here. I'll take you. See, I got a light.' He waved the flashlight reassuringly. 'Let's just get this open to let the water out and we'll be off in a second.'

The guy just stood there.

The boilermaker supposed if he hadn't spent a good piece of his life in boiler rooms the smoke might have scared him crazy too.

'Come on, fella,' he said gently, extending his hand.

Funny. Up close, in the back glow of the flashlight, the guy didn't look that crazy or panicked. And his eyes were cold as a cop rousting a bum. The boilermaker had a sudden feeling he'd made some sort of mistake. He knew it a moment later. The guy was wrapping a pair of arms like steel cables around him, crushing the air out of his chest, then lifting his two hundred and twenty pounds right off the deck and carrying him to a deep shaft down which the hose water was gurgling like a sewer.

The Otter climbed down the shaft after the body and pulled it back up to the deck, where he confirmed in the beam of his flashlight that the man was dead, his skull fractured in the fall, the first so-called innocent American he had killed in the war. His victims in New York had been, until now, Bundists and Sinn Feiners whose incompetence, vanity, or just plain foolishness endangered his own position. Of course, there were no innocents in war. Only enemies.

He shouldered the body and walked with it until he found a likely depository – a blackened stairwell where a feeder tank had exploded from the heat. He left the body there, as if the man had been blown down the stairs,

62

and headed up, hoping to find the promenade deck and firemen whose hoses he would follow off the ship. On B deck he noticed another barn door open. He risked the time to pull it shut and screw down its stops.

There were no firemen on the port-side promenade. Forward, the fire blocked access to crosscorridors. Aft, escape was blocked by crashing fireboat jets and more flame. The slip was jammed with fireboats and ice floes. He climbed out of a broken window between the water jets and the flames and scanned the water for a safe landing.

The crowd gave a sudden cheer. Two men were lowering themselves down the sheer hull in one of the *Normandie*'s lifeboats. Gates watched, holding his breath, praying a shift in the flames wouldn't burn the falls. They landed among the ice floes and rowed to the shore. As an eager mob pulled them up onto Twelfth Avenue, a third man plunged from a broken promenade deck window sixty feet down to the slip. A tug steamed towards his splash, and the crowd cheered again when the crew fished him from the freezing water.

Gates took one more look at the ship's awesome list and shambled into the crowd. Sliding on frozen hose water, tripping on snake nests of hoses welded by the ice to the cobblestones, he headed towards the pier. The navy would have a command post in or near it where he could report the depth of water on C deck.

A beefy civil defence volunteer in a shiny new rubber coat planted his bulk in Gates's path and demanded to know what Gates was doing behind police lines without a pass. Before Gates could answer a second volunteer threw a blanket over his shoulders and yelled over the clatter of the fire pumps that he had seen Gates come down the ladder from the ship.

'He has to have a pass – '

'Shut the hell up, you idiot.'

A pretty girl in a Red Cross cape pressed a container of coffee into Gates's burned hands. They hurt so badly he almost dropped it. She caught the container deftly, the coffee splashing her gloves, and helped him raise the hot, sweet liquid to his lips. Her eyes were wide with excitement, bright as diamonds. Gates mumbled, 'Thanks,' and continued towards the pier.

Bells clanging, ambulances streamed in and out of the area, loading stretcher cases and delivering doctors and nurses from Roosevelt and St Clare's. Hundreds of dazed workers and firemen waited their turn with the medical people, wrapped in army blankets, coughing and spitting black phlegm. Those that could gripped cardboard coffee cups and chewed mechanically on doughnuts brought by the volunteers.

Battered by the roar of the pumpers, Gates circled the wrong way around the fire engines and ambulances and found himself back at the hook-and-ladder truck where he'd started. The *Normandie* was listing fifteen degrees – a horrible angle, like a silent scream.

3

Gates dumped his coffee and climbed up onto the fire engine to see over the crowd. He spotted a cluster of military hats near the pier and jumped down and headed for it, slipping and sliding on the ice, careening into cops and firemen, and asking for directions to the naval command post.

Several tried to stop him, but he lunged free, losing his blanket, ran some more and sprawled headlong on the frozen cobbles. He was back on his feet and breaking into another muddled run when he saw Charlie Collins a few feet in front of him, doubled over, vomiting. Though he had a bleeding gash on his forehead and was fighting to breathe through a racking cough, Charlie shrugged off an ambulance attendant.

'I'm okay . . . just a little smoke. Take one of those burned guys.' He wiped his mouth and saw Gates shambling toward him. 'Hey, Junior. You're all wet.'

His clothes were frozen stiff like Gates's. A *Daily Mirror* photographer snapped a shot of the ambulance attendants pulling Charlie's stiff sleeve. He shrugged them off.

'Why waste an ambulance?' He threw his free arm over Gates's shoulder. 'Come on, Junior. We'll take a cab over to Roosevelt.' He lurched away from the *Normandie*, dragging Gates with him.

'Let *go!*' Gates yelled. 'Where's the navy command post?'

'Longchamps. Thirty-fourth and Fifth.'

'Let me go, Charlie. I got to find them.'

'There's some navy brass over on the quayside.'

A pair of official-looking black cars were parked beside

a crowd of officers in greatcoats on the concrete apron at the foot of the *Normandie*'s bow.

'I tell you, Junior, I'm gaining a fine appreciation for what went wrong at Pearl. What a bunch of birdbrains. Come on. You're a mess, we're going to the hospital.'

Gates jerked free and ran towards the quayside.

An ensign stopped him by the cars. Gates explained who he was and what he had seen in the ship. The ensign told him to wait while he relayed the information to his superiors.

A sigh seemed to swell through the mob. The fire was blistering the grey paint on her midships funnel. The soft, almost poignant sound seemed to quiet for a moment the roaring fire pumps, the tug whistles, the sirens, the droning planes. Cops, firemen, volunteers, dazed and injured workmen, stunned sailors and thousands of on-lookers stared transfixed as the new paint peeled away from the old and revealed the *Normandie*'s original funnel colours – the proud red and black that told New Yorkers whenever she'd come up the Hudson that an old friend was back in town.

'Mr Gates.'

The ensign motioned to Gates to join him on the quayside. He introduced him to a navy captain whose eyes kept flickering like a pendulum from the leaning bow to the fireboats pouring water onto the superstructure.

'What do you want, Mr Gates?'

'I represent Prince and Gates. I just got off your ship. She's got three feet of water on the port side of C deck. There are two barn doors forward on C deck – the first-class embarkation port and the Plymouth embarkation port – both closed. I couldn't reach them . . . the heat. I suggest burning them open from the outside.'

The captain's eyes shifted from the fireboats to the bow to Gates. 'It's out of our hands.'

Gates thought he hadn't heard right. He waited for more, but the captain looked back at the slip.

'Captain, we *have* to drain that water.'

The captain answered without looking. 'We're at the mercy of the New York City Fire Department.'

'If you can't drain C deck, may I respectfully suggest you scuttle her?'

The captain said nothing.

'I mean it . . . she stands a better chance on the bottom.'

'And how are my men supposed to find a strange ship's sea cocks in the dark? She's a thousand feet long, Mr Gates. And my men have been aboard only two weeks.'

'I'll find them,' Gates blurted, surprising himself, even as he weighed his chances. Charlie would come with him. They'd have as good a chance as anybody. 'I did a survey for the Navy Department. I know her as well as any of your people. I'll find them.' Brave talk . . .

The captain turned his back.

'Please, captain, give me some volunteers and I'll bring a couple of mine.'

The ensign was shaking his head.

'It's not as dangerous as you think,' Gates said. 'The fire can't penetrate that far down. She's close to fireproof on the lower decks.'

'We've already asked permission to scuttle her,' said the captain. 'But the New York City Fire Department said no.'

'But you're the captain. She's your ship.'

'It's their fire, Mr Gates. Excuse me.' He walked away, and when Gates tried to follow, the ensign blocked him. They started to argue. The ensign said that traditionally the senior fire department man was in command at a fire. Gates shouted back that even the best firemen couldn't understand the real danger of a ship fire, and that the navy had to protect its ship.

'Tell it to the admiral when he gets here,' the ensign replied bitterly, and Gates realized he was trying to tell him that his captain wouldn't act without orders from higher up and those orders weren't coming. Gates said, 'There isn't time to wait.'

'Don't blame me, goddamn it. I'd go down with you. I'm an engineering officer. I know C deck as good as any civilian naval goddamned architect. But I'm not in command, so get off my back, mister.'

A sudden, grinding tremor rattled the quayside beneath their feet. The startled ensign pointed at a gigantic iron bollard – one of the mooring cleats that anchored the *Normandie*'s docking hawsers.

The bollard was moving.

'*Look.*'

Gates was already looking and he couldn't believe his eyes. This wasn't a crumbling 1880s East River freight dock, but a North River super-pier built for the *Normandie* and *Queen Mary* when Mayor LaGuardia took office, and now the *Normandie*, leaning from the pier, was pulling the bollard out of its reinforced-concrete footing like a lamp plug from a socket.

Gates scrounged a rubber firefighter's coat from an exhausted battalion chief sprawled in the back of an ambulance. A woman on the Salvation Army soup truck found him wool mittens while he gulped a mug of scotch broth. He couldn't find boots, but when the angry engineering ensign saw him shivering at the perimeter of the navy command post he brought Gates a knitted cap. Gates ignored the ache in his frozen shoes, hoping that as long as his feet hurt, the pain meant they weren't frostbitten.

Dusk came early, as the fire still burned, and when it was dark and the smoke that gushed the full length of the *Normandie*'s scorched and shattered superstructure glowed deep red, the fire department wheeled in a special searchlight truck. Its beams swerved through the night, swiping the gigantic hull, lighting the fireboat spouts and the smaller streams pouring back into the slip and hardening to icicles in the bitter wind.

Across Twelfth Avenue the ranks of the onlookers swelled as staff left midtown offices. Tens of thousands stood from Forty-fourth to Fiftieth Streets, beating their hands, stamping their feet. Mounted police, their horses snorting cold breath, held them to the east side of Twelfth and called for reinforcements, while inside the barricades hundreds of volunteer air-raid wardens milled about the ice-crusted fire area demanding credentials and shouting orders at anyone not in uniform. Gates got rid of one zealot who accosted him four times by claiming he worked for the FBI. Moments later he saw the police disperse a gang of wardens who were shoving real FBI agents behind the barricades.

'Mr Gates!' The ensign who'd given him the cap waved him onto the quayside. 'Captain wants to see you. Right inside the pier.' Gates ran, wondering if the captain had changed his mind. He found him shrugging into a rubber coat. 'Are you in as bad shape as you look, Mr Gates?'

'I'm fine, sir.'

'Good. Both my lieutenants got hurt showing the firemen around. Fire's almost out. If you still want to be a hero you can come aboard with me and help with the damage report.'

'Will you scuttle her?'

'It's not my decision any more. It's up to Admiral Anderson. Are you coming, Mr Gates?'

'Thank you.'

'What the hell for?'

Followed by a retinue of stunned midshipmen, they squeezed up the first-class gangway past fresh units of firemen stringing new hoses while the weary firefighters they were relieving rolled up the old. The cold air stank of damp and smoke and burnt paint.

Gates was appalled. He'd never seen a flame-gutted ship. Judging by his expression, neither had the captain. The fire had rampaged down to C deck, destroying what little the *Lafayette* conversion had left of the cavernous first-class dining room. Burned wires dangled from black ceiling frames. Burnt insulation hung from gaping holes in the bulkheads. The sloping decks were thick with sodden ash and broken glass. On B deck nothing remained but scorched steel and dirty, misshapen lumps of heat-fused glass, copper and lead.

But what was worse, and Gates knew it was much worse, was the water on the port side. Four feet on C deck. Three on B. And, according to a city fireman he asked, six feet deep in parts of D deck. Six feet deep and all the cabin portholes were welded shut. 'It's running out those big doors front and back,' said the firefighter, but Gates was not reassured. The harbour would just as easily pour *in* those doors if the *Normandie* listed much more.

Another fireman reported that the fire was out on the promenade deck, but still burning on the upper deck. Gates, the captain and his staff waited at a stairwell that was flowing like a strong creek until the fireman allowed them up. The main salon, where the fire started, the smoking room, the main lobby, the writing room and library and winter garden were all devastated. Nothing of glass, wood or fibre remained.

Her decks were canted about twenty degrees. The captain remarked that the list seemed to have remained the same for the last hour. Gates said nothing. The tide had gone out. Right now she was sitting on the bottom, weighted down by the hose water. Her test would come at midnight as the tide rose again. The question was, would she rise with the tide or flood, and the captain knew it. Gates had already heard his orders to cut holes in her sides to try to drain the water that was dragging her over. His officers responded with a curious lethargy – shock, Gates supposed, victims of a sort of contagious misery and disbelief – and there'd been more talk about clearing it with the fire department. Again Gates volunteered to take a party below to open blocked ports and flood her ballast tanks, and again the captain refused.

Smoke still swirled in the dim emergency lights the fire department had rigged, but it was thin and one by one the killing water spouts ceased rising from the fireboats. As the first pumps shut down, an eerie silence descended on the ship, broken only by a constant watery gurgle and the distant hum of portable generators on Twelfth Avenue. Midships on the listing *Normandie*, five hundred feet from shore, the ferocious activity wound down. Firefighters slumped wearily, axes trailing on the deck, hoses flattening, sinking into water, freezing stiff whenever the air touched them.

It was quite dark except for flashlights and the scattered islands of emergency floodlights. A navy photographer came up the stairs and whistled amazement at the destruction in the grand salon. He unleashed a string of flashbulbs that popped and flared and cast leaping black shadows on the scorched, seared walls.

Flame suddenly spat from a hole in a wall. The spent firemen dragged high-pressure hoses to the outbreak and drowned it. They ripped spun glass and ground cork insulation out of the offending wall with hooks and axes, scattered the debris and warily prowled the ashes, hosing down hot spots, stalking the fire, fighting to the death a relentless, treacherous enemy.

Sickened, Gates stumbled after the captain's retinue as they worked their way back off the ship.

'The chief's got his fire out and the naval people will watch the ship,' proclaimed 'The Little Flower', Mayor Fiorello LaGuardia.

The newspaper reporters had to crowd close to hear his high-pitched voice over the roar of the pumps the navy had rushed aboard the *Normandie* to help drain the water. District Attorney Frank Hogan, the Commissioner of Docks and the Chief Engineer of the Dock Department flanked His Honor. Gates had seen LaGuardia earlier in near-hysterics trying to control the civil defence mob, but now the mayor seemed the embodiment of the able elected official explaining the experts to the press gathered on the quayside.

'How bad is it?' asked a reporter from the *Sun*. Was the list as serious as it looked?

The mayor glanced over his shoulder at the precariously balanced bow. 'It's very tender,' he replied judiciously. 'See how she's listed – and now the job is to pump the water out and that's what we're doing.'

'Was it sabotage?' several reporters shouted at once.

'District Attorney Hogan has already begun his investigation.'

'What about the navy?'

'What does the *Telegram* want to know about the navy?'

'Will they investigate too?'

A beatific smile creased the mayor's unshaven jowls. 'Mr Hogan will conduct a quick, thorough, *intelligent* investigation into the question of whether the fire was sabotage, criminal negligence or . . . gross stupidity.'

The mayor went back inside the pier, but the reporters stayed near the ship, eyeing her list and talking in subdued tones. Gates listened as some reminisced how before the war they'd board the incoming *Normandie* from the pilot boat to interview socialites and movie stars arriving in New York. Not even the *Queen Mary* carried celebrities as the *Normandie* did and the French Line always supplied interview lounges with well-stocked bars and a sumptuous lunch table . . .

The Atlantic tide moved up the Hudson and crept up the *Normandie*'s flanks. Gates watched with a morbid fascination, until the bitter wind drove him for a moment's shelter into the pier building. The cops guarding the door didn't notice because they, like the rest of the small crowd inside, were gaping at Mayor LaGuardia, who was screaming at a rear admiral – a white-haired, stiff-backed officer Gates didn't recognize.

'*I* insulted the *navy*? The navy, sir, insults New York City, which just happens to be the hub of all Allied transport. Whether you realize it or not, sir, the Port of New York

72

enjoys the confluence of the Hudson River, the Erie Canal, the Great Lakes, shipping routes to the east coast of America, as well as the Caribbean, the Atlantic, and the Panama Canal to the Pacific, and also just happens to be the terminus of every national railroad in the United States.'

He took a deep breath and started again, his voice low, but building quickly. 'And through this system New York ships two of every three bullets, guns, tanks, bombers, fighter planes, jeeps, landing craft, bags of wheat, cans of meat, artillery shells and soldiers to the European and Pacific theatres of this war.

'And what is the *navy's* role in all this?' His voice had risen to the upper octaves. 'Up till today you were content to allow Nazi U-boats to sink our freighters five minutes out of Ambrose Channel – I'm not complaining, admiral, it's been damned convenient having our sailors wash up on their neighbourhood beaches. But today you've burned the finest liner in the world right in the middle of Manhattan. She happens to be New York's favourite ship. And God help you, sir, if she turns over in my best pier.'

LaGuardia took another deep breath and looked up at the rafters. Again he started quietly, and again he finished screaming. 'A man's been killed. Two hundred are still in the hospital – including a lot of my firemen – and the Japs and Nazis are going to have a propaganda field day at this great city's expense. It is my fervent hope, admiral, that Mr Hogan finds enough evidence to send you and your entire staff for a Hudson River boatride to Sing Sing!'

White-faced, he stormed out of the pier, noticed the gaping onlookers for the first time, and flung over his shoulder, 'Anybody who prints that'll be covering clambakes on Long Island.'

She was leaning more sharply, stretching her hawsers tight. The extracted bollard had long been dragged into the slip and a second had followed, booming hollowly against her hull. But despite the electric glare of dozens of sweeping searchlights, the fire damage was all but invisible from Twelfth Avenue, which made the dangerous angle look doubly unreal.

The enormous crowds had thinned slightly in the midnight cold, and as Gates walked aimlessly under the highway he suddenly spotted Charlie, returned from the hospital, bandaged and talking his way past the police barricades.

'How you doing, Junior?' His voice rasped from the smoke. 'Should have come. You look like hell.'

'I think she's going to go,' said Gates.

'Cold?' He extended a pint bottle. Gates took it. Irish. He felt warm for the first time since the fireboat sprayed him. They walked to the water's edge for a closer look at the tide. It was rising swiftly towards the barn doors on D deck even as pump water spewed over her side. The loud drone of the pumps had been going so long that Gates no longer consciously heard. He was startled by the sudden blare of loudspeakers.

'Admiral Anderson has ordered all hands to leave the ship. All hands leave the ship. All hands leave the ship.'

Gates turned angrily towards the sound, then jammed his fists in his pockets and started pacing, his head down, his eyes on the cobblestones beside the slip. 'Ordered?' he raged softly to Charlie. 'Ordered? Where the hell was the admiral of the Third Naval District when his captain needed orders? Where the hell was he when the fire department needed orders?'

'Admiral Anderson orders all hands to leave the ship.'

'He's the port captain while there's a war! He could have ordered the fire chief shot, for God's sake, if he didn't stop overloading the ship with water – '

Gates spotted Anderson sitting in a staff car on the quayside.

'I'm going to kill that son of a bitch.'

He stormed across the icy cobbles. Charlie caught up twenty feet from the quayside and pinned his arms.

'Easy, Junior. There's cops all over and some of these

74

navy guys probably know you, so relax. You pop the admiral one in the snoot and Uncle Richard'll pay for it.' He shook him. 'Relax!'

Gates went limp. 'All right, all *right*. Let go.'

'Let's go home.'

'No. Just wait.'

Charlie laid a big hand gently on Gates's shoulder. 'All right, Junior. We'll wait.'

One by one the pumps shut down as their operators trooped off the ship. Harbour water began pouring into her open ports on D deck. The drone of the pump engines ceased and Gates could hear Admiral Anderson addressing a circle of reporters from his car.

'The men have been ordered to evacuate the ship because of a dangerous list.'

'Is she going to capsize, admiral?'

Anderson looked through the windscreen and moved his head noncommittally. Behind the car, a naval lieutenant told another group of reporters, 'The admiral has ordered all hands off the ship as a safety precaution. It does not mean that the ship has been abandoned.'

'Yeah? What *does* it mean?' demanded a *Journal-American* reporter.

'Hope has not been given up, but no one can be certain what the reaction of the ship will be to floodtide.'

'Is she going to turn over?' the *Tribune* man asked.

A gangway tore loose from the pier and crashed against the *Normandie*'s hull. Steel boomed on steel, thunderous in the silence of the stopped pumps.

'She's a goner,' muttered Charlie.

Gates waited for a miracle.

The fireboats backed out of the ship.

The Otter hitched a ride on a fireboat manned by a frozen, exhausted crew that dropped him off at his own tug moored at the end of Pier 90. They and their colleagues had done their job well, overloading the ship with tons of water. He should thank them for their assistance. Looking up across the slip from the tug's low stern he saw the *Normandie* leaning towards him, looming like a Rhine castle. Awed by the sheer size of what he had attacked, he cast off his lines and steered out into the river, skirting her stern until he could see down the length of the slot between the listing ship and her pier.

The fire was out and the smoke gone, but the proof of what he had done was the shape of that slot – an inverted triangle, wide at the top, narrow at the waterline – the space caused by her inclination away from the pier. That triangle was his, and even as he watched, the *Normandie* leaned further, tearing at her moorings.

A hawser, stretched so tightly it contracted by half, snapped. Two lengths of hemp soared apart. One frayed end flailed the pier. The other lashed the ship. She pulled a second gangway from the pier, then the third.

Alone in her slip, the *Normandie* embraced the killing tide.

Gates heard a fateful clatter in the hull, the sound of a heavy object sliding down a steeply tilted deck and smashing into the port side. Suddenly a work crane tumbled off the foredeck and splashed into the slip. A long wooden boat fell next, rolling down the deck like a cucumber. It was the captain's launch.

The solitary bangs and crashes quickened pace and soon a ceaseless, overlapping chain of racket accompanied the cascade of pumps, tools, bunks, building materials and furniture as she leaned closer and closer to an impossible angle. She reached it and listed a little further, held that awful angle like a frightened breath, then toppled over as quiet as a sigh, and lay down gently on her thousand-foot flank.

4

The trombone player at the Rainbow Room noticed that
the pretty girl in the green dress had noticed him too. Her
eyes found his each time she passed the orchestra. They
were a startling shade of light blue, pure as the centre
of a gnarled and sea-beaten iceberg he'd seen from the
U-boat that brought him to America to operate a radio
for the Otter.

Her partner whirled her past the bandstand and she
said loudly, as if she wanted the trombone player to hear,
'What a marvellous orchestra!'

English accent. Maybe one of the secretaries at the
British government offices down below in Rockefeller
Center. Thousands of English worked there – including
counter-intelligence – which made Herr Otter's *meldekopf*
hidden on the roof such a great joke on the British.

He began anticipating her circuits around the dance
floor, waiting for her smile. She appraised him with a
steady, open look. She was interested. He'd played the
clubs in Berlin long enough to know that look. It was
the same on either side of the Atlantic, and either side
of the war.

He lost sight of her reddish hair suddenly among the
dancers.

Between quick glimpses at his music and the band
leader, he searched for her among the triple tier of tables
that ascended from the dance floor. She was wearing
a green like the green in this vast room of glass and
polished metal and coloured lights playing on the ceiling
set sixty-five storeys above Manhattan like a fantastic
ocean liner gliding through a smooth night sky.

He took the Miller solo for 'Careless'. They played 'Stardust' next and the girl came back with a different man, a stocky blond built like a fire hydrant and dancing like one, too. Now the grin she gave him was rueful. If he'd been a customer and not in the band he'd have taken it as an invitation to cut in.

'The Rhumba Jumps!' ended the set. The break piano player sat in, the customers drifted off the floor to eat supper. The trombone player propped his instrument against his chair and left, carrying a long black trombone case under his arm.

He hung back as the band traipsed through the kitchen, heading for a smoke, then turned suddenly into a corridor and unlocked a door. Alone in a service stairwell, he hurried up five flights, pushed through a fire door at the top and caught his breath as he looked around the near darkness. Checking that he had his key, he let the door lock behind him and stepped into the night.

A breeze played across the top of the seventy-storey skyscraper. The city was dimmed out slightly but still not enough to eliminate the glow that silhouetted freighters for the U-boats at sea. On the roof of the RCA Building the glow was reflected down from a low cloud cover. He could see his own hands clearly, and in the distance the silhouettes of the NBC radio broadcast antennae that bristled at the south wall like empty music stands.

Scattered among them were the tall, spiky overseas directional antennae beamed at Europe. The American networks linked up with the BBC by some of those aerials. By others, it had received live reports from European correspondents before the United States had entered the war. He knelt at the foot of one and opened his trombone case.

In the bulging horn end was a compact battery-powered radio transmitter. He turned it on to warm the tubes and plugged into a hidden receptacle at the base of the beam antenna. In the narrow end of the instrument case was a wire player which was connected to the transmitter. A soft green light glowed between the transmitter and the wire player – a luminous-dial chronometer adjusted regularly to Naval Observatory time.

He waited until the transmitter tubes glowed hot, like burning cigarette tips in the night. Placing his fingers on the wire player switch, he watched the chronometer. When the second hand started an exact five-minute interval, he turned on the player. Two small reels turned. The recording wire passed silently through the playing heads for six seconds. He rewound the wire, waited exactly two minutes and ran it again. Including the first burst – which had doubled as a fine-tuning beam for the Hamburg receivers to home in on his signal – total exposure had been twelve seconds. If they were alert, the American monitors might know that a clandestine signal had been transmitted to Germany, but twelve seconds wasn't enough time to locate its source.

'*There* you are.'

He leaped up in panic, skidding on the gravel roof and trying desperately to see every way at once. The nightmare was on him – trapped four thousand miles from home with an illegal transmitter, forged papers and not a single word to explain or cover himself.

She called again and he saw to his astonishment the English girl tottering across the roof gaily waving a cigarette. She looked off-balance on spike heels and awash with martinis. As his pulses steaded he saw she had no wrap. Her bare shoulders glowed white as a shining moon.

'I thought I saw you come up here.'

He moved quickly towards her, away from the apparatus. 'You're not supposed to be up here. It's a restricted area.'

She threw her head back and laughed. Her throat was very white. 'I won't tell if you won't tell.'

He got a grip on his fear. Of all the crazy times for a broad to come looking for action from the band. Somehow he had to coax her downstairs, but gently, so she would meet him later. He smiled a greeting. His heart had ceased pounding when he saw the shadows emerging from the dark beneath the south wall. He gaped, stunned, as they moved stealthily towards the antennae. For an instant more he was paralysed with astonishment. They'd used the oldest trick in the book, and he'd fallen for it.

But why did they go to the trouble? They already had him trapped. Why had they used the girl? There was no escape – the Otter's wire! They wanted his message. The girl kept him off-guard, gave them time to surprise him before he could destroy it – he dived to the wire player, scrabbled painfully on the coarse gravel and ripped out the precious reel. He heard them running. He threw it into the night.

The tall one jumped, levering himself up the chest-high wall at the edge of the roof. His long fingers splayed wide, feeling the air like wings, and closed on the reel. He slid down the wall and crashed to the roof. Springing back to his feet, he pocketed the wire and joined the circle forming around the German. There were two others, a stocky blond built like a fire hydrant, and an older man with a reddish moustache and a menacing expression. The blond spoke and the German's blood ran cold. If the Otter didn't kill him for this, these men would.

'Pack it in, mate. Before you get hurt.'

English. He was through. Britain's fierce secret army in New York City – hundreds, maybe thousands, of intelligence agents – operated by the same rules as in Europe. They'd rip him apart for information and throw his remains in the river. He thought of the Jew from California. The Gestapo had discovered him in Austria looking for his parents – a musician with a union card and a valid American passport and no family but his missing parents – the ideal candidate to disappear so that the Abwehr might give the Otter another radio agent in New York. Even his trombone had value – American-made, not German. The Jewish musician, when his time came, must have felt this alone.

The worst part was he knew nothing. He'd never seen or even spoken to the Otter by telephone. He had nothing to give them, but they would never believe that until he was dead. They circled warily to ten feet, positioned as they'd earlier been around their table. Two men to his right, the girl and the tall man who'd caught the reel to the left, nearest the edge of the roof.

'Right you are, mate. Just keep very, very still and slowly raise your hands.'

The sleeve pistol was four and a half inches long and weighed a ton at the end of a long night of holding up the horn. It also escalated the risk of being captured, but he carried it because the Remington double-barrel breech-loading cartridge derringer served, like a talisman, as a small object between himself and immobilizing fear.

'Look out — '

She was fast. She called out her warning even before he could complete the down snap of his arm. The derringer slid from his sleeve into his palm, but the British were already at him, forcing him back and spoiling his grip on the gun. It rolled in his hand. He took a second step back, buying time to wrap his finger around the spur trigger while he brought the stubby barrels to bear.

His heel banged into the trombone case. He tripped, windmilling backward into the antennae, and fired blindly. They scattered from the blazing muzzle.

He ran at the girl, caught a quick gleam of animal intelligence in her startled eyes. Her dancing pump came off the roof in a black patent blur, but he sidestepped the lightning kick and was on her before they could stop him. He grabbed her from behind, wrapping his arm around her chest and jamming the derringer into her neck.

He started backing across the roof, dragging the girl with him, hurting her to control her. And to punish her for tricking him. 'Come with me,' he called to the men. 'Stay close. I'll kill her if I can't see you.' They exchanged glances, did as he ordered, fanning out, but not enough to threaten him. He retreated to the door he'd come up through from the kitchen.

'Stop.'

The stopped, again exchanging glances.

He tightened his hand. 'Listen to me . . .'

She nodded, her breath coming in short gasps.

'Take the key from my right-hand trouser pocket.'

Her obvious pain gave him some sense of control of the impossible situation. He began to hope. If he could continue to hold them by this door while he got it unlocked, pushed through it, and locked it again, he might have enough of a head start before they re-entered the observatory to get down to the street level or the subway and out of the building.

'*Get the key.*'

'I can't move my arm.'

He loosened his own arm but kept his hand clawed around her breast. The men were watching closely. The tall one was wary, tight. The older one, the leader, strangely impassive. The blond man who'd done the talking was clenched with rage. 'I'll kill you for this.' He actually took a step forward, which the older one stopped with a whipcrack command.

The control was making the German heady. The panic and fear of a moment past had evaporated in a new glow of power. The girl still hadn't reached for his pocket.

'*Get the key,*' he repeated, hurting her with his fingers.

Her hand descended jerkily into his pocket and he couldn't resist. 'Just the key. You can have my cock later.'

The blond man made to move again, and the other two reached to restrain him. She felt around his pocket, brushing his cock, jerking away as if she were burned, feeling through the coins, cigarette lighter, spare mouthpiece. It was taking too long. The pleasure of control was going.

'Hurry *up*.'

He didn't bother to hurt her this time. The gun against her throat was enough. Her hand moved convulsively.

She whimpered with pain and for a moment he puzzled over what was hurting her. He was cupping her breast like a lover, not squeezing at all, just reminding her he was there, and yet she was whimpering and clenching her body as if she hurt badly.

And then it was he who hurt with a deep, searing agony.

The smell of burned cloth and hair came to him, and he screamed as his trousers spouted flames. He tried to pull the trigger . . . the bitch had ignited his cigarette lighter and held her tongue while the searing flame had caught . . . but his pain wouldn't let him. All he could do was drop the gun and run.

They came after him as he beat the flames, burning bare hands, fell down and rolled over and over. The pain made him want to double up and hold himself, but sheer terror gave him strength to keep rolling, to stumble to his feet, to make a run for it again. They followed him through the thicket of aerials. He gained a bit on them and scrambled up the wall at the roof edge. Eight hundred and fifty feet down, the city fell away as if seen through the back end of a telescope.

The tall one was first through the aerials. He grabbed his foot. The German tore free, kicking him in the face. Below, taxi lights darted about the dimmed streets like glow-worms. The kick thrust him off balance. He leaned far into the night, his tuxedo flapping, cigarettes tumbling into the wind.

They lunged for him, and he reflexly kicked them away before he realized that they were trying to save him. One shoe was scrabbling at air. His other slipped from the ledge. He noticed a blur of swiftly rising dark windows. He thought he heard the beautiful English girl cry out to him . . . forgiving him for hurting her? . . . but the voice hovered beside him on the long plunge earthward until he knew it was his own, shrill with terrible anticipation.

In a secure room at the back of a block of adjoining suites on the twelfth floor of the Hotel Meurice on West Fifty-eighth Street, Cordi Grey threaded the late German agent's reel into a wire player. She worked awkwardly, her burned hand hastily bandaged, her fingers stiff with excitement. This was a real breakthrough.

One of her high-heel shoes lay by the door, the second in the middle of the room, kicked off as she ran in with the wire. Still wearing her green evening dress, she looked as if she'd stepped off the dance floor into the ladies' lounge. Three months in New York had finally yielded something important for the secret British intelligence group coded Group M, for Meurice.

Duncan Haig, who had a welt darkening his cheek where the German's derringer had clipped him, began disassembling the shortwave transmitter on a workbench littered with wire leads, alligator clips, test instruments and electrician's tools. He was Group M's boffin – a technical wizard – whose expert skill included radio and electrical engineering. Duncan, too, was still dressed in evening clothes, but his blond hair was rumpled and his shirt bunched around his thick waist. They had come directly the eight blocks from Rockefeller Center with the German's trombone case full of radio apparatus. Mark St George and Weatherburn – the latter their group leader – had stayed behind to search for the body.

Cordi played the wire, was surprised and disappointed to hear nothing but a very short burst of high-pitched squeaks, followed by silence on the rest of the wire. She played the silence to the end, then rewound and listened again. The room lights dimmed for a moment.

Instantly, Cordi took one of Weatherburn's revolvers out of her desk and levelled it at the door. Duncan had rigged an intrusion-warning pressure-sensitive floorplate under the carpet in the front hall. He was too engrossed in the German's radio to react to the alarm, but he looked up a moment later, as if sensing Cordi's gun.

Weatherburn rapped his quick-four knock, opened the door with his key and marched in, nodding approval at Cordi's gun and giving a bleak glance from under his bushy ginger eyebrows at Duncan, which said where was his. Duncan held up pliers and soldering iron, but had the good sense to say nothing. Weatherburn could be obsessive on the subject of security.

'He landed in the eleventh-floor roof garden,' Weatherburn announced in his thin, tenor voice. 'Damned good luck. We got him inside before anyone saw.'

His thick, neat ginger moustache practically shouted professional army, and he had the weathered, ruddy complexion that Cordi associated with the sort of officer who'd done more service in the field than at a desk, the sort referred to as 'a man's man'. The fact of the matter was he'd spent little time in the regular army after World War I.

No one knew his entire background, but details she'd picked up during her training, after he had recruited her for the Secret Intelligence Service, included a story that he'd joined the special police in Ireland – the Black and Tans – when he was demobilized. After the Irish troubles, and before he had joined Intelligence, he had worked for a special unit of the Colonial Army that put down the periodic rebellions that flared up against the Raj in the late twenties and early thirties.

He was of smallish build, and quick in his movements, but with slow, patient eyes – the eyes of a hunter, like a leopard, which would rather set an ambush than chase. His bushy brows were flecked with grey, but his thinning hair was close enough to her own hair colour to let them pretend they were father and daughter – an occasionally useful deceit with an odd feeling of truth; he hadn't, of course, given her life, but he had saved her life and when she looked at the little bantam of a man she often recalled the first time she had seen him in Geneva walking calmly out of the dark, his hands filled with flaming pistols like a cinema cowboy, gunning down the Germans who'd already killed Alec and were dragging her into their car.

Then after saving her life he'd got her out of Switzerland, explaining that a German agent named the Otter had destroyed the BBC station that Alec had converted into a clandestine radio for British agents in Europe. Recruitment had been a simple matter. Weatherburn had remarked on her range of languages, and Cordi, the war made suddenly personal by Alec's death, had asked to join whatever secret group it was that Alec had served. Since her training, which Weatherburn had personally supervised, they had worked together, forming with Duncan and Mark the group now called M in America, which continued the hunt for the Otter.

Mark St George, Weatherburn's very tall and elegant personal aide, came in after him like a favourite hound. As with the older man, his eyes gave everything in the room a fast once-over before he closed the door. He looked at Cordi, who nodded that she was all right.

'Interesting radio, sir,' said Duncan. 'A new version of their standard *Afus*.' The *Afus*, *Agentenfunk*, was a suitcase agent-radio, shortwave, built by Telefunken. A new model suggested that the *Afus*, and likely the agent himself, had arrived in New York recently, but Weatherburn ignored Duncan to speak to Cordi.

'That was rather foolhardy, my girl. He might have shot you.'

'I didn't see many knights galloping to my rescue.'

'He had us . . . as they say . . . over a barrel,' Weatherburn chastised her. 'Now the man is dead and we don't know who he was sending for. Too bad you let him grab you – '

'He surprised me. I tried to stop him getting past and never thought it was me he was after.'

'You do tend to forget you're a woman . . . How's your hand?'

Cordi held up the gauze bandage. Getting hurt took some of the sting out of feeling stupid. 'Duncan put Unguentine on it.'

'And the . . . rest of you?'

'The rest of me is sore but intact, thank you.'

'Any luck with the recording wire?'

'Nothing yet. It's just a bunch of squeaks. Do you want to hear?'

'Later. What's this about a new radio, Duncan?'

'Well, it was obviously set up to transmit the information on the recording wire. There's no telegraph key. It would have sent the magnetic impulses on the wire normally used to activate a loudspeaker.'

'I don't know what you're talking about, but I'll take your word for it. But if there's no telegraph key, how would he reply to questions from the receiving station?'

'There's a place for a key, but no key. Did you find anything in his pockets?'

'His pockets were holed, thanks to Cordi.'

Duncan smiled. Weatherburn said he was going to report the night's action, and Mark followed him silently through the door. While Duncan heated a soldering iron and went back to the *Afus*, Cordi threaded the wire player and turned it on.

It emitted a rapid stream of high-pitched bleeps that sounded like a record player speeded up a hundred times, and it stopped as suddenly as it had started. She reversed the machine and ran the wire again. Six seconds of high-pitched bleeps, then silence. She had earlier tried reversing the wire with no better results. She turned if off and stared at the ugly machine.

The room was silent, except for Duncan's self-congratulatory murmurs whenever the transmitter surrendered a secret comprehended only by himself. Six rooms stood between this room and the outside hall door.

Its one window was double-shuttered. An ultra-modern calculating machine occupied the rear wall, and a powerful shortwave receiver filled the closet. The rest was armchairs and an overstuffed settee that got increasingly uncomfortable on long nights, hot plate and kettle, cupboard, desks with file drawers and telephones.

On the rare occasions the shutters were open, the window offered a narrow view north, showing a slice of Central Park through an alley slit between the Essex House and Hampshire House hotels on Central Park South. Cordi, Mark and Duncan had rooms in the Meurice complex, but Weatherburn, whose cover required that he entertain, kept a penthouse apartment in the Hampshire House, on whose high, copper-green peaked roof they had secreted one of their monitoring antennae.

Suddenly Cordi heard a new sound. Duncan was staring silently at the transmitter with his head in his hands, but through the shutters came a muffled clatter, the hooves of a horse pulling a hansom cab on Central Park South. The animal was passing the alley at a quick trot, and its shoes sounded on the street like a Morse telegraph key.

'Duncan?'

'What do you *want*?' He got up and peered suspiciously at the player.

'I want the wire to play more slowly.'

Duncan went to his workbench and fished through his junk box. He unplugged the wire player's cord, cut it, stripped the ends and connected them to a bulky box with a round knob. When he turned the knob, the wire reels picked up speed gradually like a locomotive's drive wheels.

'Bless you, Duncan.'

'Don't overdo it or you'll burn the switch out.' He went back to the transmitter while Cordi reversed the machine and played the wire again and again at increasingly slower speeds.

Ten minutes later, when the alarm lights dimmed, she was almost too excited to remember the gun. It was

Weatherburn and Mark. Weatherburn sank wearily into a chair. 'How about the wire?' he said.

'Listen!' Cordi pushed the play button. 'Here is what he sent. Remember Duncan said the same electrical impulses that sound on the recorder stimulate the telegraph key.'

The machine uttered six seconds of squeaky high-pitched bleeps.

'Sounds like Donald Duck,' Mark said gravely.

'It baffled me,' said Cordi. 'Then I remembered something offhand one of the instructors at Bletchley said about burst transmission. Duncan put this speed knob on the machine.'

Cordi twisted the knob. 'Listen to it at five times slower.' She let it run for several seconds, shut it off and rewound the wire.

'Goofy,' Duncan said, coming over and sitting on the edge of her desk. 'Do another.'

'Ten times reduction,' said Cordi. 'Listen.' The machine uttered a staccato clicking, and the others sat up straight.

'Morse,' said Weatherburn. 'How did he do it?'

'He recorded the message from a telegraph key. Then he speeded up the wire recorder and rerecorded it on a second recorder at ten times speed onto this wire. Whoever received the transmission in Germany would do what we've just done and have his message – a full minute of transmission sent in six seconds.'

'I couldn't make it out,' said Mark.

'I thought Duncan could take a crack at the cipher with the machine.'

'Get to it, Duncan,' Weatherburn ordered.

Cordi rewound the reel. 'Wait. Listen again.'

'Do you expect me to pull the code out of the air?' asked Weatherburn. 'Let Duncan use the machine.'

Cordi played the wire and the Morse chattered again. '*Listen*. His fist? The telegrapher's hand? Don't you recognize it?'

They strained towards the recording. A slow smile . . . as much as he ever allowed . . . spread across Weatherburn's ruddy face. 'Is it him?'

Cordi nodded. '*I think it's the Otter's fist.*'

'Get cracking, Duncan!'

Duncan donned earphones and jacked them into the wire player. He quickly transcribed the Morse code into a jumble of letter blocks, the German's cipher, which he fed laboriously into the calculating machine, which in turn chattered busily away.

They were all trained telegraphers and to their ears a telegrapher's 'fist' or 'hand' – the pattern at which he set the short and long signals of Morse code – was as distinctive, and revealing, as a signature.

'Do you suppose that could have been him on the roof?' asked Cordi.

Weatherburn shook his head emphatically. 'You'd be dead, young lady, if it had been. Besides, we've never known him to use a gun. Also, we know that the trombone player joined the orchestra last summer, and we were reasonably sure that our man was in England until the Japanese attacked Pearl Harbor.'

'We don't know that,' said Cordi. 'We have wire recordings of his hand transmitting from this country on and off since '39.'

'*Similar*,' said Weatherburn, raising a cautionary hand. 'We don't *know*. In fact, until I heard this, I suspected he was still in England, laying low, while we came wild goosing to New York.'

'More than similar,' argued Cordi. 'Do you know what I think? I think he's been in New York *and* England.'

'Back and forth.' Weatherburn nodded. 'I hate to say it, but I've thought of that too.'

'But how?' asked Mark.

Weatherburn shrugged. 'U-boat. Or access to *our* transport. Convoys or even courier planes. Frightening. Because if that's how he does it, then he's among us. Which is why we four can trust no one. Duncan, what the devil is taking so long?'

Duncan muttered. 'He encoded from German.'

'Shall I have a crack at it?' asked Cordi.

'You can do the German,' Duncan said. 'What a language. No wonder they breed mathematicians. How the hell else could they communicate than by numbers?'

'If it's going to take much longer,' Weatherburn called sourly, 'we'll parachute Cordi into Abwehr HQ for Admiral Canaris's translation.'

'We shouldn't have let him send,' Mark said quietly. They'd learned that the musician had been transmitting from the RCA Building, but neither where nor how he connected to the overseas antennae, and had lost valuable minutes tracking him to the roof when he had disappeared in the kitchen.

'Never mind,' said Weatherburn. 'We'll keep his demise to ourselves, watch his room. Who knows what'll come sniffing around for his services? And no one will know that we know what the message was. Damn it, Duncan, should we go home to bed?'

'I've got it deciphered, sir. It's the same cipher they've been using since January. He signs off "Otter".'

Cordi scanned the German for its overall meaning. She forced herself to concentrate as she wrote the sixty-second, twenty-word message on a notepad.

'He's reported the convoy that sails tomorrow.'

'What? That's odd. Let me see it.'

While Weatherburn scanned the message, Mark got up and laid a long, thick-knuckled hand on Cordi's shoulder. 'Atmospherics were terrible today. The signal probably didn't even get through to Germany . . . '

Weatherburn looked up and repeated, 'Odd.'

'What's that, sir?' Duncan asked as he turned off the calculator and the machine sighed to a silence.

'Herr Otter has always been too important for this sort of thing.'

'He describes the convoy's cargo, as well as its departure hour,' Cordi said hotly. 'I'd hardly call it *that sort of thing* . . . What more do the U-boats need?'

'There's a dozen German spies in New York who do this sort of work. They transmit on weak portable sets to South America, where the German legations relay it to Berlin. Half don't get through. This just doesn't seem up to the Otter's style. He's not a spy who snoops about for the bits and pieces of information, Cordi. He never has been. He's a saboteur, and a damned good one. A master intriguer. I presume none of you have forgotten how he diverted a lorry load of our own aerial bombs to level an East End dock that the Luftwaffe had missed. Or how he obliterated our supposedly secret radio station in Geneva.'

Cordi nodded reluctant agreement.

Weatherburn got to his feet and began pacing between the calculating machine and the shuttered window. He'd shed his weariness like a coat and now chopped the air with quick hands as he returned to the theme he'd expounded on earlier. 'We're dealing here with Admiral Canaris's personal creation – I'm sure of it – a master saboteur with *carte blanche* to destroy whatever he sees fit and with all the support of the Reich behind him. That makes even reporting convoys small potatoes for him. He'd like us to believe that's all he's up to, but it's something bigger. He's established himself in New York and we are, I'm convinced, going to hear a good deal from him. For all we know he's infiltrated legitimate groups in New York. For that matter he could be inside British Security Coordination itself, which is why you three are here under the deepest cover and why I'm the only officer in BSC who knows about you or this room, other than the person I report to.'

Weatherburn paused at the window, opened both shutters and peered out at the dawn light spilling into the alley.

'And since *we* don't know *his* name,' said Cordi, 'try not to blunder in front of the Fifth Avenue bus, *sir*.'

'There's nothing funny about security,' snapped Weatherburn. 'Apparently I haven't impressed it enough on any of you how precarious our position is, how vulnerable we are to infiltration and betrayal. For God's sake, do you think we're the only people who can play this game? Do you think the double cross MI5 pulled on the Nazis in England couldn't also be worked against us? Do you think the Germans are stupid? Do you?'

'No, sir.'

'You'd bloody well better not or you'll wake up one day strapped to a chair in one of their interrogation rooms. Can you tell me for sure that the doorman downstairs wasn't put there by the Otter? How about your taxi driver, Mark? Or the chap beside you in the pub, Duncan? How about you, Cordi? How about the police inspector you interviewed this afternoon? Who does he really report to?'

5

The Coast Guard seaman manning the Hoboken naval pier gate had a new uniform, a polished sidearm, a clipboard and orders to check everybody's pass, no exceptions. Escort craft were loading stores and ammunition, so the chief had made a big deal about strict security, but so far the detail boiled down to a sore arm from directing trucks and saluting officers. Then a New York City taxicab drove into the gate yard and a very pretty girl hopped out and all of a sudden things were looking up.

'I'm going out to the *Lewiston*,' she announced airily, pausing to adjust her hat and soft auburn hair in the reflection of the guard shack window. She had an English accent and a white bandage around the fingers of one hand. Satisfied that her shoulder-cut bob was in place, she turned to him with a smile. 'Where is the ship docked?'

'Can I see your pass, ma'am? Please?'

'We're doing an OB,' she said. 'My pass is in the recording car and they're not here yet. I've come ahead to select the sailors to be interviewed.'

'Yes, ma'am,' he said doubtfully, without a clue what she was talking about. She had white-on-white skin and when the sun glinted on her hair it was almost red. She seemed to understand his confusion, and smiled again.

'I'm a BBC correspondent, don't you see?'

He looked at her blankly.

'The British Broadcasting Corporation. We're doing an outside broadcast. I'm a radio reporter.'

'I get it, yeah. But I don't think I can let you out there without a pass, ma'am.'

'Now I'd be so grateful if you could tell the engineers when they get here in the recording car that I've gone ahead to the *Lewiston* and they should follow. You'll show them where to go?'

'I think I better ask my chief.'

'Thank you,' she said, peering past him at the cobblestones and rails which led to the pier. 'And could you ask him to escort me out there? I don't think I want to walk past all those sailors, alone.'

The Coast Guardsman caught a whiff of her perfume riding lightly on the river breeze. The idea of an ape like his chief petty officer escorting this girl anywhere was more than he could stand. He slammed the main gate in the teeth of an incoming trailer truck.

'I'll take you, ma'am.'

Her smile was thanks enough. She had long legs and walked fast despite her high heels, and he found himself almost trotting past the warehouses as he brandished his clipboard. 'Your name, please, ma'am. I have to log everybody in.'

'Grey. Cordelia Grey . . . Here's the pier. I can make it from here on my own, thank you. Which is the *Lewiston*?'

'At the end, tied crosswise.' He recovered enough courage to ask what her interviews were about, but she just shook her head and kept going.

Trucks were blaring back at the gate, but he stood where she left him, filling her name into the log, staring after her and wishing he was a little older, a lot richer, and, damn it, an officer. She was tall and lean, in a fitted skirt, her hands in her pockets holding her coat open to the fading morning sun, and if the whistles and catcalls she drew from the seamen and stevedores on the ships and cranes bothered her, she didn't show it.

His buddy, who'd gone to take a leak, came up behind him. 'Who's she?'

'One of our British allies.'

The second Coast Guardsman stared wistfully, ignoring

the chorus of angry shouts at the gate. 'Why'd we wait so long to get into the war?'

The pier was wooden and old, its planks scuffed thin and sun-shrunk so that the river gleamed through wide joints. A mile across the Hudson was the Manhattan skyline, the sunlit buildings spiky clumps against a rapidly greying sky. The river was crowded with tugs and freighters and grey warships trailed by soft streams of white smoke. On either side of the pier were longer and broader piers covered with railroad track and freight cars and shunting engines, typical of hundreds of national railroad eastern terminus points that overshot the Jersey waterfront, and vivid reminders why the Otter had come to the Port of New York.

Halfway along the naval pier, Cordi Grey stopped a moment, puzzled. The ship tied crosswise at the end was not the escort carrier she had assumed her brother's *Lewiston* would be. It was, instead, a fair-sized three-island freighter of about eight thousand tons, looming much higher and bulkier than the naval DEs and corvettes pressing against the dock like scrawny fox pups nursing.

She walked closer, but when she could see its full length beyond a corvette which had blocked her view, she stopped again, disturbed by the unlikely sight of an aeroplane perched on its bow, a Sea Hurricane so incongruously placed that at first thought it seemed it must have crashed on the freighter's foredeck. It hadn't. The fighter was intact astride a catapult, poised for flight.

Then Tom came galloping down the gangway, his lanky gangling stride unmistakable even at that distance. Shouting her name, he ran to her. Cordi applied a smile over her fear. He gave her a brotherly hug and a kiss on the cheek, vastly disappointing the watching sailors, then stepped back nervously.

'How'd you get a pass?'

'I told the guard I was doing a story.'

Tom was sporting a black eye he hadn't had when he'd arrived in New York the day before yesterday. 'Where's the recording car?'

'The man thinks it's coming with my pass. What is this ship supposed to be?'

'What happened to your hand?'

'I poured the kettle on it. I get so confused out here. The taps turn the wrong way. The light switches go up instead of down. Now will you kindly explain this ship?'

'What do you think of her?' he asked lightly.

Size was all the freighter had going for it. Rusted, sea-battered and dock-bruised, it looked a poor match for the North Atlantic. As for German U-boats, she knew now why Tom, with a few drinks under his belt yesterday, had dubbed her 'tonnage-in-waiting'. But her condition was hardly the worst of it.

'It's not an aircraft carrier,' she said.

Tom grinned, obviously nervous about misleading her. He was a year older, but since the war he had gradually assumed a new role of little brother, a change both recognized and neither questioned, though only Cordi understood why.

'There's no fooling the BBC. How many women would have noticed the severe shortage of aircraft.'

'Not to mention the lack of a flight deck,' she shot back, angry and sick with fear for him. 'Take-off must be rather diccy.'

'Not so. I just rev up the motor and the steam catapult chucks me off like an intelligent cannonball.'

'Or a loud drunk.'

Tom grinned again. 'She's a CAM, as you probably already know. Catapult Armed Merchantman or Catapult Aircraft Merchantman, depending on who you're talking to. Perfectly safe. In actual fact it beats trundling down a pitching flight deck praying to gods you never heard of for air speed before you run out of ship. Besides, the few escort carriers we've got are tied up with Russian convoys, so the CAM is all we've really got until we build some more carriers.'

'How do you land? . . . oh, Tom, how did you get into this?'

She hadn't cried since early in the war, and she was astonished to feel hot tears burning her eyes. It was knowing that the convoy had been betrayed, knowing that she couldn't tell anyone. And even if she did break every rule of security – rules that if Alec had obeyed instead of being so naïve, as they all were early in the war, he would still be alive – and gave Tom information exposing, compromising herself and by extension Weatherburn, Mark and Duncan, threatening all of them and their mission because airmen were so often captured alive by the enemy . . . even then the convoy would sail.

Cordi turned away, blinking into the sun, clinging to the middle ground of hope that the radio signal hadn't penetrated the atmospherics. But still her eyes filled and across the Hudson the skyscrapers seemed to melt and the ships on the river turned to an impressionist's daubs.

Tom joked apologetically for allowing the fear between them. 'Not to worry. Being the only pilot aboard makes me *senior* pilot. It already looks as if I'll be elected president of the airmen's mess.'

Cordi wiped her eyes with her bandage. 'Sounds like a smashing opportunity to recommend yourself for a VC . . . I presume you haven't told Mother.'

All their lives she and Tom and banded against their mother's gloom, sided with their father, who'd lost as much in the World War and more, lost through every day of a marriage to a woman who regarded him as her second choice since her first husband had been killed. His life too had been in ashes after the war. But afterwards he had learned to take pleasure in success, money and the love of his children. He had even encouraged Cordi's friendship with a somewhat raffish, unconventional Alec – knowing full well where it was going, but knowing too that Alec was a decent person who would encourage Cordi to use her talents to be more than just another well-educated young wife and mother.

Well, the war had seen to that. Whatever she was, she wasn't a mother, barely a correspondent any more, years from being the pacifist her mother had tried to make her, light-years from the actress she had once wanted to be. Except maybe not so far from acting. This work with Weatherburn – this pretending and concealing – was done best by dissemblers and thieves, but well enough by actors too. She had met all sorts in training. Some were adventurers, most were patriots. For her, though, it had started personally with Alec killed by the Nazis in Geneva, and she'd turned professional under Weatherburn's infuence in order to survive. Professional. Hardbitten? A façade – part of the job, less a part of the woman . . .

Tom looked up at his plane standing at the start of the catapult like a long-legged bug drying its wings. The catapult girder was less than three times the Hurricane's length. 'Of course not. And I certainly didn't intend to tell you either. I never thought you'd get past the gate. No one else has.'

'I guess he was impressed by the BBC. And almost everybody wants his name on the radio – now, how the devil does all this work? When do you fly?'

'One hopes never. But if Jerry's U-boats hit the convoy from four directions and the escorts can't contain them, I pop up, locate the bastards, strafe any stupid enough to remain on the surface and drop depth bombs on the rest.'

'And then what?'

'When we've finished with them I patrol for a couple of hours hunting more U-boats. Good chance there, if they haven't been in radio contact, because they're not expecting a plane out in the middle of the ocean.'

'Then what?' asked Cordi, knowing the answer but hoping that somehow Tom would make it sound better.

'Well, when I'm out of fuel I fly back to mummy here and ditch alongside. She picks me up. I put on dry clothes and have a cup of hot tea and a kip. Nothing to fly until we reach England.'

'The plane sinks?'

'It's expensive, but if I save one freighter carrying twenty American airplanes in her hold, I've paid my way.'

'And if *you* sink too?'

'Down with my ship? Not bloody likely – '

'You know what I mean.'

Tom looked at a line of freighters steaming downriver, heading for the Lower Bay, where they were forming up the convoy. He took a pack of cigarettes from his grease-splattered flying jacket, passed one to Cordi and lit both. 'I've ditched before.'

Cordi nodded. The fact was, Tom was lucky and in that they were blessed. He'd ditched two Spits during the Battle of Britain and both times had been pulled from the Channel without a scratch.

'What's happened to your eye?'

Tom grinned. 'The Germans in Hoboken are beating up British seamen. The ship's crew invited me along for a little retaliatory *blitzkrieg* last night.'

'I hope they did better than you.'

Tom held up scabbed knuckles. 'There's one German-American who'll be sipping his knackwurst through a straw.'

She went with him up the rickety gangway. Tom took her to the captain, a round and florid old Scot with dying eyes. He insisted they share a dram, poured the whisky with trembling hands and promised Cordi in a hollow voice that he'd 'keep an eye on the laddie'.

'Rather more casual than the Royal Navy,' Tom said as they left the bridge. 'Damned little sir-ing, as you can see.'

'He looks a wreck.'

'Walking dead. Sometimes the captains don't sleep for the whole voyage. And they're not young men to start with.' He showed her his cabin, a wooden cubicle in the fo'c'sle with a curtain instead of a door – 'in case I have to exit quickly' – the gun tubs aft, midships and bow 'manned by the finest amateurs', and finally, at Cordi's insistence, his Hawker Sea Hurricane, a big single-engine fighter with a massive three-bladed propeller, twelve machine guns and four cannon. Bomb racks had been fitted under the wings.

Cordi took off her coat and climbed up the catapult track for a look at the cockpit. Tom scrambled up the other side and slid the plastic canopy back so she could see the instruments.

'Do you know when they'll send you back to New York?' Cordi asked across the cockpit.

'Soon. They want to stick me on the ferry service.'

Cordi felt a spasm of relief. Tom had done his share of dogfighting over water. He deserved a rest, delivering American-built planes to Britain.

'Are you staying in New York?' he asked.

'It looks that way, at the moment. Someone has to inform an anxious empire what the Yanks are doing for us.'

The freighter discharged a blast of its whistle. Tom looked back at the centre island, where the bridge was located. 'We're getting underway. I'll walk you to the gate.'

'I'll watch from the pier.'

'It's going to rain,' her brother said. The greying sky had darkened and the sun was gone. Cordi shivered and climbed down from the catapult and put on her coat. Tom walked with her to the gangway. 'Go on home now.'

'I want to watch . . . Will you visit Mother and Dad?'

'I hope so, if they don't just turn me around.'

'My love to them.' She opened her handbag and handed him a heavily wrapped package. 'Sugar and tea.'

'I would have brought them from the ship.'

'Bring them something else then. Maybe you'll still have fresh eggs.' She stood on tiptoe and kissed him. They bumped noses and he held her awkwardly. She wanted to say, I know the Germans sent a signal to the U-boats, but she couldn't, and once again she reminded herself that it wouldn't have made any difference anyway, that the convoys had no choice but to try. So what she said was, 'Take care. Don't go flying if you don't have to.'

'I'll keep it to the minimum, believe me . . . Say, I hope your assignment works out. It must feel good to be out of England.'

Cordi shook her head. 'They're too smug here. They haven't a clue what it was like.'

'They'll be bloodied before it's over. Pearl Harbor was no picnic.'

'I'm sorry. Sometimes I feel like a sour old maid.'

The whistle blew again, a cry taken up in chorus by the other ships around the pier. Tom took her arm and walked her slowly down the gangway as rain blew in from the river and the sailors began singling up, releasing all but one mooring line fore and aft. Cordi saw tugs streaming towards her brother's ship.

'That's it, Cordi.'

She gave him a last hug. The sailors hurried him back aboard and retrieved the gangway, pulling it into the ship and locking the bulwark. The tugs wheeled the old freighter away from the pier, urged it towards midstream. The skyscrapers had already vanished in the rain, and Tom's ship followed them, leaving Cordi alone to think how much less it would hurt to say goodbye to a lover with whom she could bury her grief in passion.

The sharp dry bite of hot glass and molten solder peppered the back room at the Meurice. Duncan Haig was shuttling between his workbench and the radio receiver in the closet, stringing wires while Cordi, Mark and Weatherburn sifted the results of their inquiries into the presence of the Otter in New York City.

Cordi had spent the past two days in the *New York Times* morgue. Weatherburn had buried himself in BSC records at Rockefeller Center. And Mark had gone through a charade of interviews with New York City Police Department sabotage squad detectives.

'If,' he said, 'we presume that the Otter is in New York, then random events in the Port of New York could be considered to take on a pattern of destruction.'

'Quite a list,' said Weatherburn. 'Look at this – January third, less than a month after Pearl Harbor, Manhattan Pier 83 was swept by fire. Burned to the waterline and if there hadn't been a lucky shift of wind the fire would have destroyed the Forty-second Street ferry terminal beside it. That would have checked the flow of the thousands of workmen who service the commercial and naval piers along the West Side of Manhattan and Jersey towns of Weehawken, Union City, Jersey City and Hoboken.

'Five weeks later the *Normandie* burns under extremely suspicious circumstances, and now blocks two of the super-piers. That leaves only the *Queen Mary* and the *Queen Elizabeth* to ferry American soldiers to England.'

'We've still got the *Aquitania* and the new *Mauritania* – '

Weatherburn cut Duncan off with an impatient, 'Not at fifteen thousand men a clip.'

'Fifteen *thousand*?'

'Starting this summer, is what I'm told. They're already working on the loading drill. The major part of a division and impedimenta.'

'Fifteen thousand men. Can you imagine a sinking?'

'The *Mary* will show her heels to any U-boat built.'

'Touch wood.'

'The *Normandie*'s an incalculable loss. Terrible blow to French morale. Slap in the face for the Americans. And a first-class propaganda coup for the damned Hun.' ('Hun' was more appropriate for World War I, but to Weatherburn a German was 'a damned Hun', never mind the time, or place, or war, or the fact that 'Hun' had always been more a popular newspaper term rather than a front-line soldier's.)

'In March we had an outbreak of freighter fires in the Brooklyn Erie Basin. Nearly a fire a night. British ships lost cargoes of sugar, rubber and timber, as well as thirty Grant tanks.

'In April, the port seemed unusually quiet, except for the smaller fires – some accidental, some obviously set by Irish dockers, German-American Bundists and the ever-present racketeer-extortionists. But ten miles up the Hudson River a goods train bound for the Chelsea docks derailed into the river with a cargo of Rolls-Royce Merlin aircraft engines built on licence by a Buick plant in Detroit, Michigan. With the labour and equipment shortages the recovery of the engines is going very slowly.'

Weatherburn slumped wearily back into his chair, his eyes hooded. 'He was quiet in May.'

Duncan Haig painted bare wire and a connector with liquid flux, held the tip of a coil of solder above the joint and touched his hot iron to the solder. A melted silver bead dropped a quarter-inch to the connector, and a thin white line of acrid smoke curled around the tool and climbed to the ceiling. 'Wonder what he's got planned for June?'

Mark St George stirred uneasily.

'Yes, Mark?'

'Well, sir, no one has come up with absolute proof that these events are sabotage – '

Weatherburn cut Cordi off before she could possibly agree with Mark. 'The Americans have committees investigating the *Normandie* fire. They'll find proof. I'm rather sure of it . . .'

Mark had a diffident way of standing his ground, unlike the more pugnacious Duncan, who would bluster but give in, or Cordi, who would challenge Weatherburn head-on and if that failed would turn him with a joke or a smile.

She liked to think of herself as equal parts forthright and adaptable.

Mark said, 'Yes, but on the other hand Mr Frank Hogan, the District Attorney of New York City, conducted his own investigation the night of the fire and concluded negligence.'

Mr Hogan has a city to pander to,' Weatherburn replied. 'I'm aware that the *Normandie* fire could have been an accident, but I can tell you that the Office of Naval Intelligence has received indications that the fire at least might have been sabotage. The Americans have got investigative committees from the Congress, the Senate, military intelligence and ONI. British Security Coordination will keep us informed of their progress, but until they find no proof of sabotage I'm assuming it could have been.'

'Well, as for the Pier 83 fire,' Mark said, 'only the New York Police Department sabotage squad is investigating and every newspaper report I've read quotes authorities who call it, too, an accident.'

'The newspapers always do that,' snapped Weatherburn. 'You can't trust the American papers any more than you can ours. The Americans are petrified of appearing vulnerable on their home soil. Pearl Harbor was a terrible blow to their sense of isolation. They can't bear the idea that they're vulnerable like everyone else. They'd much prefer to believe there is no sabotage, even at the expense of allowing a saboteur his head.'

'I think you're right there,' said Mark. 'They want to fight overseas, not here.' And thought but didn't say, not that I can blame them for that.

'And remember,' said Weatherburn, 'how obsessed the Americans are with the idea of gearing up for this war. You know – industrial giant awakening and all that. All personified by Rosie-the-Riveter factory types – '

'Somebody had to wake up,' Duncan said. He was the only member of Group M up from the working class – his father being a railway engineer, his education red-brick.

In the month they'd been in New York he'd become an ardent admirer of the Americans, who, he'd told Cordi, made him feel *equal* for the first time since he'd entered grammar school.

With boarding school education and well-off parents in the arts, Cordi sympathized but had no first-hand experience of what Duncan was talking about.

'And, God bless them, they did,' said Weatherburn. '*Our* job is to clear the way for those tanks and planes they build to get to England. That's what our fight with the Otter is about. Transport and communication. Admiral Canaris has sent him to wreck this harbour. He's doing his damnedest. We're going to stop him . . . How's your machine coming, Duncan?'

'Almost ready, sir.'

'Tell Mark and Cordi what you told me.'

Duncan proudly held up the German agent's transmitter-receiver. 'Note one standard-issue Hun spy transmitter-receiver – *Afus*, short for *Agentenfunk*, agent-radio. Late model, a bit more powerful than before, fifteen watts up from ten. Nothing too remarkable, except that it's been modified to fit in this instrument case and when you move this little lever here, which looks exactly like a catch to seat it firmly in the trombone case, we find it changes the radio's frequency. Ordinarily it transmits at around 14,500 kilocycles and receives in the range of 14,400. But move this lever and she jumps to 19,000 kilocycle transmit and 18,900 receive. What the Yanks call a whole new ball game.'

'Why would that lever be disguised?' asked Cordi.

'Because it's a bloody private line.'

'Don't you see?' Weatherburn said. 'Canaris has given the Otter his own special frequency so his signals don't get mixed up with the regular spy traffic coming into their overseas station at Hamburg. A private line, monitored by a special operator, ready for those short bursts. A private line. And thanks to Duncan, we've got his number.'

Weatherburn had a habit of letting his enthusiasms, as well as his irritations, fall on one member of the group at a time. Mark, Cordi noticed, was getting a bit annoyed at Duncan's attention. He asked, 'Do you mean that the four of us have to share watches, monitoring our receiver twenty-four hours a day? Doesn't sound very practical.'

Duncan looked like he could barely contain himself, and Cordi said, 'I suspect that Superboffin has come to the rescue again.'

'He has that,' said Weatherburn. 'When he's done fiddling with those bits of wire we'll be in possession of an automatic monitoring device tuned to the Otter's frequency.'

'How?' asked Cordi.

Duncan shook his head. 'I wish I could take credit for all of it, but all I've really done is marry a pair of rather exotic radio inventions. Thirty years ago, when Marconi learned that the *Titanic* had sunk ten miles from a ship whose radio was shut down for the night, he tried to invent a device to make an untended radio alert an operator if distress signals were being received. By the time he succeeded, ships' wirelesses were routinely monitored round the clock, so the device was never marketed. I've connected Marconi's automatic radio alarm to our double antennae radio direction finder that pinpoints a radio source by triangulation. A signal beamed on the Otter's frequency will activate our direction tuner. Our tuner will register the relative bearings of his source from our aerials on Hampshire House and our number two aerial on the Cunard Building downtown. Draw those two lines of bearing on the map here, and where the lines cross will be the Otter's antenna.'

'What are those little drums with the graph paper?'

'They started life as barographs — for recording atmospheric pressure hour by hour. I've connected their inkers to the RDFs and God willing, it should record the direction of the strongest signals received on the Otter's frequency. So if you walk in here and see that the machine has gone

107

off, lay the two bearings on the map, hail a taxi, and go arrest the bugger.'

'But wait for the rest of us,' Weatherburn interrupted drily.

'Seriously,' Duncan said, 'we ought to get a neighbourhood and even a fair idea of the street. The point is, we don't have to be here all the time. Our receiver may not be as sophisticated as the Americans' big coastal listening stations, but they've got to scan the entire shortwave spectrum while we can concentrate on the Otter's special frequency.'

'What if he uses that burst technique again?' asked Cordi. 'What can you possibly locate in six seconds?'

'He's got to send at least twice, and my machine starts homing instantly.'

'But we can't just sit around waiting for the Otter to radio Hamburg,' protested Mark, and Cordi agreed. 'We don't even know that he's got another radio.'

'Wouldn't you? Four thousand miles from Germany?'

'I suppose,' Cordi said. 'But we've got to do more.'

'Of course we're doing more,' said Weatherburn. 'I don't believe for a minute that we'll catch the Otter himself at a radio station. But we'll get a lead on him from the agent sending for him. Even if we do nothing more than cut him off from Canaris, we've accomplished something. How long can he survive alone?'

'That depends on his cover,' said Cordi. 'If, for example, he's set up as an American citizen with an appropriate job, he might do very well.'

Weatherburn looked intrigued. His eyes roved away from Duncan's workbench, skipped over the receiver and settled on Cordi. Mark St George said, 'The papers and background would be extremely elaborate.'

Weatherburn shook his head. 'Not too elaborate if he's Admiral Canaris's private boy. He's got every forger in the Third Reich at his command . . . An American. Interesting . . .'

'Not only papers,' said Cordi. 'But all the trappings. The

reality of it. A home, possessions, friends. Not so much a spy as a traitor.'

'Are you suggesting a native-born American?'

'Or an agent planted so long ago he'd seem like an American.'

Weatherburn nodded. 'Why not? We know that Admiral Canaris roamed the world through the thirties setting up his submarine supply bases. And his spies. I don't know that he was ever in New York – '

Cordi said, 'It doesn't matter whether *Canaris* was here. The Otter could still be an apparently respectable New Yorker with a meticulously created background that's had years to age.'

Duncan Haig put in sceptically, 'Wife, cat, children and dog all landed on Long Island by U-boat?'

'Don't be thick,' Weatherburn told him. 'Cordi's onto something here. Canaris and the German-American Bund have each had a long time to set up an entire family – including your dog, cat, wife and child – waiting on the Otter's arrival.'

'And maybe a business to support them,' said Cordi.

'Or if not a family,' Mark added, 'an adeptly buried infrastructure with communicators, paymasters and bully boys standing by for the Otter to take command.'

They sat quietly, digesting the notion to the busy clicking and scrabbling sounds of Duncan's small tools and the muffled clatter of hansom cab hoofbeats on the street past the park. 'Which is why,' Weatherburn said finally, 'you trust no one but each other. And me.'

Cordi was still smarting from his rebuke about security. She said, 'That leaves about eight million suspects in New York. Who do we start with?'

'Who do *you* suggest?'

'Obviously people with a knowledge of transport, particularly ships. Harbour operations. Maybe a man in shipping. Someone connected highly enough to know about cargo movements.'

'How about a tugboat captain?' Duncan said.

'That's not so far-fetched,' said Cordi. 'He'd have the access, the knowledge, and the right to take his boat anywhere in the harbour.'

'They're a small fraternity,' said Weatherburn. He'd begun scribbling notes. 'It should be simple to check up on new members. Very good. Who else?'

'Shipfitters?' said Mark.

'Too broad a group to be useful right off. And, frankly, I can't see the Otter using an ordinary workman's occupation as cover. It would limit him too much.'

'Shipyard managers, then.'

'Railroad traffic managers,' said Cordi. 'Lorry dispatchers, harbour operations, et cetera, et cetera, et cetera. Quite a list by the end of the day.'

Duncan shuffled past, spread arms draped with trailing wires. They stopped talking to watch him finish as he crouched by the radio receiver and connected the wires to the automatic radio alarm, the wire recorder, and the drum graphs for recording signal direction. He got up, wiping his hands on his work trousers, and looked expectantly at Cordi, hoping she'd be impressed.

'Done. Now all we have to do is wait for the Otter to tell Admiral Canaris what he's got laid on for June.'

6

But two weeks later, when they learned what the Otter had done and that he had already told the chief of the Abwehr, Duncan's automatic radio monitor was still silent. The wire recorder remained poised at the beginning of a blank reel, and the slowly turning drums had inked only smooth, unwavering, overlapping lines that showed no direction but the passage of time.

Cordi Grey reported to an office on the eighth floor of the RCA Building on Weatherburn's orders and used her British Broadcasting Corporation cover at the NBC receptionist's desk. The woman directed her to a sound studio where Cordi have several times performed non-cover, legitimate work, broadcasting live reports linked up with London.

The studio itself was dark, and she found Duncan and Mark waiting in the greenroom next door. Mark was sitting on the shabby couch, smoking. Duncan had his face pressed to the glass as he peered into the engineer's booth. 'They've got a disc recorder in here.'

'So?' Mark offered Cordi a cigarette from his silver case.

'So I'd like to get my hands on it,' Duncan muttered, steaming the glass. 'It's a damn sight more sensitive than the wire recorder I put on the monitor.'

'But can it stand such hard use?'

Duncan turned angrily on Mark just as Weatherburn hurried in and explained why he had summoned them. He seemed extremely upset.

'I've brought a naval lieutenant. He's just flown in from England. You know the route – Scotland, Labrador, Montreal – so he's fairly exhausted. He was sent to inform

111

BSC what happened to his convoy. He assumes you're another group of BSC agents – all right, sit with Mark on the couch.'

They did, Cordi in the middle. Weatherburn turned off all the lights except a reading lamp that he directed onto a straight chair near the door. 'I don't want him to see your faces.'

He went out and returned with a slimly built officer about thirty years old wearing a naval uniform so impeccably maintained that it was hard to believe he'd made the journey standing in trains and lying in the belly of a bomber. But his weariness showed in his eyes, deep-set in a weathered face, and there he looked much tireder than even the long haul from England should have made him. His eyes reminded Cordi of the Scots captain on Tom's *Lewiston* – brimful of death on a thousand endless nights.

'Lieutenant Naill. If you would be so kind to repeat your story for this group.' Weatherburn stood beside the chair, at the edge of the light. Naill sat very properly, not even blinking, and Cordi recalled her father describing a full lieutenant in the Royal Navy as a man who could administer a fair-sized colony on short notice.

'I am first lieutenant and asdic officer on the destroyer HMS *Claymore*. My ship met up with a fast convoy eight days out of New York, on the Chop Line. Our group relieved the Canadian escorts. Two days later in mid-ocean four ships exploded within moments of each other and quickly sank. While the convoy continued my ship led two others on the hunt for the U-boats.

'*Claymore*'s asdic made no underwater contact. Nor did the other escorts'. Asdic operators heard nothing on their listening devices, no returns, no screws. Look-outs reported no periscope sights, no wakes. Even the convoy's CAM plane spotted nothing from above. It gradually became apparent that we'd lost the attackers. At dark we broke off the attack. While catching up with the convoy we traded notes by signal lamp and discovered that not one of our soundbeams had actually made contact with a U-boat or anything like a U-boat for even an instant.'

'Is that unusual?' asked Duncan Haig.

'Yes, sir,' Naill answered the voice in the dark. 'We certainly don't sink them every time, but we usually make some contact before the water gets too riled by the depth bombs. Only when we were back on station did we learn why. Which is the reason I've been flown here.

'It was the opinion of all the men rescued from the water that none of the sunken ships had been struck by a torpedo. We'd had a severe gale the night before and many of the crews were in their holds, rearranging cargo that had shifted or broken loose. There was a severe loss of life when the explosions occurred, but the survivors were unanimous on one point. They swore to a man that the explosions occurred *inside* their ships.'

Duncan interrupted again. 'How could they tell the difference between an internal explosion and a German torpedo?'

'These chaps have been running the U-boat gauntlet for close to three years now. Many have been torpedoed before. I rather think they'd get the hang of it after a while, wouldn't you say?'

Duncan resented the upper-class, understated manner of an officer like Naill. Cordi touched his knee to keep him calm and Weatherburn stepped in to smooth it over. 'Go on, lieutenant.' He was as upper-crust as Naill, but his rough, outdoor manners offset that for Duncan.

'Thank you, sir. The fact is, we interviewed the sailors carefully and I'm of the opinion they're right in contending that the explosions came from within their cargo. The explosions each occurred in the depths of the midships hold. They sank like scrap iron.'

'Well, what are you saying?' said Duncan.

'Apparently the ships were sabotaged.'

'In New York?'

'That's beyond my knowledge, sir. I wasn't here for the loading.'

'They were *betrayed!*' Weatherburn said, coming now into the circle of the light. 'Betrayed in port before they reached the sea.'

'It would seem that way, sir. As I suggested.'

Cordi asked, 'Did you say that all the ships sabotaged were on the perimeters of your convoy?'

He seemed surprised to hear a woman's voice. 'Yes, ma'am.'

'Do you think that odd?'

'It seems to indicate that certain cargoes were vulnerable.'

'How so, lieutenant?'

'The convoy moved essentially as a large square. Eighty ships. Eight columns of ten each, with escort vessels circling off the corners of the square. Our procedure in forming up is to screen the volatile carriers such as oil and petrol tankers and ammunition and arms carriers inside a perimeter of bulk and dry carriers. All the explosions detonated in dry carriers.'

'What do you mean by dry?' Cordi asked.

'Sugar, rice, rubber. One had machine tools.'

Cordi tried to think of related questions, to put off asking the one she was afraid to ask. 'Was the sugar in bulk?'

'I believe it was in sacks.'

'And the rice?'

'Sacks. The rubber was in barrels and the machine tools, of course, in crates.'

'So the common denominator among the sabotaged ships was that they all contained cargoes carried aboard rather than poured.'

'I'm not sure I follow you, ma'am.'

'What she means,' interrupted Weatherburn, 'is that individuals operating cranes and forklifts or carrying sacks on their backs, placed the cargoes in the holds. Assisted by the trusting sailors.'

114

'Were there any U-boat attacks on the convoy?' asked Mark.

'None,' said Naill. 'The Nazis have been concentrating on the American coast of late. What with the city lights to silhouette the freighters and the Americans' refusal to employ convoy defences, it's too good an opportunity to pass up.'

'. . . Did your convoy sail from New York on the thirteenth?' Cordi finally got up the nerve to ask.

'Yes, ma'am.'

She steeled herself. 'Did you say that the *Lewiston*'s CAM pilot went up?'

'The CAM? A fiasco.'

'Oh?'

'He nearly crashed on take-off because the ship was pitching so badly in heavy seas. The catapult let loose a sheet of flame. It didn't harm the plane, of course, but with the explosions all around, some anti-aircraft gunners on the merchant vessels assumed that the plane had strafed the *Lewiston*, causing the flame, and they opened up on the CAM plane, never stopping to think where a German plane would come from in the middle of the Atlantic.'

'They *shot* him?'

'The fellow was a superb pilot. Pulled her up in time, dodged the anti-aircraft fire and rolled the plane over a few times to show the gunners who he was. He flew around for a couple of hours supporting our search. When his fuel was up he ditched beside the *Lewiston*.' The weary looking lieutenant displayed emotion for the first time. Disgust. 'Of course there were no U-boats so the whole thing was such a bloody waste. The seas were impossible. He took one into his cockpit as he slid back the Perspex. They said the plane literally disappeared. Poor devil never had a chance.'

Naill waited, peering uncertainly into the stifling silence, into the dark where Cordi covered her mouth, crushed her lips against her teeth, and held her scream.

She squeezed her eyelids so tight shut that sparks stormed in front of her eyes. Opening them, she saw Weatherburn move briskly into the light. On the couch, Mark felt for her hand.

'I'll take you to your next appointment, lieutenant.' Weatherburn opened the door and Naill rose, still staring into the dark, wondering what he had done.

'*Wait.*'

Naill turned gratefully to the hard, dry sound. 'Yes, ma'am.'

'I have more questions. Has this . . . ' A heavy numb feeling closed around the words in her throat. She forced herself through it. 'Has this sort of thing happened before, lieutenant? I mean, have you heard of internal explosions mistaken for torpedoes on other convoys?'

Naill sat down again and peered towards her voice. 'Odd you should ask, ma'am. I've been reviewing in my mind other sinkings I've observed. We naturally attribute an explosion, particularly one at night, to a German torpedo. But it seems likely that some of the occasions on which we've found absolutely no sign of a U-boat could have been sabotage.' He added after a moment, 'It would certainly be an interesting line of inquiry.'

'Yes, it would,' said Cordi. She felt her voice thickening beyond control. 'How long could this sort of thing have been going on?'

Naill looked abruptly exhausted, his last reserves dried up. 'I've been on escort duty since September '39. I can think of a dozen sinkings since then that could have been this sort of midships, deep-hull explosion from within.'

'Before the United States came into the war?' asked Weatherburn.

'Since the war began.'

'Westbound as well?'

'Outbound, carrying rubble as ballast . . . yes, now

116

that you mention it. But more homebound, for obvious reasons. Ships are one thing for the Germans. Ships *and* cargo are quite another.'

'Why'd you ask if there were any U-boat attacks on the convoy?' Cordi asked Mark.

Lieutenant Naill was gone and the lights were on, but they'd remained on the couch.

Mark eyed her closely, then said, 'I had a hunch that the message we found on the wire wasn't sent to tip off the U-boats. The Otter sent it to Canaris, not as a tip but as a report of what he had already done. And I'll wager Canaris didn't even pass it along to U-boat Command. This way there'd be no mistaking who sunk the ships; his man would get the credit.'

'Very good, Mark,' Weatherburn said. 'Excellent insight into the Hun mind. The bastards.'

Cordi was suddenly fed up with Weatherburn's silly anachronisms, his Colonel Blimp attitude, his childish denigration of a fierce and clever enemy. But then he surprised her, adding in a gentle voice, 'Cordi, I think I can wangle space in a bomber so you can go home and see your parents. Would you like that? They'll soon know about your brother . . .'

'I'd rather stay here. I prefer to get started on this. *Immediately.*'

'How do you propose doing that?'

She waited until she could trust her voice. 'The first question is, who loaded the ships?'

'BSC will start the legwork on that. We'll follow up their best leads. But tonight I really think you ought to let us take you home and put you to bed with a stiff drink.'

'No, I want to be by myself.' She shoved blindly out of the door into the maze of radio studios and offices. The halls were brightly lighted, filled with normal people going about the normal work of broadcasting. Great nationwide link-ups stemmed from here. London beamed in nightly to include this American ally in programmes for the empire. She felt ten thousand miles from the empty stretch of cold sea where her brother lay.

A thought came ... all the years she'd fought her mother's fears and timidity and railed at her precautionary cold distance suddenly seemed callous years. Now she too had lost everything. Her lover Alec in Geneva, and now Tom. A physical pressure to cry swelled deep in her throat and collected behind her eyes.

But she wouldn't cry. She wouldn't follow the route of fear.

7

Steven Gates's drawing table was tilted at an eight-to-one incline, lighted from the left by the window as well as a lamp for cloudy days and long nights. Hard against the left side, his T-square marked the constraints of physics with a stern horizontal line. An orderly litter of triangles, dividers, scales, slide rule, compass and pencils waited to test those limits while his French curve ruler, whose logarithmic ellipses and spirals swirled like waves on the buff drawing paper, tempted the imagination.

Gates had sketches of a new lightweight gun mount for a destroyer escort taped to the board. He was trying to shave weight from the DE's foredeck to improve its sea-keeping abilities, hunting the fine line between a turret strong enough to support a four-inch gun yet light enough to keep the convoy escort's bow above water while it was icing in a North Atlantic gale.

The navy's first solution had been to mount smaller, three-inch guns and lend the entire class of DEs to the British Western Approaches Command, which reported that German U-boat commanders were delighted with the weapon. The refit was an interesting challenge because Prince and Gates's handbook of scarce resources contained a long list of exotic lightweight metals behind Japanese lines, but Gates was gazing vacantly at the *American Glory*. The model sat on a filing cabinet, beneath a corkboard thick with newspaper clippings.

'We're late for the launching,' called Richard Prince, running into Gates's office. Impatiently he tapped the gun mount sketches. 'We're late and so is that.'

'Five minutes. Sorry.' Gates hurried through the sketch,

putting on paper what he had already settled in his mind, and entered the specs with a trained neat hand while his uncle paced around the room. He glanced up once and saw Prince holding the model in his arms while he read the newspaper clippings.

The photographs Gates had collected of the *Normandie* burning four months ago and the file pictures of her steaming at sea revealed the homage that Prince's design paid the French liner. They painted her fate in frozen sequence. Smoke belched from the sixty-million-dollar liner in the early morning-after photos. Then the afternoon editions showed the pride of their profession sprawled on her side like a gravely injured whale tangled in harpoon lines of frozen hose water. A forlorn cluster of orphaned lifeboats huddled in her lee.

The ice had melted in later shots of torch-wielding salvage workers cutting off her raked stacks and removing the hastily mounted gun tubs. There were no pictures in the recent accounts of the committees inquiring into what had happened, nor of those debating her fate – to be cut up where she lay, or salvage attempted.

Prince had sat on the salvage inquiry and Gates had begged him to fight for salvage. Prince and William Francis Gibbs, as the doyens of American naval architecture, had swung their considerable weight to try to save the *Normandie*, as had an angry Mayor LaGuardia. But Gates's delight at the decision to try to raise her by controlled pumping – a job which would take at least a year – was tempered by the disappointing reports on the cause of the fire.

One by one the various investigating committees had concluded 'negligence'. Fortunately the Office of Naval Intelligence report had not been released yet. Gates had testified in secret before the ONI committee, and ONI, he was sure, would find overwhelming evidence that the *Normandie* had been sabotaged.

'Done.'

He shrugged into his jacket, and on the way out through the main drawing room – a vast bright and open space with a hundred and fifty tables – he handed the sketch to a young draughtsman.

'Give me principal views and these two sections.'

'You want this yesterday, Mr Gates?'

'Last *week*. Haven't you heard there's a war on?'

'Might as well be funny if you can't say please,' Prince remarked on the way to the elevator.

They had two floors of a modern twenties building on Church Street in lower Manhattan with views of the harbour, north light for the draughtsmen, and a short walk from the navy procurement offices in the Federal Building. Gates hailed the cab. His uncle said, 'Brooklyn Navy Yard. Navy Street gate,' and Gates added, with a smile for Prince, 'Step on it. Please.'

Bars, greasy spoons and flophouses occupied the crumbling tenements outside the brick walls of the United States Naval Yard. The cab stopped by a sentry in a massive iron gateway. The armed guards greeted Gates and Prince by name, slapped a temporary pass on the windscreen and waved them through. Gates guided the driver towards the shipway, where their new aircraft carrier waited. Shipways and dry docks, foundries, railroads, machine shops, marine barracks and a power plant sprawled across two hundred acres of land and water, clutching a sharp elbow of the East River called Wallabout Bay.

This was the crucible, a proud and ancient shipbuilding city a quarter-mile from Manhattan, two miles from the Upper Bay confluence of the East and Hudson Rivers and fifteen miles from the sea. The first steam-powered warship had taken life here one hundred and thirty years ago – the paddle-driven, thirty-two-gun *Fulton*.

Steven Gates found his own history in the yard. He had driven his first rivet here amidst the deafening cacophony inside a steel hull, had cut his first carbon steel plate with an acetylene torch, met his brother-in-law Charlie here, and drunk his first boilermaker in one of the grimy bars outside the brick walls where the shipfitters' beer-and-rye concoctions had been invented.

Eight thousand shipfitters had worked here his first summer, a third from the WPA. Today thirty thousand were building for war, and he was still here, to his surprise – and disappointment, because the one ship they'd never built here was a liner. More specifically a projected beauty called *American Glory* that had never got off the drawing board.

The cab moved slowly along the road crowded with men walking towards the ways and pulled up next to a black Packard limousine parked beside the scaffolded bow of the carrier poised to slide into Wallabout Bay.

'The Strattons are here,' Gates said, recognizing their friends' car and waving hello to their driver, who, to the Strattons' good fortune, was too old to be drafted or work in a defence plant.

Prince paid and they climbed out.

'There's Vera.'

High atop the launch ceremony platform Steven Gates's mother looked like a flower, her silk dress plucked at by the wind, the sun shining on her light gold hair. The platform rose halfway up the carrier's lean flared bow, from which a striped ribbon dangled a dark green bottle of champagne.

Yard workers were standing by on the ways and applying a final coat of thick grease to the rails. Thousands more, given time off for the ceremony, were gathering the length of the seven-hundred-foot hull.

'Everything ready but us,' said Prince, pausing for a long, proud look at her bilges, then stepping back to glimpse the distant screws. He'd been here half the night and most of the morning.

'And the tide,' said Gates, nodding at the current slowing for the slack.

122

Prince clapped him on the back and they hurried up the scaffold steps, Gates taking them two at a time in his growing excitement. The yard spread before him, low and broad with cranes spiring the sky. Long sheds and partially formed hulls littered the ground. Water glinted in slips open to the bay, and smoke and steam danced in. the air to the staccato bang of riveting guns and the clatter of shunting engines moving raw steel on the shipyard's railroad.

Gates's uncle caught up, short of breath. 'Next time I'll build a lower ship.' They climbed the last flight of wooden steps together. Gates took his uncle's arm but dropped back as they reached the platform. This was, after all, his uncle's day.

Some two dozen waiting people broke into greetings when Prince appeared and crowded around him. Gates saw the old four-star admiral of the yard, and the newly appointed rear admiral of the Third District . . . the man Gates had blamed for doing nothing at the *Normandie* fire, in true blue navy tradition, had been promoted. He also identified a number of civilian managers and businessmen on the platform, some subcontractors and their wives, a congressman and then people he knew well – Wallace Stratton, Sr, an old friend of the family who was representing the Secretary of the Navy this day, his wife, whom Gates called Aunt Louise, and their son Wally, Gates's oldest friend. Gates's sister Kay was there with her husband Charlie Collins, and Vera Gates, his mother and Richard Prince's sister.

Richard Prince reached back for Gates announcing, 'We're sorry we're late, but Steven needed a few minutes to invent a new turret. You'll like it, admiral.'

'I'll like it a lot more when your ship is off my way so I can start a new one. How are you, Dick? Haven't seen you since this morning.' He turned to the others. 'You'd think the Brooklyn Navy Yard had never launched a ship before the way he's been hanging around here. Guess he doesn't trust us.' Gates went over to his mother and kissed her. 'You look lovely. Excited?'

'Nervous.'

'She's afraid the bottle won't break,' Kay said. Kay was tall and slim like Gates, and both had planes and angles to their features that made them look stronger than their mother, who seemed almost ethereal except for her intense, sparkling eyes.

Gates said, 'See that man by the ribbon. He'll bash the bottle with a hammer if you miss.'

'So they told me, but I'm still nervous.'

Her son-in-law Charlie Collins pushed into their circle. 'Listen, Vera, I worked on this ship.' He leaned over the railing and patted the steel prow. 'Don't hit *this* spot. It won't take too much pressure . . . And how you doing, Junior?'

'What's that thing around your neck?'

'It's a tie,' Kay said. 'Leave him alone, he's had enough ribbing from those characters he works with down below.'

'We're about ready,' called one of the civilian managers. 'Mrs Gates, if you'll stand here, please, and the gentleman here will hand you the bottle when the congressman finishes speaking.' He stepped back and let the photographers take the pictures of the man with the bottle after they failed to persuade Vera Gates to show them some practice swings.

The admiral of the yard took up the electric switch which would actually release the last shackles holding the ship and signalled the men on hydraulic rams to give her a nudge if needed. Richard Prince spoke by telephone with the foreman leading the men below.

'We're ready, admiral. Slack tide.'

A warning bell clanged to clear the ways.

Vera Gates summoned up a loud, clear voice that seemed too strong for her slight frame. She stood tall and cocked her arm and looked very purposeful and for a second Gates saw the beautiful young woman his father must have married.

'It is an American tradition to name aircraft carriers after honourable battles.'

Gates was astonished to see the flaring bow give a sudden tremble. Somebody muttered, 'Jesus Christ, there she goes.' The ship had started sliding.

'*Mother*,' said Kay.

'I see it,' Vera Gates murmured through clenched teeth. She stepped forward, raising the bottle. 'I name thee, *Niagara*.'

The entire platform was shaking and the space between it and the bow increased from inches to feet. Vera Gates threw the bottle after it, calling out, 'May you carry brave men to swift victory.'

The bottle struck the prow squarely and exploded in a thick spray of creamy white bubbles, and the crowd cheered her accuracy as *Niagara* hurtled towards the water.

Gates and his uncle pushed to the rail and watched intently. Only under enemy fire would she make a voyage as dangerous as these few feet from dry land to deep water when for an agonizing moment she hung suspended like a clothesline between her bow still on the way and her floating stern.

Niagara shoved a huge wave into the bay. Giant drag chains roared after her, slowing her even as she pushed the waiting tugs backward. When the tugs finally stopped her, blowing angry black smoke from their tall stacks and frothing the water behind their sterns, the *Niagara* floated high and empty on an even keel.

'Seems to float,' Richard Prince said.

'Nice shot, Vera,' said Charlie, and Prince turned to his sister. 'And very nicely said, too.'

'"Swift victory." Perfect for a carrier.'

'Charlie helped me.'

Gates looked at his brother-in-law, a little surprised. The betrayal of the Spanish Civil War had left Charlie dubious about accomplishing anything by war, and the

125

Nazi-Soviet non-aggression pact of '39 – shortlived though it turned out to be – had left him sick of causes. Charlie shook his head and ran a hand through his thick black hair. 'Your idea, Vera. I just helped put some words to the tune.'

Wally Stratton came up. 'Hey, Steven, we're invited up to the admiral's for a drink.' He was a round-faced man with deep-set, sad hound-dog eyes, and judging by the colour in his cheeks he'd had a few already. 'Congratulations, she looks great.'

'Better congratulate Uncle Richard, Wally. I just helped on this one.'

'Not from what I heard. Everybody says those broad bilges were your idea.'

'Stolen straight from the *Normandie*. How the hell you been? How's the new job?'

He braced himself for an unhappy reply. Wally Stratton, his oldest friend . . . they'd played together since childhood, their families' country places abutting at Lloyd's Neck. Wally had been educated at Harvard, was sensitive, erudite, and at the age of twenty-six he was a failure. He'd even failed his draft physical, but he'd surprised everybody by wangling a commission in the volunteer Naval Reserve and now spent his weekends on coastal defence patrol, doggedly shadowing convoys and searching for U-boats from a slow-moving navy blimp. He was wearing his navy uniform today, with the naval balloonist's insignia on his left breast – a winged foul anchor, like the regular naval aviator's pin except that the balloonist only got one wing.

Just before Pearl, Wally's father had installed him at the Maritime Commission, which set shipbuilding policy for the American Merchant Marine.

'In a word,' Wally now said, answering his friend's question, 'hell. Lots of hell. The French – those two or three dozen who haven't yet bellied up to the Nazis – are having fits over their precious *Normandie*.'

'What are you talking about?'

'Well, first they abandoned her here and – '

'The French didn't abandon her, Wally. I went aboard last year. The skeleton crew was great. You should have seen their fire watches. That ship was loved, Wally.'

'Yeah, well I was there the day the skeleton crew put on a band concert under the West Side Highway so they could pass the hat for lunch money. The French were thrilled to hand her over. But now that she's a charred hulk blocking two of the longest piers in New York, they've decided she was their national symbol. A sort of floating Eiffel Tower. You should hear them, old buddy . . . It's a matter of *honneur français*, which translates to the frogs want their money. I told Howard . . . he's – '

'I know who he is.' Gates was getting annoyed, in spite of his recognition that there was more than a little truth in what Wally was saying.

'Well I told him, give her back to the French right now. Let them try to raise her. Of course, they'd probably pull the pier down in the process if they're as bad at salvage as they are at war.'

'I imagine they're pretty good at salvage. They're certainly good at building ships – '

'Then how come the *Normandie* was so unstable?'

'She was *not* unstable,' Gates said. 'She had a hell of a long righting arm. She was a snappy roller – '

'I heard she was a top-heavy bathtub. That's what everybody's saying.'

Gates took hold of Wally's arm. 'I sailed on her six times, damn it. She snapped back like a destroyer. *Okay?*'

'Okay,' Wally said, squirming away and staring at his friend.

'Steven . . . we're going now.'

'She wasn't unstable,' Gates repeated, and stalked across the ceremony platform and took his mother's arm.

'What's the matter?'

'Nothing.'

With a last look at the *Niagara*, which the tugs were coaxing alongside a fitting dock, they went down the scaffold steps and worked their way through the milling shipfitters to the Strattons' car. The driver was standing guard over his gleaming charge, and it was clear it would be a while before he could turn the car around and drive out of there.

'The others went ahead, Mr Gates.'

'Let's walk,' said Vera Gates. 'It's just over there.'

They left by the nearest gate and walked up a narrow street to the admiral's house. It was surrounded by iron fences and sat on a big lawn.

'What have they done to the woodwork?' his mother whispered as they walked through the entrance and main hall. 'It's all layered with paint.'

'The navy gives it a new coat every time the yard gets a new admiral, which is about every two years.'

'Who decorates these rooms?'

'The admirals' wives,' Gates said, enjoying her interest. It had taken her almost ten years to accept the idea that his father had disappeared after the stock market crash. But then she'd suddenly begun to use her artistic sense, studying interior design, and two years ago, to her son's surprise and delight, she'd taken on a job doing a friend's apartment.

'Every two years?'

'Smile. Here comes the latest.'

'No wonder she wasn't at the launching.' Vera glanced around the rooms again, and by the time they had reached their hostess she was able to say with a convincing smile. 'I *love* what you've done with your flowers.'

The party was outside on a stone terrace aswarm with bees and blooming shrubs. The smoking naval yard, clearly visible from the porches, was blocked from view by the house, as was the Manhattan skyline. The party could have been somewhere out on Long Island's North Shore. Gates got his mother a drink and when she began talking with a pair of naval officers, Wally Stratton advanced on Gates again, waving a glass and apologizing with a floppy smile.

'Forget it,' Gates said. 'Sorry I got hot under the collar. How's the blimp?'

'It's a gas, pardon the lousy pun. It's really great. You ought to come up with me sometime. You got to see the harbour from the air. It's like a beautiful machine with a million moving parts.'

'You go weekends?'

'*I* do, but the ship is up every day. We volunteers relieve the regular crews. I suspect we're more a deterrent than anything else, but it keeps the Germans honest and makes the merchant sailors feel better. They ought to at least get a break in sight of land, right. You want to come along some weekend? I can get you aboard.'

'Soon as I get one off,' said Gates. 'Say, who's the brunette?'

Wally gazed owlishly over his glass. 'Why don't we find out?'

Women, Gates knew from long experience, were often attracted to Wally's vulnerable manner. As was usually the case, Wally got to talk with the brunette while Gates was left with her date, a close-mouthed ensign who reluctantly admitted that he worked for the Office of Naval Intelligence but only after he realized that a civilian with Steven Gates's job held a higher security clearance than he did.

'Do you know Lieutenant Ober?' Gates asked. 'He and I discussed the *Normandie* fire.'

'Ober's been made a lieutenant commander. Shall I say hello for you, Mr Gates? He's a very good officer, by the way.'

'Sure, you could do me a favour and ask him what the hell is going on with the *Normandie* investigation.'

'It's over.'

'What did they find?'

'What did you say your clearance was?'

'I'll show it to you.' Gates pulled out his wallet and showed him his US Navy clearance. 'Top secret.'

The ensign was impressed.

'No big deal, it's just hard to talk to a marine engine designer like my uncle without getting into classified stuff. Anyway, so you know you can trust me. So what's going on? What did Ober finally conclude?'

'Negligence.'

'*What?*'

'Yeah, they're blaming two of the officers aboard at the time. The ship was a mess. Too bad for them, but somebody had to take a fall.'

'That's crazy – '

'You can't charge negligence, Mr Gates, without fixing blame – '

'I don't mean that, damn it.'

'Then what are you talking about?'

'Forget it.' Gates turned away. He brushed past his uncle as he stormed out of the house and jumped into a cab that had just disgorged its passengers at the admiral's front gate. 'Federal Building. Church Street, Manhattan.'

Richard Prince, following him, yanked the door open before the cab could pull away. 'What's going on? Where are you going?'

'I got to see somebody in town.'

'Do you mind explaining? You ran out of there like the house was on fire.'

'Uncle Richard, I just have to go see somebody and – '

'Steven, is it something I can help with? Would it help to talk a minute? I've never seen you so upset. If you meet somebody the way you are now you're going to put both feet in your mouth for sure. Come on. We'll get a drink and walk this off.'

Gates reluctantly got out of the cab. 'I don't want to go back in there.'

'Stay here, I'll bring a couple of glasses. Canadian Club?'

130

'Sure.'

Prince returned in a moment with two glasses. Gates thought better of it and handed his to the marine guard.

'Thanks, Uncle Richard, I'm fine. Come on, I'll fill you in.' They walked down to the yard gate, showed their passes and strolled beside the empty way, which workmen were already preparing for the next keel.

'Back in February, the day after the *Normandie* burned I went to ONI and told them I thought that the *Normandie* fire had been purposely set.'

'Sabotage?'

'Sabotage, arson, call it whatever you want. Somebody set the fire and somehow channelled the smoke down to the boiler rooms.'

Prince took a sip from the glass. 'Go on.'

'The fire spread too quickly to be an accident.'

'It started in kapok – '

'That doesn't explain why so much smoke got to the boiler rooms. The forced-draught fans should have pulled most of it into the furnaces, down the funnels, but the smoke went directly into the engine room. I'd guess that some elevators are down on E deck. The elevator shafts could have acted as reverse chimneys.'

'What did ONI say?'

'They said they were investigating. And they told me to keep it under my hat. Later they called me back for an official deposition, and asked me not to testify at the congressional hearings.'

'Which you didn't?'

'I thought ONI was a lot better qualified. And the guy I saw wasn't old-line navy. They'd brought him up from the volunteer reserve. He was a little standoffish, even after I dropped your name, but he listened and he at least seemed reasonably bright.'

'What's his name?'

'Ober. Lieutenant Percy Ober. I just heard he made lieutenant commander.'

'Don't know him,' Prince said.

Dressed in a well-tailored uniform and brandishing a pipe, Lieutenant Percy Ober had reminded Gates of a wealthy academic, the kind he'd seen at Yale who taught, wrote and lived well on a private income.

'He didn't really understand the chimney action drawing the smoke down to the boiler rooms,' Gates said, 'but he seemed a little more interested in the doors.'

'What doors?'

'When I saw how badly the ship was listing I opened some outer doors to drain the hose water.'

'You went back into the fire?'

'I opened about ten doors on the promenade. A lot of good it did.'

'Is that how you burned your face?'

Gates touched the quarter-sized white circle. 'Yeah. Me and Don Quixote. I walked into a fireboat jet. It tossed me across the promenade like a damned snowflake.'

'Why'd you keep this from me? Why didn't you tell me at the time?'

'I didn't want to bother you. You were in Oregon at the Kaiser Liberty Ship Yard. And then you were so busy with the *Niagara*. Anyhow, when I got off the ship the doors were closed.'

Prince reacted like Lieutenant Ober, with mild interest. 'What are you saying?'

'I'm saying I opened the doors to let the water out and somebody closed them.'

To Gates's annoyance, Prince repeated Ober's objection. 'But you were hundreds of feet away on the shore. Obviously you couldn't have seen the doors through the smoke at such a distance.'

'I know . . . I admit I didn't see the doors themselves, but only two or three streams of water were pouring off the promenade. There should have been ten.'

Again, Prince reacted like the intelligence officer. 'But wasn't it getting dark by then?'

'I also opened a couple of cargo ports below decks. One of them might have been closed too, but I couldn't see for sure. I'm much more positive about the promenade doors.'

'Steven, don't get sore, but I think the last time you sounded this sure you said there wouldn't be a war.'

Gates looked away angrily. 'I didn't *want* a war. I was hoping we could build the *Glory* – '

'So was I – what's your reason this time?'

He had a reason, a crazy reason – the man in the stack. He hadn't told Lieutenant Ober because the only way to challenge the generally held opinion that the fire was an accident was with facts, and his eerie impression that the man in the *Normandie*'s funnel had been observing, when he should have been escaping, was a notion, an impression – never mind how strong – not a fact. His uncle was watching him, obviously not convinced.

'I'm just *sure*,' Gates said.

'So what are you going to do?'

'I'm going to ask Ober what's going on. Why didn't they at least follow up my evidence, flawed as it might be.'

Prince turned around and steered Gates out of the yard. 'Don't go off half-cocked. If you need some help, I'll speak to some people for you. But stay in channels. You know the navy.'

With his promotion to lieutenant commander, Ober looked less academic.

'My aide tells me you're upset.'

'I am. What happened to my testimony? What's this about no sabotage? What about the cargo doors I opened? Who closed them?'

'The report hasn't been released yet.'

'Are you telling me that the report doesn't say it wasn't sabotage?'

'No. It says that certain officers were grossly incompetent.'

133

'They were, but that wasn't all. They didn't start the fire.'

'They might as well have.'

'Tell me something, Commander Ober – '

'Whatever I can,' Ober said. 'Then I'm afraid I must ask you to leave. I've got a lot of catching up to do in New York.'

'Is it perhaps just more convenient that it isn't sabotage?'

Ober sighed. 'What do you want me to say, Gates?'

Gates stood abruptly, his arms stiff at his sides, his face pale. 'I want you to look me in the eye and tell me that the navy pursued a vigorous, honest investigation of the causes of the *Normandie* fire.'

Ober looked him mildly in the eye. 'The navy pursued a vigorous, honest investigation of the causes of the *Normandie* fire *and* the subsequent capsizing of the ship.'

Gates shook his head. 'And did they report all the conclusions?'

'All. Satisfied, Gates?'

'No.'

Ober shrugged and picked up some papers from his desk.

'And you shouldn't be either. Because whoever sabotaged the *Normandie* isn't going back to Germany to collect his medal. He's going to stay right here in New York and do it or something like it again.'

Ober shook his head. 'We're hitting our stride, Gates. No more sneak attacks. If he exists – and I'm not accepting that he does – but if he exists and stays and tries it again he'll wish like hell he hadn't. We're ready for anything they try to pull.'

'I don't believe you. You're faking. You don't have the foggiest idea how the *Normandie* fire started or how to stop another sabotage attack. What if he tries for the navy yard? Do you want to see that carrier of yours go up in flames on the ways? Or how about a magazine explosion in a heavy cruiser? That ought to light up Brooklyn.'

Ober stood up.

'Get out of here, Gates. Nobody can prove that fire

didn't happen because of carelessness and bad planning. Besides, it's over. Like I said, we've got a war to fight.'

'I *know* that, Commander Ober. I'm not a fool. But I was and still am convinced the *Normandie* was the finest creation of engineering in the world. She's the perfection of a hundred years of industrial invention. She was beautiful. And she was elegant. In every sense.'

Ober sighed and sat back down. 'Gates? If you're that fired up about her why don't you go help raise her?'

'I just might do that, but – '

'But please leave the saboteurs to us.'

'I can't,' Gates said. 'You don't believe that she was wilfully destroyed. Look, for God's sake, we're on the same side. But you didn't see her die. You hate the *idea* of Nazis and Japs but it's not personal with you, Ober. You can't believe that one of them did this *right here in New York.*'

Ober shot back, 'Don't tell me the war's not personal. I joined the reserve in '41.'

'Big deal. You ran up a reservist burgee on your sailboat mast. Prince and Gates stopped *all* civilian work in the Fall of '39.'

'Are you telling me you made more money designing yachts and garbage scows than the navy pays you?'

'I'm telling you that we gave up building the finest liner the world has ever seen. Or *will* ever see if we can finish this war and get back to her.'

Ober looked at him. 'Even finer than the *Normandie*?'

'Even finer than the *Normandie*.'

Ober picked up his pipe. 'So that's it?'

'You're damned right that's it. At least part of it.'

'Sorry I can't change the world, Gates.'

Gates reached for the door. 'Don't worry about it, Ober. You don't have to change anything.'

'What's that supposed to mean?'

'The Nazi agent who did in the *Normandie* is going to change it for you.'

8

On the river, a thousand feet from Twelfth Avenue, the Otter burrowed deep into the overturned chambers of the *Normandie*'s stern. The capsized ship lay at an eighty-five degree angle, almost flat on her side, and stinking of old smoke, burnt paint and charred cork. Decks and ceilings, hurled upright, had become walls. And walls, tumbled on their sides, had turned into decks and ceilings. He moved on gloved hands and padded knees. In the low, dark, glass-littered halls every stateroom door led to an open pit.

He reached down into the dark for their latch handles, lifted them shut, and prowled on, strewing man-traps . . . a weighty sheet of jagged glass propped against a ceiling fixture made a guillotine; where the junction of fore-and-aft and crosswise corridors formed a chasm fifty feet deep that smelled of foul river water, he concealed the hole with a length of carpet.

Booby-trap injuries wouldn't stop the salvage but they would at least instil fear in the workmen, slow them down. But such efforts at sabotage were irritatingly small, what the Americans called penny ante. He had to do more. He had to attack, but what target? The port was so big. Where were they vulnerable?

The fallen ship exerted a special hold on the Otter. It was his handiwork. He kept coming back to it, overwhelmed by the sheer immensity of what he had destroyed. Indeed, nothing he had achieved in the months since the fire came near to matching it, not even derailing the train when the boxcars spilled into the river in a spectacular necklace of splintering wood and shrieking steel.

She weighed heavily on him, cramping his imagination, but he told himself there was sound reason to return. The military potential of the great hull was still awesome. Salvaged and refitted, it could transport fifteen thousand troops in a single Atlantic crossing at speeds no U-boat could hope to match. A field division with equipment in four days, while isolated, battered Germany had only the strength of the men in her borders to replace the casualties of her three-front war.

Access to the fallen ship was easy, despite the Coast Guardsmen, army troops and police camped on the pier. The Rik van Slough cover let him roam at will. The morning after the fire, while the other contractors were still hustling around New York trying to replace their lost equipment, he had appeared with a work crew and burning outfits and bid for the contract to cut away the US Navy's deck-gun emplacements.

Van Slough Salvage had stayed with the job as the navy accepted bids from scores of contractors to lighten the ship by ordering the stacks dismantled and the sundecks cut away. The work gangs, including his own legitimate employees, stayed in their own work areas, and so far had left the interior of the hulk to the Otter. As well they might, he thought, because it would take a special brand of lunatic to stray where he had strayed.

Oil coated every surface the tide touched. Splinters and shards from the mirrors and decorative glass that had sheathed the walls gleamed jaggedly in the beam of his flashlight. He had a spare light attached to his belt. Though he had crept in and roamed the echoing black spaces for many nights, and he knew the *Normandie* as she then lay better than any man in the city, even he would never find his way back without a light. Entering another corridor, he identified it as a service passage because it had less broken glass than the lavishly appointed accommodation levels. He crawled aft. Water gurgled close below.

A star glowed in the dark as he crawled to an open

porthole in the curve of the stern. It was one of many ports the welders hadn't capped before the fire, and he knew that any they'd left open on the down side would drive the salvors crazy. Fresh air poured through the broken glass. He pushed the shards out with the butt of the flashlight and rested, his eye roving over a patch of river framed by the port.

A tug passed. And another and another, running upstream, laying white wakes in the light of a quarter moon. Several followed and his interest quickened. Then, ghostly, a shadow moved across his vision from up the river, a great grey shape, filling the night sky, and a second, as large, and a third and a fourth, and he saw what the tugs had come for. Freighters waiting up the Hudson had weighed anchor and were crowding downstream on the tide, forming up yet another Atlantic convoy.

Of the three eighty-thousand-ton liners that existed in the world, he had destroyed one, this one. Singlehandedly. Larson and Walsh were unimportant; explosives experts like the redheaded Larson only existed to be recruited by the bolder and more imaginative; as for Walsh – the fanatical Bundist of mixed Irish and German blood whom Uncle Willy had planted in the Third Naval District procurement office – disaffected clerks had performed minor forgeries for various reasons since the days of the Roman Empire.

Walsh's forgeries had expedited the delivery of the flammable kapok life jackets days early. The proper note of official panic in his forged additional instructions – a memo allegedly from an admiral – had ensured they were stacked in the salon instead of left where they should have been on the pier. Even the late hour the day they arrived had given Larson a chance to set his incendiaries among the bales while the contractors argued about overtime. But the *source* of the splendid destruction was the Otter. And yet ... even though the *Normandie*'s charred hulk blocked New York's longest piers, and all the world could see the Allies' failure and the Otter's victory, war material continued to move, almost as if nothing had happened.

The port still gathered arms and food . . . built, loaded, sheltered ships and spewed them into the sea. *That* was his failure. A failure of imagination – the imagination that was supposed to set him above ordinary recruits, prove he was a leader, his father's son, the saviour of a desperate Germany.

He'd lived outside the Fatherland, and the exile . . . bitter as it had been . . . gave him large insights into the ways the world worked. He could see how a simple drive east had gone wrong and entangled the Reich in a three-front war that grew more ruinous each day as her enemies gained in their might. So, too, he could see that Germany's last chance to extricate herself was to drive home her U-boat advantage on the Atlantic and demand cease-fires in Europe and North Africa the moment Moscow fell.

But that U-boat advantage was thin, and the Americans were building more ships every day. So the challenge and opportunity fell to him – to choke the flow of Allied arms and personnel here at its source. Sinking a single great ship had not been enough. He should have sunk the liner in a channel to block the port. But that was a job for a submarine, and New York Harbour was too shallow to hide a submarine large enough to cross the Atlantic.

Uncle Willy had warned him that the sheer size of the port could break his spirit. Brooklyn alone was one of the major shipping centres in the world, and it was only a part of the Port of New York. It was true. He had smashed at New York with all he had, and yet a few days later the city returned an uncaring leer at him.

Disgusted, he turned away from the porthole, only to be arrested by a new shadow gliding upriver from the sea – a spectacle that mocked him more than the forming convoy, as if it had been staged by a prescient practical joker in Third District harbour operations who'd somehow guessed that the Otter was at this moment mourning his own unimportance. The shadow blotted the night sky, the river, the Jersey waterfront. Even the convoy, still filing by like the links of a chain, hugged the Jersey side to give the newcomer a wide berth.

He recognized the *Queen Mary* by her square bow and wedding cake cluster of decks that fronted her superstructure even before he saw the distinctive profile cast by her three funnels. Slowly, the tugs eased her into the far side of Pier 90. Already the Otter could hear the gangways clanking against her hull, the grate of her cargo ports opening and the furious rumble of trucks and winch engines as the Americans raced to provision her for another voyage. Tugs pushed oil barges into her slip. If she followed her recent pattern she would turn around in four to five days and take another load of soldiers to Ireland. He could radio Hamburg, but he doubted that the U-boat commanders would make better use of his information about this ship than they had done before. It wasn't worth the risk of signal interception.

He stood up in a cold space that echoed his steps and walked in the light of his flash. The deck, a former bulkhead, was painted grey and the odour of fresh paint was stronger here than the omnipresent smell of smoke. The paint appeared ripply – smeared and streaked with brush marks – but before he caught its meaning he had already shifted his weight to his leading foot.

He jerked back from the window, too late.

The glass, which had taken the paint poorly, shattered. He dropped the flashlight and tried to cover his face as he pitched forward, breaking more glass. And then he was falling through darkness, falling into sheer black, falling longer than was possible, falling forever.

There was time to cringe from the steel that waited in the dark, time to know with certainty that he would die. He landed in water, and even as he thought he was saved, it closed over his head, so cold that it stunned him, and he was sinking rapidly, still falling, pulled down by his heavy work clothing, choking because he'd yelled involuntarily from fear and shock and cold.

The cold pounded him rigid and still he sank, powerless to move his arms and legs. He hit bottom, face first, and the burst of pain in his nose goaded him like fire. He balled his knees under him and pushed up from the slime, kicking and clawing for the surface. His clothes dragged him back down. He was out of air. He tore at the buttons, ripped them loose and struggled out of his coat. It pinned his hands behind his back, and he sank again, kicking the water and ripping at the sodden cloth. He swam heavily, kicking and stroking with his last strength, pulling himself to the black surface where he gulped the cold air and fought to stay afloat.

He pulled his spare flashlight from his belt.

The beam soared high. He was treading water in an immensely tall and narrow cavern. An upended deck and ceiling formed walls, close on either side, but the roof was at least forty feet high and curved down like a dome fifty feet away. The roof, formerly the skin of the hull, was studded by huge, closely spaced windows separated by steel struts.

He swam to a round protrusion – a winch barrel wrapped in heavy manila line – pulled himself onto it, and collapsed, teeth chattering, heart pounding from the struggle. Slowly he caught his breath. His face itched, and when he rubbed it, it felt worse. Spun-glass insulation in the water had entered his skin. He knew from experience there was nothing to do but let it work itself out.

He darted his light about – risking it being seen from out in the river – and played memories of the *Normandie*'s rooms through his mind, laying the memories on their sides, trying to figure where he was. The size of the space and the aft location put him in mind of the third-class dining room, but the winch was the giveaway.

This was the huge aft mooring compartment where her

stern hawsers were stored. Half the cavern was underwater, half above. The arching windows had been the row of tilted, square ports that curved around her behind like the after castle-windows of an old wooden frigate —

And suddenly the Otter knew that the *Normandie* would serve him again, and in the process help him finally to bring the Port of New York to its knees. The newspapers had likened the wreck to a huge discarded toy or a beached whale, but somehow he had always seen the wreck as a dead horse . . . all right, why not a dead *Trojan* horse?

The arching windows were the same beneath the opaque water — huge, open doors to a dark and silent underwater cave. An invisible lair. An Otter's lair. Next door to the *Queen Mary, and big enough to hide even a fair-sized submarine.* A submarine to sink the *Mary* not by a pier, but in the mouth of New York Harbour, choking it, and all that tried to pass through it, to death.

9

He removed the trip from the glass guillotine, opened the stateroom doors and dropped the carpet down the deep shaft he had concealed – undoing anything that might arouse suspicion. Until now he had not cared whether the investigators who had swarmed around the pier had finished inquiring into the fire, but suddenly it mattered that none suspect sabotage.

Then he remembered that eight hundred feet forward of the dark cave and five decks below – or rather sideways – the forward baggage elevator sat at the bottom of its shaft where he'd left it to draw the smoke. The location of the car didn't matter. The investigators would blame it on bad luck ... except, damn it, for the fuses he'd loosened in the elevator motor room. Those would scream sabotage louder than any propaganda broadcast from Berlin. He'd better get to those fuses before they did ...

Gates went by twice in a taxi, marking how she lay. This was the first time he'd brought himself to see her since the fire. He felt embarrassed. She looked like a beautiful woman who'd died with her skirts hiked up around her thighs.

The fallen liner sprawled diagonally between Piers 88 and 90, her stacks and sundecks stripped. The navy had tried to hide her behind a plywood fence, but the ruin was starkly visible from the West Side Highway, where traffic – thinned by gas shortages since the U-boats had sunk most of the coastal tankers – still knotted up passing the *Normandie*.

The *Queen Mary* had just docked on the other side of Pier

90. Police, soldiers and armed Coast Guards were blocking off Twelfth Avenue, so Gates's already-exasperated cab-driver had to circle around to Forty-fifth Street after he got off the highway in order to drop him near Pier 88. A token force guarded the *Normandie*'s fence. Gates flashed the navy's ID he used to enter Third District shipyards, and they waved him through.

The *Normandie*'s bottom faced the pier. Her flank swelled fifty feet out of the water. Her bow pointed into the north-east corner of the slip and blocked what had been the *Queen Mary*'s berth. Eleven hundred feet out in the river, her stern pressed tight against the French Line dock. She had shattered the end of it with her rudder. The pier building, set back from the edge of the dock, was undamaged, but several dock pilings had been destroyed. Gas and compressed-air hoses and torn-up mooring cables webbed the bulbous hull like harpoon lines that had hauled a great whale to the surface.

Behind her, the *Queen Mary*'s stacks loomed over the roof of Pier 90, the Cunard pier. The three colossal, battle-grey cylinders were sporadically venting steam, the pressure released with a fitful roar, like a huge animal worried by a death of its own kind nearby.

'*Hold it.*'

Gates started. Work had stopped for the night and he thought he was alone, but a voice had hailed him from the shadows. A light hit him in the eyes and a Coast Guard fire patrol was suddenly on him, four seamen and a petty officer carrying flashlights.

'Got any ID, mister?'

Gates showed his navy ID again, and again they accepted that he belonged. When they had walked off, Gates headed onto the pier along the narrow footpath between the pier building and the edge of the dock. Halfway out was access to the fallen ship – a single gangway, jury-rigged from one of her own boarding ways, which was still gaily emblazoned 'French Line', and a slapdash extension of planks and girders of the sort of rough but serviceable passageway found on any marine job site.

Gates looked in both directions. The area was deserted. No one challenged him as he climbed up the gangway and onto the *Normandie*'s flank. There was a cool wind off the river, and as he climbed higher he could see a long line of freighters heading downriver to form up a convoy beyond the Lower Bay, their running lights winking in sombre anticipation.

He found a few crude wooden shacks perched atop the *Normandie*'s flank. He walked across the vast hull, across its pools of light, and located the stairs he'd seen from the highway that led down her vertical deck to a catwalk. Far below in the slip, a second village of work shacks floated on barges. Float cranes were moored in the slip, and empty barges into which the cranes would hoist what was now scrap steel from the liner.

The catwalk was a temporarily rigged platform for the burners to cut her steel from, as well as a passage which ran fore and aft, bow to stern. It was slung twenty feet above the barges, and a second catwalk hung below it at water level. An eight-inch water main ran alongside, and the catwalk bulged every hundred feet at a fire-hose station.

Gates descended a second stairway to the lower catwalk, which placed him at the water and almost on the centreline of the ship. He turned right and walked forward, hugging the vertical deck and ducking into shadows so he could not be seen from the slip, from Pier 90 or the highway.

His goal, the forward baggage elevator shaft, pierced the ship horizontally, with a slight tilt downward. A pool of floodlight illuminated the opening, and Gates had no choice but to step through it as he entered the shaftway. The light spilled in a short distance, but beyond that the elevator cables, clustered in the centre at shoulder height, pointed endlessly into darkness.

Gates pulled a flashlight from his pocket and entered

the shaft. The beam faltered beyond a dozen feet, a murky yellow spot fed grudgingly by old batteries. He reached for the cables and his hand came away greasy. He hadn't thought to bring gloves, and he discovered he'd worn the wrong shoes. His feet were sliding on the guide rails.

The fallen ship was eerily quiet. Though a liner at dockside did not move perceptibly, small noises, the sense of her banked fires, some slight cant indicated that she floated. But the *Normandie* lay dead as a stone. Gates felt deeply frightened by the silence, the vastness, and the thick dark. She smelled of sewage and burned cork. He forced himself down the shaft, leaning back against the slope, bracing himself on his heels and holding the elevator cable like a lifeline.

The Otter ran through the ship. He was soaked from the fall, and his wet clothing chafed and clung to his limbs. He found a stair tower and plunged into it, thinking it might be a faster way forward than through the glass-strewn corridors. The stairs pitched impossibly horizontal, but he dragged himself along their railings and climbed sideways into the *Normandie*'s depths . . . past the accommodation decks, through the service decks, dense with the odour of meat the navy had loaded, rotting in the cavernous refrigerators, and into the vast ventilating compartment above the motor room.

Water swirled close below, black and oily and speckled with flotsam. Turned on its side, the steel deck-grating between the ventilator compartment and the motor room stood like a grim arras in a church built for siege. The Otter shone his light through the chinks in the grating and saw the tops of the starboard electric motors. As an engineer he marvelled that neither of the gigantic machines had been wrenched off its mount. He climbed onto the struts of a catwalk railing that hung a few feet over the black water, determined his direction by putting the grate – the lower deck – on his right, and headed forward. He passed the motor room and, getting the rhythm of the struts' spacing, entered the ventilator space above the number four boiler room. Half the *Normandie*'s boilers were underwater, as were half her ventilator fans.

He moved sure-footedly along the struts, holding his light in one hand, balancing with the other, picking up speed until he was running hard, leaping from strut to strut, tossing the light from hand to hand as he ducked fixtures, cables, fire hoses that came suddenly into his path. He hit a patch of grease, slipped and started to fall, caught himself and raced on. He felt exhilarated. The *Normandie* would serve him again. And the Otter would stopper this port like a cork in a bottle. *Uncle Willy, you were wrong*. New York would forever remember the Otter.

He came at last to the forward bulkhead of the ventilator space and puzzled a way out, which involved entering the forward boiler room and pulling himself up a crazily angled stairway. It took a while to get his bearings, to figure out where he was in relation to the baggage elevator, and a while longer to get to a corridor he'd remembered. It was broad, having been used to move steamer trucks and large crates, so he could now stand erect.

And then he saw the baggage elevator, still open, lying partly submerged with light streaming through its open ceiling. Intent on locating the compromising fuses, he didn't notice that the light was moving until he had climbed into the elevator motor room and screwed tight the fuses. He crawled back out and stood up in the corridor. He froze. Something was moving in the elevator shaft. Exhilaration crystallized into hard purpose. He slipped back into the motor room, pocketing his flashlight to free his hands.

Gates descended the dark sloping shaft, gripped by fear but propelled through it by anger at the *Normandie*'s stillness. No view he had seen of her, neither newspaper pictures nor newsreels, nor his sight of her tonight from the highway, had conveyed her death as did this ghastly silence.

The elevator cables ended suddenly at a system of pulleys hooked to a pair of massive, crossed girders on the roof of the car. Gates's heart jumped . . . the first thing he noticed was that the ceiling panels were missing. To facilitate loading? Misplaced in the confusion of converting? Fallen out when the ship capsized? *Or* ripped out by a saboteur to draw smoke down the shaft?

He climbed over the girders and into the car itself. The panels were not in it. He played his light over the elevator control. Its plates were intact. He had been half-expecting to find the wire torn apart. But the car's doors were open, another piece of evidence that favoured sabotage. Had the government investigators even bothered to come down here?

He stepped out of the car into an overturned hallway. Somewhere along it would be the elevator motor room. He shone his light at his feet and saw an open oblong pit. A doorway. He knelt and looked in. It was the motor room. If you wanted an elevator to stay at the bottom of the ship, this was the place to sabotage it. Water – the ebb of the tide on which the *Mary* had docked – gurgled through part of it. He put down his flashlight, lowered himself through the door, and felt with his feet for a hold. He hit something soft and slipped –

A loud crunching sound prefaced a bolt of pain behind his ear, and he fell, reaching for his flashlight because everything was turning dark. His fingers, though, had already let go of the door frame. He felt himself floating down towards the gurgling tide, his arms spread out like wings, his head exploding as bright as a star in the blackest, coldest night.

10

The Otter threw the body into the water, where it floated face down, buoyed momentarily by an air pocket in its raincoat. The wallet he'd torn from the man's clothing was expensive pigskin. Riffling through it, he came upon the name. Gates. Steven Gates.

It rang a faint bell . . . Steven Gates . . . He poked his flashlight at the dark until he found the body, still floating. Blond hair splayed on the filthy water. Gates had a US Navy document that gave him *carte blanche* to enter Third District naval installations. Very handy. The Otter put it in his pocket.

A business card. Engraved, 'Prince and Gates – Naval Architects.' Of course . . . he remembered nearly three years ago, days before the war – the last crossing of the *Normandie*. Uncle Willy had provided an annotated first-class passenger list, identifying the rich and powerful, culling the pretenders. Richard Prince was a leading expert in high-pressure steam marine propulsion, and confidant of the United States Navy planners. The Otter had cultivated Prince and his young nephew. Steven Gates had seemed very young and caught in the sway of his illustrious relative. The Otter recalled him as a gentle type with a stubborn streak. Gates had obviously fallen hard for the English BBC girl, the one who'd turned up later in Geneva, the beauty with the startling eyes and an independent air that had reminded the Otter of his mother. Valuable people, the Prince and Gates family.

He looked at the water. Gates had disappeared except for the tails of his raincoat. Funny coincidence. Or was it fateful opportunity . . . ?

He tended to believe in fate, though he tried very hard to control his own destiny. Still, so much of his life had abruptly turned out to be directed by forces outside himself, as he had learned at nineteen on a day of fear and loss in Austria. The day the Austrians executed his mother. It was 1934. They had hanged her for her part in the assassination of Austrian Chancellor Dollfuss and the failed Nazi coup against the Austrian dictatorship, which denied political union with Germany. Fiery, brave and single-minded she had died for the German cause of *Anschluss* four years ahead of its time.

Uncle Willy had appeared at great personal risk beside the raw grave. He had just been relieved of his battleship command and had been put in charge of the Abwehr, Germany's intelligence service. It was winter. The Austrians had debated executing a woman for nearly six months after the male members of her Nazi terrorist cell had been hanged. The ground had not yet frozen, but snow quickly whitened Uncle Willy's shabby navy coat. He was distraught, and the Otter's relief at seeing his old protector quickly turned to confusion, hurt, and then a kind of exhilaration as Uncle Willy unfolded what he had been groomed for all those years . . .

But first he told the Otter how he had loved his mother, how they had met in the World War when he was a spy in Italy . . . how *he*, Wilhelm Canaris, was the Otter's father . . .

The mysteries of his childhood – why his mother didn't marry, where the money came from, why they so often travelled with 'Uncle' Willy on his trips to Holland, Spain and Switzerland but never Germany, where he had his family – were suddenly explained that day by his mother's grave. But it was more than a man providing for his bastard son. Far more. For years Uncle Willy had had a plan for his son . . .

Gates woke up in bright lights. His head was split with pain like an axe between his eyes. His throat felt on fire. A nurse was holding his head over a toilet bowl. She smelled medicinal. He was vaguely aware that when he was done being sick she cleaned his face with a washcloth, laid him out on a bed and hovered nearby while a doctor examined his skull. Sometime later, another face moved into the light.

'Can you hear me, Mr Gates?'

'Yes.'

The face drifted in and out of his vision, a clean-shaven man in his twenties, a serviceman's tie knotted about his neck. The vision melted. His throat ached.

'Can you see my hand?'

A hand popped into his vision, and the effort to make his eyes focus caused his head to throb cruelly. The hand loomed. He brushed weakly at it. 'Yeah, kind of. What happened?'

'Maybe you can tell us.'

'Where am I?'

'Armed Guard Center, Pier 92.'

'What? How'd I get here? That's the Coast Guard, isn't it?'

'That's right, Mr Gates. I'm Lieutenant Bristol. Security. What were you doing on the *Lafayette*?'

The navy name for the *Normandie*. It jolted Gates back to memory. 'How'd I get here?'

'Mr van Slough brought you in.'

'Who's he?'

'He's the guy who saved your bacon, Mr Gates. You almost drowned.'

Gates saw a large, round amiable-looking face slide into his view.

'Remember me?'

Gates was still grappling with how he'd got here, but van Slough was familiar, which made things even more difficult to understand . . . 'Didn't we meet on the *Normandie*?'

'Twice,' van Slough said. 'The second time was tonight.'

Mr van Slough found you floating at the bottom of an elevator shaft.'

'What were you doing down there?' Gates asked.

'Mr van Slough is a salvage contractor,' said Bristol. 'He was *supposed* to be there. But you weren't, Mr Gates. You want to explain?'

'I showed my clearance to the guard.'

'Not for this job, Mr Gates. You conned the guard. You had no business down there and you know it. You want to tell me about it or you want to wait in the brig for the cops?'

'Oh, come now,' van Slough said. 'I can vouch for Mr Gates. Why don't we just find out what happened to him?'

'I don't know,' Gates said, closing his eyes. 'I think I fell on my head.'

'Wait a minute,' said the Coast Guard lieutenant. 'I still want to know why he was inside the ship at night.'

Van Slough came to his defence again. 'Who cares if it was night? There's no difference inside the wreck night or day. It's always pitch black. Why do you think I was in there too? I save the daylight for outside work.'

'Yeah, but you're in the business, Mr van Slough. What were you doing, Gates?'

Gates let the discussion wash over him. Anything to lie still and make his head stop hurting. Keeping his eyes closed, he answered with the story he'd put together before he went into the ship. 'It's sort of private. Can I count on you to keep it to yourself, lieutenant?'

'If it's something illegal you can count on me to take you down to the nearest precinct – '

'It's not illegal,' Gates said. 'Look, my firm is trying to get a leg up on a refit commission.'

'I don't follow.'

'If the salvors manage to raise the *Normandie*, Prince and Gates would like to design the refit. To make her a troop carrier. I figured it would be worth a look around to see

152

how the salvage is going, get a notion about the problems ahead of time.'

He opened his eyes. 'Did your uncle send you, Steven?' van Slough asked him.

Gates shook his head. Which hurt like hell. A new wave of nausea came over him. 'No. He doesn't know about it. And that's why I'd appreciate your keeping it to yourself.'

Van Slough looked relieved, as if he hadn't wanted to imagine Richard Prince doing anything even remotely underhanded.

'There's nothing wrong with it,' Gates said.

'Good business,' said van Slough, nodding. 'That's how you stay ahead of the competition.'

'Yeah, well, next time, Gates, get a pass. You know what strings you can pull. Why don't you just pull them instead of sneaking around giving me problems?'

'I'm sorry.'

'And don't go in alone. If Mr van Slough hadn't come along you'd be dead.'

'I'm sorry. You're right. I'd like to get out of here, if I could, please. I want to get into a bed.'

'All right with you, lieutenant?' van Slough said.

'Okay.'

'Think you can sit up, Steven?'

Gates swung his legs gingerly off the bed. Pain drilled through his head; he felt nauseated again. Rik van Slough, the Otter, took his arm, helped him stand and locked a powerful arm around his waist. 'Come on, let's get out of here. Good night, lieutenant. Thanks for everything.'

'Thank *you*, Mr van Slough. You want I should call you a cab?'

'Thanks. You've got everything blocked off around the *Queen Mary*, haven't you?'

While they waited at the main door for the taxi, Gates noticed that van Slough's clothes were as wet as his. The Dutchman grinned. 'We look like a pair of bums, don't we?'

'I think I owe you a lot.'

Van Slough laughed. 'We'll work something out. How's your uncle?'

'Busy as hell.'

'Say hello for me.'

'Glad to. We'll have you up for dinner. Can I get you at the ship?'

'Sure. Or call the office. Van Slough Salvage, over in Hoboken. Here.' He took a soggy business card out of his pocket. Gates put it in his equally soaked wallet. The cab arrived. They got in and van Slough said, 'I'll drop you off.'

And then it came back to Gates . . . 'By the way, did you happen to notice that the ceiling panels in the elevator were missing?'

Van Slough had been looking out of the window as the cab pounded across the cobbles of Hell's Kitchen. He faced Gates intently. 'No, I didn't.'

'Wonder where they went?'

Van Slough turned back to the window, then broke into his open, easy laugh. 'That conversion job was closer to anarchy than the Russian Revolution.'

'Did you work on her?'

'Sure. I had a scrap removal contract. They were cutting excess steel.'

'I know,' Gates said. 'My uncle and I did a preliminary survey for the navy. Were you aboard the day she burned?'

'Yeah. I got caught below decks. How about you?'

'I was there.'

'Too bad. A beautiful boat.'

The Otter took the cab to Harlem after dropping Gates at a private house on East Fifty-fourth Street. The five-storey building on a carefully tended block between Lexington and Park was a reminder of how much influence he had lost by failing to befriend Richard Prince and Steven Gates after they had crossed together on the *Normandie*. He had started well, but when the British blundered into war over Poland, what should have been a year of careful preparation in New York exploded into a frantic battle.

He had stayed out of it, kept busy setting up van Slough, uneasy with the poor quality of the German spies ... Bundists, Nazi sympathizers and Irish Sinn Feiners who attacked British shipping with a fury marked by an excess of enthusiasm and a scarcity of professionalism.

Uncle Willy kept asking him to get out while he could, but he had continued to rebel until Van Slough Salvage Corporation was fully established. Then to Sweden, via South American freighter, to give van Slough a base in that neutral country. And then, at last, to England for Uncle Willy, where he operated for the first year of the war making forays into Europe, aided by Uncle Willy's superb false documents.

In the autumn of '40, when all but the Luftwaffe knew that the Battle of Britain was over and lost, Uncle Willy had let him return permanently to New York, with a warning that he did not have much time before the Americans found some excuse to enter the war, to salvage an organization from the wreckage strewn by the British shadow army. He'd made two clandestine trips to England, but New York had become his territory, as originally planned, until the war was won, or the van Slough cover was blown, or the Otter was dead ... So here was a second chance to cultivate Prince and Gates. Except what was Gates doing aboard the wreck?

He put Gates from his mind and told the cab driver to drop him several blocks from an apartment he kept near Sugar Hill – one of the pleasanter safehouses he maintained around the port – where he stripped off his wet, smelly clothes, bathed and dressed. Restless, though it was late, with the idea of the submarine and the Trojan horse coursing through his brain, he went out again.

He prowled the boisterous bars, drinking his favourite Scotch and milk, and eavesdropping, as was his habit, to

155

hone his ear for American English. He spoke German, the language his half-Italian mother had demanded; Italian, which he had learned as a child in Italy and in the Italian expatriate communities in Vienna and Switzerland; Dutch and Spanish, which he'd picked up when his mother had followed Uncle Willy on his trips to Holland, Spain and the Argentine; and English, which Uncle Willy had insisted he study in school. The Otter realized, looking back, that Uncle Willy had known for a long time who the enemy would be. But even he must have been surprised that Germany had entered a war in the east. He'd not insisted that the Otter learn Russian . . .

He moved on, prowled the streets some more, toying with the notion of finding a woman. There was one in particular that he kept going back to, his 'vice', or weakness . . . ? Her name was Casey, or at least that was what she called herself. She was a street hustler instead of one of the brothel girls he ordinarily preferred, and fiercely independent. He had recruited her to relay messages, but she was also his favourite whore in Harlem, with a long lean body and a matter-of-fact inclination to please that seemed to stem from true professional interest in perfection – an attitude towards sexual performance much like his own approach to his profession.

But though she had no idea who he was and no knowledge of what the messages contained or where they came from, it was still terribly risky to let her see his face, to go to her more than once. Uncle Willy had taught him to analyse his habits regularly in order to relieve the mental pressure of surviving in enemy territory.

Dutifully he had analysed the situation he had allowed to develop with Casey. She was good, but not that good, and it certainly wasn't any form of love or even friendship. As far as she was concerned he was just another ofay john flashing money. He realized that his 'vice' could be a subconscious desire to be caught . . . the ultimate relief . . . but he decided instead that patronizing this girl was a way of pretending, for a few hours, that his life was not on the line every second he lived in the enemy camp, a method by which he could be Rik van Slough for a few hours with nothing more serious to worry about than how to hide excessive profits from the tax auditor. And as such, it had a fine relaxing effect, rejuvenating him, which possibly outweighed the risk. But he kept his visits to a minimum, and she was his *only* 'vice', he told himself. (Was this how Uncle Willy had met his mother?)

But tonight the idea of the miniature submarine – the *Seehund* – kept intruding, the details flowing like a tidal surge. And halfway to the 'Market' on Seventh Avenue where Casey plied her trade, he realized that despite his preference for letting a major idea sit for a few days before taking it up, there would be no Casey tonight. No indulgence.

He settled at a corner table in a noisy nightclub, and began committing the details to a cocktail napkin, penning numbers in a tightly disciplined hand. His broad shoulders shielded the numbers as he hunched over the little table drinking more Scotch and milk, looking up now and then to gaze at the dance floor awash in cigarette smoke and moving lights.

On a fresh napkin he enciphered his calculations for radio transmission to Hamburg. It was a considerable order. The harbour channels were deep – dredged to thirty-six feet – but the bays were shallow. Many places in the middle of New York Harbour, a man could stand miles from shore. He needed speed and range. There'd be seconds to aim, no time to reload and a long, long run to rescue by a waiting submarine in the open sea.

A considerable order. Even for Uncle Willy. But to make it possible the Otter could offer Uncle Willy's *Unterseeboot* engineers limitless electricity and compressed air in the bowels of the *Normandie*.

And the target was worth the whole war.

11

'It seems hopeless,' said Weatherburn. 'Twenty thousand people in New York have the sort of proximity to shipping that we've agreed upon as possible covers for the Otter. Cordi, you're late.'

'Sorry, sir. I was all the way out at the Bush Terminal when I got word.'

'Call in more often. We don't have that many meetings. You can get here on time.'

Cordi sat on the couch beside Mark. It was two weeks since they'd learned about her brother's convoy, and a month since the Otter's radio message. She had devoted herself to the search for the source of the sabotaged cargoes, warehouse by warehouse and manufacturer by manufacturer. The tedious work was worthwhile only if performed methodically, but numbed by loss, she was insensitive to discomfort and therefore in a perfect frame of mind to trace each empty lead to its empty conclusion.

Weatherburn, always impatient, was suffering from a bad case of frustration. He was smoking heavily, lighting one from another, and his nervous voice was pitched higher than normal. This was the third meeting this week, bringing her and Mark and Duncan off the street, where they should be, to watch Weatherburn pace edgily about the room and chop the air with his nervous hands.

This time, though, it sounded as if he had a real purpose.

'We must narrow the search. And I think I may have found the proper focus.' He snatched up a thin pile of typescript from one of the desks, flicked off a paper clip and passed the sheets around.

'The Otter slipped in and out of England several times

158

since the spring of '40. And Cordi suggested that he must be rather well-established in New York to pull off the sort of attacks we've credited him with. Therefore, we're looking for a man well-connected in transport who has also visited England in the past two years.'

Cordi examined the first sheet, a list of names particularized by addresses, business affiliations, ages, and dates arrived and departed from Great Britain. Many were starred, indicating more than one visit.

'Wait a minute,' Duncan said.

'Yes?'

'What good is this lot if the Otter came and went by U-boat?'

'Every time?' Weatherburn asked scornfully.

'Why not? We parachute agents into Europe. We don't send them through Nazi immigration.'

'For God's sake,' snapped Weatherburn, 'America was neutral until last December. A man with the right cover could easily have penetrated Immigration. Still could if he's buried deeply enough. No, Duncan. Once, maybe, by U-boat. But not more. Can you seriously imagine U-boat Command allowing their boats to be commandeered at the whim of a single spy? Not likely.'

'But I thought that Admiral Canaris has influence with the U-boats,' said Cordi.

'But almost none with U-boat *Command*.' Weatherburn went to the single window, cracked the shutters, and peered out. When he turned back and faced them the familiar vein in his forehead was pulsing again. 'It's occurred to me that we make a mistake assuming that the totalitarian governments operate as trimly and orderly as a scientist's laboratory. By their nature they must be as riddled with dissension and personal ambitions as any combination of men supposedly working together for a common purpose. The enemy isn't all that different from us. Imagine for a moment what Western Approaches Command would say if I kept asking to borrow a destroyer escort for a couple of months at a clip? Well, that's precisely what U-boat Command would tell Admiral Canaris, don't you see? This Otter has travelled through normal channels. And that makes him one of the people on this list. Now let's get started.'

Cordi wanted to get out of the Meurice and back to Brooklyn. The meeting bubbled around her ... Mark, Duncan and Weatherburn comparing names, discussing possibilities, choosing suspects who seemed worthy of investigating, considering ways to check their backgrounds. Weatherburn had worked quickly since they'd arrived in New York, and he had contacts with the New York police, naval intelligence and the FBI.

'Cordi,' he now said sharply.

'Beg pardon?' She'd been thinking about Tom ...

'I said,' Weatherburn repeated testily, 'which names will you start with?'

'I'd rather finish my warehouse survey first. Sir.'

'It can wait. Go through the list.'

She riffled the papers, and her eyes focused on something familiar, dimly recalled. 'Here's a name. I can't quite ... ' His company name seemed to leap off the page. The suspects were listed alphabetically. She went backwards to the right page, then ran her finger down the column. Ford, Ferguson, Gabriel, Garfield, and there it was. Gates. Steven. P. For Prince, his uncle's name.

'Here's one I know. Met him on the *Normandie*.'

Weatherburn leaned over the back of the couch and pointed with a nicotine-stained finger. He had little wrinkles on his knuckles, like brussels sprouts. '*Three* trips to England. Who the hell is he?'

'A naval architect. Prince, his partner, is his uncle. I think they're quite prominent.'

'Have you seen him since?'

'Of course not, I returned home immediately – wait! He rang me in London. He rang me up that winter. I got the message when we came back from Switzerland.'

160

'Did you make contact?'

'No.'

'Why not?'

'I was in a terrible state . . . after Geneva. Then you sent me into training.'

'I wish you'd mentioned it at the time, Cordi. We were all instructed to use our American contacts to the limit. We needed friends then, you may recall.'

Cordi looked at her hands. 'I didn't think I could control the situation so I didn't risk it.'

'I see. Mr Gates popped you off to his cabin, did he?'

Beside her, Cordi felt Duncan grow tense. Mark noticed and smiled at the ceiling. Cordi elbowed him and said to Weatherburn, 'As a matter of fact, sir, he popped me off to the motor room to show me the ship's motors.'

'You're joking.'

'I am not. They happen to be electric – which, he said, was very unusual on a liner – and he was extremely proud of them. The third night out he led me into the depths of the ship, down tunnels and shafts you'd never dream of. He'd studied her at school and knew his way through her.'

Weatherburn was intrigued. 'Knew the ship, did he? What's Gates like?'

'He had some dreams of building a new liner called the *American Glory*.' She told them how he had taken her down to his stateroom to show her a model of the ship. He'd held it like a baby as he explained each feature.

'It looks rather like the *Normandie*,' she had said, and he had answered like a lecturer at university . . . 'Her bilges – this part below the waterline – are broad in the waist, like the *Normandie*. The breadth adds buoyancy so we could narrow her bows. But she's faster, bigger and more beautiful than the *Normandie*.'

'Like the *Queen Mary*?'

'She's got a cruiser stern like the *Mary*'s but she's faster and bigger and more beautiful than the *Queen* too.'

161

Weatherburn said, 'You seem to remember quite a bit about him.'

'I didn't at first. So much has happened since. It was another life.'

'Were you sweet on him?'

Cordi looked at him. The old boy had moved into territory he knew only by the maps. She said, 'We had an awfully nice time,' and recalled how grim it had turned when the *Normandie* started zigzagging through suddenly treacherous waters. What a strange four days to be in mid-ocean. Her radios were silent for safety, and no one knew a thing about what had happened in Europe. Most had stayed in their cabins. But Steven, in a way, had fought the gloom. They'd danced across empty floors and taken long walks on deserted decks.

'Will he remember?' asked Weatherburn.

'I remember him.'

'Mark, you handle Gates – better yet, I'll do it.'

'I'd hardly call him a legitimate candidate for the Otter,' Cordi said.

'They're all legitimate candidates until proven otherwise. And he has more than a few of the credentials. Familiarity with ships, easy access, trips back and forth . . . Charm and even a love of ships is no disqualification. Perhaps just the opposite. And you could hardly ask for a deeper plant . . . '

Cordi shrugged, shook her head and flipped back a couple of pages. Charlie Collins, she noted, wasn't listed. She turned to the last page . . . 'Here's another one I know, sir . . . this van Slough. I met him, too, on the same voyage.'

Weatherburn looked. 'Dutch passport?'

'East Indies,' Cordi said. 'Djakarta, I think. He was a salvage diver, as I recall . . . I had the impression he was working for the French Line.'

'Well, he lists his business here as Van Slough Salvage based in Hoboken. Dutch? Convenient way to mask a German accent.'

'He had a very faint accent.'

'We'll follow him up. Djakarta? Behind Jap lines. Rather convenient.'

'Salvage is a small world,' Mark said. 'We ought to be able to check him out.'

Cordi wore a severely cut suit, but let her hair fall freely to her shoulders. The combination opened a lot of doors along the Brooklyn waterfront. From Weatherburn's list she had chosen businessmen located around the Erie Basin and the Bush Terminal.

'Please tell Mr MacMillan' – and before him, Stein, Doyle, Fiorello, Sloane and Raucher – 'that Cordelia Grey of the BBC wishes to discuss the possibility of a radio interview.'

Once inside, she found overworked, often frantic executives torn between a killing schedule and the flattering prospect of a News Talks Unit descending on his office to broadcast his thoughts on war production to three-quarters of the English-speaking world.

MacMillan was a grain agent and Weatherburn had expressed particular interest in him because he was very young and travelled often. Five trips to Liverpool since the Nazis had invaded Poland. And he had access to a broad range of cargoes shipped to England. He was a man in his twenties, bulging prosperously from his waistcoat and quite pleased to spent a few minutes with a pretty girl. He told her right off that he often went into Manhattan for what he called 'a relaxing late lunch at a good hotel.' The half-dozen telephones on his desk rang constantly, and he answered each after an apology to Cordi for interrupting his description of how the grain-shipping business worked ... 'New York's always been a grain port, of course, but with the war I'd say we're doubling or even tripling the volume passing through this town. Midwest grain – corn, wheat, rye, barley and oats – comes either across the Erie Canal and down the Hudson River by barge or directly to New York by train. Here at the Erie Basin we also handle a lot of rice from the South, and to answer your last question before the phone rang, the stuff in sacks comes mostly from the south. Rice brought up by coasters and transferred to Atlantic freighters.'

'Directly?' asked Cordi, her heart sinking at the thought that the explosives could have been hidden before they reached New York.

'Oh, no. A broker buys from the southern producer and sells it here to an exporter or to an English company or directly to your government or mine, depending how that deal's been made. The grain is off-loaded into whomever's warehouse and then loaded into whomever's seagoing freighter.'

'Wouldn't it be simpler to transfer the cargo from the coaster to the Atlantic freighter? I've seen it done like that in Rotterdam. They load from the Rhine barges directly to the freighters.'

'Maybe so, but business doesn't work that way here. Who's going to organize that when the system already works?'

That MacMillan might be the Otter's agent, or the Otter himself, seemed absurd, but that was just why the problem was so enormous. A good cover could well resemble this busy office. In the end, she had to rely on her instincts about the grain agent, his open willingness to talk, his manner, even the way he came on to her, in order to recommend whether to investigate him further.

'Do you own warehouses?'

'I'm an agent. I don't own anything – except my dad's forty-year reputation in the business.'

'What if you need to store some rice in sacks?' Cordi asked. BSC was positive that explosives had entered the ships *inside* the cargo.

'I know who's got space. That's my job, knowing where there's space in warehouses and ships and who wants what. Producers, warehouses and shippers . . . I bring them together . . . Well, does the British public want to hear about Fred MacMillan?'

'We'll have to get back to you, but thank you so much for your time.'

Home at the Meurice late that night, she found the back room empty. She started to brew a cup of tea to take to bed when she noticed that Duncan's machine had been in operation. The drums of graph paper had recorded a pair of direction lines within the hour. And the disc recorder, which had replaced the wire recorder, had cut a partial disc.

She approached it warily, trying to remember exactly how Duncan had said it worked. She checked each step as she went so as not to destroy the evidence accidentally, and when she had removed the acetate disc and put it on a player, her heart leaped to the squeal of speeded-up Morse.

Torn between trying to decode the message and examining the radio direction finders, she decided first to go to the drums and transposed the direction lines to the map. The bearing relative to the antenna on the Hampshire House crossed the bearing relative to the antenna atop the Cunard Building at a point in midtown. Four blocks east of the Meurice and ten or eleven blocks downtown. Park Avenue. At Forty-eighth.

She went to her room, slung a packed bag over her shoulder and was on the street an instant later, the long day forgotten. Halfway to the indicated point of radio transmission she remembered she hadn't left a note. Well, they'd figure it out. She had.

Duncan's machine wasn't, as he'd said, all that precise, and when she came to the block indicated she found three grand old apartment buildings shoulder to shoulder on either side of Park Avenue. The bearing lines had converged closer to the west side of the wide street, so she went to the middle building on that side, waited until the doorman ushered her through the foyer into a sumptuous lobby of burnished wood, and when he asked whom she wished to see she had passed him a ten-dollar bill – a bit more than a day's salary – and murmured that 'the gentleman I'm seeing doesn't want it known. Now if you would just take me to the sixteenth floor, please . . . '

He looked at her sharply, apparently decided she wasn't a hustler, pocketed the money, relieved the elevator man and took her up himself.

Cordi waited until he had closed the door and she could hear the machinery move again before she headed down the hall on the sixteenth floor to a stairway, which she took to the roof. It was a maze of chimney pots and shaft housing, like a Paris roof made enormous, and she searched it for an hour with a flashlight before she was satisfied there was no antenna.

The buildings on either side were a full storey lower. She put on the overalls and crepe-sole shoes she'd brought in the bag, chose the roof to the north, shined her light down to locate a safe landing place, climbed over the wall between them, hung by her hands and dropped. She hit hard, stinging her feet and making a mess of the overalls against the sooty wall.

In Europe, where the distances were so much shorter, a toilet chain on a high floor made a good antenna. But from America, a radio operator needed much more height. She wasn't expecting another antenna as blatant as the commandeering of the RCA overseas directional, but as it would have to be rather large, she was hoping for a permanent installation. If it weren't, then the operator would have already disassembled it.

She checked all the various pipes first, as she had at the first building, and the electrical leads. A lightning rod atop the water tank crossed the roof and went over the side of the building. And then she found a second 'lightning rod' lower down the elevator house. It disappeared down one of the chimneys that stuck out of the roof like a crowded Stonehenge.

The next afternoon, a Saturday, Cordi and Weatherburn sat in the back of a taxicab watching the building on Park Avenue where she'd found the antenna. Building records Mark had checked at City Hall that morning showed that the flues serviced a line of bedroom fireplaces. Which apartment of the luxury building the particular flue Cordi had found descended to, no one could tell, but a list of the building's occupants, obtained for Weatherburn by BSC, revealed the name of a man in whom British Security Coordination had taken an interest earlier in the war.

'There he is,' said Duncan, who was slouching behind the wheel wearing a cabbie's flat cap and looking sullen. 'The white-haired man with the girl. Same old codger the doorman showed me this morning. The girl's supposed to be his daughter.'

Cordi pressed against the glass for a better look.

De Villeneuve had come to New York right after the war broke out and had mixed with New York society from whom he'd raised money, supposedly for the Free French exiles in England. BSC had looked into his activities because rumour had it he'd had fascist leanings in France, but De Villeneuve had suddenly stopped fund-raising, and after a time BSC called off the investigation for lack of activity.

De Villeneuve was impeccably dressed, very polished. His daughter was beautiful, dark and slight.

'Cocky-looking bastard,' Weatherburn said. 'Ought to put the screws to him. That type breaks easily. Daughter's a tasty-looking dish, I must say.'

'Why don't I put on some decent clothes and chat her up?' Duncan offered, subtlety to the winds.

'We'll see,' said Weatherburn. 'Her name's Elise. What's he carrying?'

'It looks like a lady's overnight bag,' Cordi said.

'They're hailing a cab.'

'Follow them.'

It was a short ride. The cab went down Park, through the General Building, and stopped at the upper entrance to Grand Central Station. Duncan eased up behind, and after De Villeneuve and his daughter had walked through the doors, Weatherburn offered Cordi his arm and said, 'Daughter, my dear?'

'Don't mind if I do.'

They strolled into the station. De Villeneuve and his daughter were going down the broad stairs to the main concourse. They watched from the marble railing above. The Frenchman bought a ticket at the Hudson Line windows. Cordi and Weatherburn followed them to a gate where a Quebec Pullman was posted. They watched them head out onto the platform and board the train.

'Now what?'

'This is perfect,' Cordi said. 'What a chance to search the apartment.'

'Wait,' Weatherburn told her.

The conductors began calling 'Aboard!' and as the train started to roll, De Villeneuve stepped lightly off and blew a kiss. He stood on the platform, watching until the train's two red lights were lost in the tunnel, then headed back into the station, head down, hands in his coat pockets.

'Wish me luck,' said Cordi.

'*What?* Where are you going? Come back here – '

But Cordi had already darted away, hurrying, then running towards the platform, converging with De Villeneuve at the gate. She ran into him full tilt. His coat, which he'd had draped over his shoulders like a cape, slid to the floor. He ignored it and took Cordi's arm.

'*Pardon, mademoiselle.*'

'I'm so *sorry* . . . the train . . . '

'It is gone – '

'Oh my God, my bags are on it. I just went to make a call.'

'*Mon Dieu.*' The Frenchman was still holding her arm, and Cordi leaped into the opening with a torrent of French, repeating she had gone to make a telephone call and now her bags were on the way to Quebec and she was stranded and what in the world was she going to *do* . . . ?

'You are French?' asked De Villeneuve, and Cordi met his eye for the first time and saw that he found her attractive. It was going as planned . . . 'No. English. My father was with the embassy in Paris while I was a girl. I spoke French for years there.'

'Your accent is marvellous. What is your father's name?'

She momentarily froze. Stupid. Bull it through. Close to the truth. 'He was very young then and quite minor to know important people in Paris. Just a third assistant *chargé* . . . oh, my God, what am I going to do?'

'The thing to do is go home and telephone who it was that was waiting for you to get your bags and go tomorrow.'

'No, no . . . you don't understand. I don't live here. I'm working in Washington for the British Embassy . . . I'm a secretary . . . and I know no one here and I've checked out of my hotel . . .'

Within minutes she was in a cab riding up Park Avenue, trailed by Duncan and Weatherburn in their cab, and telling De Villeneuve what a treat it was to converse in French once again.

He repeated that her accent was remarkable. He was elegantly handsome, no question, and wearing the headiest cologne she'd ever smelled on a man or woman. He had several empty bedrooms in his elegant apartment.

He showed her the telephone, and she called the long-distance operator, asking for a made-up number in Quebec, and instructed the mystified householder who answered to pick up her bags at the train and she'd be up the next day or the day after. He took her to one of the bedrooms and brought her a robe and a negligée that, he said, belonged to his daughter.

'Unfortunately I have a dinner engagement – '

'Oh, I'll be just fine here. Thank you so much.'

'Ah . . . come *with* me.'

'No, thank you, but I couldn't. I haven't any clothes – '

'Perhaps one of Elise's evening dresses will fit you.'

'No. No, thank you, I'm really very tired. You go on. I'll be fine here.'

'I'm not sure I should leave you alone,' he said, his voice trailing off as if he were thinking aloud. Cordi repeated that she would go directly to bed. De Villeneuve studied her for a moment. Cordi looked away and pretended to yawn. He shrugged and went to his bedroom – where the antenna would be – to dress for dinner.

She waited anxiously in the drawing room, flipping through a magazine. When he reappeared in evening clothes she was struck again by his undeniable elegance. He repeated that it troubled him to leave her alone and as she protested that he shouldn't worry she still couldn't tell if it was simply good manners on his part or if he was worried about the apartment's secrets.

With a final shrug he took his stick and top hat. Cordi held his cape for him. 'Good night, then, *mademoiselle*. The kitchen is down that hall and there is champagne in the refrigerator. Please take what you like.'

Cordi stood by the door as he left, waved, smiled and nodded as he entered the elevator. She listened to it descend until she was sure it had gone down to the lobby. She went immediately to his bedroom. She was halfway to the hearth when she heard the front door slam.

Cordi whirled about and ran back to the hall. He was hurrying down it, his face concerned. He looked startled to see her coming from his room. 'There you are.'

'I got lost, I'm afraid . . . it's such a big apartment . . . '

'Yes, of course.' His eyes darted past her in the room to the fireplace.

'What happened?' she asked.

'Halfway down in the elevator I thought to myself, I can't possibly leave that young lady all alone . . .'

'What about your dinner?'

'I shall cancel it. We will have supper in. I shall make something you will love.'

They went to the kitchen and he bustled about cooking an omelette that he graced with champagne and truffles. 'Tinned, I'm afraid, but such is the price of war.'

As he served it in the dining room by candlelight Cordi heard rain on the windows and wondered if Weatherburn and Duncan were standing in it, watching De Villeneuve's lights. He poured more champagne and she sipped slowly, despite his entreaties that good wine should be quaffed, not sipped.

De Villeneuve brushed his lips against her neck as he helped her up from the table. She pretended to ignore it and put some space between them.

'Please don't stay in tonight for me,' Cordi said. 'I'll go to bed early. I was tired before, and now the champagne's gone to my head –'

'No, I think it's begun to rain. I tell you . . . Let's have a nightcap and then I shall send you off to bed.' He led her to the study, lit a fire and more candles, and poured brandy. Cordi resigned herself to fending him off for a decent interval before she could excuse herself. They talked about Paris. He asked what Washington was like this spring and she answered as best she could from magazine pictures of the Japanese cherry trees. They both knew Berlin – she'd visited a school friend there – and her father had taken her on an assignment to Buenos Aires.

'The most beautiful women in the world are in Buenos Aires,' said De Villeneuve, adding with a smile, 'though possibly I've found an exception.'

Cordi began a smile, and he leaned over quickly and kissed her on the lips. She pulled back wondering how far she would have to go. He was as old as her grandfather, a colonel in the Home Guard. And then she reminded herself that it was her idea to come here. The consequences were her problem . . .

De Villeneuve's hand came closer, preparing to cup her breast.

'Please don't,' she said very quietly. 'I'm sorry . . . really . . . but I think I'd better go to bed.'

De Villeneuve shrugged, smiled his disappointment. 'I'm sorry, of course. I'll show you the way.' He put a screen in front of the fire and led her to her bedroom, where he kissed her hand and continued down the hall to his own. Cordi undressed and got into bed, feeling too nervous to sleep. An hour passed. The apartment was silent. Two in the morning and even the street sounded distant, like a stream on the far side of a hill.

She put on Elise's robe, opened her door and listened. The hall was still. De Villeneuve had left a night-light in the bathroom nearest her room, which provided a pale yellow path to his door. She crept down the hall, hugging the wall to avoid creaking floorboards in the centre. His door was open a crack and she stilled her own breathing to listen for his. Her heart started pounding in her ears. She steadied herself, listened again. There, like an old bellows, short but regular. He was asleep.

She eased back to the bathroom and closed the door to block the light, then knelt by his door, listened again, gently pushed the door open and started to crawl across the rug. The rustle of the satin robe sounded like thunder to her. She undid the belt, slipped out of it and continued crawling. She passed the bed, bumbled into an armchair she'd forgotten. Something fell from the table beside it and landed with a muffled thud. De Villeneuve awakened.

'Is that you, my dear?' he asked sleepily.

Cordi froze, praying he would go back to sleep. No luck. She heard him feeling around for the bedside lamp. She did the only thing she could do. When the light flared on she was standing naked beside his bed.

De Villeneuve smiled. 'You have changed your mind.'

172

Cordi said nothing. What the hell could she say?

'A woman's prerogative. Come.' He slid across the bed and opened the lace coverlet. Cordi looked at her robe heaped near the door, a million miles away. She slipped between the sheets. De Villeneuve reached for her gently but swiftly. He caressed her thigh with one hand and her breast with the other, leaned close to her mouth, whispering, 'What do you like?'

Cordi, trying to pull away without seeming frantic about it, said, 'Champagne.'

'Now?'

'To relax me.'

De Villeneuve looked at her for a long moment and an edge of hard light deep in his eyes told her this was indeed the right apartment. She half-expected him to produce a revolver and announce that the party was over.

Instead he smiled his damned knowing smile and said, 'Of course, *mademoiselle*. To relax.' He got quickly into a silk robe, as if ashamed of his sagging body, and he hurried out the door. Cordi launched herself off the bed and knelt down on the hearth.

She couldn't see far enough into the dark fireplace. There were candles on the mantel. She looked for matches. If there was an antenna she'd try to subdue him, tie him up, and call Weatherburn. He was, after all, an old man. If there wasn't she would run like a sacred virgin. She found matches in a lacquer box, lit the candle and thrust it into the fireplace. De Villeneuve had done a messy job of it. A metal fitting curved out of the flue and disappeared into a big chip in the firebrick.

She drew the curtains and raised the window shade to signal Weatherburn. She put on the robe as De Villeneuve walked in, hands filled with a silver champagne bucket. He saw the open curtain, saw the matches she'd left on the hearth, threw the bucket at Cordi and dived across the bed, reaching for his night table. Cordi managed to duck

173

the champagne, hurled herself across his back and got to the night table first. Rolling off him as she pulled the gun from the drawer, she clicked off the safety and levelled it at his head.

De Villeneuve looked terrified. 'Who in the name of God are you?'

Her robe had opened. She closed it with one hand and backed away, watching his eyes, keeping the gun close to her own body. There were footsteps in the hall. Weatherburn already? The girl De Villeneuve had left at the station sauntered into the bedroom calling in French, 'You're awake, I'm so glad. I left the train at Albany, *chéri*. I came home.'

Elise stopped dead when she saw Cordi. She was younger than Cordi by a few years, barely twenty, strikingly beautiful with black hair and dark eyes that had now grown enormous. Cordi backed further away and gestured for her to sit by De Villeneuve on the bed. Did she know her father's secret?

'*Bastard.*' She ran from the room screaming. Cordi was momentarily too startled to move, until De Villeneuve started to get up. She turned the gun back on him. 'Sit down. Call her back.'

'You don't understand,' he said. And then the girl was back, brandishing a kitchen knife, charging at Cordi. Cordi sidestepped and backed away, showed her the gun. Elise ignored it, slashing wickedly, screaming French obscenities.

And then De Villeneuve made a move. Cordi was off-balance, but it was Elise he was going for, not her . . . and then she understood that Elise's rage was the rage of a betrayed lover. The girl slashed at De Villeneuve, who fell back with a cry of pain, clutching his hand, which was suddenly spewing bright red blood on the creamy carpet. Elise screamed again that he was a bastard and went for Cordi.

She didn't want to shoot the girl, who, after all, was an innocent in all this .. and then Elise was on top of her, slashing. Cordi caught her arm, twisted out of the knife's arc, and threw the girl against the wall. As she did so, she dropped the gun. De Villeneuve went for it. Elise had dropped the knife when she fell. Now she turned her attention to De Villeneuve, biting and scratching. And then abruptly, she stopped and collapsed in his arms, crying as though her world had ended.

Cordi picked up the gun. De Villeneuve looked very sad. When Cordi told him to get back on the bed he ignored her, and kept on stroking Elise's hair and murmuring for her not to cry.

It seemed that De Villeneuve, *au fond*, was more lover than spy. How terribly French, she thought.

Weatherburn and Duncan came in moments later, guns drawn. Duncan gaped at Cordi. 'We came in as soon as the daughter arrived,' Weatherburn said. 'Afraid she might be part of it.'

Cordi closed her robe. 'Daughter? I'd like a chat with your informant.'

'You've been at him all night and half the morning,' the BSC doctor said. 'He's an old man. If you don't let him get some sleep soon he may well die.'

'Then perhaps you'd better stand by with some sort of injection, doctor, because he's holding back something and I'm going to get it. He's hiding something. Or somebody.'

'Well, I wouldn't get rough with him if I were you.'

Weatherburn said nothing, returned to the pantry, where they'd confined De Villeneuve for the interrogation. The Frenchman slumped in a straightback kitchen chair, holding his bandaged hand and watched over by Duncan and Cordi. Weatherburn motioned them aside.

'Monsieur De Villeneuve.'

De Villeneuve raised weary eyes.

Weatherburn leaned over him. 'You've admitted the names of German agents you've served with your radio.'

'*Oui, monsieur.*'

175

'We've checked your claims with the FBI and culled our own records. Every one of them has already been arrested, jailed or hanged.'

De Villeneuve said nothing.

'You're a pretty clever chap. You managed to avoid being apprehended at their message drops. In fact, so clever that you're still hiding something.'

'*Non, monsieur*. Nothing.'

'I was thinking perhaps that Elise might know more than you've let on. I was thinking we might question her.'

'I told you. The child knows nothing. Don't hurt her. Please.'

Weatherburn shrugged. 'It might be the only way to find out if you've told the truth.'

Weatherburn was convinced that the girl knew nothing. He made an abrupt about-face, to shake the last of it out of De Villeneuve. He smiled. 'Would you have any objection to remaining at home with your lovely companion?'

'What do you want – ?'

'What you have not told me.' Weatherburn sat back and waited, watching the Frenchman's face.

'He'll kill me . . . '

Weatherburn's chest tightened painfully. 'We will protect you. After all, we want you to continue your radio services, though we'll shorten your transmitter range considerably. Now, what have you forgotten to tell me?'

'The Otter . . . ' De Villeneuve could barely whisper the name.

Weatherburn struggled to make his voice sound calm. The Frenchman was obviously terrified.

'Who is the Otter?'

'I don't *know* . . . he has only used my radio twice – '

'What does he look like?'

'I have never seen him.'

'Where does he drop his message?'

'He does not use drops like the others. He transmits himself. He makes me leave my apartment before he comes.'

'Have you ever watched to see him?'

'After he calls the first time, he telephones a coinbox an hour away.'

'Where?'

'He tells me when he calls. He tells me to go to Continental Avenue in Forest Hills. Or a bar in the Bronx. Or the Yonkers. I go. The telephone rings. It is he. I wait. He calls back when he is done. Then I go home.'

'Where do you drop the messages that come in for him from Germany?'

'He does not receive messages. He only transmits.'

'What language does he speak on the telephone?'

'English.'

'Could he be American?'

'I'm a Frenchman. How would I know such a thing on the telephone?'

'When he calls, do you take Elise with you?' Weatherburn was reminding De Villeneuve that he hadn't forgotten the hold he had over him.

'Of course. I would not leave her. But she doesn't know why – '

'Of course . . . What do you tell your doorman? Do you alert him that this man will go to your apartment while you are out?' That could be a flaw in the Otter's cut-out system. The doorman might provide a description. Something they had from no one else. But De Villeneuve, his eyes cloudy with fatigue, shook his head.

'No. He has a key to the back door. The service entrance.'

'To the building?'

'To my apartment. I don't know how he gets in the building.'

'In other words he could enter your apartment without anyone knowing?'

'Whenever he chooses.'

Weatherburn did not think too much of this frightened Frenchman. He had been wondering why the Otter trusted him . . . Of course . . . it was Elise, the same hold that he was exerting now. 'You're afraid of him.'

'He killed two radio operators, *monsieur*. Because he did not trust them. And others. Bundists. Some he betrayed to the police.'

'To whom does he send?'

De Villeneuve hesitated. 'I do not know . . . when they prepared me I began to have the idea that it was for someone of great importance. Admiral Canaris's deputy himself sent me a note wishing me luck – '

'How did you get into this work? You hardly seem the sort.'

'Perhaps that is how, *monsieur*. I am personable, I have been told, not threatening. And what I lack in courage I make up for with a good mind. I am a very good operator – '

'Yes, yes, I'm sure you are. I repeat, who does the Otter send to?'

'Considering the importance of this mission, and that Canaris's own deputy sent me best wishes, I think it might even be to Canaris himself . . . '

Canaris himself . . . it would explain the Otter's insistence on sending his own messages . . . 'Was the Otter in New York before you?'

De Villeneuve hesitated. 'I don't know. I just . . . I don't know. He came to me shortly after I arrived.'

'But he could have been here earlier?'

'Certainly, *monsieur*.'

Weatherburn interrogated him for another hour, going over and over the information, extracting more detail about his impressions of the Otter, which amounted to little more than a man with a threatening attitude and an air of command. Finally, when the exhausted Frenchman was drifting into incoherence, he said, 'All right, that will do for now. My people will tell your Elise that we broke into your flat while you were out and planted the girl that she saw.'

'She will not believe that, *monsieur*.'

'That's your problem. I want you to resume your life just as it was. You are to be on call for the Otter. We'll be nearby, twenty-four hours a day. Understood?'

De Villeneuve, amidst a stream of *mercis*, assured him that it was.

Weatherburn left the pantry, issued instructions, and went to see his superior at Rockefeller Center. The Old Man was pleased.

'We'd better come up with something juicy to feed back to his control.'

'I beg your pardon, sir,' said Weatherburn, 'but I'd rather hold off on the false information for a while, if you don't mind.'

'But didn't you say that the whole point of taking this fellow so quietly was to feed misinformation to the Abwehr?'

'I did tell you that, sir, but now I'd much prefer to get this Otter first, sir.'

'What makes him so special?'

'Neither we nor the FBI have caught him, sir. That makes him very special indeed. You've seen my reports – ships and dock fires, unaccountable explosions, derailments, the apparent sabotage of convoy cargoes . . . ' Weatherburn let his voice trail off, leaving his superior to endorse his conclusion. The Old Man, however, was not easily led. 'Fires, derailments and explosions are inevitable in an overworked harbour. Almost ordinary occurrences, if you think about it.'

'Certainly, sir, but I suggest that if Admiral Wilhelm Canaris put this Otter in New York, he'll be up to bigger things than ordinary sabotage. Much bigger.'

'But didn't you say that your people picked up the transmission from the Frenchman's radio?'

'Yes, sir. Apparently the Otter sent it himself. By the fist.'

'What did he say?'

'I don't know.'

'Why?'

Weatherburn tugged unhappily at his moustache. 'The Otter seems to have used a different cipher this time, sir. I'd guess the key is privately held by him and Canaris. The sort of thing he'd use only for the most important communication. Uncrackable unless he sends a great mass of material that the calculating machine can analyse.'

'And he's not likely to do that, is he?'

'No, sir. In my opinion he's sent an important message launching his new project, whatever it happens to be.'

'Can you make a *guess* about its nature?'

Weatherburn had been up all night. 'A very loud explosion in the last place we'd want to hear one.'

12

'I'm telling you that door's shut tighter than a virgin's pussy,' said the navy salvage diver. 'That door *ain't* open.'

His name was Norman and he was drunker than Gates, but not, Gates thought murkily, by too much. They stood shoulder to shoulder, Norm's workboot propped on the bar rail beside Gates's polished black wingtip in a Twelfth Avenue seamen's bar that had been taken over by the *Normandie* salvage crews. The place was jam-packed, loud and smoky, and neither the crowd nor the smoke had thinned for hours.

'I have reason to believe that door is open,' Gates insisted.

'You calling me a liar?'

'I'm talking about B deck. Port side. Second barn door aft of the bow.'

'It's closed.'

'It can't be.'

The navy diver put his glass on the bar and straightened up. 'You *are* calling me a liar.' He swayed slightly and added as an afterthought, 'you son of a bitch.'

'Watch it,' Gates said. 'I don't care if you're wrong about the door, but watch your mouth – '

'Sonny, you want to step outside or apologize here?'

Gates thought about it. As near as he could remember, they'd been drinking since five-thirty and it was now . . . he looked around and located a clock glowing like the moon in the smoky haze . . . Jesus Christ, it was now ten-thirty. He'd been haunting these bars talking to workmen about the fire. Norm was one of several dozen divers who'd begun clearing the hull of wreckage and non-bearing partitions. They'd struck up a friendly conversation when Gates asked if Norm had dived in the forward sections, but now the navy diver was bunching up his thick arms.

'Sonny, I been down there. It's forty feet under water and ten feet in the soup. I stood on the goddamned thing today. If it was open, I woulda stood in mud. Now are you telling me I don't know soup from steel plate?'

'Maybe you mean the door furthest forward,' said Gates.

'Goddamn it, now you're saying I'm stupid?'

Gates's lips felt numb. 'I didn't say that . . .'

'Yes, you damn well did. Listen, I don't mean the forward door. It's closed too, by the way.'

'I know.'

'Fuck you, you know, you haven't been down there.'

'Watch your mouth,' said Gates.

'You say that once more and I'm going to hit you.'

'Watch your mouth.'

The punch started near the floor. Gates saw it coming, rising lazily, almost in slow motion, but he was too drunk to move. It glanced off his chin and grazed his cheek and knocked him back onto the next drinker. The diver swung again, but the punch missed completely. Things then started moving quickly, and Gates found himself sitting on the sidewalk, his head ringing.

'You okay, Steve?' Norm was sprawled next to him.

Gates held his jaw. 'Yeah, just fine.'

'Hey, listen,' Norm said, pulling himself up with the help of a lamp-post, 'let's us get ourselves some supper.'

'Yeah. Good thinking.'

They found a diner that cooked steaks. Halfway through the apple pie and coffee Norm started in on the door again.

'Forget it,' said Gates.

'You don't believe me.'

'I just know it's open.'

'How do you know?'

'I opened it during the fire. To let the water out. So I know it's open.'

182

'Maybe it closed when she turned over.'

'It's a sliding door. How the hell would it close? I screwed the stops down. Couldn't have closed . . . unless somebody . . . I wish like hell I could see it . . . hell of a piece of proof to hand Commander Ober . . .'

'I'll take you down,' Norm said.

Gates looked at him. 'What do you mean?'

'I'll take you down and show you the door. What the hell else would I mean?'

'I'm not a diver.'

'I don't care.'

'They won't let me go down.'

'They're not going to know.'

'The hell they're not.'

'Are you calling me a liar?' The diver grinned this time.

'You're drunk.'

'So are you, you son of a bitch. You don't think I'll take you down.'

'You're crazy. We'll both kill ourselves.'

'No sweat. Long as the tenders are sober.'

'Let's have some more coffee.'

'Good idea, Steve. Now you're thinking. I'll fill you in on a couple of details. Hardest part'll be getting through the front gate.'

They headed for the ship at midnight, practising walking straight.

The *Normandie* was lighted up with arc lamps from the pier buildings and high points on her hull. She looked the same forlorn, oversized tank model she'd looked since they'd attacked her superstructure, but there were more shacks on her flank and a thicker carpet of barges surrounding her in the slip. Work inside and outside the ship had moved to three shifts.

'Got any dough?' asked Norm.

Gates checked his money clip. He had taken to cashing large cheques for walking-around money because his questions about the *Normandie* were leading him into places that didn't cash cheques or extend credit, far away from the world of private clubs and obliging restaurants.

'Got about a hundred. What do you need?'

'Five to start.'

'What for?' Gates handed him the money.

'The doorman,' Norm said with an appreciative stare at Gates's roll.

The Coast Guard stopped them at the gate to Pier 88.

'Where you guys think you're going?'

'Monte Carlo,' Norm said.

The guard gave the money a headwaiter's lightning scrutiny as it disappeared in his pocket. 'Real high rollers.'

The *Normandie* resounded with the roar of mud pumps. The mud spewed out of her into waiting barges from dozens of holes in her vertical deck. Deep inside her divers guided the suctions.

Gates and Norm climbed steep wooden steps from the pier, crossed her swelling flank, then down another set of wooden steps to the main catwalk and down more steps to the slip. They walked across a string of barges and gangplanks and entered an enclosed barge, a cafeteria-mess hall that housed Monte Carlo – a twenty-four-hour crap game, literally floating – that served the round-the-clock salvage crews.

Gates and Norm threaded their way through tables of cards and dice. The diver stopped at a pot-limit poker game. Three navy divers, a tug captain and a skinny bookkeeper in steel-frame glasses watched silently as a sixth man, a Coast Guard Shore Patrol chief petty officer, dealt a hand of five-card stud. Norm jabbed the diver, who raked in the pot.

'Hey, Jack. I got to talk to you. Cash in, I need a favour . . . hey, Ronnie, you losing?' he asked another diver.

'What does it look like?'

'You come too.'

'What for?'

'Tell you outside.'

Outside, the diver introduced Gates and said, 'My buddy Steve here wants to get a look at B deck up front.'

'So let him look.'

'In the water.'

'What do you need us for?'

'He ain't a diver.'

'You guys drunk?'

'Yep. Loaded, in more ways than one. Steve, show 'em.' Gates peeled off fifty dollars for each of them, grateful he'd brought enough cash for bar-hopping.

'You and Ronnie take him down and I'll tend him. Okay?'

'Sure.'

'Steve?'

'I guess so,' Gates said, awash in second thoughts, and sobering quickly.

As they climbed to the catwalk and walked forward Jack said, 'I suppose Norm told you, you can't see anything. It's pitch black down there, night or day.'

'I know that.'

'What do you want to do?'

'I want to see if the second barn door is closed.'

'It is.'

'It can't be.'

Jack shrugged. He might be a crazy man, but at least he was a crazy man with money.

'Can he use your suit. Norm?'

'Yeah. Little big but it'll fit.'

Gates looked nervous.

'No sweat,' Jack said. 'It's not open sea so the current's not too bad, unless the tide is running, which it ain't tonight. We've cleared most of the busted glass out of the way so your hose is pretty safe. And it's only forty feet deep, so you don't have to worry about pressure and bends.'

They shanghaied a couple of tenders on the way to the

cargo elevator shaftway that served as a corridor into the fallen ship and walked into A deck, where the diving suits were stored. Gates had seen hardhat suits in operation but only at a distance, and the details of keeping water out and air in were a mystery. Ronnie and Norm helped him into one while Jack stood look-out for unfriendly foremen. 'You ought to have long underwear for the cold, but you won't be down that long so it don't matter. Here.' He tugged a brilliant red knit watch cap from his pocket and pulled it over Gates's head. The other divers were wearing the same red hat, like a badge. They dabbed grease around his wrists to make a good seal. The single-piece suit was made of layers of rubber and twill that fitted Gates from toes to neck, with tight-fitting cuffs at his wrists and two plates bolted to the cloth around his neck. To counter the buoyancy of air inside they gave him heavy brass-soled boots and a garland of lead weights for his waist, which he could release by tugging a lanyard.

Ronnie and Jack got into their suits. Norm checked that the way was clear and they hurried down to B deck, carrying their helmets and clomping in the heavy boots. The tenders were waiting, having strung lines down from the air compressors on the hull that contained insulated telephone wires, air hoses and strong lifelines wrapped together in hemp.

'Ready?'

Gates gazed into the black water. Oil and sewage swirled on the surface. Norm attached a line to his headgear, a beaten copper helmet with glass eyes forward and on either side. The eyes were protected by a steel latticework, like miniature sewer plates. 'Okay,' Norm said, 'inside here's a valve to vent your air. You just lean your head left to push it open. Don't forget. Otherwise you'll blow up like a balloon. Just hit it with your head. Like breathing. Easy.'

Norm lowered the helmet over his head and locked it to the corselet over a quarter-turn. Air rushed in. He gulped at it and heard Norm tinny on the telephone speaker.

'Relax. If you got any problems I'll pull you right up. Relax. You're breathing too fast. You're okay.' Gates nodded. He could hardly see anything through the bars.

'You hear me?' asked Norm, looping a guide rope around his waist.

Gates nodded again. Norm came around and peered into the front eye. 'Say something, damn it. I can't see your head in there.'

'Sorry. Yeah, I'm fine.' The helmet seemed small.

They sat him on the edge of the diving platform, a wooden platform a few feet above the water. 'Okay,' said Norm. 'It's you and me, kid. Hold hands with Jack and Ronnie and tell me your troubles.'

'I can't see much.'

'Don't matter. You won't see nothing where you're going.'

They grasped his arms and lowered him into the water. It closed over his head, and everything turned dark. He flapped around with his arms until Jack and Ronnie took his hands and Norm said on the phone, 'Just relax, Steve. Vent some air. No sweat.'

He felt sudden terror at the dark and the confinement. He knew immediately how claustrophobia could stop a man from diving. But this was the *Normandie*. He tried to concentrate on other senses. He felt his body pulling down in the suit. When he pressed his head against the escape valve he heard the air bubble out. He couldn't see the bubbles, couldn't see anything. He closed his eyes. No difference. The water pressed against his chest. He felt cold. He was suspended in nothing. Suddenly he was rising.

The phone startled him. 'You forgot to vent, Steve — okay, skinny passage coming your way. Ronnie's going first. Let go his hand. He'll take your foot.' Not wanting to, Gates let go.

Ronnie's glove travelled down his leg. His exhalations sounded louder. The ink black was stupefying. Ronnie

187

pulled his boot. Gates brushed something in the dark, slid his hand along it. It felt like a wooden timber. Ronnie was pulling him past it, Jack pushing from behind.

'Wait,' Gates said.

'What's the matter?' Norm said.

'What's this thing they're pulling me through? Shouldn't be here. This is a wide hallway.'

'Hang on, I'll ask.'

They continued descending. Norm came back on the phone.

'Don't worry about it. They're shoring a bulkhead – know your way around pretty good, don't you?'

'Pretty good . . . '

'You're almost there. Jack just hit bottom.'

Gates felt a hand slide up his leg, drawing him down. His boots sank into soupy mud and then hit steel with a hollow thump. He was standing in total blackness forty feet beneath the surface of the Hudson River.

'How you doing, Steve?'

'Okay. Fine.'

'Jack says you're standing on the door. It's closed, see.'

'Tell Jack to let me feel along the edge.'

Jack and Ronnie steered him to the right, bent him down and tugged his right hand. Through the glove, and through a half-foot of liquid mud, he felt the lip of the barn door cargo port. He moved his hand along it, found a stop, then the top of the door and followed it on his hands and knees, with Jack and Ronnie guiding him, for twelve feet to the other side.

'Hey, Steve? Did I tell you it was closed or did I tell you it was closed?'

'You told me it was closed.'

'Is it?'

'It's definitely the door I was talking about and it's definitely closed, but I can't figure out why.' He mentioned the last for Norm's sake. He had a very good idea why it

188

was closed and he was going to tell Commander Ober about it first thing tomorrow morning.

He was still on his hands and knees and he'd touched a stop. He tried to turn it, but it was frozen, screwed shut. How could the door have slid shut against the stop he had screwed tight in the fire? Impossible, and that clinched it. Ober was going to get a telephone call as soon as they reached the surface –

Blinding pain ripped his hand.

'What's the matter, Steve?'

'My hand. I got something in it. Right through the glove.'

'Oh. Probably a hunk of glass. Nothing to worry about.'

Gates heard him call to the other tenders. 'Hey, tell 'em Steve wants to come up.'

They hung around the first aid shack cracking jokes with the nurse while a sleepy pharmacist's mate removed a long glass splinter and looped stitches through Gates's palm. Gates worried about infection from the sewage in the water, but the others were casual.

'Happens all the time,' said Norm. 'Never heard of a ship with so many windows.'

'They weren't windows. They sheathed her walls with decorative glass.'

'Oh, yeah?' Norm grinned at the nurse. 'Listen, dear, we need some help getting this man to a bar for medicine. When do you get off?'

'I got to make a call,' Gates said.

'They got a phone in the back,' said Ronnie. 'What are you drinking?'

'Order me a beer.' He handed Ronnie a five-dollar bill. 'And buy the guys a round, I'll be back in a few minutes.'

Gates shouldered his way through the crowded bar. He felt tremendous – the exhilaration of the diver multiplied by the discovery of the locked door. He fumbled a nickel into the phone with his left hand, as his right was wrapped in gauze bandage, and took Ober's card from his wallet with his teeth.

189

The telephone rang a long time. Gates glanced at his watch.

Ober answered sleepily.

'What is it?'

'Commander Ober?'

'Speaking. Who is this?'

'Steven Gates. I spoke with you about the *Normandie* fire – '

'Do you know what time it is?'

'Three a.m. I found out something you'll want to know – '

'Tell me at the office, for God's sake.'

'I just made a dive to B deck. One of the cargo ports I'd opened to let the water out has been closed.'

'Are you sure?'

'Absolutely.'

'That's interesting, Gates. Can you send me a *brief* report?'

'Can do!'

Gates ran out of the bar, flinging apologies over his shoulder, and rushed home. He brewed a pot of coffee to stay awake and spent the rest of the night writing the report in his uncle's library. He included several illustrations drawn to scale so Ober could send a diver down to confirm what the saboteur had done.

He ran into Ober a few days later at a War Bond ball at the Waldorf that he'd had to attend because Kay and his mother were on the organizing committee. Ober was barely civil, and when Gates asked him if he'd confirmed the information about the door, the ONI man turned on him.

'You know, you're becoming a pest, Gates. I went back and looked at the newspaper and official navy photographs taken before she capsized. That door was closed all along.'

'*Not* all along. I opened it.'

'You got confused, Gates. Or scared. Or something. Excuse me.'

Gates watched him stalk across the ballroom. There were more uniforms on the floor than dinner jackets. For the first time that he could remember he felt out of place in New York. He went to the bar. Wally Stratton lurched up and repeated his invitation to go up in the blimp.

'Want to hit some bars,' Gates said.

'Good thinking. A ballroom full of four hundred biddies is no place to dally with married ladies. Or get too smashed. Get our coats, I'll find some girls.'

He found four of them and they worked their way east, shedding women along a route of bars and saloons whose floors changed from carpet to parquet to linoleum to sawdust. When they had reached wet sawdust they were down to one girl, firmly affixed to Wally, who was waving his silver-headed walking stick at the El and remarking loudly that the street belonged to the people . . .

'I'm going home – '

'It's only three . . .'

'Thanks for coming along.'

'You were a barrel of laughs.' Wally rode off and Gates started walking, zigzagging the blocks of his neighbourhood. It was a cold morning for summer and he stuffed his hands into the pockets of his lightweight cashmere coat.

He turned east on Fifty-fourth into a greying line of dawn. Halfway down the block, yellow light splashed warmly from the morning room onto the cold sidewalk. Uncle Richard was already up. Gates drew nearer and caught a glimpse of him holding a coffee cup in one hand and a telephone in the other, standing, head bent, then pacing in and out of sight, talking to someone like himself in another light room on a dark street, middle-aged, energetic and deeply concerned. He stared at the bay window and half-wished his uncle would turn to the glass and see him and wave him inside.

Slowly he turned away and headed west into the wind. A cab came along and dropped him across town at Eleventh Avenue. He walked the last block, yawning and shivering.

His hand was throbbing at the stitches. Wooden police barricades still restricted pedestrian traffic to the east side of Twelfth Avenue. An army unit was out in force patrolling the blocks around the pier. Gates stopped at the barricade and gazed under the highway at the fallen ship looming over the plywood fence.

A soldier bearing a carbine with a bayonet fixed eyed Gates's evening clothes and remarked, 'Looks like the joint's done jumpin'. Better go home and out of those fancy duds or someone'll do it for you.'

Gates nodded, the soldier tossed an easy salute and resumed his round . . . leaving Gates, not so incongruously, with a memory of his father provoked by the man's comment about his 'fancy duds' . . .

He'd left home in the weeks between Thanksgiving and Christmas, 1929, when Steven was thirteen. He'd had a midnight-blue chesterfield draped over the arm of a dark business suit, as if he were running to catch a cab to the office, but Steven knew there was no office by then and knew with a child's surety that his father wasn't coming back.

'Take care of your mother,' he'd said. 'I'm sure you'll make a better job of it than I have.'

He'd gone to the door and down the front steps, then turned back and looked up at Steven, his brow wrinkling in puzzlement, as if he still wondered what had happened. It had been cold and he'd slipped into his coat with the grace that characterized all his motions. 'Find something useful to do,' he had suggested, smoothing his velvet collar. 'Like your Uncle Richard, for instance.'

Something useful . . .

Workmen began arriving at the pier, walking from the trolley and ferry terminals at Forty-second Street. The soldiers lined up around the gate while the Coast Guard checked passes. Gates crossed Twelfth Avenue and edged closer in the confusion until he could see through the entrance the slip itself, which was coming alive with workmen running along gangways, and boats shuttling from barge to barge, and booms hoisting materials.

He gazed into the slip, penetrating with his mind's eye the forty feet of water, the thirty feet of soupy mud and silt beneath it, the hard-packed, claylike mud under that, the hard pan of boulders, clay, sand and gravel, and finally the sloping New York bedrock, a prong of which, left by the builders of the super-piers, pressed dangerously against a forward section of her hull. The *Normandie* would have to be luckier than she'd been since the war began to rise from those cloying layers.

A smart, clean tug ploughed jauntily into the slip. She bore the name *Hollandia* and was remarkable for her small size, less than sixty-five feet, and her polish. The white letters on her stubby black stack were VSS. A diesel-electric boat. Brand new. VSS. Van Slough Salvage? *Hollandia*, van Slough's ancestral Holland. Then he saw Rik van Slough step out of the pilothouse to direct a crew tying up. He reached inside and stopped engines. The black exhaust stopped jetting from her stack. Gates watched, an idea forming ... 'Something useful' ... He about-faced under the highway into the first open chandlery he found.

He bought a navy pea jacket in the seaman's shop, thick socks and a flannel shirt, twill pants, gumsoled, over-the-ankle boots and heavy leather work gloves.

'Got a place I can change?'

The bemused clerk led him to a little toilet in the back. Gates pulled his scarf through the sleeve and hung his topcoat from a nail in the wall. He took off his jacket, his bow tie, his shirt – careful not to drop the pearl studs, moving in deliberate counterpoint to his racing mind – his pants and his evening pumps. The new clothes scratched. He folded the old into a pile, asked the clerk to wrap them and told him he'd pick them up later.

Then he emerged into the cold morning and walked over to Pier 88, blinking a bit bleary-eyed at the sunlight slanting over the highway, elbowed his way among a knot of workmen and flashed his navy pass on the way in. He hurried out on the pier, crossed the swell of the hulk and clambered down the catwalks and gangways to the slip, where he picked his way across barges and planks until he reached van Slough's tugboat.

The Dutchman was issuing orders to a barge crew. When he was done he stepped into his wheelhouse. Gates jumped aboard and climbed up to the wheelhouse.

'Rik?'

'What are you doing here?'

'I want a job.'

'Oh? Doing what?'

'I want to work on the salvage.'

Van Slough leaned against the big brass-rimmed wheel and eyed Gates dubiously. 'You're not a salvage man.'

'I can handle a burner. I worked three summers at the Brooklyn Yard and two on subs at Electric Boat.'

'You're crazy.'

'Are you turning down a trained burner who'll work for shipfitter's wages and happens to be an engineer? I'll throw the engineering in for free.'

'I don't know, Steven. It seems like a waste of your talents.'

'Let me worry about my talents.'

'*Ach*, it's crazy.'

Van Slough moved suddenly, catlike, across the wheelhouse. He grabbed Gates's unbandaged hand with his own massive fingers, rubbed his palm and held it to the light. 'You're not in shape. Look at your hands.'

'I'll be back in shape in a week.'

'Two months is more like it.'

'What if I bring Charlie along, too? I'll get him out of the yard. You're not going to tell me *he's* not in shape.'

'What's he doing at the yard?' the Otter asked. He was interested as van Slough because good men were hard to get and he had noticed when he had met him aboard

194

the *Normandie* that the big Irishman's hands carried the dozens of small burn scars of a longtime shipfitter.

'He's a welder.'

The Otter shook his head. Something wasn't right. 'Kay told me on the ship that Charlie was a Rhodes scholar. I gather that's an honour. He went to Cambridge, or someplace, before the Spanish Civil War. Then why is he working as a welder?'

'Charlie doesn't want to be a boss. He's a man of the people.'

'So why did he marry a rich girl like your sister?'

'I'll tell you what Kay told my mother. They fell in love, and it's worked damned well for six years.'

'Is he a communist or something?'

'Mostly, I think he's an idealist, but after his disillusionment with old lost causes he just wants to get back to earth, to work with his hands and be left alone.'

The Otter stepped back and eyed Gates. Charlie Collins . . . a considerable bonus, if Gates could bring him. As for Gates himself . . . he had a different plan for Mr Steven Gates. The Americans were adapting quickly to war and, it seemed, as quickly to intelligence and counter-espionage. He could feel the pressure against him building. He'd have been captured already if he hadn't eliminated so many weak links in his operation so early on.

Already he'd lost his best radio operator – disappeared – not a clue where he'd gone. Had the British got to him? Or was it the Americans?

He had other radios. That was not a problem. Yet. But how close were his enemies? The trouble with his plan to use the *Normandie* as a base from which to launch a submarine was that it locked him in place for a long time. Which made him a kind of sitting target.

He looked at Gates – so damned earnest, and certainly no agent – and thought of a stalking horse unknowingly drawing fire while the real attack formed behind it.

13

Salvage, Gates decided, was shipbuilding in reverse. A movie run backwards. The last that had gone aboard was the first removed. The *Normandie*'s palatial public rooms and deluxe cabins had graced her hull like a sumptuous crown. But now the superstructure was deadweight – killing weight – and her only hope of new life lay in merciless amputation.

Gates had been hired during the final stages of the stripping of her stacks and upper decks. Each ugly, gaping hole he cut from her plate steel made the ship that much lighter so that her hull and engines might one day stand and float when she was finally hollowed out, sealed and pumped dry. Such, at least, was the theory of controlled pumping. But the *Normandie* was an eighty-thousand tonner, weighted down by an extra burden of countless thousands of tons of mud and wreckage, and Gates knew of only one ship even a third of her size that had ever been raised – the twenty-eight-thousand-ton *Hindenburg*, pride of the Kaiser's scuttled fleet at Scapa Flow, and she'd been broken up for scrap.

He worked at a feverish pace with an oxyacetylene burner bucking and hissing in his hands and the hot summer sun beating on his back. He pushed hard, trying to force his body into shape. Charlie had come with him, as Gates had promised van Slough, but it wasn't a labour of love for Charlie and he was already in great shape, so when Gates rushed back to work after lunch, Charlie wedged his shoulders into a corner of blackened steel and read the newspaper.

'Hey, Junior. You taking any more destroyers on sea trials?'

'You know damned well I'm not.'

'Yeah, well if you change your mind, Abercrombie and Fitch is advertising a thing from England called a Vitabuoy coat. Guaranteed to keep you afloat for three whole days.'

'Regardless of freezing to death in ten minutes?'

Charlie shook out the paper, leaned close and pretended to study the advertisement. 'Well, let's see . . . *forty-five dollars?* Oh, cut in the 'naval officer style' – have to be for that price. Doesn't say anything about freezing to death, but it's got a flameproof inner lining.' He barked a laugh.

Gates flipped his mask in place and resumed cutting. When he finished, and the piece was ready to fall away, he signalled the bellman on a barge-mounted steam derrick, who lowered a length of cable which Gates looped around the piece. The derrick hoisted the piece away and lowered it to one of Rik's barges in the slip. An engineer came by and made a note in a log. In order to calculate the fallen ship's centre of gravity, an estimate was made of the weight of the scrap taken off.

Hollandia was working twelve-hour days, shuttling Rik van Slough's four barges between Pier 88 and his Hoboken scrapyard. He was taking advantage of the tug and tug pilot shortage to tow other subcontractors' barges as well, and to keep *Hollandia* going he was teaching Gates to handle her in addition to Charlie and an old captain he'd taken out of alcoholic retirement.

'Hey, Junior?'

Gates had started to lower his mask again, but something in Charlie's voice made him stop. 'What?'

'What are you going to do when Uncle Richard gets home?'

Gates shrugged. 'I don't know.'

The day after Gates had quit, his uncle had been ordered to Washington State. He had gone to the new shipyards in Oregon and California, consulting on Liberty ship production, and was presently in Washington, D.C., which meant he'd soon be back in New York.

'Do you think I should move out of the house?' Gates asked.

'I think you ought to go back to work with your uncle.'

'I won't.'

'He hurts, Steven. Give him a break.'

'I hurt too. I can't help him.'

'Then you better move out.'

'I guess you're right. It would be kind of awkward. I'll find something near here.'

Charlie folded his paper and picked up his burning mask. 'Plenty of apartments with all the dames in town going along with their new soldier boys.'

Gates shrugged again and glanced towards Twelfth Avenue. They'd hung catwalks on the nearly vertical decks, strung work lights out from the shore and installed an eight-inch fire main. Still, a city fireboat was stationed in the slip . . . they'd had insulation fires almost daily, touched off by the oxyacetelyne outfits.

'You going to sunbathe or cut steel, Junior?'

Gates lighted his outfit. Charlie had an infallible sixth sense for knowing when a boss was coming, and Rik van Slough was a hard driver.

Gates and Charlie took a cab home. As they climbed out a man in a dark, square-cut raincoat was banging the bronze griffin knocker on the front door. 'Who's that?' Gates said.

'That, Junior, is almost certainly a cop. Pay the cab.'

Gates shoved a bill at the driver and ran after Charlie, who was sauntering up to the house with a casual smile Gates didn't believe. He caught up with him just as he reached the cop, and at the same moment Paula, the housekeeper, opened the door and Kay came down the front hall stairs, sliding her hand down the polished banister and waving happily when she saw Charlie. Her face changed when she saw his expression.

'Help you?' Charlie said.

198

The cop found himself in a circle between Charlie and Gates on the outside and Kay and Paula in her black dress and lacy white apron on the inside. He had a big broad face with a high brow and receding hairline, wide cheeks and small, unrevealing eyes.

'If you're Mr Charlie Collins, you can.'

His voice was a monotone. He was built short and broad and when he turned and faced Charlie he seemed to turn all in one square piece. 'Police,' he said. 'Detective Tweed. May I come in?'

'Do I need a lawyer?'

'You tell me.'

'Don't be smart, I'm sick of you people being on my back – '

'Charlie, take it easy.'

'What's it about . . . the *Normandie* fire?'

'What makes you think that?'

'Listen, you're at the end of a long line of boneheads been after me and others I know about. The FBI's even been here. Not to mention private eyes working for the US Senate committee and investigators from the DA's office and last and least the Office of Naval Intelligence, which, when you look at the record of the last eight months, suggests a contradiction in terms. I should have known New York's finest would come sniffing around when the rest of 'em were done. What are you, sabotage squad? Scraping the bottom of the barrel?'

Gates started working on a straight face. Charlie Collins's was a show you could charge admission for.

'You guys are all the same. When you can't find the real culprit you look for somebody to pin it on. I can see you running your fingers down the list of guys aboard the ship that day and, *look here!* This character Collins was in the . . . horrors . . . Abraham Lincoln Brigade. Goddamned commie. He did it. And looky here! The commie's boss has an accent. Says he's Dutch but he's probably German. Says he's from the East Indies but all his records are in Jap

199

territory. Jesus Christ almighty, they did it together. The kraut lit the match and the commie blew on it.'

'Knock it off, Collins. I agree, we are scraping the bottom of the barrel. That's why I'm here. No, I don't think you started that fire, but you hung out with some hard types back in the thirties, and you got an assault record from the union fights and my captain wants me to check you out. Just tell me where you were during the fire and can the jokes.'

'Charlie, will you please be quiet and talk to him?'

'Okay, okay. What do you want to know?'

'Let's sit in the morning room,' said Kay. 'Would you like tea, officer – '

'Tweed, Mrs Collins. Jim Tweed. Thank you, I would. I'll make this as quick as I can. We're just trying to tie up the last loose ends of the case.'

Gates couldn't help liking the detective, or admiring his cool in the face of Charlie's anger. Kay led the way up to the large second-floor parlour they called the morning room. She pulled a bellcord, indicated a chair for Tweed and asked for tea when Paula appeared. A bay window faced south and yellow light slipped in and out of the room as the sun moved between Manhattan's skyscrapers.

Tweed pointed at the model on the mantel. 'What ship is that? I don't recognize her.'

'The *American Glory*,' Gates said. 'My uncle and I were building her when the war began.'

'The great designer works with me cutting steel on the *Normandie*,' Charlie growled. 'He's a little crazy. Hey, maybe he did it . . . maybe *he* helped the commie and the German – '

'Charlie, shut up.'

'What do you want to know, Tweed? You want to know what happened? Nothing. The navy screwed up. The civilian contractor screwed up. And there was a fire. That's it, and nothing that the War Department or the navy or the Senate or the House or the FBI or the

200

DA or even the New York Police Department — sabotage squad or homicide or bunco — says can change that.'

'We still believe that we should follow every lead — '

'Why?'

'Because,' Gates put in, 'if it was sabotage, then the saboteur is planning something else.'

'Right,' said Tweed.

'Junior, you *are* nuts. Tweed, why pick on such easy targets? You're not going to catch any Nazi by bothering people like me. I'm used to this stuff. Lived with harassment most of my life — it goes with the territory. But don't try to put it to the Dutchman.'

'Van Slough?'

'He's a hard-working guy and scared of cops. He thinks you'll intern him.'

'I'll make this quick,' Tweed said. 'Where were you when the fire broke out and what did you do?'

Charlie sighed elaborately.

'I was aft, burning off some pantry doors down on E deck, starboard side. I extinguished my outfit and ran like hell. I got lost when the lights went out. I got soaked and almost got frostbite. Finally I got out a cargo port amidships on D deck, down a gangplank and onto the pier.'

'Where was van Slough?'

Charlie sighed again. 'I didn't even know he was on the ship. I wasn't working for him then.'

'Did you see him?'

'*See him?* There were three thousand guys running around in the smoke. Even if I had seen him I wouldn't have known him. We'd met once on a trip back from England before the war. I didn't know the guy.'

'Have you talked to van Slough about the fire? Since then?'

'Sure.'

'Where was he?'

'Crazy fool almost got himself killed trying to rescue a

welding machine. He has a high respect for private property. Especially his. That's what took him so long to get off.'

'What took *you* so long?'

'I had to stop a second. No big deal.' He looked away.

'To do what?'

Kay spoke up, with her hand on his shoulder. 'Officer Tweed, he stayed an hour on that ship unpinning some poor man who got hurt when a bulkhead fell on him.'

'No big deal,' Charlie mumbled.

'What was his name?'

'We didn't talk much and it was kind of dark so don't ask me what he looked like.'

'You and he went off together?'

Charlie nodded. 'I carried him off and put him in an ambulance.'

'So you must have seen his face then.'

'I was puking my guts out. We had a little smoke.'

'Is there anything else?' Kay asked coolly.

Tweed stood up and said no.

Kay rang for Paula, who brought his coat and hat. Halfway out of the door, he turned back and asked Charlie Collins, 'What happened to van Slough's tugboat?'

'The engineer told me he backed her out of the slip. She didn't have a fire nozzle so she was just in the way.'

'She had a monitor when I saw her the other day.'

'He installed the nozzle after the fire. Said he wanted to be ready to help next time.'

'Next time?'

Gates said, 'I'll walk you out.'

On the sidewalk he said, 'Let me say a word for Charlie. He's drawn a lot of flak because of the Spanish War. He was fighting Nazis six years ago, and it doesn't seem fair. He can't even get a commission in the army.'

'Don't worry about it,' said Tweed. 'I got what I came for.' He started to turn away, but Gates said, 'Wait. What have you found out?'

'About what?'

'The fire. Do you think it was sabotage?'

'I'm just following the leads I'm told to.'

'But what do you *think*?'

'I leave the thinking to the lieutenant.'

'Come on, Tweed. You can still have an opinion.'

'Contrary to what Mr Collins thinks, I try not to form opinions until I see all the evidence.'

'How about a guess? Why did it spread so quickly? How did all that smoke get down to the boiler room so fast? How come so much water got trapped on the upper decks?'

'You're the expert, Mr Gates. You're the ship designer.'

'I don't design ships any more, I'm working on the *Normandie*.' And what was he going to do when his uncle came back and he had to move out? He talked about it to Tweed, mostly to try to sort out his thoughts.

'Where you going to live?'

'Over by the docks.'

'Find anything yet?'

'Haven't looked. I hear there are lots of places.'

'That's for sure. Give me a ring, I can save you looking.'

'You know a place? All I want is a furnished room.'

'I got three of 'em.'

'What do you mean?'

'I own a rooming house. Twelve rooms for rent, three empty. I'll give you a good price. It's clean. I know what you're thinking ... not too many cops own rooming houses. I inherited it from my mother. Give me a call. I'd like to have you. Add a touch of class to the place.'

Sunday morning at a quarter to five the Strattons' yawning chauffeur drove Gates and Wally to the Naval Air Patrol Station at Rockaway on the ocean edge of Queens. Wally had telephoned the day before and Gates had decided to forego a long Sunday sleep for a shot at sub patrol.

The car rarely exceeded thirty-five, a pace set to conserve gas and tyres, so by the time they arrived the ground crew was already dragging the floating air ship out of its dimly lighted hangar. A mobile tether secured its blunt nose while men with ropes held down the tail. It loomed impossibly huge in the dark sky, but Wally said it was only a quarter of the length of the *Hindenburg* zeppelin which had crashed at Lakenhurst before the war.

A mixed crew of trainees, regular navy men and volunteer reservists like Wally trooped into the cabin which hung from the belly of the helium-filled balloon. Wally introduced Gates to the skipper, a regular navy lieutenant who scrutinized his clearance papers and welcomed him aboard. They could use, he said, an extra pair of eyes.

Wally and Gates took view-ports side by side in the stern of the cabin, which was about thirty feet long. The rest of the crew took other ports, including one in the cockpit with the skipper. An undocking officer flashed a light from the ground. The signalman responded on the skipper's command, the engines, idling quietly, rumbled louder, the ground crew let go the stern lines and the bow tether, and the blimp nosed softly up to the dawn.

Climbing a few thousand feet, they were over the coast when the sun rose and heading southwest along the Rockaway sandbar that formed the north wall of the immense Lower New York Bay.

The submarine nets across the mouth of Ambrose Channel were open. Picket boat wakes pointed like arrows at the freighters entering and leaving the harbour. Wally pointed down. The army gun crews at Fort Tilden on the Rockaway bar were conducting a Sunday morning gun drill. The long, black barrels of a sixteen-inch battery swept the harbour approaches while anti-aircraft clusters popped out of sand dunes and wheeled cannons were dragged around the beaches by tractors, leaving trails crisscrossing in the sand. They all appeared like toys from the blimp.

The blimp turned southeast and headed out over the two-thousand-foot open gate in the submarine net and into the Atlantic. Below, far from land, bobbed a red object, the permanently anchored Ambrose lightship marking the channel. 'How'd you like to be sitting on that?' Wally asked. 'Waiting for a U-boat?'

They spotted a lone ship, made for it and signalled with a light. A short bright burst was returned.

'Most of the job is challenge and identify,' said Wally. 'Goes on all day.'

They passed over the lone ship, a rusty tanker, four thousand tons, Gates guessed, then spotted another ship and another and another, until it was apparent they'd found an inbound convoy. A pair of flanking destroyers knifed through the waves, old four-stackers, World War I survivors that Gates knew should have been melted for scrap in 1932.

'Hey, look at that,' shouted a machinist's mate, and the sight of a wounded ship caused a flurry of excitement aboard the blimp. A freighter, six thousand tons, heeling sharply and down at the head but still making the convoy's slow six or seven knots. The blimp continued to circle until the last ship was in sight of the Ambrose light, then wheeled ponderously around, pitching and swaying like a boat badly anchored, and headed out over the sea.

They'd been out of sight of land for several hours when Gates asked, 'Don't you get bored?'

'Sure, sometimes. But I get mixed up in other stuff. Last week somebody got sick the last minute, so they asked me along because I spoke German.'

'German? What kind of range does this thing have?'

'Not this. It was a joint ONI-FBI raid with some state police thrown in . Top secret. There's some strange stuff going on. We drove way out to Long Island and raided a field hospital the Bund had built for the German invasion. It was incredible. A great big stone building . . . '

'You sure you should be telling me this?'

'You're not going to tell anybody . . . I just wish something would happen on this thing. Like you said, it can get boring . . . '

Wally Stratton would get his wish . . .

A critical flaw in his path to hide a miniature submarine inside the *Normandie* developed unexpectedly at one of the weekly subcontractors' conferences aboard the wreckmaster's barge in the slip. The wreckmaster, who chaired the meetings, was Captain Tooker, a salvage veteran. He wore a white shirt and tie, as well as his omnipresent hat. He had a truculent W. C. Fields nose screwed onto an otherwise mild face.

Captain Tooker announced that the clearing-out, the catwalk and staging and passage construction as well as the steel removal were moving along on schedule and that a survey had begun to determine where to place the watertight bulkheads. The Otter listened intently. The salvors were preparing to divide the vessel into fourteen separate compartments, which meant there was a strong chance they would seal him out of the stern . . . which was to be his lair.

The interior of the fallen ship was enormous; all the Empire State Building's offices, halls and elevator shafts would fit inside. And more than half the space was under water. Subdividing was the only way that the salvors could isolate the leaks to be patched – the hundreds of air and cargo ports in the downside of her hull, the hundreds more pipe openings, stairways, boiler uptakes and machinery hatches that riddled the promenade deck at the points where the salvors were removing her superstructure.

Tooker explained that he intended to extend the vessel's own watertight steel bulkheads with massive timber and concrete bulkheads constructed under water from the ship's skin to several feet above high tide, and to those parts of the promenade deck strong enough to take the load.

'Yes, Mr van Slough?'

206

'Captain, the promenade deck does not extend all the way aft to the stern. Will the watertight bulkhead extend to B deck or all the way to A deck?'

'Can't tell you now. That's one of the areas we'll be surveying.'

'Thank you, captain.' The fact that the stern mooring compartment was riddled by a circle of big windows wouldn't stop the salvors. Though large enough to admit the miniature submarine, the holes were nothing compared to the huge turbine and boiler room hatchways that had to be patched on the promenade deck.

Worried, the Otter strained his cover trying to stay a step ahead of the salvors, but since no ship as big as the *Normandie* had ever been raised, the engineers were making decisions day by day as divers explored the precise locations of stanchions, deckhouse, frames and bulkheads in the opaque water.

He made his own examination of the stern.

He inspected the above-water half of B deck and was relieved to find the deck strong enough to resist a hydrostatic head of thirty feet – the pressure that Steven Gates had told him the bulkhead would have to hold to stay watertight. Which meant that the sealed portion of the stern could stop at B deck, leaving access to the aft mooring compartment. When he got nervous and inspected A deck – the ceiling of the mooring compartment – it, too, looked strong enough.

He eavesdropped on the consulting engineers as they trooped out of their strategy meetings, and haunted the waterfront bars where the salvage workers speculated about the job. When he discovered that the gang of navy divers hung out at Baldwin's uptown on Broadway he stood rounds of drinks there, talking into the night, steering the conversation towards the bulkheading plans.

Nobody could tell him. Seriously worried, he considered hiding the sub elsewhere, but port security was tightening daily as the Americans embraced the idea of being at war.

He'd be a fool to count again on that lunatic disorder which had allowed him to destroy the *Normandie* two months after Pearl Harbor. Not while men like Tooker were in charge.

Tooker worried the Otter. They called him the Old Man, an accolade not lightly bestowed, and nothing he had seen so far suggested Tooker didn't deserve it. It was generally agreed that the salvage master was the best in the business – as good at his job as the stumblebums who'd fouled up the troop ship conversion had been bad. The Americans were getting in gear. Which meant the Otter's time was shortening.

Uncle Willy had predicted early that they would bring awesome industrial might to bear, but that was only textbook logic. It was quite another thing to see them. To see how good they were at it. How they enjoyed it. What concerned him most was their motivation. It wasn't just patriotism. They liked the *action*.

He could have admired them for it if it didn't make them so dangerous. Couldn't they understand that their excitement and optimism came from their wealth of land and coast – which was all Germany wanted? Room for her energies and her destiny. Room to do and be in her hemisphere what the Americans had done and were in theirs. His mother's *Anschluss* speeches had said it all. Political union. Crazy as she was, she knew that only Germany could save Europe from itself.

His position in New York demanded reassessment. Van Slough Salvage, launched with healthy infusions of Abwehr money, was thriving. He'd made a name for himself around the port and that was fine, because broad roots looked deep. His agent Hank Larson, the redheaded saboteur who'd helped ignite the *Normandie* fire, was another plus. Larson was the best of the Bundists the Otter had recruited from the shambles created by the British and the FBI; a brilliant craftsman with a good business head, intelligent, ambitious and willing to do anything for money – including, which was rare, taking a bold initiative.

The trucking operation that Larson had set up in Brooklyn with the Otter's money was proof of that. The people they had left in charge were predictably running it into the ground, but that was a small price to keep the Otter's face and van Slough's name in the clear. And T and C Trucking paid its way doubly by hauling stolen and black market goods for the Otter's profit and by giving him solid connections with New York's criminal elements – the various 'mobs' in Brooklyn and New Jersey, some of which were so powerful that they had clear access to the waterfront, including naval installations, through the various unions they controlled.

For the Otter, the racketeers were a source of false papers, forged passes, and even explosives, which they sold to him on the mistaken assumption that he was as patriotic and Nazi-hating as the next black marketeer – a profiteer, not, God forbid, a spy. And what they couldn't obtain, Glenn Walsh in Third District naval supply often could. So his main cover was solid, he had two dependable agents – as dependable as agents ever could be, and neither of them knew his cover – as well as secret ownership of a trucking business.

Less certain was radio contact with Germany. Communications was a serious problem, heavy with risks, and would be until Uncle Willy had delivered a boat. But with the trombone player vanished, or ignoring his drops, he only had the Connecticut *meldekopf* through which he received Uncle Willy's messages by a foolproof cut-out system; and to transmit, Kroner and De Villeneuve – the old Yorkville Bundist and the opportunistic French fascist were his weakest links.

Neither radioman knew his name, of course, nor a single fact about him, but they did know he existed. When either fell to the FBI or the British, as one day they must, New York would turn very dangerous. Which was why he had no choice but to hide the submarine in the *Normandie*. No place in the harbour could be as safe, with the noise of the boat masked by the noise of the salvage and a ready supply of compressed air and electricity, and the last place anyone would ever imagine to look.

Could he manage to slip the submarine under the overhanging of the *Normandie*'s stern, hide it outside the ship in the mud? No. Divers would be down there, patching. And again during the dewatering – jetting mud away from the hull to shake the grip of suction. He decided the solution lay in Germany. He hated the exposure of using the radio, but he had to risk it to put his case to Uncle Willy to speed things up and deliver the submarine before the *Normandie* was sealed.

14

Gates huddled by the taxicab window, watching Harlem's dawn turn pink as they sped down a nearly deserted St Nicholas Avenue. Van Slough passed his flask. 'Take a snort. We'll get coffee at the job.'

His slightly thickened Dutch accent was the only clue that Rik had had even more to drink than Gates. They'd begun the night at Small's Paradise, had hit a bunch of smaller jazz clubs Gates had never noticed before and finished up at what Rik had billed as the best whorehouse on Sugar Hill.

Seconds later, it seemed, Rik shook him awake. The cab was stopped in front of his rooming house. The sun had cracked the horizon and was shafting the length of West Forty-sixth Street. A row of identical stoop banisters blazed like piano strings in the nightclub spotlight.

Rik clapped his big hands. 'Hop to it. Work to be done.'

Gates staggered up the stoop and three flights to his room on the second floor, where he changed into his work clothes, hoping he'd find Rik passed out on the stoop so he could go back upstairs and sleep. But Rik was waiting, very wide awake.

'You'll be fine with some breakfast.'

Doubting that seriously, Gates followed him to a diner on the corner of Tenth. They shouldered through crowds of workmen and sailors and took a table.

'Coffee,' said Gates.

'Bring him ham and eggs. You can't work on coffee.'

Gates forced down breakfast at van Slough's urging, topped it with coffee. They walked two blocks up and over to Pier 88. Beyond the *Normandie*'s flank three massive grey stacks loomed over Cunard's Pier 90, the north boundary of the slip.

'*Queen Mary*'s in.'

She had not been the previous night, but she was here now, a massive grey ghost of the sea, home safe from some part of the war, docked secretly and already provisioning in haste. She had left New York months ago, and rumour had it that she had taken eight thousand American soldiers to Australia.

'Let's have a look at her,' said van Slough.

'I thought we had to go to work.' Gates didn't want to look at the Cunarder, but Rik insisted. They walked up Twelfth and past Pier 90, where Coast Guardsmen stopped them from getting closer.

Rik seemed annoyed. 'We'll see about that. Come on.'

The morning shift was filing into Pier 88. Gates and van Slough elbowed through, showed their passes, hurried out to the end of the pier, where Rik usually moored *Hollandia* when he slept in Manhattan instead of across the river in the apartment over the office at his Hoboken scrapyard. Gates had asked why he didn't rent a place in Manhattan – he certainly could afford it – but Rik had said it wasn't worth the trouble. If he couldn't find a girl the nights he stayed in the city, he could always sleep on the tug.

It was one of the odd things about the Dutchman. Despite his scrap business and the big contracts he kept landing on the *Normandie*, he seemed essentially rootless. The apartment at the scrapyard was as spare as Gates's own room in Tweed's house; he kept several changes of clothes in the tugboat, like a travelling salesman living out of a suitcase. Having worked with him all summer now Gates had the impression that Rik had no friends except himself and Charlie, who were little more than occasional drinking companions and then only at Rik's invitation.

What did he do when he wasn't working? Gates had heard the rumours that Rik dealt in the black market – and certainly he would disappear with the tugboat for a day or two at a stretch, hauling who knew what – but anyone making big money was suspected of being in the black market and trading in gasoline or coffee or meat or whatever happened to be in short supply that week. Gates put little credence in the talk.

Charlie was already aboard *Hollandia*, drinking coffee from a cardboard container. 'Jaysus, look at the two of you.'

'Crank her up,' said Rik, stripping off his suit and pulling work clothes from a locker while Charlie called down to the engineer, another of the old Irishmen Rik had hauled out of retirement when the draft began cutting a swath through the river crews.

Charlie winked at Gates. 'Junior, you're going to hell in a handbasket.'

'You were invited.'

'Nice talk to your sister's husband.'

'Cast off,' ordered Rik.

He took the helm and swung *Hollandia* past the fallen *Normandie*, around Pier 90 and right under the *Queen Mary*'s stern. Oil barges were hugging her great flanks, pumping in the tons of bunkerage she'd burn on her next run through the U-boats. Long jagged strips of grey paint were missing from her waterline, testimony to the speed at which she'd been driving through the oceans.

Charlie joined Gates at the tugboat's bow deck. 'I wonder if they'll ever get her?'

'One's *enough*,' said Gates, looking back at the *Normandie*. All that remained of the ship that had once made the *Mary* the second boat on the Atlantic was a thousand feet of muddy, blackened steel, her two starboard propellers clawing motionlessly at the sky.

The Otter said nothing.

'Okay, let's get to work.'

There'd been less burning since the superstructure was gone, but van Slough had contracted to remove debris from those after-sections of the hull still above water. Gates and Charlie spent the morning inside the stern on A deck, tying bundles of wrecked furniture which Rik's other men hauled up through a cargo port and lowered to his barges.

Then came a call to pick up a machinist crew at Bayonne that was detailed to spray rust preventative inside the starboard inboard electric motor, which was repeatedly breached by the rising and falling tide. They combined the river crossing with lunch, which Charlie cooked in the galley, then helped the machinists – three grey-haired old men – wrestle their equipment down a sloping elevator shaft into the *Normandie*'s propulsion room.

Charlie trundled a fifty-gallon drum of penetrating oil on a hand truck and Gates followed with the spraying machine. While the machinists set up their work lights, Gates and Charlie went back for the brutally heavy air compressor and the rest of the drums, then stood by as the machinists opened the motor housing and climbed inside for a close inspection.

They had only one helper among them, a common sight with the labour shortage, so Gates climbed into the motor with them to pass tools and snake the spray machine's hoses. When the motor had been sprayed they carried everything back up the sloping shaft, hoisted it down to *Hollandia* and ran the machinists back to Bayonne.

The sun was setting behind the river fog of white smoke by the time they were headed back to Pier 88. Gates was at the helm. Van Slough stood beside him, lining up tomorrow's work and commenting on the subtleties of steering the tug, which he always did when Gates or Charlie steered – instructing them in the boat handling he'd learned pushing salvage tugs around the Orient. Gates traded a quick, private smile with Charlie. For all his knowledge, Rik was a clumsy pilot. He blamed the people who rented his tug for the scarred fenders and mashed barges he was forever repairing, but the truth was he did most of the damage himself.

'What's that?' he asked, catching the smile.

Gates said, 'Looks like the *Mary*'s leaving soon. That was fast. Probably just going to the army terminal.'

'How do you know she's leaving?' asked Rik.

Gates nodded at the powerful diesel tug overtaking the smaller *Hollandia* and veering towards Pier 90. 'The *Marie Moran* takes the number one berthing position on the *Queen*.'

'Is that so?'

Gates turned *Hollandia*'s big helm – a five-foot circle of spokes with a smooth brass rim – and throttled back to berth against a barge beside the *Normandie*'s stern, docking the boat with only minor complaints from Rik.

The Dutchman had bought a beauty. She was a diesel-electric with all her controls at the helm. She required a single engineer below instead of the two- and three-man crews aboard the steam tugs, and in a pinch one man could operate her alone from the pilothouse. Gates found pleasure in learning to handle her well, even though he knew that poking about the harbour in a tug shorter than the size that required a licence was a far cry from warping onto a moving ten-thousand ton freighter when a split-second mistake in timing would drag the low stern under water, flood the engine room and sink the tug like scrap iron.

His eye roamed from the *Marie Moran* under the grey *Mary*'s stern and back to the fallen hulk. The princess of the Moran fleet had also once taken number one position on the *Normandie*.

A week after the night the *Queen Mary* sailed with ten thousand men, Gates and Charlie Collins were eating lunch on the catwalk that ran the length of the *Normandie*'s vertical promenade deck. When they were done, Gates stretched out in the sun with his shirt off and Charlie read the newspaper, calling out the news that interested him.

'The pier fire? Last week in Brooklyn? Turns out some clown was smoking on top of about forty thousand bags of copra. Oh, look here. Somebody opened the skylights. Thought they'd let the smoke out. Bright.'

'Who opened the skylights?'

'They don't know. Everybody says they were closed before the fire. Made a hell of a chimney.'

'Aren't they investigating who opened them?'

'Who's going to admit something that stupid?'

Gates felt footsteps reverberating on the catwalk. He sat up, his legs dangling fifty feet above the dirty water. It was Rik.

'I won a subcontract to clear the debris from the stern.'

'We're doing that already,' said Charlie.

'*Under*water. I'll be diving.' He squatted down between them. 'Listen, you guys. I'm going to need you to take charge topside. I'll split the crew and make you both foremen.'

'I want to learn to dive,' said Gates. 'I heard they're going to start a school.'

Charlie said, 'You know something, Junior? You ought to go back to Uncle Richard. He's hurting, he needs you.'

'Not till the *Normandie*'s raised.'

Rik nodded. 'You're a good worker. I'll miss you, but Charlie's right. I spoke with your uncle. I think he blames me and I don't want that.'

'Are you firing me?'

Rik looked at him. Gates returned his gaze. The Dutchman's eyes reminded Gates of prisms. They revealed different depths at different angles.

'Because if you are, I'll just go to the main contractor and get another job. I'm staying on this ship.'

Van Slough's eyes turned opaque. He nodded. 'All right, Steven. Stay.'

The Otter dropped a nickel in the slot and dialled the Frenchman. 'May I come and see you tonight?'

216

De Villeneuve's response was a startled breath. 'I . . . I have company. Can't it wait until tomorrow?'

'No,' said the Otter. 'Wait for my call at Gage and Tollner in Brooklyn. The phone closest to the men's room.'

'Well, I really do have company . . . I'll need a little time.'

'One hour,' said the Otter, and hung up.

Was De Villeneuve coming unstrung?

Concerned, the Otter went to one of his safehouses – a tenement flat between Seventh and Eighth near Times Square. He'd chosen the neighbourhood because it was a fringe area where neither working clothes nor a business suit would look out of place among the mechanics, the elderly poor, the young salesmen and the struggling actors who inhabited its rented rooms. He put on a dark suit appropriate to Park Avenue and started to walk across town, thinking that New York lost its unique spirit when it dimmed its lights.

The sudden mournful howl of air-raid sirens set his brain racing . . . had he conjured the sudden animal wail in his mind by recalling the past? A deep and hollow scream, rising and falling like carousel horses, pried up chaotic echoes of the Spanish War and the London Blitz and set his heart pounding with memories of hunkering down in the enemy's shelters from German bombs.

The heavy drone of aircraft left the Otter rooted to the sidewalk while around him the city blackened in defence. The street lights went out all at once. Windows disappeared jaggedly behind hastily drawn curtains. The sky grew visible, a clear night, no moon, but thick with stars seldom seen above New York. The planes sounded closer.

While shafts of light shot up from the horizon, searchlight beams stroking the sky like long fingers, and converging abruptly, focused hard and silver on a single airplane as tiny as an insect. A second battery swerved to it. And a third. The Otter thought he heard a far-off rumble of anti-aircraft fire, but no flak exploded.

Police cars and civilian defence trucks were screaming through the streets, and the wardens were out in force now, herding people off the sidewalks into hotel lobbies. The Otter stepped into the shadows of a phone booth, holding the door open to keep the light off. It was four long blocks to De Villeneuve's Park Avenue apartment. He dodged a warden and ran into the subway and caught the shuttle to Grand Central, where he called De Villeneuve's apartment. No answer. He dialled again. De Villeneuve picked up the pay phone at Gage and Tollner after eight rings. He was out of breath. I'm sorry. I'm sorry. The blackout, we – '

'Have the oyster stew,' said the Otter. 'And a full dinner. It will be a long night.' He hung up and took the Lexington IRT one stop to Fifty-first, where he cautiously emerged up to street level and, hugging the shadows, worked his way past the wardens and police to a telephone booth across Park Avenue from De Villeneuve's apartment. In his pocket was a key to the service entrance gate. He held the booth open to keep the light off while he watched.

Pairs of civilian defence wardens were marching along the sidewalk, surveying the deserted avenue. The only light was from the stars and the sporadic flicker of the wardens' flashlights and the horizontal slits in police car headlamps. The blackout would make it easier than usual to slip through the service entrance unnoticed by the doormen fifty feet down the sidewalk.

He marked each car parked along the avenue.

The wardens made him uneasy. If there was a watch on De Villeneuve's building it could be a man in a warden's uniform. An armband and a helmet on the head and they were in business. He watched them cruise. One pair walked the block, about-faced, walked back.

He had mastered clandestine movement in Spain, spying for Uncle Willy in the enemy Republican strongholds of Madrid, and later, Barcelona. He had met real fear for the first time in Spain – fear of torture and death if the anti-Franco loyalists caught him – and he had learned how to control his fear by holding to his belief in his superiority over the enemy. He'd learned to conquer the loneliness that destroyed most other spies by creating a cover personality of the bluff, hearty soul who was naturally surrounded by friendly people. And he had met death. Not the noisy death of street insurrections he'd known as a boy in Italy and Austria, but swift death that swooped like a hawk, silent until the last moment, when what seemed like a warning was actually an announcement of what was already happening.

On their third pass, the wardens changed their patterns, veering suddenly towards a parked car near the service entrance. On came their flashlights, which they pointed into the car. The Otter saw a man inside the car, and before they extinguished their lights, he saw the man pull something from his jacket.

A police car passed slowly, blocking his view. When he could see the parked car again, the wardens were backing away. He could not swear to it, but for a moment it seemed as if one touched his forehead in a deferential salute.

It could have been a trick of the eyes. But one thing was not a trick. Whoever was in the car hadn't got out, hadn't been ordered into shelter until the air-raid drill was over. Who was he? Air-raid drill organizer? Police? Newspaper reporter? Or an overanxious or self-important counter-espionage agent who had made, in a split-second decision, the mistake of not getting out of the car and going where he was told but flashing some sort of ID, which impressed the wardens and gave him away?

If that were the case, the man would not be alone.

The Otter backed out of the booth into deep shadow and inched his way back towards Lexington Avenue. Halfway there somebody turned a light on in a window and in the moment it took to blot it out with a curtain a warden came running towards the offence. He ran into the Otter and gave a yelp of surprise and flicked on his flashlight and shined it in the Otter's face. The Otter closed one eye and squinted the other, protecting his sight, slapped the light out of the warden's hands, and ground it beneath his heel.

'Hey, what are you doing on the street? Let's see some ID, mister.'

He'd learned to enjoy death in a peculiar way. There was little pleasure in feeling it in his hands, holding life as it ceased. He was not a murderer. The pleasure was in the instantaneous reversal of a threat. To survive was a matter of killing first and never allowing the enemy to see the threat.

He had sufficient identification. But how many were watching De Villeneuve's building? The warden knelt to find his flashlight. 'Let me help you,' said the Otter, kneeling beside him and taking hold of the man's throat in his huge hands.

He deposited the man's wallet, helmet and armband in a garbage can and continued to Lexington Avenue, where he again boarded the uptown IRT, averting his face from the change clerk, and rode it to the Eighty-sixth Street stop in Yorkville.

As he had suspected, there were few wardens out in the German-immigrant neighbourhood, and none on the tenement-lined side streets. It was a working-class neighbourhood and people here had already gone to bed. Whereas civilian defence had blanketed De Villeneuve's midtown area for maximum newspaper coverage of the air-raid drill, the Otter saw only a single prowl car on his walk to Kroner's. He found the radio repair shop shut for the night, crossed the dark and empty street and walked through Kroner's building into a backyard and up a rear fire escape, following a route he had used to watch Kroner when he had first recruited the German-American Bundist.

The sirens had stopped, but the all clear had not been sounded. Between the buildings, where the police could not see, light spilled from the occasional window. The Otter kept in the shadows, climbed to Kroner's apartment and jimmied the window lock with a four-inch steel pry he had left hidden on the fire escape.

Kroner came to investigate the noise. He had an unconcerned expression on his innocent moon face, as if his wife had sent him and he didn't expect to find anything wrong. He'd got balder and a trifle more stooped. His eyes widened, almost comically, at the sight of the open window. The Otter reached in, grasped his robe, clamped a hand over his mouth and pulled him into the dark.

'I want your radio, Herr Kroner.' He uncovered Kroner's mouth.

'Let me go, my wife's in the next room —'

'Where's the radio?'

'In my shop.'

'Ten minutes.'

The Otter pushed him back into the room and hurried down the fire escape. He crept up the inside stairs and hid where he could see the pay telephone in the hall. Kroner hurried past it without a glance, and the Otter silently followed.

He waited until Kroner was in the shop, with the door shut, and watched for light, but none escaped his blackout curtain. He knocked, with a final look at the empty street, and slipped a stocking over his face. He did not seriously fear that Kroner would betray him. He was a devout German, and besides patriotism, Uncle Willy had given the Otter a club over the German emigré in the form of his son, a German soldier. Unless . . . probably until . . . young Kroner was killed on the battlefield, the Otter had a powerful grip on the father, promising protection — or death — to the son.

It was a dusty little shop with a curtained back room. Kroner had the walls lined with wooden shelves, which held

221

repaired and waiting-to-be-repaired radios, gramophones and electric clocks. He eased past the Otter, who practically filled the small customer space, and moved behind the counter.

With a smile turned inward as if for his own enjoyment, Kroner stood on a box and lifted several table radios off the highest shelves. Each bore a cardboard repair tag, recently dated, with customer's name and notation of deposit received. He set them on the counter side by side, and still embracing his private smile, unscrewed their wooden cases.

Four commercial radio frames had been drastically rebuilt as the components of a long-range transmitter-power supply, amplifier, transmitter and receiver. Kroner joined two pieces of metal lying in a junk box on his workbench and displayed a workable-looking telegraph key.

'This is all very clever, Herr Kroner.'

'Thank you, Herr Otter.'

'But you've managed to hide five dangerous items instead of one.'

'I did – '

'An enemy agent searching your shop would have five opportunities to find your secret. Not one, *five*.'

Kroner looked at the floor. 'I hadn't thought of that, Herr Otter.'

'Fix it tomorrow. Where's the antenna?'

'In the cellar.'

'That's six.'

'Yes, Herr Otter.'

Kroner led him down to the cellar and opened the coal furnace fire door. He shined a flashlight inside and showed the Otter that a fitting extended down from the flue.

'It goes up the chimney. Twenty-five metres. When you want to transmit I will attach the transmitter here and connect an additional seven metres of rigid antenna to the top of the chimney.'

Just like De Villeneuve, thought the Otter. What was it that made amateurs sleep with their incriminating evidence? Did they think everyone else was stupid, or were they just lazy?

'And what will you do if I come in winter?'

'Extinguish the fire, Herr Otter.'

'And the building? What about the heat? Won't the other tenants complain to the super?'

Kroner looked embarrassed. 'My shop doesn't do so well. I am the super. I pay the rent.'

'Hook it up.'

The Otter had already enciphered his request to Uncle Willy to deliver the miniature submarine as soon as possible. He had made it blunt and short and he carried the letter sequences in his head. Kroner connected the radio components, fussed over the wiring, then self-importantly pronounced it ready. The Otter flexed his fingers, practised two runs on the dead key, then flicked the transmit switch and set a fast chain of V's – Dit dit dit dah dit dit dit dah dit dit dit dah – to alert the Hamburg station that he was on the air.

'Sit down, Kroner. It'll be a while.'

Kroner sat on a broken-back chair beside the furnace.

'Herr Otter. My . . . my boy?'

'Fine, the last I heard.'

'I'm very worried.'

'Don't be. He was promoted. Lieutenant.'

'Why didn't you tell me before?'

The Otter watched Kroner closely, wondering if he should kill the man. But Kroner now only shrugged and murmured plaintively, 'I didn't think the war would last so long.'

'It has just started, Herr Kroner.'

It came through. The go-ahead.

He had a fast hand, a phenomenal one hundred letters a minute, so his message filled the air for less than eight seconds. Too little time, he was sure, for a tracking station to home in.

Once an hour he turned on the receiver. They would be searching the Reich for Uncle Willy. He travelled as always and he might be anywhere in Europe. But this night he was not. At four the receiver chattered a long burst of enciphered Morse into his earphones.

The Otter was bitterly disappointed and angered by how casual Uncle Willy seemed. He apologized for taking so long to approve his plan. He said he needed time to find a submarine. And time to prepare the ground – by which, the Otter assumed, he meant time to cover his back in the unpredictable ballet of German secret service rivalries. The Otter hunched over a notepad, deciphered the last of the long reply. It was a promise. *You will have all you need.*

The Otter felt the blood drain from his face. Did Uncle Willy realize what he had said? Word for word, the last message Uncle Willy's predecessor at the Abwehr had sent to the Otter's mother, word for word the last message she had carried from the German consulate in Vienna to the chancellor's office where the Austrian Chancellor Dollfuss lay dying, prisoner of the German patriots who had shot him to achieve *Anschluss*. But 'all they needed' never came – no troops, no bombers to finish the coup. And instead of Germany achieving political union with Austria in 1934, the patriots were hanged – four men and the fiery German-Italian woman who had been Uncle Willy's mistress and the Otter's mother. It was from her raw grave that Uncle Willy had taken him away . . .

The Otter raised his fingers to his face. The stocking mask was slick with perspiration. He fumbled for the radio switch. Had Uncle Willy any idea of how dangerously he was exposed? He began scrabbling at the telegraph key. He hit the hot tube cover. He jerked away, but the pain in his burned fingers was real. As he reached again for the power switch he smelled the hot tubes and the damp odour of the basement. And felt the coolness of the damp on his face. They were real. Slowly, the fragile arrangements deep in his mind regrouped – thin glass tubes sliding into flimsy glass slots.

The receiver chattered. The Otter looked at his fingers and realized he had been transmitting gibberish. So that Uncle Willy wouldn't worry he sent a quick message in clear text. WHERE IS YOUNG K?

The answer came immediately and the Otter, already on an upsurge of relief, now was pleased that Uncle Willy kept close track of the thin threads that formed the fabric of his security. When Kroner awakened, as the Otter was disassembling the radio, he was able to say, 'I asked about your son. He's fighting with the Afrika Korps.'

'With Rommel,' said Kroner. 'That is an honour.'

'To be sure.' The Otter started up the stairs, determined to be out of the vicinity while Kroner clambered around the roof disconnecting the top of the antenna.

'Herr Otter? There is something I should tell you . . . '

The Otter turned sharply to the new tone in Kroner's voice.

'The other day a man brought a radio to be repaired. The radio was . . . junk. *Drek*. But his clothes were fine. And I wonder what such a man is doing, coming to my little shop.'

The Otter started slowly down the stairs.

'My friend Hans on Ninety-second Street thinks the same man came to his shop, too . . . Herr Otter, I said *nothing*.'

'Why did you wait until now to tell me?'

'I wasn't sure.'

'They will hang you as fast as they will hang me. Remember that, Kroner. And don't think you can buy your life by telling them about me. You know nothing about me. You don't know what I look like. You don't

225

even know the colour of my hair.' He shook him, hard. 'Hide the radio. *Now*.'

When he arrived at his safehouse in Harlem he thought about Kroner. The radio was valuable. Vital, if he had lost the use of De Villeneuve's radio, as he feared he had. And the risk really was all Kroner's, because what he had told the Bundist was accurate – Kroner knew *nothing* about the Otter, except for the fact that he existed. He did not know his ciphers, his van Slough cover, his plans, or even that his radio signals were beamed exclusively to Admiral Wilhelm Canaris. Indeed, it was highly doubtful he had ever heard the name Canaris.

The Otter went to his refrigerator and started to mix a Scotch and milk. Even if he never used Kroner's radio again, it had a psychological value, just knowing it was there. It was strange, he thought, but for a while, when he still had all his radios, he had had greater access to Uncle Willy, an ocean away, than when his mother was alive.

Uncle Willy couldn't help this time. He couldn't rush the submarine. The *Seehund* would never arrive before the salvors had made their decision about sealing the stern mooring compartment. The Otter was back where he had started, alone in New York, waiting, and still at the mercy of the salvors' decision.

Worse than where he had started. De Villeneuve looked blown. One less radio. He couldn't be sure, but checking into him would be dangerous. He had to write the radio off. As for the Frenchman, if he was blown, he had already done the only thing he could do to him – admit to the enemy that the Otter existed. No point in killing him – or Kroner – and risk the potential telltale consequences of committing murder, police investigations . . . Better to let the enemy wonder why he had not shown up. And wonder about the slain air-raid warden. German agents

226

didn't kill air-raid wardens . . . His existence in New York was finally, it seemed, known to the enemy.

Weatherburn watched the Park Avenue service entrance from an unmarked car. Mark St George covered the back stairs on De Villeneuve's floor, standing like a statue except for the occasional opening and closing of his fists, an action less of impatience than the desire to keep his body loose. Duncan waited in the apartment with De Villeneuve and Elise.

They had returned after two, when the restaurant the Otter had ordered them to had finally closed. As the night wore on, the Frenchman grew increasingly distraught. The Otter had neither shown, nor telephoned again.

'You must believe me. This is how we always did it.'

'We believe you.'

'He said he would come in an hour. I called you immediately.'

'We know he called,' said Duncan. He and De Villeneuve spoke English, which Elise apparently didn't understand.

'I would not make all this up,' said De Villeneuve.

'You'd be stupid if you did.' It had been a long, long night, and Elise's pouty lips had been driving him crazy for hours. She was obviously not pleased with De Villeneuve's performance under stress. Duncan saw that the girl was inspecting him with careful, sidelong glances.

The telephone rang. De Villeneuve picked it up when Duncan told him to. He listened intently, his aristocratic face assuming long, deep lines of disappointment.

'It's for you.'

'Yes?'

'Go to bed,' said Cordi. 'He had another radio. We picked up some transmissions from over on the East Side.'

'Where?'

'It was too shallow an angle for the bearings. It covers a huge area. Weatherburn says to pack it in.'

'Does he think we spooked him?' asked Duncan.

'He thinks somebody did.'

Cordi hung up and looked at the transcriptions she'd made from the disc. A meaningless jumble of ciphers. And then a strange pair of phrases sent in clear. Some sort of code words.

WHERE IS YOUNG K? had been beamed to Germany. NORTH AFRICA was the reply. Cordi went to bed. She would be back to the Brooklyn warehouses early in the morning, though she had begun to suspect that the Otter had used some other means than a warehouse to smuggle his explosives into the cargoes set aboard the freighters in Tom's convoy.

She heard Weatherburn and Mark clump into the suite a while later, but stayed in her bed. Let them sort out the radios. She was on a better track. But she couldn't ignore them. Weatherburn started shouting.

A dead man had been found a block from De Villeneuve's. A robbery victim, it was thought, until the police discovered he was an air-raid warden.

'Damn fools,' she heard Weatherburn say. 'First they roust me out of my cover, then one of them blunders into the Otter and frightens him off. And it takes the police three hours to discover the body. He's probably on his way to Germany by now.'

Gradually Mark calmed him, and Cordi stopped listening.

Steven Gates slipped into her mind, and lay between sleep and dream. Mark had found him, of all places, on the burned *Normandie*. It was rather strange. He was working as a labourer. Stranger still, Rik van Slough was there, too, a salvage contractor who'd got rich on the war. Weatherburn had turned up rumours that Rik was somehow tied up with the black market. But strangest of all, Steven and his brother-in-law were working for Rik. 'Closes the circle, doesn't it?' said Weatherburn.

15

A row of shacks and work huts clung to the fallen *Normandie*'s starboard flank like a shantytown on a blasted hill. Snaking around them were electrical, water and compressed-air lines. The superstructure had been cut away to the waterline, exposing her promenade deck, which plunged vertically to the slip. A string of barges stood alongside. Cranes were still heaping debris into a few, but most of the barges were receiving thick gushers of mud that spewed from a dozen hoses thrust out of the deck hatches. The salvage site thundered from the air-lift engines pumping mud and shattered glass.

Gates sat by a bollard at the edge of the jetty, his back to the fence, watching the swing shift swarm over her as the sky and river reddened from the setting sun. Under the roar of the pumps he heard footsteps approaching at a familiar quick-paced rhythm that he couldn't place in the context of the salvage job. He saw the bulging briefcase first, then his uncle stepped around the bollard and looked down at him with a grave smile.

'Hello, Steven.'

Gates scrambled to his feet and grasped Prince's hand. 'What are you doing here? How are you?'

'I'm fine. I'm looking for you.'

Gates took a step back. 'How'd you find me?'

'The guards told me you usually hung around after your shift.'

'You look tired,' Gates said, debating whether it would be too much to ask Prince to help him go over Ober's head.

'I feel like a rusty tug pushing the *Queen Mary* with a

broken propeller. But you look wonderful. This outdoor work agrees with you, though you also look like you've been doing a bit of drinking.'

'The divers are a drinking crowd.'

'How's the job going?'

'Not bad, except every ten minutes one of the air lifts sucks up an armchair or an old piano and a diver's got to go down to clean the suction. And two more divers have to go with him to protect his hose from broken glass. Kind of slows things down.'

'Is she moving at all?'

'Settling a hair in the stern, just like you said she would. The bow's coming up a few degrees. Seesawing on that rock knob.'

'She's not going anyplace,' said Prince. 'But Lord knows what that rock is doing to her plates ... Is the mud firming up?'

'Not yet.'

'Charlie mentioned it looked like it might never. It has to, or you'll never patch her.'

'Charlie's a pessimist.'

'I should know that by now.' Prince cleared his throat, started to speak, and stopped as if he'd thought of something else. 'Mind if I sit down?'

'Here's a board for your back.' Gates slanted a piece of scrap against the fence and offered his uncle a hand as he eased himself down to the quayside. When he was settled, Gates sat beside him.

'Thanks.'

They sat for a while in silence, watching the mud stream down and the tugs passing on the reddening river.

'How's van Slough doing at the diving?' Prince asked abruptly. 'He's been hanging around the house with Charlie, but we haven't seen much of him lately.'

Gates weighed the question. 'Rik is a very different person when he dives. Tense. Short fuse. I think it scares him.'

230

'That's a way to stay alive at it.'

Gates said nothing. The sky was turning darker red and the floodlights gleaming from Pier 90 were edging paths across the slip. A shift of wind carried an autumn chill, and Prince shivered.

'Are you aware of the sinking figures?' he asked. 'No, I guess you wouldn't be. They're not releasing them to the press. The U-boats are killing us. Four *million* tons of shipping sent to the bottom so far this year. England's running out of food and weapons. It's getting worse.

'The Nazis started the year with less than a hundred boats operational and the latest we hear is they've built close to two hundred more. Doubled their attack fleet, at least. And Rommel's on the move again.'

'Then you are asking me to come back.'

'No. No, I'm not. You don't owe anything. Not with the work you did on the escorts. You contributed plenty of ideas. Now it's up to the shipyards, and the sailors.' Prince looked around. His gaze fell on the catwalk that ran the length of the liner's vertical deck, fifty feet above the water.

'What are those old geezers doing up there?'

A dozen grey-haired men in white shirts and straw boaters were marching along the catwalk. A few wore cardigan sweaters but they marched in close, purposeful formation like veterans at an Armistice Day parade. They right-faced and disappeared inside an open hatch.

'Fire watch,' said Gates. 'They hauled them out of retirement from the New York Fire Department. They're firing men for smoking.'

'Good. About time they ran this job right.'

'Nine months late,' Gates said, wondering if this was a good opening to talk to his uncle about sabotage.

'Damnit, Steven,' Prince said harshly. 'Come on back to work.'

'But you said –'

'It doesn't have to be for me. Work for anybody you want. But do *your* work. Please. Come back.'

'As soon as the *Normandie*'s raised.'

'Goddamn it, Steven, you're as irresponsible as your goddamned father.'

Gates was shocked. In all the years his uncle had never uttered a single word against his father.

'You're running away, just like he did – '

'He had nothing left when the market crashed – '

'Neither did anybody else. We all lost.'

'He was an innovator, he risked so much. Losing it all so fast was more than he could take – '

'Did your mother tell you that?'

'Yes. He practically changed the business of selling stocks single-handedly. Maybe it hurts more to fall from the edge – '

'Changed the business of selling stocks? What do you mean by that?'

'He saw what a selling tool the telephone could be,' Gates said defensively. 'You know that, Uncle Richard, he brought stocks to ordinary people – '

'He ran a boiler room.'

'A boiler room?'

'He sat fifty fast-talking salesmen at a table full of telephones and they dialled everyone in the book and sold them worthless stock at blue-chip prices.'

'I know what a boiler room is. He didn't do that.'

'I *saw* the place,' Prince said. 'It looked like a bookie joint, except it wasn't as honest.'

Gates sat numbly listening to the mud pumps roar. He wished his uncle hadn't told him.

'Your father wanted to borrow money against the Lloyd's Neck place. But it's half mine, so he couldn't take it from your mother without my permission.'

'I wondered how come we didn't lose it,' Gates mumbled.

'He dragged me down to Wall Street to show me the firm – that's when I saw it – to persuade me to put up the place. It wouldn't have made any difference if I had. The firm was already gutted by margin calls. He was in

232

worse than his greediest customers. It's not that your father was really greedy. He was just an overgrown child. Your grandfather was a tough old pirate and your father was a pirate's spoiled child.

'Now what about you, Steven? Will you come back to work?'

Was that why he had gone dutifully along in his uncle's footsteps? Gathering accolades to deny being the child of a pirate's child? Was this why he wanted to answer his uncle *yes*? Yes, he would leave the *Normandie*, resume their partnership? Was *no* nothing more than trying to break that pattern, stubbornness?

'I can't, Uncle Richard. I'm sorry.'

Richard Prince ran a hand through his grey hair, abruptly stood up, slammed his briefcase on the bollard and brushed off his trousers.

'What are you doing about the draft? They sent forms around.'

'The board gave me an essential occupation deferment for working here.'

'All right.' He started away.

Gates shrugged. In his fashion, he too was fighting a war.

And among the enemy, the *Normandie*'s destructor was a living, breathing human being. He'd dealt with the navy so he knew it for the huge, headless entity it was, which made it hard to direct his rage at the men the navy blamed. Admiral Anderson came as close to a single villain as any in Gates's mind. Typically, he'd been promoted. Revenge would undo nothing. But a saboteur loose in the city . . .

He hated fighting with his uncle, and put the thought out of his mind . . . replaced it with the thought of Cordi Grey. Hardly a week went by that he didn't think of her, or think he saw her on a street, or in a bus or the back of a cab. Auburn hair would catch his eye the way a melody line appeared over and over in the same song.

233

In fact there *was* a song, 'Looking Around Corners for You . . . '

She and the *Normandie* lay entwined in his memory, woven too tightly to separate them. He walked home to the rooming house, brooding on how the joy of both had slipped as far from his grasp as the unbuilt *American Glory*.

Jim Tweed was sitting on his front steps, as he often did in the evening, propped back on his elbows, nodding hello to the men who passed and smiling at the women. He and Gates had talked a few nights about ships. 'Turning a bit nippy for a beer, but you're welcome to one,' he said now.

'Are you still investigating the *Normandie* fire?' Gates asked bluntly.

'Umm . . . we kind of ran out of leads. If you can call guys with funny backgrounds like your brother-in-law real leads. I think the captain was kind of glad to back away from the whole mess after the ONI said it definitely wasn't sabotage.'

'ONI doesn't know what it's talking about. I gave them the best lead they had and they didn't know what to do with it.'

Tweed gave him a flat look and sipped his beer.

'Remember I told you I opened some ports to drain the hose water out of the ship?'

'I remember you told me.'

'Well, I thought all along that some of the doors I'd opened on the promenade deck were shut.'

Tweed watched a car go down the street.

'I was diving and —'

'Diving?'

'Yeah. Some of the divers took me down for a look. It just happened. No big deal.'

'If you say so. Want a beer?'

'No . . . so I'd told ONI about the promenade deck doors. When we dived I found one of the big cargo doors was also closed. *A door that I had opened.*' He waited but Tweed said nothing. 'A door I had opened and *locked* open was closed. Take my word for it. I told ONI immediately and they thanked me and now they're coming out with this report that says it wasn't sabotage. I can't believe it.'

Tweed said, 'Can I take your word that it's the same door?'

'Absolutely.'

Tweed was silent for a while, then went in for more beer. When he returned he said, 'Got to remember, Steven, how crazy it was at the fire. Flames and smoke spook people. Make them do funny things. We all know how people run back into burning buildings. How sure are you that it was the same door?'

'I sailed on that ship six times. In college I studied her plans like a divinity student reads the Bible. And I did a survey of her for the navy before the war and was in on some of the conversion work. I know that ship better than any ship except the one I want to build. I know her like you know your house.'

'So you think it was the same door.'

'No doubt in my mind at all.'

'Interesting.'

'Damned right it's interesting.'

'What are you going to do about it?' Tweed leaned further back on his elbows and smiled at a pretty girl who passed under the street light and smiled back.

'I don't know what to do. ONI won't listen any more.'

'Who'd you talk to there?'

'Lieutenant Commander Percy Ober. Know him?'

'Heard of him. Knows how to get along. A real hotshot.'

'Who do I tell? Your captain?'

'You can tell him,' Tweed said, 'but he's closed the book on the fire. Everybody has. The war's moved on.'

'But if there's a saboteur – '

'Then he's still around,' Tweed finished for him.

'Could you do something?'

'The captain's given me a full plate, Steven. We have to investigate every fire and accident that has anything to do with the war. And seeing as how the port feeds the war, that means almost everything. If a crane operator's got a hangover and drops a load of pig iron on a tugboat, we gotta make sure he isn't a Nazi. The same goes for all fires, derailments and explosions. I'm still working on the Forty-third Street pier fire.'

'The one the papers said wasn't sabotage.'

'They say that about every fire. They have to, there's a war on, but we have to make sure. If that pier fire had jumped the alley it would have wiped out the ferry terminal.'

'Then you think there's a saboteur in New York –'

'More like a bunch of them.'

'Nazi agents –'

'More likely some nuts, plus some Bund-type fanatics. But I don't buy a real-life German spy.'

'Can you do something to help me about the *Normandie*?' Gates asked again.

'I'll nose around a little . . . ' Tweed watched the traffic. 'Cars are starting to look old,' he said. 'You can telephone a lot of people it would take me weeks to see without a warrant. Navy people. Government people. Rich people. Even some of your brother-in-law's crazy friends. If you really want to check some stuff out, ask around. Use what you know. But be damn sure about that door.'

'I'm sure.'

'Did you ever find out about that elevator? Remember you said there might be one at the bottom of the shaft?'

'It was there,' said Gates. 'But nobody thought it meant much.'

'It seems to me like you've got four lines of inquiry –'

'Four?'

'In order of their likely results . . . The men with the burning outfits that actually ignited the fire. The reasons why the life jackets got aboard early. Who brought that forward baggage elevator down to the engine deck? And who closed the door you say you opened?'

Gates looked at him. 'Can I – '

'Talk to me about it? Sure. Ask advice? Sure. Use my name? No.'

'Where do I start?'

'Put on some clean clothes, for God's sake, and start acting like who you are.'

When the navy tenders began setting up a diving stage in the stern mooring compartment, the Otter knew that the survey was closing in on him. It was impossible to dive clandestinely in a hardhat suit . . . it required a tender to handle lines and a compressor pumping air . . . so the Otter contrived a way to dive publicly.

At night he collected chain from around the wreck and dumped it in the water in the aft mooring compartment. He warned the survey engineers that he had discovered a tangle of mooring chains beneath the water and that he volunteered to undertake the dangerous clearance job himself, asserting that no diver knew this part of the ship as well as he did.

He dived with an underwater gas cutting-torch. It took several days, during which he repeatedly refused offers of help on the grounds that it was too risky a situation for more than one man to work at a time. The busy surveyors were grateful to van Slough for the opportunity to let their hard-pressed divers work elsewhere on the wreck.

After he pronounced the mooring compartment safe, producing as evidence lengths of cut chain he had secretly lowered into the water, the surveyors sent down their own divers. The men spent a day in the black water and reported topside that a number of frames were missing on A deck, weakening the structure. The surveyors assumed that the frames had been removed for some reason during the chaotic troop ship conversion, and another round of oaths was loosed at the anonymous idiots who had let the ship burn, leaving ports open, decks jammed with debris, and scaffolds blocking holes that had to be patched.

The surveyors deemed the A deck ceiling too weak to support the expected hydrostatic head during controlled pumping and decided to finish off the sealed portion of the ship's stern at B deck. The after-mooring compartment would not be sealed. Its vast ring of windows would remain open. Open to the tide – and to the Otter's submarine.

16

All the fire reports included the testimony of the men operating the burner that ignited the life jackets, and Gates doubted that Nash or his helpers, Armstrong and Larson, could tell him anything they hadn't already told the House, Senate and naval investigators.

Tweed's second suggested line of inquiry seemed more promising. Why had the flammable kapok and burlap bales arrived at the *Normandie* early?'

Gates told Rik van Slough he wanted to do some design work at the office and asked to be transferred to the four-to-twelve swing shift. Van Slough said he had no objection . . . his better workers tended to be family men who preferred the day shift and Gates's relentless dedication to raising the *Normandie* might balance out the looser swing shift.

Telephoning people he knew at Third District HQ, Gates ran down a lieutenant, jg., in the Third's office of procurement who, his contacts said, had had some sort of involvement with the shipment. He went to the townhouse, checking first with Kay that his mother and uncle were out, and collected a dark business suit, an autumn-weight overcoat and the right shoes. The jg. was easily persuaded to leave his beaverboard cubbyhole and walk down Church Street for lunch at Fraunces Tavern, though he made no secret of his surprise that a full partner of Prince and Gates wanted to entertain someone as near the bottom of the chain of command as he.

Fraunces Tavern stood at the corner of Pearl and Broad Streets. The jg. admired the early Georgian Colonial mansion, so Gates explained how it had been restored and pointed out the Dutch influence in the shape of its dormers. The restaurant on the ground floor was packed with Wall Street bankers and shipping men. The captain greeted Gates by name, the bartender remembered he drank Canadian Club; the jg. was duly impressed. He waited until he had a drink in his hand, then he asked, 'Mr Gates, what's all this about?'

'I'd like to talk about a couple of things. We're both busy and lunch seemed like the best time.'

'Fine with me. What do you want to talk about?'

'Some procurement practices in the Third District.'

The jg. put his drink down. 'You got the wrong guy, Mr Gates. I buy potatoes and carrots for ships and shore stations. That's kinda different than locating armour plate for Prince and Gates.'

Gates saw no reason to say he no longer worked for his uncle.

'I know that, but someone told me you used to purchase life jackets.'

'Sure. Used to. I can tell you who to talk to, but he should be sitting here, not me.'

The jg. was about two years younger than Gates with a shavetail haircut and a shiny college ring. University of Wisconsin. An ROTC grad, probably.

'Let me ask you one thing,' he said, watching the man's face. 'How come eleven thousand life jackets were delivered to the *Normandie* two days ahead of schedule?'

The jg. shrugged. 'We had a thousand-foot liner getting ready to put to sea after being laid up for two and a half years. That's like sending Hoboken to sea. Tons and tons of stores from food to building materials to . . . life jackets had to go aboard. Plus, there's a war on and things are kind of crazy anyhow. I got into the navy last summer, right? After I graduated. The biggest thing I did before Pearl was lead a detail checking fire extinguishers in shore installations.'

'Just confusion? You're sure?'

The jg. didn't seem to hear him. 'They subpoenaed all the manifests and shipping orders and decided it just happened. Should have left the life jackets on the dock until they were stencilled to go in the cabins, but they didn't. Maybe they figured they'd put them in the cabins on the way to Boston.'

No chaos like the chaos of a new ship, Gates knew. Except the chaos of a conversion job. It was easy to believe that the fire was an accident, the capsizing inevitable. He might believe it himself if it weren't for the doors. And the man in the stack.

'Why you asking?'

Gates signalled the waiter to refill their drinks.

'I don't know, I guess I've been thinking that the *Normandie* was very unlucky.'

'How so?'

'Unexpected last-minute burning was done in a room full of unexpected, highly flammable kapok, which arrived ahead of schedule on a job backed up for weeks, while new hose couplings hadn't arrived to replace the old couplings the contractor had already removed. That's a string of coincidences you could fly a kite on.'

'Or it could be just a lot of bad luck, combined with a lot of fouling up.'

'Which is what all the investigations said,' Gates said.

'There you are.'

Gates asked for a menu when their new drinks arrived. He studied it briefly. The jg. read it line by line.

'Are these prices by the week?'

'Have a steak,' said Gates. 'Before they're rationed.'

'I just might do that. On my salary steaks are rationed all the time.'

Over coffee, Gates asked, 'Could you get me photostats of the orders and invoices for the life jackets?'

Trucks had delivered the eleven thousand kapok life jackets that had arrived early at the *Normandie*, which interested Gates because heavy, bulk shipments were so much more easily moved around the harbour by barge, particularly when they were headed for a ship. The navy had ordered the life jackets from a manufacturer in Brooklyn, Reliant Flotation, one of the several Brooklyn cordage houses that had supplied rope, twine, cable, cork floats and rafts and life jackets to the navy for decades, and was suddenly trebling production to try to meet the war demand.

Gates had a conversation with a talkative Reliant production manager, arranged by a mutual contact at the navy department. Reliant had supplied the life jackets from stock, both inventory and material already slated for delivery elsewhere, because it was a rush order and no one wanted to disappoint the navy on such a large purchase.

'That was for *one* ship, remember. Never had an order that size in our lives.'

'How much time did they give you?' Gates asked.

'None. I'm not kidding. The ship was originally supposed to sail to Boston on the first of the month. February, right? It looked like the navy intended to buy the jackets there, from a Boston outfit. But she didn't sail on the first. So about the third or fourth we get this order. First by phone, confirming we could supply, then written purchase orders sent by messenger. I guess they figured it would be a way to make up for lost time by supplying the jackets here before they sailed. Didn't want 'em stencilled or nothing. Just wanted 'em. Right now. I didn't think we'd make it. Thought we'd miss the boat for sure.'

'Is that why you sent them by truck?'

'No. That was the navy's brainstorm.'

'What do you mean?'

The production man shrugged.

'Look, you work for the navy?'

'Sure. They buy ships.'

242

'So I'm not going to sit here and run down the navy, but you know as well as I that they can do some dumb things.'

'Can and do,' said Gates. 'What did you have in mind?'

'We move eleven thousand life jackets onto that pier down there. And we're getting ready to hoist them onto the first empty barge we can get our hands on, and who pulls into the front yard?'

'Who?'

'Some shyster trucker with ten of the sorriest looking trucks you ever saw and a handful of purchase orders from the navy. We're loading barges and some clown in procurement sends trucks. I got on the horn and started yelling and they told me that's the way it was. So we moved eleven thousand life jackets back through the building out the front door and onto the trucks. Trucks were breaking down and we had to post a man here all night just to watch the stuff they left sitting around. Took 'em two days. I kept thinking that if the navy hadn't stamped all the orders Rush things would have got done faster. Then they stick 'em in the main lounge and burn the ship down. What are you going to do?'

'So actually they ended up at the ship early?'

'That's 'cause nobody at the ship knew they were coming.'

'What do you mean?'

'If they knew they were coming they would have been ready for 'em, right?'

'Did you get paid?' asked Gates.

'Sure. Not our fault they burned.'

'Could you show me the invoice?'

Gates compared it to the photostatic copy the jg. from procurement had given him. They looked the same. 'Is this the invoice you sent with the life jackets?'

'Right. And here's the purchase order the navy sent us. What's that you got there?'

'Copies.'

243

'What for?'

'Just checking things.'

The production manager took back his copies of the orders and invoices. 'Anything else?'

'Thanks a lot. You were a big help.'

'You know something, I don't know if you are who you say you are, but this company's been doing business with the navy a long time and we intend to keep on doing business. What the navy orders from Reliant they get. Top quality and accurate measure. I know it's just your job, checking up, but go bother some of the new boys who just popped up since Pearl. We been around a long time before this war and we'll be around after.'

Gates bought another lunch for the jg.

'Reliant's copy of the purchase order was stamped Rush. And the Rush stamp was initialled E.M. Who's E.M.?'

'E.M. E.M. No one there now. Must have been the traffic manager. That's who would say Rush. Oh, Ed Mullaney. Left the supply office about six months ago, I'd say. He was gone from there before I left that branch of procurement.'

'Where'd Mullaney go?'

'Beats me. Maybe he got drafted.'

'He's not navy?'

'No, civilian ... How are you getting on with the *Normandie*?'

'Coming along.'

Gates spent a week of cramming nickels into pay phones, pounding the sidewalks of lower Manhattan, and putting the arm on old friends in the navy to track down the traffic manager who had initialled the Rush stamp reproduced on Reliant's copy of the purchase order. People were helpful but busy, and it often took hours to complete a single contact. Mullaney hadn't been drafted, nor had he even left New York, but he'd changed jobs three times

244

since he'd left the supply office. The sort of free and easy movement from job to job which would have hinted at instability before the war was becoming commonplace.

Mullaney turned up at last in the harbour operations section of the Third District service office, which supplied US and Allied naval vessels with pilots, tugs, piers or anchorages, ordnance, fuel, food and repairs. When Gates had finally talked his way into the hectic operations room he found Mullaney in civilian clothes shouting into the telephone.

'What? A tug pilot drafted by the *army*? . . . Jesus Christ, I'll get back to you.' He slammed down the phone, picked it up and started dialling again, oblivious to Gates's 'excuse me.'

Gates waited while Mullaney shouted his way through a series of secretaries and aides and up a chain of command like a salmon fighting upstream. The operations room commanded a spectacular view of the harbour – the flats of Brooklyn beyond the Manhattan towers, the black cranes of the Navy Yard Annex in Bayonne, New Jersey, distant Staten Island marked by white church spires, and through the Narrows, a hazy glimpse of the empty eye of the sea.

'Somebody's crazy,' Mullaney yelled in the phone. 'We got a thousand vessels a month in this port and another five hundred naval craft, not to mention about one *million* railroad floats and every damned thing that moves in this harbour is moved by a tugboat. You're goddamned right I'm shouting. You get those pilots out of boot camp or I quit.'

He slammed the phone down again and noticed Gates.

'What do you want?'

'These your initials?'

'Yeah. E.M. Ed Mullaney. What about it?'

'Why'd you stamp them Rush?'

'What?' Mullaney grabbed the photostat copy of the shipping manifest and shook it in the light. 'Life jackets?

245

What the hell are you bothering me with life jackets for? Who are you?'

'You sent these to the *Normandie* and you stamped them Rush.'

'The *Normandie*? That was a year ago.'

'Eight months.'

'I'm not in that office any more.'

'Just tell me why you stamped them Rush.'

'There must have been a rush.'

'They got there early, remember?'

'Remember? How the hell am I supposed to remember stamping one manifest eight months ago? Probably somebody said they was in a rush, so I stamped them Rush. If they said they was in a hurry, I'd have stamped them Hurry.'

'Why'd they go by truck instead of barge?'

Mullaney squinted at the windows and picked up a set of long-range binoculars. 'Faster.'

'Did you order the trucks?'

'What do you think I am? The navy historian? Go ask the trucker.'

'Do you – '

'Jesus Christ, look at that,' Mullaney growled, focusing on the Narrows. Gates made out the square, grey shape of an aircraft carrier filling the crowded channel between the Bays.

'I've known he was coming for two days and I still ain't got a berth to put him in, thanks to the *Normandie* using two, or a tug to put him in it.'

'Are you sure these *are* your initials?'

Mullaney was already reaching for a telephone. For an instant his bloodshot eyes met Gates's. 'Who the hell else is going to sign my initials?'

Gates telephoned the Third District supply office, where the orders for the life jackets had originated, said he was Steven Gates of Prince and Gates and asked for help.

'Yes, sir, Mr Gates.'

'I'm trying to check an invoice number.' The copies of the orders that the jg. had given him had not been stamped Rush, while the copies at Reliant had. He wanted to see the original orders.

'Expecting something?'

'Something we got last winter. Or should have.'

'Shoot.'

Gates read the invoice number.

'Yeah, that goes back a ways. Want me to call you?'

'I'll hang on.'

He waited and twice put nickels in the pay phone in the hall of his rooming house, praying each time the clerk wouldn't come on and then hear the coin bells.

'Still there?'

'Yes. Find it?'

'I found the number, but I don't know what it has to do with you.'

'What do you mean?'

'It's for life jackets. Eleven thousand of 'em.'

'That sounds a little screwy. What ship were they for?'

'*Lafayette.*'

'*Lafayette?*'

'Yeah, you know. The one that burned last year? The *Normandie.*'

'Of course I know,' Gates said. 'It was February. We worked on the job, but we didn't order any life jackets. There must be some mistake.'

'I don't know what to tell you, Mr Gates.'

'May I come up and see it?'

'I don't have the papers here. I just checked the traffic reports.'

'Where are they?'

'We've been moving the old stuff out to dead files in Queens.'

'Well, you can get them, right?'

'Take a week. Why don't you check your numbers again?'

247

'I really have to see them . . . want me to talk to your supervisor?'

'No. No, I'll get them.' Son of a bitch, the clerk thought.

'Can I come up Monday?' Gates asked, pressing the advantage he'd discovered in the clerk's apparent fear of his superior.

'Yeah, okay. Better make it Tuesday. But be sure to ask for me. It's a crazy house here. Nobody else'll know what you're talking about.'

'Sure . . . what's your name?'

'Walsh. Glenn Walsh.' And, he thought, the Otter was going to have his ass for this. Ass, hell. His life.

17

You are too vital to be linked to your own network.

It was Uncle Willy's first rule and the Otter obeyed it.

The Otter's only communication with Larson and Walsh was a one-way system that he activated himself. Neither the arsonist nor the navy clerk could contact him. Neither his cover name, nor his face, nor his safehouses were known to them. Nor had he provided message drops. He contacted them. At random. Without warning.

If they were in trouble, he couldn't help them.

He did not rescue captured functionaries. He merely listened for the anxious note in their voices that said they had been turned against him by the enemy. They were conveniences, less valuable than radiomen, who at least were a link with Uncle Willy.

If they had information, it could wait.

Larson and Walsh were not in place to gather information. Uncle Willy had provided them to implement actions that the Otter initiated. As such, it was the arsonist and the clerk who needed to hear from the Otter, not the other way around. If the one-way communication system had any flaw, it was that the Otter occasionally got a good deal of bad news at once . . .

He telephoned Glenn Walsh at his navy office, then called him again at a pay phone across town on South Street during Walsh's lunch hour. The Otter made both calls from pay phones. The navy clerk was extremely upset. Unlike Larson, Walsh had no fear of being arrested for his forgeries, but he had a powerful fear of failing the Nazi party. Walsh was a fanatic, which meant that the Otter could, and did, ask more of him than others. When Uncle

Willy learned that Walsh had taken a personal oath of allegiance to Adolf Hitler, he had had the Abwehr forgers concoct a letter purportedly from Hitler instructing Glenn Walsh to obey the Otter's orders as if they were his own. Walsh had believed deeply enough to go for it.

'Hey,' he exploded. 'I thought you'd never call in time. Some guy wants to see the life jacket invoices.'

'So? You had to give them to the investigators.'

'But this one says he isn't an investigator.'

'Who does he say he is?' the Otter asked calmly, thinking this was trouble, and thanking Uncle Willy once again for teaching him about severing connections.

'Naval architect. Prince and Gates. He says he's Gates himself. I stalled him until Tuesday . . . What should I do, sir?'

'I will give you instructions before Tuesday. *Heil Hitler.*'

Brooklyn was huge, the size of Chicago, and though it was best known as the 'home borough', with endless tracts of residences, each of which seemed to have at least one star in the window for a boy in the army, Brooklyn was also a vast manufacturing and shipping centre, which by the end of October Cordi Grey had come to know quite well.

Seven months after her brother's death, Cordi had traced all the routes taken by all the cargo which had been loaded into the four ships sabotaged in his convoy. British Security Coordination had already concluded that a saboteur or saboteurs unknown had somehow managed to elude the dock guards and secrete the explosives aboard the ships. Cordi had been freed up to mine the richest prospects. No luck.

She had worn her British Broadcasting cover so thin that in order to keep hunting on the Erie Basin and Bush Terminal piers she had had to conduct several actual radio interviews and feature reports, which were broadcast in England. But even the appearance of the recording car driven by Mark and the instruments in the backseat presided over by Duncan couldn't explain all the time she spent there, and towards the end she'd noticed that various people were saying hello to her as if she'd become a member of their community.

MacMillan, the grain agent, was one whom she had interviewed. He'd picked up the programme from London on a shortwave. And this time when he asked her to have lunch in Manhattan, she agreed. They ate at the Plaza, in the Palm Court, where she had insisted they meet because it was too open and light to be misconstrued by him as a trysting spot. She had been wondering if she'd gone about her search in the wrong way – or, rather, had searched for the wrong thing.

'Are you involved with the black market?' she asked bluntly.

'What? Me?'

'I'm not about to tell anybody, I just wondered.'

'Sure, I'm involved the way most people are. I give my butcher all my meat coupons at the beginning of the month and slip him a few bucks the way I always did and get all the steak I want. I know some people who can usually sell me gas, for a price. And I have enough friends in the food business to get me coffee. What do you want? Cigarettes?'

'That's not what I meant.'

'I know, but that's all I know about the black market. I got plenty of legal business to keep me happy.'

'Where do the black marketeers get the things they sell?'

MacMillan shrugged. 'Stolen stuff. And fresh stuff bought directly from farmers. Local. And maybe bought under the table from the big suppliers. Meat packers . . . The mob's in on it.'

'Is stuff stolen on the docks?'

'If it isn't nailed down. And from warehouses. And from trucks.'

251

'Trains?'

'Doubt that. Railroad police have a pretty firm hold on the trains.'

'When you send grain by truck do you worry that it might be stolen?'

'I don't worry, but I keep a close track of the weights. I mean what's to stop a driver from pulling into another warehouse before he goes where I sent him.'

'I was wondering about that,' Cordi said. 'Who does your trucking?'

'Depends. There's old reliable and there's quick and dirty and most everything in between. Short haul. Long haul. Though I use mostly short haul, from the warehouses to the docks. Brooklyn's full of truckers.'

'Speaking of firm holds and under the table, Mr MacMillan, that's my leg, not the restaurant's.'

MacMillan let go with a sheepish grin. 'Sorry . . . at least you didn't call me quick and dirty.'

'That was an oversight,' she said, gathering her bag and gloves.

'I'm sorry. Really. What can I do to make it up?'

'Nothing, thank you.' She started to stand. MacMillan leaped up, concern on his fleshy face.

'Come on, Cordi. Don't leave sore. I'll do anything – '

'Anything?' She permitted him a thin smile.

'You name it, sweetheart, it's yours.'

'How about a list of the mob truckers?'

The Otter called Larson at the Long Island aircraft plant where he had placed the arsonist after the *Normandie* fire, and left a message. He wanted to see where Larson stood before he dealt with Walsh's problem with Steven Gates.

Flaunting his brilliant mechanical skills and natural leadership, the talented Larson had worked his way up to foreman and claimed to be setting up something really big. Too slowly, in the Otter's opinion, but he had let the redhead go his own way because his plan for the *Normandie* and the *Queen Mary* was much more important than the disruption of a single aeroplane factory.

'Trouble,' said Larson when he answered the pay phone in the next town the Otter called an hour later from another pay phone in the Fiftieth Street IND subway station. Larson's chief flaw was that he was greedy. None of Walsh's *Vaterland über Alles* for him. Just cold cash.

'What trouble?'

'The clown at the trucks' – he meant the dispatcher whom he'd made a partner in the T and C Trucking business – 'says somebody's watching the trucks.'

'Who?'

'A girl.' Larson tried to sound unconcerned, but he was concerned enough to report it.

'What are you talking about?'

'He says they been hanging around the yard and followed him home once. He figures it's the Canarsie mob muscling in. Bright.'

'What else did he say?' The Otter had of course never met the man, but Larson knew him well, having installed him in the trucking business. 'The guy's shaking in his boots. Doesn't know what's going on. He thinks they had accents. I says, what kind of accents? He don't know. He thinks maybe English. The clown's from Brooklyn. He knows it ain't Brooklyn, so he thinks it's foreign. It could be Park Avenue or Timbuktu . . . You want me to torch the joint?'

'No. You stay away.' Ordinarily the Otter did not risk acting as his own firebug, but Larson was no fighter, and there was a greater risk of him being captured by whoever was watching the truckyard; nor was Larson capable of including the dispatcher in the blaze. No, T and C was one 'joint' the Otter would 'torch' personally, when the time came. 'Do not return to T and C ever again. *Is that understood?* '

'Sure. Take it easy. I don't want to go back. I just thought you'd want it torched. You been talking about dumping the place.'

The Otter wanted to hang up, but he still had a few more

253

seconds of safety before a tap could trace this phone, and he thought he detected something wrong in the redhead's voice. 'How is your job?'

'Coming along . . . '

'Then what's the matter?'

'I'm not too sure how to tell you this, but I think I might get married.'

A second jolt. How long had the war been going that such a thing would happen? He'd been using Larson since '39. Over three years.

'Who is she?'

'A widow. Husband got killed last summer at Guadalcanal.'

'Big insurance policy.'

'Yeah, but that's not it. I been kind of seeing her on the side since he went overseas.'

'She sounds like a perfect cover,' the Otter said, and hung up.

Larson loved money. If he thought he had enough with his bride-to-be he might not want to work for Germany any more . . . well, worry about that later . . . Right now he had to be concerned about who was watching the truck company. The mob did not use women. Especially women with English accents. Unless they'd suddenly got more sophisticated than he thought possible . . . Then who was watching?

Whoever it was, he would give them a show they'd remember. And they might even get to meet Mr Steven Gates.

'Show Gates any papers he wants to see. Then point him towards the trucker.'

'Send him to T and C *Trucking*?'

'Are you questioning my orders, Herr Walsh?'

'No, sir. Of course not.'

'*Heil Hitler*.'

'Glenn Walsh?'

'Mr Gates?'

The navy clerk had the original purchase order on his desk, which was in a corner far from the lightfall of the nearest windows in the lower Manhattan Third District supply office. Walsh was in civilian clothes, a white shirt greying at the cuffs and a dark, frayed tie that looked as if he slipped it over his head each night rather than untying the knot. He was a pale, spindly man in his forties with thin, greasy hair, chipped front teeth, and eyes a bit brighter than Gates was accustomed to seeing in file clerks as far down the ladder as this one. There seemed to be a little extra space around his desk, as if over the years the other clerks had subconsciously edged away.

'Here you are, sir.' As on the telephone, Walsh's voice had an officious-sounding drone.

'Is this the original?'

'Yes, sir. The original stays here. The manufacturer gets his copy. Receiver gets his. Shipping gets his. Navy in Washington gets theirs. And procurement here in New York gets one, too. But this stays here. Until it goes into the dead file.'

It was stamped Rush. Like Reliant Flotation's copy.

Gates handed it back, disappointed. 'let me ask you something. Whose initial is this by the Rush stamp?'

Walsh read the entire form aloud in his drone, ending with: 'This is Admiral Anderson's signature or his secretary's and these initials say E.M.'

'I know that. Is that Ed Mullaney?'

'E.M. Ed Mullaney.'

'Do they look like his initials?'

'Yes. But this is for life jackets. That's not what you wanted . . . what *did* you want?'

'We'd ordered some structural steel put aboard. We can't find out if it got there before the fire. We're afraid it didn't and it just disappeared, but somebody's got to pay for it.'

Walsh nodded. 'I see what you mean . . . sit down a second, Mr Gates.' He dragged a wooden chair over from his neighbour's desk and waited until Gates had settled in it. He hated these rich types. The clothes on the guy's back cost more than a month of his salary. National Socialism would end inequities with a single blow. The Gateses would be swept aside, put where they belonged.

'What's up?' Gates asked.

'This is just between you and me, but a lot of stuff heading for the *Normandie* disappeared after the fire if it was already in the trucker's hands. They said they delivered right before the fire, that it was on the ship someplace.' He watched Gates. This was tricky stuff . . . Gates was lying about the steel's disappearance. It was about as genuine as the purchase order which he had forged himself, along with Admiral Anderson's supposed letter demanding a Rush order for the life jackets.

'You're saying I should go to the trucker?'

'Right . . . I don't know what good it'll do you, your steel's already on the black market. In fact, your steel's probably already been put into some civilian building project. You're going to have to write it off. *Unless* you can prove the trucker took it.' He picked up the purchase order. 'Funny about the purchase order number. Almost seems as if the trucker was setting up to divert your steel ahead of time. Who is this T and C? Do you deal with them often?'

Walsh sat back and watched Gates try to keep his lie going. Maybe he could push it harder. 'Do you know them?'

'No, I think it was the first time we'd used them.'

Walsh leaned closer. 'Don't say you got this from me, but I hear T and C is thick with the mob. A lot of them are.'

Gates got up quickly and reached to shake hands. Walsh was surprised by the callouses on Gates's palm. Gates thanked him, hurried out between the rows of desks. Walsh watched him go, then looked down at the papers on his desk to hide his smile from the other clerks grinding away at their desks, oblivious to the drama around his. Cogs.

He had followed his orders to the letter. He too might

be a cog, but in a far superior movement. He did what he was told, he accepted that his was not to understand but to do. But in this case even a cog could guess that his superior had plans for T and C Trucking that would do Mr Steven Gates no good.

Lunch aboard the Führer's special train, thundering east on cleared track from Berlin to East Prussia, took swift, unexpected and increasingly vicious turns, and Admiral Wilhelm Canaris began to doubt the wisdom of his latest resolve to broach the difficult subject of the SS mistreatment of Jews and Slav civilians. Unfortunately, he'd already committed himself by requesting a private conversation after Dönitz and Raeder left.

So far he'd drawn the least fire, but he knew from experience that his situation could turn as suddenly bad as Grossadmiral Erich Raeder's and U-boat Admiral Karl Dönitz's. Ironically, the naval officer's discomfort stemmed from a bad performance by Hitler's favourite army general in the desert. Because they were with him at lunch when the disappointing news about Rommel had arrived, Hitler had a convenient target for the blame.

Canaris hunched down in his chair like a steer turning its bony haunches to the wind. Hitler had been in a good mood. He'd spent the early part of the meal expounding the virtues of a vegetarian diet, then switched his monologue to the Russian campaigns, which commanded so much of his enthusiasm that Canaris worried about the imbalance. Then an aide had interrupted with a long dispatch from North Africa.

Rommel had stopped moving again. This time at Alam Halfa, south of Alamein, where British reinforcements — fresh troops and new tanks — had stopped him cold eighty kilometres from Alexandria. He'd had Egypt in his grasp, but the British kept bringing in more reinforcements, and now it was feared the Allies might try to land in French Tunisia.

Hitler read the dispatches and accompanying reports. Then read them again, aloud, spitting his sarcasms, firing questions and slashing through Raeder and Dönitz's attempts to respond. He already had answers.

'How did those reinforcements get to Alexandria? Well might you ask. Did their battleships run a German naval blockade? No, Grossadmiral Raeder, they didn't need battleships, since yours are all in Norway. Ah, Admiral Dönitz knows? Was a vast convoy cut to ribbons by a pack of U-boats and by bad luck did a couple of ships stagger through? No, Admiral Dönitz. The British reinforcements did not have to travel by convoy.' He waved a sheaf of reports and Canaris was satisfied to see his own agency's buff-coloured reports among them, carefully distilled from his Cairo agents' observations.

'No,' Hitler shouted. 'They aren't concerned with U-boats. They send their reinforcements by Cunard passenger liner.'

It was more complicated than that, by far, but Canaris had emphasized the role of the express liner in his report. The ploy seemed to be working magnificently. He hunched lower, content to let the papers do their work.

'New Zealand soldiers and American tanks sailed into Alexandria on the *Queen Mary* as if the year were 1925 and the German navy a ragtag collection of torpedo boats and garbage scows!' He angrily waved Canaris's report. 'Half a regiment and a hundred and fifty American tanks. Can you explain this situation, Grossadmiral? What should I do? Put Rommel in charge of the sea, too?'

'*Mein Führer* —' Raeder began hesitantly, stroking his thick jowls.

Hitler cut him off. 'And don't tell me it's the Luftwaffe's responsibility! What about you, Admiral Dönitz? Where were your U-boats? Are your captains waiting for Cunard-White Star lines to print schedules?'

Dönitz said, 'Express liners are too fast to pursue on the surface and next to impossible to hit with a torpedo.

The answer, *mein Führer*, is to continue developing a high-speed U-boat.'

Old Raeder rumbled ominously.

'Are you breaking wind or delivering yourself of an opinion?' Hitler snapped at the Grossadmiral.

Raeder stiffened. 'The problem is not a pair of fast liners. The problem is where they come from.'

'And where is that?' Hitler asked with dangerous quiet.

'A single port. The enemy's most vital port.'

Canaris sat up straight, intrigued, and Dönitz's hard features turned wary.

'Go on,' said Hitler.

'I have a plan, *mein Führer*. I propose a breakout from Norway. The *Scharnhorst*, the *Gneisenau*, the *Hipper* and the *Tirpitz*. Once out in the Atlantic, they will strike like lightning, where no one expects.' His aristocratic gaze swept the railroad car like a cavalry sabre. '*New York*.'

Dönitz was stunned. Canaris just stared. Was the old admiral that desperate to get his bottled-up surface ships into action? Even Adolf Hitler looked a bit awed. 'How would you get through the Denmark Strait?'

'I will coordinate the attack with weather reports from Admiral Canaris's agents in New York. Night and fog will be our allies — '

'No,' Canaris blurted, feeling Hitler's gaze fall on him. 'I have no agents in New York.'

Raeder turned on him angrily, but Hitler cut him off. 'Your courage is admirable, Grossadmiral, but since you lost the *Bismarck* I am a lion on the land, but a coward on the sea.' Canaris had broken the spell. Without accurate weather reports such a raid was doomed to being sighted in the strait between Iceland and Greenland.

'The *Kriegsmarine* would proudly sacrifice itself to end the war victoriously,' insisted Raeder.

Canaris didn't doubt it. No other unit in the Reich had the *esprit de corps* and the training of the German navy. If they got past the guns at Sandy Hook they'd blast the docks of Brooklyn, Manhattan and New Jersey to matchwood and sink the equivalent of four convoys at their moorings.

Hitler shook his head. 'Even if you could – and of course, you would lose all your ships – it would not serve victory. The important battle is in Russia. When it is won we will cease hostilities elsewhere and consolidate. No, Grossadmiral. Brave, but foolhardy.' He turned to Dönitz, who'd gradually relaxed as he saw that Raeder's bid had failed. 'What will you do about the express liners, Admiral Dönitz?'

Canaris listened to Dönitz promise Hitler he'd make every effort to sink the *Queen Mary*. He knew, and Dönitz knew, it would never happen unless she strayed by chance into a U-boat's sights at the moment it was ready to fire torpedoes, but it didn't hurt to promise.

'What about the *Queen Elizabeth*?'

'Yes, *mein Führer*. Then the *Elizabeth*.'

'I don't *care* about the order,' Hitler told him, fingering the dispatches again.

'Yes, *mein Führer*.'

'What do you think, Admiral Canaris? You know something about submarines.'

Canaris took the opportunity to put the U-boat chief in his debt. For some reason Dönitz hated him and had for years. His enmity had been a factor in Canaris leaving the *Kriegsmarine* for the Secret Service. Canaris presumed it went back to the days when Dönitz had briefly served under him in the navy. He said, 'There was a time when I knew a good deal about submarines, but not so much any more since Admiral Dönitz has improved them so.'

Hitler persisted. 'What do you think of Admiral Dönitz's chances of sinking the liners?'

'I think the British liners are worthy targets and sinking them will produce both real and propaganda value. And I would never doubt that the admiral could do it.'

Dönitz's face never changed.

Hitler glanced at the dispatches again and abruptly dismissed Raeder and Dönitz. When they had left the car and the door had closed on the clatter of the wheels on the track, Hitler said, 'What do you want to talk about privately?'

'*Well?*' Hitler was growing impatient.

Canaris thought quickly. 'A small matter, *mein Führer*. My South American agents report that the Brazilians are angry over the sinking of two ships.'

'Let them keep their ships out of the war zone.'

'I'm told that they're considering declaring war against us.'

'Hah. The Reich trembles.'

Canaris wished he hadn't started on this tack. 'Unfortunately, if they do declare war they will allow the Allies use of their air bases. If that happens, the Allies will drive our surface raiders out of the South Atlantic.'

'If! If! If it happens, Dönitz's U-boats will make short work of that problem. He's a strong one, that Dönitz. A man of iron. Dönitz can be depended on. Iron.'

'Yes, *mein Führer*.'

Canaris started to leave, but Hitler stopped him with a sarcastic laugh.

'Destroy New York Harbour?' He puffed his cheeks like Raeder's and corkscrewed a finger at his head, pantomiming that the Grossadmiral of the *Kriegsmarine* was crazy. 'Aren't you sorry you recalled your spies?'

'Yes, *mein Führer*,' said Canaris, pretending not to hear the sarcasm, and leaping on the opportunity he spotted in Hitler's chance remark. 'The enemy strength flows through the harbour.'

Canaris backed out of the dining car, struggling not to show Hitler his sudden excitement.

He had not, of course, recalled all his New York agents, only winnowed them out. And the best had survived. Compared to the counterespionage army the British had moved into New York, he was pitifully thin on the ground.

But the British were in a defensive position in New York, while his swift, unpredictable Otter had nothing to defend – like Germany herself with limited resources and no ships to bring more.

Old Raeder had inspired him. Germany couldn't fight a long war. She had to win at a stroke. And just when he thought the time for sudden strokes lost forever, the stolid old Grossadmiral had offered a mad, brilliant idea that meshed precisely with a madman's rational plan.

And madman the Otter was, at least in his obsession to cover his tracks. In the process the Otter had done more damage to the Abwehr's meagre New York network than the FBI and the British Security Coordination combined. Admittedly the *Normandie* was a great victory, as were his dock fires, his shipping reports to guide the U-boats and his strategic explosions, but the price – in betrayed and murdered agents the Otter decided were unacceptable risks – was high.

Canaris had been laying groundwork very slowly. Stalling, the Otter had accused in his last signal, which had been half-plea, half-angry demand. Canaris had put him firmly in his place, as only he could, but it was true that he had been reluctant to commit himself to the Otter's plan, afraid of the consequences of success. Now Raeder's wild, bold plan swept away those fears and showed Canaris that the Otter's plan for an attack on the *Queen Mary* in New York Harbor could indeed end the war like a death-stroke.

Book II

18

A faded wall of mustard stucco and arched green shutters speckled with salt corrosion stood close to a street of similar four- and five-storey warehouses in Red Hook. An arrow and a sign pointed the way to T and C Trucking into an alley beside the building, long and narrow and overhung by loading booms that extended from the roof above each line of shutters.

Gates went down the alley and found a driveway that passed behind the building into a broad truckyard, blue with exhaust smoke and echoing motors and the shouts of drivers. A second sign, peeling like the first, announced 'Office'.

The dispatcher sat behind a wooden counter open at both ends.

'Steven Gates. I called earlier and – '

'What do you want?'

'I'm not sure who I spoke to when I called, but told him I'm checking an invoice that went astray.'

'You spoke to me and I told you I didn't know anything about it.'

Gates stopped being polite. 'I'm not going anywhere until you show me a copy of this invoice.'

'Oh yeah?' He stood up and yelled down a hall. 'Roscoe! Slack!'

Gates said, 'You want to strong-arm me, I'll bring the cops.'

The dispatcher sat down and pretended to read papers on his desk. Two big men came into the room. Each had prize-fighter's scar tissue bunched hard and white over his brows.

'Throw him out.'

'Okay, buddy. Out.'

Gates knew he had no chance against the two of them, but he'd at least slow them down with a bluff. 'I told the man here I'll be back with cops.'

'Yeah, well just make sure you bring enough.' The man threw a punch and Gates sidestepped and caught the second punch square in the mouth. He staggered, raised his hands, and the second one sank a fist into his stomach and doubled him up.

'Want more?'

'I just want to ask – '

Roscoe slapped him open-handed aside the ear, sending a dart of pain down his neck. Slack feinted with both hands and when Gates had blearily dodged both, sank a fist into his stomach.

'I just – '

Again, a slap across his nose that made his eyes water. He dodged the blow to his stomach, but in twisting exposed his back. A kidney punch drove him to his knees.

'More?'

Gates steadied his breathing as he dialled the pay telephone. He noted his own bloody fingerprints on the door. He wiped his mouth. His handkerchief came away dappled scarlet. There was more blood in his nose. On the third ring Paula answered with her familiar placid dignity.

'Gates residence.'

He thought he could hear the clock ticking peacefully in the muffled quiet of the front hall. 'It's Mr Gates, Paula. Is Mr Collins home yet?'

'Are you all right, sir?'

Paula had been with his mother before he was born. There was no fooling her. Gates didn't try. 'Get Mr Collins, please.'

His arm hurt like hell where they'd twisted it as they

marched him out the alley, and he tasted a steady flow of salt from a deep cut in his lip. His side ached.

'What's up, Junior?'

'I need help, Charlie.'

'Where are you?'

Gates gave him the address.

'That's in Red Hook, for God's sake.'

'No kidding.'

'You in trouble?'

'Sort of. Can you bring Rik, too?'

'No. He's on the tug. Somebody rented it for the day and he went along to make sure they don't beat it like the army did last time.'

'I don't know if one of you is enough.'

Charlie was silent for a moment. 'I'll tell you when I get there.'

'I'll spring for a cab.'

'I should think so. Red Hook, for God's sake. Stay put and don't mouth off at anybody.'

Charlie arrived dressed like a longshoreman, complete with a watch cap, and when he lifted his windbreaker to replace his wallet in his hip pocket Gates saw a loading hook swinging from his belt. He glanced up and down the street.

'You're slumming, Junior.'

'I went into a place to ask a couple of questions and — '

'What kind of questions?'

'About the life jackets that burned on the *Normandie*.'

'Oh, great. And they thought you were blaming them for the fire.'

'They didn't give me a chance. Just slapped me around and threw me out on my ass.'

'It's a custom down here. Why waste breath talking when you can hit somebody?' He looked up and down the street, inspected Gates's lip, which had stopped bleeding, and groaned at the bleak warehouses. 'You're out of your element, Junior. Which one is it?'

267

Gates led him to T and C Trucking and down the alley. The drivers in the yard stared but said nothing. Charlie paused at the entrance to the office. 'If I tell you to do anything, do it fast. And be ready to run like Jesse Owens.'

He pushed the door open and held it for Gates. The dispatcher was alone behind the counter, on the telephone. He saw Gates and put his hand over the mouthpiece. 'I told you to get out of here – '

'One simple question,' said Gates. 'Who told you there was such a big rush to deliver the *Normandie*'s life jackets?'

'I don't *want* to answer your simple question. Can't you get that through your head? *Slack. Roscoe.*'

The two men lumbered in. Gates realized that neither was much smaller than Charlie. They stopped short when they saw Gates.

'Throw 'em out,' said the dispatcher. 'And this time I don't want to see him again.'

'Gangway, Junior.' Charlie shouldered past him to face Roscoe and Slack. 'All right, my buddy here's going to ask his questions and we're going to listen.'

Slack crossed the room fast and threw a punch at Charlie, who stepped under it, hammerlocked his arm behind his back and rammed his head into the wall. Slack fell to the floor. Roscoe flicked out a shiny loading hook.

The room turned quiet. Out in the yard the trucks had stopped moving, no sound except from one unattended engine idling as the drivers and loaders gathered around the window. Gates stared at Charlie, whose face had turned as hard and expressionless as the man's with the hook, hardly believing he'd started all this. Charlie motioned him back into the dispatcher's cubbyhole. Gates felt the dispatcher move beside him, and looking down saw him slide open a drawer and reach in. His fingers worked through stacks of dollar bills, towards the wooden butt of a gun.

Charlie faced Roscoe in a low crouch – outthrust shoulders and knees protecting his groin and belly – and pulled his hook from his belt. Roscoe glanced at the fallen Slack, assumed a similar crouch, moved towards Charlie.

Gates watched the dispatcher's fingers close on the gun butt, pull it out of the drawer, thumb back the hammer. It clicked softly, he raised the barrel over the counter – Gates grabbed the telephone and smashed the dispatcher's wrist with the heavy receiver. The dispatcher yelled, dropped the gun and ran out the other side of the cubbyhole.

'Nice going,' Charlie said. 'Don't touch the gun. Kick it under the counter. Easy.'

As he turned to watch Gates kick the gun out of the way, Roscoe swung his loading hook. Charlie moved aside with a liquid twist.

'Mister,' Charlie said, 'I got a fat wife and six kids. I don't see much of a future for my balls. How you feel about yours?'

Roscoe swung again. Again Charlie sidestepped, but this time he swung back, a sidearm sweep that went towards Roscoe's groin. Roscoe scrambled away and lowered his hands. Both hands were still at his waist when Charlie hit him with his empty fist and sent him sprawling.

'Ask your questions, Junior.'

'The dispatcher beat it,' said Gates, pawing through the drawers. The files were in a mess. He found manila folders separated haphazardly by handwritten tags and stuffed with flimsy copies of purchase orders and invoices.

'Here it is. *Lafayette.*' Gates pulled apart the folder and looked in. 'Empty.'

'How about *Normandie?*'

Gates slammed the A-to-L drawer shut and yanked out M-to-Z. '*Normandie.* Here it is.'

Gates pulled out four flimsies. A receipt for the eleven thousand jackets delivered. The shipper's copy of the manufacturer's invoice. The shipper's copy of the navy purchase order, stamped Rush, and clipped to it, the carbon copy of a typed note. 'Show at Pier 88.'

Why? To get them aboard the ship? It was all that was new. All he had to show for getting beaten up and dragging Charlie to Red Hook. He sensed movement and looked up to see Roscoe lunge off the floor, loading hook arcing through the light.

'Charlie, look out —'

Charlie fell against the counter, which crashed off its footing and pinned Gates to the wall. He could feel the ripple of Charlie's bone and muscle as he tried to lever himself out of range. The hook slashed down and bit deep into the wood an inch from Charlie's hand.

In the second it took Roscoe to tear it loose, Gates saw the blood rise in Charlie's face. He wound up and swung his hook backhanded. Roscoe screamed as the tip tore through his cheek.

He tried to crawl away and collapsed in blood. Charlie followed, raising the hook high over his head.

'Charlie.' Gates heard his voice as if from a stranger. He grabbed his arm and held on until he felt Charlie regain control. Police sirens sounded in the distance. Charlie hustled him over the fallen Roscoe.

'Move, Junior.'

Gates saw blood on Charlie's hand, thought he'd been hurt, then realized it was Roscoe's. There was more blood on the floor, a puddle by Roscoe's face. Charlie grabbed his arm and pulled him out the door.

'Run.'

They ran through the truckyard, scattering the gaping stevedores, down an alley, over a board fence, up a ladder and over a low roof and out onto a street, where they slowed to a fast walk.

'In there.'

Charlie shoved him into another alley and they repeated the process of crossing backyards to yet another street. The sirens howled past on Van Brunt Street and faded rapidly in the direction from where they'd run.

They walked to the docks along the Erie Basin and ducked

into a seaman's bar, where they ordered boiler-makers like two men just off work.

Charlie drank the shot of rye with shaking hands.

'Saved my bacon, Junior. Thanks.'

'Sorry I got you into it. I didn't think it would get that bad.'

'Wait'll Rik hears this.' Charlie laughed.

'Don't tell him.'

'Why not? He's okay.'

'I don't want what I'm doing made into a joke. I appreciate your help but I'd just as soon nobody else knew.'

'Sure, Junior.' He signalled for refills.

'Charlie?'

'What?'

'Would you have killed that guy?'

Charlie caught Gates's eye in the mirror behind the bottles and held it. 'Sure.'

'Why?'

''Cause I was crazy for a minute – listen, what are you going to do next?'

'I'm not sure. I'm kind of stuck.'

'I told you before, you're out of your element.'

From a flat roof atop the next warehouse Cordi Grey and Mark St George watched the police cars careen into the T and C truckyard. An ambulance arrived with a bell clanging. Two men were carried out of the office and loaded into it. One had a bloody bandage on his face. The ambulance clanged away and the police started pushing the truck drivers around, asking questions that no one seemed inclined to answer.

'Why were you there?' asked Weatherburn.

Mark answered, 'Cordi discovered that this same trucking company had made deliveries to all four of the ships that were sabotaged in Lieutenant Naill's convoy. We spent a couple of afternoons on the next roof watching them. We intended to come to you for permission to break into the premises tonight. As we were about to leave Gates and Collins came into the place and ran out shortly afterwards. Apparently they attacked some men inside.'

'Are you sure it was Gates and Collins?'

'I recognized them from last month when I checked them out at the *Normandie* salvage site. And Cordi knew them from years ago.'

'Cordi?'

'That's right, sir. It was them. I got a good look when they ran out.'

'What do you think?'

'I'm astounded.' What she thought was that she wished she had got a better look at Steven's face. It was him, for sure, but she had been far away. 'I want to go into that trucker's tonight.'

'Goes without saying,' said Weatherburn. 'All of us.'

A hard, cold wind swooped off the Upper Bay and rattled the steel shutters in the darkened truckyard. They had used the taxicab to come out here and had left Duncan in it to watch their backs. Weatherburn had insisted on weapons . . . he knew the area.

Mark did the locks. Cordi and Weatherburn waited silently in opposite corners of the yard. Thirty or forty trucks were parked in tight rows, so closely that Cordi wondered how their drivers got out. Mark whistled softly. She moved to the door and Weatherburn pushed her through after Mark, followed and shut it.

'Lower the shades.'

He pulled the one on the door and Cordi edged through the dark towards the insubstantial square patch of greyness which was the window. The mechanism was old, and the shade flew up with a bang and flapped around the roll the instant she released it.

Weatherburn did not smile in the dark.

'I've got it,' Cordi murmured. '*Wait*.' Holding the shade, and moving it an inch from the window frame she peered into the yard. 'Someone's coming.'

Weatherburn locked the door with a barely audible click, and Mark came up behind Cordi. 'Where?'

'Coming from behind that lorry. There.'

'One, sir,' Mark whispered.

From the dark, Weatherburn said, 'How the devil did he get past Duncan?'

'Came in from the other side.'

'He's coming to the door,' Cordi said. The figure, hunched low and glancing over his shoulder, darted across the yard. A key scrabbled around the lock, snicked into it and turned the bolt with a loud snap. The door banged open. The figure hurried in and shut it quietly and threw the bolt.

Cordi heard him move across the room confidently, as if he knew his way. A spring creaked – the swivel chair behind the counter – and a drawer slid open. From where she stood by the window, she could hear him breathing now. Mark and Weatherburn had faded to the corners.

The man's breath came in quick gasps, as if he'd been running. She heard the rustle of paper, something dropped. He turned on a flashlight and dropped to his knees to pick up a gun. It was the truck dispatcher she'd seen go in and out of the building, who, Mark had learned, was actually an owner-manager of the business.

A truck with a broken muffler started noisily in the yard. Gears clashed and the sound leaped closer as the truck scraped the side of the building. Cordi couldn't be sure what had happened, but the dispatcher knew. He turned on the lights and tried to get the door open, but the truck was blocking it. He turned, scared, making for the opposite door, when he saw in the flood of light Cordi and Weatherburn and Mark.

He was startled, then momentarily relief came over his face before he resumed his calculating look. He reached into his pocket. Mark, who was closest, slapped the gun out of his hand and grabbed his arm, just before an explosion in the yard blew shredded glass through the window shade.

Cordi picked herself up off the floor. The dispatcher was running down the hall. Mark had blood on his face and Weatherburn was laying motionless over the counter. Outside the window the night was red with fire.

'Get Weatherburn,' she shouted at Mark. He shambled across the room, wiping blood out of his eyes, and picked up the older man. Cordi went after the dispatcher.

He turned right at the end of the hall and she heard him pounding up a flight of stairs. Another explosion shook the building. Cordi looked back. Mark had made it into the hall with Weatherburn. 'Follow me,' she called; 'he must know a way out.'

It was a hope, a guess. She went up the stairs two at a time, pulling herself up the banister with one hand and fumbling a flashlight out of her pocket with the other. Ahead in the dark the dispatcher went higher and higher. Cordi followed him four flights to the roof, where he bounded over the gravel, leaped a low retaining wall and fell hard with a cry of pain. She was on him in a second, blinding him with the light. She showed her gun. 'Don't move.'

'The whole yard's going to blow, we got to get out of here – '

A truck exploded with a hollow boom and the flame tips leaped out of the yard, higher than the roof. In their flicker Cordi watched the man's face, saw his fear. 'Do you know a way down?'

'Come on.'

'We'll wait for my friends . . . Did you start the fire?'

'What are you, crazy? Who the hell are you?'

'Who put the truck against the door?'

'The same people who are trying to kill me.'

'Who?'

274

'Lady, we got to get *out* of here. It's going to the next building — '

'Cordi!' Mark called.

'Here! Hurry.' Mark loped across the roof, carrying Weatherburn like an empty sack. 'He knows the way, let's go.'

Half a dozen trucks blew up in rapid succession as the fire spread along gasoline tanks. The dispatcher led them across two roofs. Mark put Weatherburn down and helped him kick in a door on a third roof.

More trucks exploded, arousing Weatherburn, who surprised Cordi by getting to his feet. He took in the situation quickly. The door crashed open and they descended through four storeys of storage lofts. Mark moved ahead at the street door and unlocked it. With one hand firmly on the dispatcher, he led them onto the cobblestoned street, then to the alley where the cab was parked. Duncan had the motor running.

'A truck pulled out just before the first explosion. I didn't know if I should follow — '

'You should have,' Weatherburn said. 'Get us away from here. Find someplace quiet.' He put the dispatcher in the back seat between himself and Mark and told Cordi to sit in the front. As the car started moving and fire sirens approached he turned to the dispatcher, who asked, 'Who are you?'

Weatherburn's voice turned silky. 'Actually, that's our question.'

'He knew nothing,' Weatherburn said. 'A dupe.'

'What if he goes to the police?' Cordi asked.

'The only place he's going is a railway station to get out of town ahead of whatever enemy he thinks tried to fry him along with his trucks. Apparently the Otter set him up in business and decided to un-set him. Of course it was done through third or fourth parties.'

'What did he tell you about Gates and Collins?'

'He said that was the first time he'd ever seen them.'

'What did he say that Gates and Collins wanted?'

'His records. The fool is so confused he thinks that his silent partners had caught him stealing.'

'Did he admit slipping explosives into the convoy cargo?' Cordi persisted.

'No. For God's sake, don't you understand? He wasn't part of it. He just thought he was. The truck, if it was his truck, would have been diverted by the Otter's people along the way.'

'So now what do we do?' asked Duncan.

'We find out what Gates and Collins were up to.'

'How?'

'How do you feel about resuming a shipboard romance, Cordi?'

Cordi stared at her dark reflection in the cab window as they crossed into Manhattan. She had wondered if it would come to this.

'Well, Cordi?'

Well, Cordi? You liked him well enough the first time around. But this was to be no shipboard romance. This was business. Try to remember that, she instructed herself as she nodded her agreement.

19

Prowling the wreck, the Otter slipped into the giant aft engine room hatchway – horizontal and therefore overhung with steel chairs and ladders poised at useless angles – and noted with pleasure that the stench of the hulk had changed. Mantling the reek of burned paint, leaking oil, rotting provisions and raw sewage was a fresh, clean-sour smell of recently sawn timbers, as, cleared of debris, the shafts and passageways echoed with the banging and hammering of carpenters building stairs, ramps, staging and scaffolds to open access into the fallen ship.

The Otter realized he had developed an odd involvement with the salvage job, beyond the fact that his success hinged on the salvors' success and that the more orderly the work proceeded on the *Normandie* the easier it was to blend in, to interact with the job. He depended on the salvage proceeding with steady rhythms and schedules, which was why staging an accident, the simplest way to eliminate Gates, was a bad idea. He could hear Uncle Willy's reaction. What animal hunts in its own den? Killing Gates outright seemed worse. Regardless of his peculiar urge to bury himself among the ordinary, Gates was not just another workman and far too many important people would demand to know exactly what had happened to the architect who'd cried sabotage. No, better to use him, manipulate him into a suspect, as he'd already begun to do . . .

He stopped to watch a navy tender lead his diver through the water to the point where he wanted to submerge. Tugging at his lines, the tender looked, despite the US Navy-issue white cap and T-shirt and the bright tattoos on his brawny arms, like a farmboy leading a rambunctious bull. Beneath the wooden diving platform the oily water bubbled in adjacent pools of exhausted air, each pool marking the spot where a man worked. The divers operated in teams, helping each other through the dark and twisted passages.

He felt suddenly unnerved. Germany had stirred up a brand of optimism on this continent that the world had not seen in a long time. The American response to the problem of a severe shortage of trained divers to salve the *Normandie* had been to open a diving school on the wreck. Two schools: one for navy men, the second for civilians. He doubted that Europeans – even Germans – could learn to turn adversity to advantage so quickly and imaginatively. The Americans seemed to *enjoy* problems. Well, it wasn't anything that could not be learned. Steve Gates was wilful, stubborn. But he was also emotional, and therefore open to being diverted. Used.

'Junior, you happen to have an alibi for where you were last night?'

Gates paused in the midst of lighting his burner and shut off the gas. Charlie sounded serious. 'What do you mean?'

'Where were you?'

'Sleeping off a headache. I get them when I get hit in the mouth a lot.'

'Did Tweed happen to see you come in?'

'I don't think he was at home. Why?'

'Junior, don't you read the papers?'

'I went to bed with a headache, I woke up with a headache, late. And I just barely got here on time, with a headache. And you're giving me a new one.'

Charlie put down his lunch pail and unrolled the *Daily News*.

'Front page. T and C Trucking had a fire.'

'What?'

'All those trucks in the yards? Their gas tanks blew. Good picture in the centrefold.'

'Was it arson?'

'Who knows?'

'Hell of a coincidence, a fire right after we tore the place apart.'

'Junior, at the risk of repeating myself, you're out of your element. The mob's got hooks into trucking. Black market. You go sticking your nose in there then drag me in and we pound a few heads, it's like poking a hornet's nest. For all you know they went in to beat up some rival guys they thought might have put us on them and the rival guys torched the joint. Or maybe the boys who owned the place figured you were an undercover cop and the heat was on and it was time to take a powder. You don't know what's going on.'

Gates lighted his burner. And worse than that, he thought, he wasn't sure what to do about it.

When Gates asked van Slough for time off – intending to look for the men who'd been doing the cutting that had started the fire – van Slough refused, citing scheduling deadlines, and put Gates back on the day shift in charge of a gang clearing rubble from the huge stern mooring compartment at the aft end of B deck.

The *Normandie*'s crew had used the mooring compartment as their own promenade, Gates remembered, a place for a smoke and a walk, out of the weather and far removed from the passengers. Tipped on its side, the ports half-submerged, chains and hawsers dangling into the oily water, it remained as isolated, the stern being so far from Twelfth Avenue that it took ten minutes to reach it from Pier 88's guarded entrance.

Gates's crew cleared the loose rubble first – broken glass, burned tools, charred manila hawsers and heaps of sodden furniture which had been stacked there during conversion and had tumbled into the water. Then they trundled in burning outfits to cut away the winches and other excess steel, lightening the *Normandie* topside.

But before Gates was allowed to hook up the acetylene and oxygen bottles and commence burning he had to get permission from the New York City Fire Department battalion chief who commanded the fire watch. A humourless phalanx of retired foremen promptly descended on the aft mooring compartment.

When Gates was finally given permission to cut, he and his shield man worked under the eye of a straw-hatted fireman old enough to be their grandfather who pointed a rock-steady fire extinguisher at the white sparks cascading from the tight blue flame. They never learned his name and the only words he ever spoke were, 'Wake up, sonny!' when a spark slipped past the shield.

Van Slough was working nearby with underwater gas-cutting torches, clearing channels through pipes, ventilators and interior walls for a watertight bulkhead between the sternmost watertight compartments. He visited the aft mooring compartment frequently, often in his diving suit, to relay instructions from the salvage engineers.

A few days after the T and C Trucking fire, he brought orders to cut one of the thick struts between the windows – enlarging an opening through which a barge-mounted crane could lift out the gigantic main mooring winch.

Gates and Charlie put their crews to work building a wooden stage from which Rik would dive to clear the underwater half of the mooring compartment. Then they dragged their gas lines onto the curved top of the hull and wrapped hoisting chains around the strut. Charlie cut while Gates held the shield.

'What did Old Man Tooker say?'

'Who?'

'Captain Tooker. The wreckmaster. He was looking for you.' Charlie brought his flame to the steel, but Gates waved him away and lifted his mask. 'Captain Tooker was looking for *me*?'

'Yeah, he was around yesterday.'

'What for?'

'Sounded annoyed to me. You may be going back to Uncle Richard a lot sooner than you thought.'

'What did I do?' Gates asked. He got no answer.

Charlie said, 'Jesus Christ, look at that.'

Gates turned, and found himself looking into the polished chrome grill of a maroon Buick suspended in a sling fifty feet above the slip. The sling was attached to a crane which lowered the four-door sedan until it was level with the *Normandie*'s hull and a dozen feet away from Gates and Charlie. A driver sat nonchalantly at the wheel. A man wearing earphones was hunched over some equipment on the back seat. A woman sat in the passenger seat.

'Ask them if this is the right place,' she said in an English accent. BBC was written in white letters on the door.

Gates put down his shield, stood up and tried to see into the car.

The driver called, 'Is this the stern?'

Cordi Grey laughed and leaned across the driver. 'Steven Gates, it *is* you. What are *you* doing here?'

The Buick lurched and swayed as a tugboat nudged the barge crane closer. 'What am *I* doing here? How about you?'

'We're doing an outside broadcast for a programme about the salvage. This is Duncan, our engineer, and Mark, our driver. Hello, Charlie. Remember me? How's Kay?'

'Where the hell did you get the crane?'

'It was floating by in the water. Listen, is there any way we can join you up there?'

Gates leaned over the side and located the grinning crane operator. He brought the car closer on Gates's hand signals. The driver opened his door and stepped onto the catwalk. Cordi slid across the seat and followed, her skirt riding up above her knees.

'We came out to do a programme on the salvage and I could hardly believe it when I saw your name on the work list. I asked where you were working and they told me I'd find you here. So here I am. I have to interview somebody, so it might as well be you. Do you mind?'

'Sure, what do you want to know? . . . Cordi, I'm so damn glad to see you – '

'Me too. Steven . . . I want to know about the salvage. Here, let me get set up and then I'll ask questions and you and Charlie answer them.'

Duncan, wearing the headphones, passed a microphone through the window. She gripped the short stick and held the four-inch perforated cylinder to her lips.

'This is a test, this is a test.'

'I'm getting you all right.'

Duncan lowered the recorder's cutting arm to a blank acetate disc spinning on a turntable.

'. . . Five, four, three, two . . . This is Cordelia Grey and we are standing on a catwalk on top of the capsized ocean liner *Normandie*, the French ship which burned in New York Harbour last February while being converted to a troopship. Now she lies on her side at a pier in this busy port. The Hudson River is a mile wide and crowded with tugs, barges, seagoing cargo ships and warships. From this port the great convoys carry food and weapons to Britain. America is the arsenal of democracy and this great Port of New York is its harbour.

'We are speaking to Mr Steven Gates, a naval architect, and Mr Charlie Collins, while they take a brief moment away from the task of raising the *Normandie*. In the background you hear the clatter of cranes which are lowering debris from the hull to scrap barges in the slip, the same slip where the Cunarder *Queen Mary* used to dock. There is a roar of heavy engines nearby. What kind of engines are those, Mr Gates?'

Gates leaned forward.

'You're hearing air compressors that run the power tools. And that deeper sound is mud pumps.'

'What's that banging? That *hiss-bang, hiss-bang*.'

'That's a pile driver. They're sinking a new mooring pole for one of the work barges.'

'I hear a lot of hammering, as though a house was being built.'

'Carpenters are building a diving stage – a platform above the water the divers will work from.'

'And Mr Collins, what is it that the mud pumps are pumping in those great dark streams into the barges?'

'Mud.'

There was a second's silence and Gates saw panic in Cordi's eyes. Dead air. He leaned closer to the microphone. 'It's actually a mixture of mud, broken glass, spun glass insulation, cork ash, cinders and large pieces of furniture.'

'Debris?'

'Some of that too,' Charlie said.

'We're pumping for two reasons,' Gates interrupted. 'To clear her hull, and to harden the mud she's lying on so that we can patch the holes in her hull – open ports. The mud is very soupy and until it firms up, the divers can't get to the holes.'

'It's difficult to describe the vastness of this fallen ship. If you could stand it on end it would be almost as tall as the Empire State Building. Mr Gates, can you explain exactly how your salvagemen intend to pick it up?'

'She'll pick herself up, when the time comes,' Gates said. 'We're removing excess weight. Then we'll seal her hull – watertight – and pump out the water. And then she'll float and right herself.'

'I can see that she might float,' said Cordi. 'But why do you say she will *right* herself?'

'Because she's a *ship*. She just doesn't happen to look like one at the moment.'

Cordi gave him a curious look before she returned the microphone to her own lips. 'And there we have it . . . men working to raise the *Normandie* to make her a troop ship again to carry soldiers from America to England so that someday free men will go back to Europe. Thank you, Mr Steven Gates. This is Cordelia Grey in New York for the BBC News Talks Unit.'

'Could I ask you a question?'

'Yes, Mr Gates?'

'What are you doing for dinner tonight?'

'Steven, it's so wonderful to see you.

Gates took her in over a glass of champagne.

With a gesture at the restaurant, she added, 'You're also as loony as ever.'

He'd found this restaurant all the way over on Ninth Avenue, which was owned by former *Normandie* crewmen. He had ordered champagne and had tried to re-create the time they'd spent on the *Normandie*, no mean task in a crowded little room with red-check tablecloths.

'Excuse the wine,' said Gates. 'But the Germans are behind in their shipments. When did you get to New York?'

'Last spring.'

'How come you didn't call?'

'I met you for five days three years ago. I'm not in the habit of calling up relative strangers.'

'I called you in London.'

'Yes, I was away. What were you doing in London?'

'Work.'

'Ships?'

'It was kind of hush-hush because we weren't in it yet, but I was doing liaison between your designers and our yards. I got involved with some of the new escorts.'

'But how did you get on the salvage?'

'Remember Rik van Slough? The Dutchman?'

'. . . Yes.'

'He's become a big operator in New York. Owns a tug and a scrapyard and a bunch of barges and God knows what else. Uncle Richard says he's going to own the harbour by the time the war is over. He gave me the job.'

'What about designing ships?'

'I'm out of that for a while.' He looked away and she recalled what she'd thought this morning the moment she'd seen him before he saw her. He was unto himself, a man alone. Lonely?'

'Do you have a girl?'

Gates turned to her and the same grin spread across his face. 'I waited.'

'I beg your pardon?'

'For you.'

'Don't be silly.'

'No, I don't have a girl. Do you have somebody?'

'I did. He was killed. Alec. I told you about him.'

'I'm sorry . . . How's your brother?'

'He was killed last spring.'

He reached across the table and took her hand. His was much stronger than she'd remembered. He'd filled out and where he'd been thin he was now lean and powerful-looking. Could he have killed German agents he didn't trust? Could he be an agent? Physically, yes. Was he tough enough? Tougher than he'd seemed three years ago. But then again, so was she.

'Do you date much?' she asked.

'Not much. I've really been working all the time. Lately on the ship and before with Uncle Richard. We went nonstop from the day we got back to New York. Uncle Richard got involved with Liberty ships and the business really grew.'

'Were you able to work on your . . . *American Glory*, wasn't it?'

'Not a line. She'd a dead duck, for a while.'

'Is that why you went to the *Normandie*?'

Gates looked at her and she thought she'd scored a truth. 'I guess . . . How long are you going to be in New York?'

'Quite a while, I hope.'

'Great. Where are you staying, the Meurice?'

Cordi was surprised. She had asked him to pick her up at the BBC studio in Rockefeller Center to lend reality to her cover. 'As a matter of fact, yes. How did you know?'

Gates shrugged. 'Always been the hotel for English actors and you said you'd been an actress. Is it comfortable?'

'Oh, rather cramped. The company took a small suite I share with Duncan and Mark. I have a small room of my own, but it's not much more than digs.'

'I'll bet it's palatial compared to mine. I live in a rooming house between Ninth and Tenth.'

'What about your family's place?'

'I left under a cloud, as they say, quitting the company. And this cop who was investigating the fire mentioned he owned this rooming house, and there I am.'

'What fire?'

'The *Normandie*. He came checking on Charlie because of his left-wing record. Turned out to be a decent guy. He's been helping me.'

'What do you mean?'

Gates hesitated. 'Helped me get settled, found me a room. Do you still dance?'

'Not much lately.'

'John Kirby's playing at the Lounge Restaurant at the Waldorf. We'll have to get dressed up some night and see if you remember anything.'

'I'm a little rusty for the Waldorf.'

'That's what you said on the *Normandie*.' Gates looked at his watch. 'Hey, come on, Muggsy Spannier's over at Jack Dempsey's. We'll catch the show and dance there.'

'Now?'

'Sure. It's just over on Broadway.'

'What do you think?' asked Weatherburn. He seemed tense.

'I don't know what to think.'

'Why the devil did you let him bring you home?'

'He guessed I lived here.'

'What? How?'

'He knew it was an actors' hotel.'

'And you believed that?'

'It was a surprise, but I think it could be true.'

Weatherburn eyed her, and Cordi was suddenly aware that she'd dressed very carefully for the evening. 'That's nice perfume,' he said. 'Still taken with him?'

'Of course not.'

'Be careful, Cordi.'

20

'Where to?' asked the cabdriver, and Gates, still looking at the doors to Cordi's hotel, shook his head and said, 'I have no idea.'

The driver nodded. 'I know what you mean. She your girl?'

'Isn't she beautiful?' Gates handed him some money. 'I think I'll walk.'

When he got back to his room, still too full of Cordi to sleep, he found a note from Jim Tweed: 'The last of the *Lafayette*'s black gang are leaving tomorrow on the light cruiser *Binghamton*. She's in the Bayonne Annex. Why don't you go ask them about that elevator?'

At dawn he telephoned Charlie at the townhouse. 'I'll be late for work.'

'Good night?' asked Charlie.

'What? Yes . . . tell Rik I'll be late . . . '

At the Bayonne Annex he found the three sailors – a boilermaker's mate, a machinist and a fireman first class – in the *Binghamton*'s gleaming new boiler room. They'd just stood down from inspection. The captain had moved aft to the ninety-thousand-horsepower turbines, and they were feeling good. Gates didn't say who he was, he just asked if they'd served on the *Lafayette*, but they knew immediately what he was after.

'We told it to the Senate. Then we told it all over again to the House of Representatives. Then we told it to the navy. Now what the hell can we tell you that we didn't tell them?'

'Who took the second forward baggage elevator down to F deck?'

'I sure as hell didn't.'

'How'd you get down to the boiler room that day?'

'We all walked. Right?' The other two nodded. 'They was moving furniture into the hold. We usually walked. The civilians always had the elevators tied up.'

'Did you try to take it up when the smoke drove you out of the boiler room?'

'Nobody gets in an elevator in a fire. Nobody with brains, anyhow.'

'Which,' remarked the boilermaker's mate, 'didn't stop Denny McGuire.'

'Who's he?'

'Third oiler. Denny figured he'd ride up and beat us to the top. You see, us four – the three of us and Denny – we got separated from the rest of the gang. We got lost on E deck and headed forward. Anyhow, we ran into the elevator and found the companionway next to it and started up.'

Gates fumbled a notepad from his pocket. 'McGuire? Denny McGuire, third oiler. Right?'

They exchanged glances. 'Yeah, right.'

'Did he beat you to the top?'

'No. He came running after us a little later. Yelling his head off 'cause the smoke is thick enough to cut and he's scared. We waited till he caught up and got out on the foredeck. I saw you there, mister, by the ladder. Then you ran back. Forget something?'

'My wallet.'

'I remember you. You didn't have a coat and you were wearing a fancy suit and freezing your ass off.'

'Yes, I gave it to a guy . . . So what changed Denny McGuire's mind?'

'About what?'

'About taking the elevator.'

'He said it was busted. But he was like that. You know, one of those guys who always blames machinery. Never his fault. I figured he just couldn't start it, the French gear was pretty weird.'

Gates felt the excitement rising, moving past the exhaustion of the sleepless night.

'But he didn't testify in any of the reports I read.'

'None.'

'Why not?'

'The day after the fire an oiler got sick on a DE heading out to cover an eastbound convoy. They grabbed Denny.'

'Where's he serving now?'

The fireman first class who'd done most of the talking gave Gates a long look. 'In a better place than you or me, sir. She took a torp down the throat off Iceland.'

Gates spent Sunday telephoning shipyards, trying to trace down the men who'd operated the burners that ignited the fire. He got nowhere. Many of the yards were operating but their office staffs had taken the day off and no one was around to check records.

Back on the *Normandie* Monday morning, he found van Slough a thousand feet out on the stern, preparing the day's diving. He'd been curt on Saturday when Gates arrived late and he was still brusque. 'I got a note saying Captain Tooker's looking for you.'

'Charlie mentioned something about that.'

'What's up?'

'I don't know. What would he want to see me for?'

'You'd better go now. He's not a man to keep waiting.'

The Otter watched Gates hurry down to the slip, where the general contractor's office barge was moored, and had a sudden incongruous memory of himself running down the slopes of some Austrian hill town, all long legs and slippery sandals, to meet Uncle Willy at the train, excited to be seeing him, but apprehensive too. Would he be allowed along with his mother when she went wherever it was Uncle Willy was taking her that summer? In retrospect it seemed he always went, but then he wasn't sure . . .

He preferred to keep Gates alive, but while much of Gates's blundering about looking for sabotage might well eventually help set him up for the fall, it was also fast becoming an irritant. He hoped that Captain Tooker would unwittingly take Gates off his hands because if he didn't, Gates, he now decided, would have to have an accident.

Immediately after the fire at T and C Trucking, he had set Gates up with Tooker, passing the word in a roundabout way about Gates's activities, mentioning at the same time Gates's encyclopaedic knowledge of the *Normandie*. It was his hope, having seen Tooker in action, that the wreckmaster would take care of Gates in the best possible way – divert him, unknowingly, from his poking around, and yet keep Gates close enough for the Otter to use him when and where the need arose.

And the need would arise. Because the pressure was on. He had lost two radios. They knew now of his existence in New York, they even had an idea where in New York. What other reason for the British to send a counter-espionage team under a phony BBC front to the *Normandie*?'

They'd made a mistake in their choice of driver. The Otter had watched the whole scene from a short distance. Uncle Willy had demanded from the beginning of his childhood that the Otter be taught to fight with his hands – the best spy was a spy who needed no weapon. The Otter had excelled, and he had recognized in Mark St George another professional, expert with his hands, even before Cordi Grey stepped out of the car. Was she still the frightened young dupe of British Intelligence she had been when Uncle Willy sent him to destroy their Geneva station?

Was Cordi Grey the girl who had been watching T and C Trucking?

Was hers the group he'd come so close to wiping out in the fire?

Likely. But three things were certain. The British were

291

on to his existence. He might be miles ahead of them, but they'd keep hunting . . .

The Otter surveyed the hull, lying at the edge of Manhattan like a fallen skyscraper. He would stay ahead. He had his lair in the *Normandie* and a shield in Steven Gates.

21

Standing quietly, waiting to be acknowledged by the legendary Captain Tooker, Gates realized for the first time how a young draughtsman would feel in the presence of the man he called Uncle Richard, wondering what the inventor of the Prince turbine and every other high-pressure marine propulsion device of the past twenty years wanted with him.

Captain Tooker was also standing, bent over his desk with his hands in the pockets of his baggy trousers. A light-coloured hat was tipped back on his head, as if he'd either just come in or was heading out. He wore a white shirt and a tie. At last he looked up.

'Gates?'

'Yes, captain.'

'It's come to my attention that several months ago you dived to the bottom of a forward section of B deck.'

Gates drew in his breath and made no answer. How in hell had he found out?

'I'm told you're not a diver.'

'No, sir.'

Then why are you diving on my wreck?

Gates said nothing; there was nothing to say.

'Don't waste my time denying it. I've already dealt with those knuckleheads who took you down.'

'It wasn't really their – '

'Have you heard we're starting a civilian diving school?'

'Yes, sir.'

'Want to train? Do you want to be a diver?'

'Yes, sir. But – ' Fear and excitement went side by side down his spine as he thought of the blackness in the helmet –

'But what?'

'I've been told I'm too light for the work.'

'Bull. Working in the dark takes more brains than muscle. They're expecting you at the school. See my secretary if you want it.'

'*Thank you*, sir.'

'Don't thank me. I need people who know what they're doing.'

Gates couldn't believe his luck. Tooker glanced at his watch and Gates began backing towards the door.

'Gates, let me tell you something about that craziness on B deck. There's two kinds of divers in the salvage business. Bold divers. And old divers. I've been in this business forty years. Three of my boys are diving on this wreck. And my old man was raising ships for forty years before I was born. And none of us – not him, not my sons, not me – have ever met an *old*, bold diver.'

Tooker looked down at his papers and made a note and Gates eased out the door. An intercom buzzed, and the male secretary answered, 'Yes, sir.' He handed Gates a letter for the diving instructor. 'Get over there. You're late.'

Gates took the letter, shook his head, still astonished. 'Just like that?' He felt his face freezing in a taut grin.

'A couple of calls from your bigshot friends helped, but the captain said something about having pulled worse stunts when he was your age.'

He called Cordi as soon as he got off the pier. She wasn't at the number she'd given him for her Rockefeller Centre office so he tried the Meurice, where after some confusion the hotel desk put him through.

'Hey, don't they know you live there?'

'There's a new man on the desk. I had a lovely time the other night. Thank you.'

'Listen, can you come and celebrate?'

'Celebrate what?'

'I'm in diving school.'

'You're joking.'

'I'm going to be a salvage diver. I got invited in by the wreckmaster. I thought he was going to fire me for making an unauthorized dive but he sent me to school instead. Come on, I'll take you to the theatre and we'll have supper at Sardi's. Have you seen *Angel Street*?'

The *maître d'hôtel* at Sardi's seated them at a banquette along the left wall. Cordi cast her eye around the busy red room and asked, 'How do you manage such a table?'

'Mostly, because they appreciate beautiful women, and partly because that old gent remembers he put his children through college on my old man's tips.' He ordered Moët.

'Again? Don't you drink anything normal?'

'Last time we were celebrating you and tonight we're celebrating the best thing that's happened to me since you.'

'Thank you twice. By the way, aren't you a little scared?'

'Damn right. Mostly of claustrophobia. Diving in a hard hat in the Hudson River is like being trapped alone in a dark elevator. Some of the guys went crazy the minute they put on the helmet.'

'What about you?'

'Scary as hell, but so far I think I can handle it . . . at least I knew what to expect; I dived once last summer. It's a common problem, complicated by the complete darkness underwater. My class started with thirty guys and is down to twenty already – '

'Last summer? I don't understand. You dived without training?'

'Craziness. Got drunk with some divers and they took me down.'

'But why?'

'. . . Just to see what it was like.' Gates looked around the room, then turned back to her. 'I asked the captain's secretary what had happened to the guys who'd taken me down. Had he fired them? "*Fire* them? You think we're going to fire two trained salvage drivers just because they're drunk and crazy . . .?"'

The chief engineer of the Deutsche Werft U-boat factory at Hamburg ran to the front gate, fear corroding pits in his ample stomach, worrying who had told what lies to whom. A frightened guard had just reported the unannounced arrival of an officer of the Reich Security Administration. Whether it was Gestapo, SS or SD, an unscheduled visit couldn't be good. He prayed to God that it was only about slave labour arrangements.

Skidding around the last corner, white shirt flapping from his waistband, the chief engineer saw a uniformed driver helping a small, hunched figure out of a large black car. He gasped relief, stopped running, stuffed his shirt into his pants and strutted to the car.

Admiral Wilhelm Canaris.

An honour. It was said that the admiral reported directly to Adolf Hitler. It was said that he ran German counter-intelligence. And it was known he had set up the *Etappendienst* – the secret supply organization that provisioned U-boats in neutral ports around the world.

But among *unterseeboot* engineers, Admiral Canaris was hailed for achievements that predated the *Etappendienst* and his work in the Abwehr. The Type VII C submarine – the eight-hundred-ton, two-hundred-twenty-five-foot work-horse of the North Atlantic raiding fleet – was the main product of the Hamburg Deutsche Werft. The VII Cs had been modified over and over, strengthened, made faster, more powerful, more deadly, but each boat stemmed from the same fine design that owed its existence to secret experiments in Spanish and Argentine yards back in the 1920s, when the Versailles armament restrictions were still enforced against Germany. And the man who'd arranged those experiments was Wilhelm Canaris.

Canaris asked to see the works. He seemed older than his fifty-five years — shabbily dressed, a short, slight, weary and rather sad-looking figure lost in an old naval greatcoat that bore neither insignia nor signs of recent cleaning. He kept it buttoned against the cold wind from the River Elbe. An aide, cheerful by contrast, attended him.

Although Canaris was sniffing into a crumpled handkerchief and obviously suffering from a bad cold, he was unfailingly courteous, speaking with soft gestures, listening without interrupting, gathering a crowd like iron filings as the engineers flocked to show him the slipways on the oily river shore, the stocks holding half-completed hulls, and the workshops where diesel engines and electric motors from other plants were tested before being broken down and reassembled in the hulls.

The Type VII Cs were succeeding brilliantly for the second time in the war. The previous year they had dominated the western approaches to England, devastating the Allied shipping that kept England in the war. Now they were supreme along the American shores, sinking the merchantmen within sight of the cities that loaded their war cargoes, although kills were down since the Americans had adopted the British convoy system in their own waters.

But, the engineer admitted, the VII Cs were small for transocean work and limited in their torpedo and fuel capacity, which was an increasingly serious problem as the English tightened their control of the sea's surface.

These limitations were addressed in the Deutsche Werft's experimental sections, and they, apparently, were what the admiral had come to see. He was extremely interested and several times startled the engineers with his up-to-date knowledge of new developments, particularly the *Milch Kuh* supply boats, a fattened Type VII modified to carry enormous amounts of fuel and spare torpedoes underwater to the Atlantic raiders.

He seemed to admire everything he saw, but when

an engineer showed him the new designs for heavily armoured conning towers and multiple-barrel and anti-aircraft guns, Canaris offered, for the first time, an objection. He repeated the engineer's last words.

'Anti-aircraft guns?'

'*Ja*, Herr Admiral. We will increase firepower until the U-boat creates a virtual flak trap no bomber could penetrate.'

'A flak trap?' The little spymaster looked amused. A small smile broke over his long face and his sad eyes brightened. 'Why would a submarine need a flak trap?'

'To fight the bomber.'

'An aeroplane?' Canaris asked, astonishment ringing in his voice.

The engineers exchanged glances. Then one ventured, 'As you know, sir, they attack our boats on the surface.'

'On the surface?'

'*Ja*, Herr Admiral.'

'But why are our boats on the surface? The Allies have aeroplanes and destroyers and corvettes with ten centimetre radar and asdic. They control the surface.'

'But to shadow a convoy until night, and to line up a shot and call in the *Wolf* pack, our boats must make ten, even fifteen knots, sir.'

'Fifteen knots? The answer is not more guns, and not heavy armour, but fifteen knots where we don't need guns. Underwater.'

Again the engineers exchanged glances. Eventually one looked side to side, like a doe sniffing the wind, and murmured cautiously, 'The Führer has postponed work in that area.'

Another concurred. 'We had a Walther engine in that boat.' He nodded at a bulbous hull with animal curves, then added excitedly, 'They sent us a defective motor from Kiel. We haven't received a replacement in months.'

Canaris nodded sympathetically. 'I imagine the Führer might change his position rather soon. And when he does,

I'm sure you'll meet the challenge. Though personally, I think you'll have better success with diesel-electrics than hydrogen peroxide.'

He watched their reactions and several faces confirmed what he had learned at other *Unterseeboot* yards. The exotic hydrogen peroxide, closed-cycle Walther turbines suffered too many problems to put them into production soon enough to help. Electric motors were excellent if they could be recharged, and a snorkel device, recently copied from the Dutch, might be the answer to running the diesels while the boats remained just beneath the surface.

Canaris smiled at the attentive assemblage. 'Show me your *'Seehunds.'*

They passed near the river on the way to the experimental *Seehund* section, and paused to watch a U-boat, returning from its mission, enter the repair yards. Her crew stood on the forward deck casing, returning the salute of the dockyard workers, their backs to their mutilated conning tower.

The officers stood on the riddled steel structure itself and Canaris thought they resembled nothing more than scavengers in a scrapyard, surrounded by twisted steel railings, blasted anti-aircraft guns, and jaggedly torn bulkheads. By a miracle the pressure hull hadn't been breached, but the bandaged officers, two with head dressings and another with his arm in a sling, attested to the ferocity of the attack.

'Terrible,' said the engineer. 'Terrible.'

'That's what comes from fighting aeroplanes,' said Canaris. 'There is such a thing as being too brave.'

Canaris thought that naming midget submarines' *'Seehunds'* was unfair to the seals. The sole connection between the ugly midgets and the graceful mammals was their ability to operate in the shallow waters of a harbour. Whereas the VII Cs had the sleek lines of hunting sharks, and the *Milch Kuh* swelled with rich mammalian nourishment, the little

Seehunds seemed all sharp edges and ugly protuberances. They bristled with jutting fins, disjointed rudders, naked propellers, and grasping torpedo racks.

Many hulls were empty shells, still in the early stages of experimental design. Others sat idle, waiting for Walther turbines. He spotted what he was looking for at a distance, and knew it immediately. Though his pulse quickened, he dutifully examined the intervening boats, moving all the while closer.

'Take the rest of them over there,' he murmured to his aide, then fell in beside the chief engineer and waited for Heinrich to draw the others off.

Canaris steered the engineer to the *Seehund* and circled it slowly. It was a flat boat, nearly fifty feet long, but less than six feet high from keel to deck. No conning tower broke its smooth lines, only a low hatch. It had four internal torpedo tubes – two forward and two aft. A skilled captain might fire his second salvo before the first hit – a distinct advantage against a capital ship, and a capability which put this *Seehund* in a superior class to her smaller sisters.

'The crew lies prone,' said the engineer. 'Steering and aiming the torpedoes is done by periscope.'

'Crew?'

'Two men. Helmsman-torpedo aimer and engineer. It can be operated and fought by one. But because of its long range and submersion time, it can carry an engineer for maintenance.'

'How much time would you need to make her operational?'

The engineer looked pained. 'We can't make her operational until the Walther engine is perfected.'

Canaris fixed him with his dark eyes and lowered his voice to a whisper, drawing the man closer. 'I want electric motors.'

'I'm sorry, Admiral. But there isn't sufficient room for the diesels.'

'Diesels?'

'To charge the batteries for the electric motors.'

'I don't want diesels. I want electric motors. I want silent belt drive. Dead silent. And I want all the batteries you can wedge into her.'

'But how will the batteries be recharged if there are no diesels for surface running, sir?'

'There will be no surface running.'

The engineer said, 'Yes, Herr Admiral,' but he looked worried. 'Sir, you still must charge the batteries. Particularly if you demand high speed underwater.'

'I do demand high speed underwater.'

'Well, how will you charge the batteries?'

'With electricity, of course.'

'But the charger will only last a few hours, especially at speed. There must be a source of electricity.'

'Perhaps a long extension cord.'

The engineer smiled jerkily, not sure it was a joke.

Canaris stroked the steel hull. 'Has she a name?'

The engineer looked relieved to change the subject. 'She's designated VB.62, but I call her the Otter.'

Canaris looked at him sharply, startled by the coincidence, but realizing quickly it could only be that. They used all sorts of animal names for the miniature submarines: Beaver, Pike, Marten. It was perhaps a good omen. He walked around the front of it and inspected the blunt bow with the broad nostrils that were torpedo tubes. 'Yes,' he said, slowly. 'I see that. She's much more an otter than a seal ... You like animals? I like a man who likes animals.'

Encouraged by Canaris's sudden warmth, and his obvious admiration for the boat, the engineer blurted, 'You might call her my pet. I designed her myself, thinking we'd have the Walther soon. She's designed to be very fast, dive instantaneously and, like an otter, stay down a long long time.'

'When can you have the electric motors installed?'

'But how will you charge the batteries, sir?'

301

'How will be our little secret,' murmured Canaris. 'As secret as everything you and I have discussed. No one is to know.'

The engineer swallowed. 'Yes, Herr Admiral.'

'No one. If anyone asks – anyone at all – you are filling an order for the Germania Werke at Kiel. My aide will create the necessary documents and stay with you until the job is finished. Speed is of the essence. As well as secrecy, which is why we will call her a *Seehund*, so as not to draw attention.'

The engineer nodded vigorously, anxious to please, but Canaris could tell he was troubled. Who could blame him? What factory manager balancing shortages of material and manpower against the *Kriegsmarine*'s voracious demands for more U-boats wanted interference from the chief of the Abwehr? What would prevent the manager, a month from now, from confessing to Admiral Dönitz that the reason for a delayed U-boat delivery was a special request from the Abwehr?

He took the man's arm and led him away from the Otter. 'You know, I was up at Kiel yesterday. An old friend manages one of the propulsion works. He could barely park his car for the crates of Walther turbines. I'll have him send you a few.'

'Thank you, Herr Admiral. Thank you.'

'Have you enough hydrogen peroxide?'

'Not a drop at the moment, sir. I'm sure we'll find some.'

'No, no, no. I'll see what I can do.' He extracted a crumpled piece of paper from his greatcoat pocket, made a note with a pencil stub and shoved the paper and pencil back into his coat.

'Thank you, sir.'

'And thank *you*. I trust my aide will be useful to you and comfortable while he is in Hamburg.'

'He'll be a guest in my own home, Herr Admiral.'

'You're very kind.' He did not say *Heil Hitler*.

His dachshunds were standing in the back of his car, their noses pressed to the glass, barking joyous welcome. He repeated final instructions to his aide and made the man repeat them twice. He got into the car, lowered the window. 'Call me if you have any doubts.'

'Yes, sir.'

'And Heinrich?'

'Yes, sir.'

'Under no circumstances are you to communicate anything about this matter by radio.'

'But surely the Enigma —'

'Nothing.'

'Allied intercepts?'

Canaris shook his head. 'The Enigma code is secure. It's not *the* Allies I'm concerned with. I don't want any of *our* allies running to Hitler with this. Not yet.'

The driver had kept the engine and heater running, and Canaris opened his greatcoat as the big Mercedes drove out of the boatworks and through Hamburg's cobblestoned streets.

The dachshunds lay on either side of him, tails curled up on the back of the seat, noses on his bony knees, their intelligent eyes fixed on his face. He stroked each behind its ears and after a while he talked to them — a habit that came from affection and a need to order his thoughts.

'Hitler will be pleased, but only by the results. It would be suicide to tell him before it is done. And my execution if he finds out. But when it is done, the Abwehr will be vindicated.' He rubbed their knobby spines. That would take care of Himmler, who was trying to absorb the Abwehr into his Reich Security Administration.

'The Americans will be sickened,' he told the dogs. 'And their transport will be paralysed. They'll blame the British because the *Queen Mary* is a British ship, British manned, British defended. The Allies will split. And Germany *will* win the war.' In his excitement, Canaris rubbed too hard and the dogs began to squirm. He told them he was sorry.

22

'Coming at you, Gates,' said the diving instructor.

Cradled in massive iron clamps, an eight-foot timber sank ponderously into the ink-black water.

Thirty feet down, Gates moved uneasily on a platform he couldn't see and raised his hands, his fingers reaching as blindly as a sea anemone. Another diver, an advanced student like Gates, working while finishing the diving course, waited on the platform – invisible. Helmet phones connected them to an instructor topside who was leading them through the construction of a watertight bulkhead between two adjacent vertical decks, step by sightless step.

The difference between working out of water and in water was the difference between fellowship and isolation. Out of the water, tools were nearby and handy, men could gang together quickly for an extra lift and pass warnings to stand clear with a shout. In the water, the diver had to carry his tools with him or waste precious diving time while those he couldn't carry or hadn't known he would need were painstakingly lowered into the dark water through the labyrinth of docks and passageways. Every warning, and even the simplest request for assistance, had to be relayed by telephone through the tenders topside and back to the other divers below. And to keep track of where he was, a diver had to memorize by touch the feel of everything he passed.

'Got it.' Gates was taller so the timber hit his outstretched fingers first. When it hung a foot below its slot, chain falls were lowered down either side of the partially completed bulkhead. Gates and his partner felt for the dangling cables and hooked them to chain bridles on the clamps. He squeezed his eyes shut and opened them again on equal darkness.

'Okay,' said the instructor. 'Push the timber against the deck frames.'

Gates had done well in the diving course because his mathematical, orderly memory helped him work in the dark, but here his light build put him at a disadvantage. The invisible student beside him was built broad and square. His end of the timber was snugged against his deck frame while Gates was still struggling.

'Ready?' asked the instructor.

'Give me a sec.' He heaved hard, nearly fell off the platform and heaved again when the swaying timber's momentum swung to his advantage. 'Okay, ready.'

'Get your mitts out of the way. Up she goes.'

The men topside hauled on the chain falls. The timber rose, sliding up the two deck frames. Gates guided the spine atop the timber into the corresponding notch in the bottom of the previously set timber. Gates felt the joint with a hook bolt he'd fished from his worksack. 'It's in tight.'

'Bolt it.'

Gates hooked the bolt around the deck frame, pushed it through a pre-drilled hole in the timber, screwed on a washer and nut and tightened it with a wrench.

'Okay, you guys. Come on up.'

'I can do some more,' said Gates.

'You've been down four hours, hotshot.'

'What's the latest on Gates?' Weatherburn asked.

'He's finished the diving school. He's working for van Slough again. Diving with him,' Cordi said. 'What about van Slough?'

'Something just came in from London this afternoon. I want you try it on van Slough.'

'Try what?'

'One of our agents parachuted into Holland reports that the Dutch underground has a test they put to people they suspect of being Germans masquerading as Dutch.'

'What kind of test?' Cordi asked.

'A word. A Dutch name. Here.' He spelled it out on paper. 'It's a resort city on the North Sea. The bloody Hun can't pronounce the word.'

'Are you having me on?'

'No. It's the damnedest thing, but the German can't get his tongue around the word like a Dutchman, no matter how fluent his Dutch, which of course is very similar to German anyway.'

'Are you sure?'

'The underground stake their lives on it.'

'Quitting time,' van Slough called, the reluctance to stop heavy in his voice.

'I'll do one more if you want,' Gates said, slumping exhaustedly on the diving platform. They'd been working side by side all day, erecting wooden forms underwater to retain the sealing cement which would be poured around the joints where the watertight bulkhead timbers butted into the decks.

'No, you won't,' Charlie said. Rik's tender, Marty, nodded agreement. 'Both of you have been down too long. Somebody's going to get hurt.'

'*Ja*, I suppose.' Rik handed his helmet to Marty and removed his brass boots. 'Okay, see you tomorrow. Early.' He hurried off in the direction of his tugboat, which, when it wasn't towing, he kept moored in the slip near the *Normandie*'s stern.

Gates hadn't moved. Charlie helped him out of helmet and suit and arranged them for the morning. Gates stood on the platform in his long woollen underwear, still not moving.

'You look beat.'

'I'm dying.'

'Does that come from chasing Cordi around town or Rik underwater?'

'He's a damned machine.' Gates bowed in the direction of Rik van Slough. 'Lord of the Stern Empire.'

Charlie's laugh echoed in the steel caverns. The Stern Empire had become their joke as van Slough concentrated his diving, cutting and carpentry crews at the aft end of the ship, having convinced the salvage company that he could keep a closer eye on his various jobs if they were clustered.

'Put some clothes on. Let's get out of here.'

The lockers were at the end of the diving platform. Gates dressed.

'Want to come home for dinner?' asked Charlie.

Gates thought about the warm dining room in his mother's house. 'Where's Uncle Richard?'

'Washington.'

'Right.'

'Don't forget to tell Kay how well I tend you.'

Less than twelve hours after Kay Collins had learned that her brother was in the civilian diving school, Charlie was out of the wheelhouse of Rik van Slough's *Hollandia* and in the same school – training to be a diver's tender. Van Slough had hired them both when they'd qualified, on the condition that he could use Charlie for other jobs once they'd found a backup tender for Gates, an arrangement which would not get back to Kay.

It took ten minutes to negotiate the wooden catwalks to the gangway in the centre of the ship and out the pier, which was crowded with homeward bound workmen and stragglers for the next shift. A pile-up around the front door slowed things further. Charlie asked if Gates had talked to the burner he'd been looking for.

'I haven't had a chance since I've been diving. He's over in the Hoboken Ship Yard, but he's working when I'm working and I can't find where he lives.'

They kept repeating a new song on the radio, 'I'll Be Home

307

for Christmas', and it was making Gates feel both lonely and romantic. Cordi worked odd hours as a correspondent, and very late on the nights that her unit beamed programmes live by shortwave to London. He telephoned Wally and talked a while and then asked to speak to his mother.

'Aunt Louise, may I bring a friend to dinner on Christmas?'

'Of course.'

'Her name is Cordi Grey, she's English and — '

'I know all about her.'

'You do?'

'Everyone wants to meet her.'

She wore a dress of green velvet on Christmas Day, and her auburn hair was a rich frame for her high, pale brow. Gates had never walked so proudly into the Strattons' drawing room — a high-ceilinged, cavernous chamber packed with antiques fetched home from Europe in a hundred years of travel. When Gates and Cordi arrived early, the still-small gathering was almost lost in it.

Wally greeted them with a lopsided smile. He was stirring a martini pitcher, which he did whenever he got drunk before his own party.

Vera Gates came in with Richard Prince and Kay and Charlie followed. She managed a quick word for Steven in the confusion of introductions. 'She looks lovely, I can't wait to meet her and I promise to be good.'

'Merry Christmas.'

'Come to the house later, we have presents for you. Be nice to your uncle. You can bring Cordi if we haven't terrified her by then. I have a present for her.'

Richard Prince was already in conversation with Cordi, and it looked by their animation as if they'd picked up where they'd left off on the *Normandie* crossing three years and four months ago. 'Hello, Uncle Richard. Merry Christmas.'

They shook hands, but Gates couldn't meet his eye. He said, 'Mother, may I present Cordi Grey. Cordi, my mother, Vera Gates.'

'I'm pleased to meet you, Mrs Gates.' She had a point of colour in each cheek, and seemed to be enjoying herself.

'Please call me Vera. It's lovely to meet you at last. Steven told me about you on the *Normandie* years ago.'

Gates reached gratefully for the martini that Wally was holding out to him.

It was a large party that reminded Cordi of Christmas in London before the war with everyone home from school and picking up where they'd left off at the end of the previous summer. She was aware of how curious Steven's family was about her. Somehow the word had got around that he was becoming involved with her. Or were they suspicious of this English girl who'd suddenly reappeared among them?

'Cordi?'

She turned around. Steven had left her to get another drink. It was van Slough, smiling down at her.

'Do you remember me?' he asked. 'Rik van Slough.'

'Of course. How are you?' she said, shaking his hand. 'Merry Christmas.'

'I was sorry I missed your radio interview. They're still talking about your method of arrival on the ship. It's very good to see you.'

He looked very prosperous and quite handsome, and he was smiling down easily at her. She wondered how he'd react when she manoeuvred him into the underground's Dutch test.

'Are you friends of the Strattons?' she asked.

'Not until today. They heard from Kay and Charlie that I was alone. They're inviting Christmas orphans, so here I am . . . '

Gates saw them together and hurried back. 'Found each other?'

'We certainly did,' said van Slough.

The drawing room filled rapidly, sprinkled with uniforms. Gates didn't recognize many of the officers, and assumed that the Strattons, like most New Yorkers this Christmas that marked a year of war, had opened their home to out-of-towners stationed in the city.

At dinner, served at two tables wedged into the large dining room, Gates and Cordi and van Slough and some younger officers were at Wally's table. Wally put Cordi on one side and a pretty girl on the other, which left Gates between one of Wally's sisters, an amiable chatterbox he'd known all his life, and a sad-faced matron whose husband had been killed recently during the Torch landings in Tunisia.

A pair of ensigns, one naval, one Coast Guard under naval command, were both reserve officers assigned to New York Harbor defence. They competed in trying to tell Cordi and the pretty girl all they knew about submarine nets and aquaphones. Gates thought they should be court-martialled for babbling.

'I get a kind of daytime nightmare. I see a German block ship steaming up the Ambrose Channel,' said the Coast Guardsman, abruptly serious.

'What's a block ship?' asked Wally's sister.

'A ship you sink in a channel to block it,' he replied. 'I see it coming in at dawn or in a fog – which is most of the time in the Lower Bay, real pea soup – when they can't see a damned thing from the forts and she's got a German destroyer covering her. And we come out in our little toy boats and the destroyer pops us off one by one and the block ship turns cross-channel and the Nazis scuttle her right in the middle. I mean, my boat's got a fifty-calibre machine gun and a one-pound heave-to cannon on it. Al Capone was better armed.'

'What would happen?'

'Close the harbour for a month.'

'Would it, Steven?' Cordi asked. Gates had been looking

down the table at her. He straightened up as the ensign turned to him.

'Here's a man who knows more about strategy than I do, I'm sure.'

'It would take a huge block ship to close it entirely. The channel's two thousand feet wide, but it would certainly slow things down. The problem for the Germans is distance. They're a long way away to bring any kind of attack. I think it's significant that the closing of the harbour for a day last month because of mines was the only time it's happened since the war began. But don't you clear entering ships three or four miles from Sandy Hook?'

'We try to.'

'Rik?' Cordi called across the table. 'Wally and I were just discussing Holland . . . ' She'd forced the conversation some to be sure Wally wouldn't blow her ploy . . . said van Slough was from Holland, she understood, and so forth . . .

'*She* was discussing Holland,' Wally said. 'I was pretending to listen while I grabbed her knee under the table – oh, Steven, you're here, I thought you were at the other table.'

'What about Holland?' Rik was smiling.

'What is that holiday resort on the North Sea?'

'Zandvoort? Near Haarlem.' He added with a laugh, 'That's the Haarlem with two *a*s.'

'No,' said Cordi. 'Not Zandvoort. You know the one I mean. It's got a huge hotel right on the beach. It looks, I'm told, like Atlantic City. You know. The one with the unpronounceable name.'

Rik picked up his wine glass and drank.

Then, instead of answering Cordi, he slowly took his wallet out of his jacket and fished inside. The others watched curiously. Cordi, Gates noticed, seemed strangely intent. Van Slough opened an inside flap. A circle was worn in the leather. Whatever he kept in that flap had been there a long time. He extracted a gold coin and held

311

it to the candlelight. The flickering flame made his fingers look as if they were shaking.

'Gold,' he said. 'An old golden guilder. The first gold I ever owned.' He picked up his wine glass with his other hand and drank again.

'What does that have to do with the holiday resort?' asked Cordi.

'I earned this guilder in that resort for being very clever when I was a boy.'

'So what *is* the name?' Cordi asked again.

'Where I won this coin? Scheveningen.'

'Come again?' Wally said.

'Scheveningen.' Rik laughed. 'Don't even try. Only a Dutchman can say that name . . . '

Scheveningen. They'd stood on the beach. Uncle Willy held the coin to the sun. It was a fortune to a boy of nine or ten. He was leaving them at the hotel for a couple of days while he toured a Dutch U-boat factory. The coin was his if, when Uncle Willy returned home from the U-boat works, he could pronounce the name of this Dutch resort. Youth, and the fact that he was already multilingual at Uncle Willy's insistence, made it a little easier, but to this day he still needed a moment's time to prepare his tongue before he uttered the word.

'Steven, why don't you try it?' he called down the table. 'An American might be able to say *Scheveningen*, now that I think of it. You New Yorkers have quite a bit of Dutch blood. *Scheveningen*?'

The others laughed, thanking Rik van Slough for sparking the conversation with something new and amusing, and turning to Gates, who, as the Otter had guessed he would, flushed with embarrassment and made an unconvincing try at the tongue twister. The others pounced on the word with fresh laughter and as luck would have it, both Wally's sister and the Coast Guard ensign did a pretty good job of getting it right. The Otter couldn't resist a wink at

Cordi as he signalled the Strattons' butler for more wine. Uncle Willy wouldn't have approved the indulgence. Well, Uncle Willy wasn't the one in the field, operating under his kind of pressure. He needed his rare indulgences to stay sane.

Late that night, after they'd left the Strattons and had a visit to the Gateses' townhouse, Gates sat with Cordi in a cab outside the Meurice and gave her a small gift-wrapped box.

'Merry Christmas.'

'Steven, this looks too small to be casual.' She held it warily, and felt uneasy.

'Don't worry, it's casual. Open it.'

She was disappointed by the way Rik had passed Weatherburn's test. She realized now that she had been hoping he would fail and be the Otter, so that Steven would definitely not be.

'Open it.'

She untied the white ribbon, slid her fingernail under the tiny binding of cellotape and carefully opened the package without tearing the robin's-egg blue paper. Inside was a black jewellery box. She weighed it tentatively in her hand. What was he doing to her? Up the street a crowd of soldiers lurched out of the back entrance of the Essex House, carolling loudly, and headed for the cab until they saw her and Steven in the passenger seat. There was another cab behind, and she had the vaguest awareness that it too was occupied, but by then she was hinging open the box.

'Driver, turn on the light,' Gates said.

'No need,' said Cordi. 'I can see by the glare. Oh, Steven, it's beautiful.' Cordi lifted a fine gold chain out of its velvet nest and dangled the pendant – a gold V, encrusted with diamonds.

'Patriotic. I thought you'd like it.'

'I love it. But I can't accept it.'

313

'I *want* you to have it. I – '

She touched his lips with her finger and pressed the pendant into his hand. 'Your're moving too fast. There are . . . obstacles ahead you can't see. Slow down.'

The Otter fingered his gold guilder as he watched them from another cab. They were having an animated conversation. Cordi was tossing her hands about and Gates kept leaning forward and sitting back.

He felt sometimes like one of Uncle Willy's U-boats, planned and invented down to every detail, from the very beginning. But at least Uncle Willy had done a good job of it. He had thought of everything for his Otter. Everything the Otter would need to survive . . . Now he watched as Cordi kissed Gates on the cheek, got out of their cab and went into her hotel. She was clever. And brave. She'd laid a good trap, but at the price of telling the Otter who she was and where she came from. Miss Cordelia Grey was no plaything of British Intelligence. She was a hunter. And a good one. She'd shaken him, catching him off balance when he'd stupidly had too much to drink. He should have guessed sooner, before she made her move.

He didn't like it . . . her coming at him from one side, backed up by how many Britishers? And Gates poking away at the other side. He'd need to turn them against each other – as he had done at the dinner table – or else get rid of one of them, even if it meant losing Gates as a shield.

23

'How is it coming?' asked Weatherburn.

'Slowly,' Cordi told him.

'Speed it up. Come along, Duncan. We'll be back as soon as Duncan shows our new American friends how to operate their radio monitoring stations properly. I can't bloody stand all this hands-across-the-sea claptrap just because there's a war on.'

When they had gone, Cordi said to Mark, 'What a mess.'

'Gates?'

'Either he's falling in love with me or he's the best actor in New York.'

'He could be both.'

'It's a mess. He's definitely keeping *something* from me. But I don't know what ... Damn Weatherburn and his silly test. I was sure it was van Slough.'

'The test is real,' Mark said. 'The Dutch use it, and they shoot people who mumble.'

'Weatherburn is making it count far too much. Isn't there anything else on van Slough? How are you doing?'

'There's an Australian coastwatcher in New Guinea who worked on salvage in Shanghai. He might know if van Slough was there. If the Japs don't get him first.'

The Otter crouched, cupped a match from the wind and lit the switch he had doused with oil. Orange flame scattered lazily over the icy rails and clumped in pockets along the movable tongues. He picked up his oil can and walked to the next switch, waited for a diesel yard engine to pass, and lit another fire. The sound of the engine and the fact that the gravel ballast around the ties were frozen solid prevented him from hearing the guards until they were right up behind him. He turned quickly.

A flashlight caught him in the eyes.

'Got any ID, buddy?'

There were two of them, their breath fogging in the cold. Coast Guard auxiliaries, the volunteers who patrolled the waterfront. One had a .45 automatic strapped to his waist outside his coat. Both carried night sticks. The Otter put down the oil can, pocketed his matches, reached deep inside his jacket and took out a railroad pass. He handed it to the nearest, the one with the gun, who read it by flashlight and gave his face the once-over. The Otter had a railroader's peaked cap pulled down over his hair, covering his brow and shielding his eyes. If the guards told him to remove it, he would kill them.

'Okay,' said the guard, handing it back. 'Cold as hell out, isn't it?'

'More like a stepmother's kiss,' said the Otter, pleased with his idiom.

The auxiliaries laughed and moved on. The Otter watched them pass through darkness to the next burning switch, then through darkness again, and another burning switch. Flames dotted the Weehawken freight yards as far as he could see, dancing in the night, each fire marking a switch, burning to keep the movable rails from freezing.

The Otter poured oil onto several fires which were already burning, relighted one that had gone out, then ducked suddenly behind a line of coal carriers. He held onto the oil can, in case he was stopped again. He had work here tonight, work which would yield an emergency *Seehund* repair station at riverside. But first he needed a railroad car; the heaviest he could find.

Spur lines scattered out of the Weehawken yards and ran down to the piers and carfloat terminals on the river shore. The piers were enclosed warehouses where goods were unloaded from railroad cars and loaded onto ships.

The carfloat terminals were open docks, where the cars themselves were eased onto barges and floated across the river to Manhattan and Brooklyn.

A single coal carrier detached from the line in the yard and began to roll. The black gondola was heaped with sharp-edged anthracite that glittered like diamonds as it passed the orange-flaming oil fires on the switches.

Ahead, a switch closed.

The gondola trundled heavily through the switch on flattened springs and down a sloping spur. Behind it, the switch returned to its previous position like a pair of bony fingers. The Otter ran after the rolling car. Pounding along the frozen ballast, he forged ahead and threw the next switch.

Shunted onto a second spur, the coal carrier left the railyard and rumbled into the night, picked up speed on tracks that led to a lone carfloat terminal in the middle of a small blighted patch in the otherwise bustling waterfront. To its south was a short stretch of burned-out piers whose charred pilings were rotting in the mud. North, a smallish dark building stood alone, unconnected to the railroad, its windows boarded, its doors sagging. The only lights in the entire blighted stretch were in the carfloat terminal, but even it had the dreary appearance of a worn-out enterprise that survived more by habit than intent.

The square iron girders of the lifting apparatus which raised and lowered the tracks to the level of the tide-borne carfloat barges stood like a miniature gate to the dimmed-out city silhouette across the river. A half-dozen loaded boxcars waited on twin rails beneath the square archway while the hoists clanked the rails down to the level of a barge, which a tug was nosing through the ice in the slip.

The Otter climbed the hand- and footholds at the back corner of the gondola, made his way across the heap of anthracite and scrambled down a ladder at the front end. The car was moving fast now, ten or twelve miles per hour – and ahead, the rails sloped sharply. There was one more switch to open. He tensed on the rungs and leaped. He landed on the ties, slipped and started to fall.

The gondola rumbled after him. He tucked his shoulder and let himself go, hitting the ties on the point and back of his shoulder, rolling over and onto his feet, running even as the leading edge of the gondola nudged his back like a giant hand. He put on a burst of speed, drew ahead, and reached the switch with barely a second to spare.

No one had bothered to light a fire on this one. He grabbed the switch lever. He'd underestimated how cold it was. He should have started here and worked his way back to the main yards before he released the coal car. He was lucky. The switch was stiff, but it moved. The rail tongues slid open. The gondola ground loudly over the old and neglected switch. He left it open – for the investigators – and watched the coal car, which was heading quickly down the slope towards the carfloat terminal, less than a quarter-mile away.

Rust coated the last stretch of track except for a narrow shiny line down the centre of each rail – the print of the boxcars a yard engine had shepherded into the terminal earlier in the day. The runaway glided ponderously after them. The railroad workers who were preparing to lock the carfloat to the terminal heard it coming and scattered.

Laden with tons of coal and rolling at twenty miles per hour, the gondola smashed into the boxcars at the end of the track. Only the first car's hand brakes was set and the impact shoved it and the second car over the edge. They dropped two feet to the carfloat. The first car turned over and crashed off the float into the water. The impact of the second boxcar tore the mooring lines and shoved the float and tug back into the slip. The third car tipped over the end of the terminal, teetered for a long moment, and slid into the water. The coal gondola landed on top of it and settled into the water until all that showed above the surface was a crown of anthracite.

From the Otter's distance the crashing of steel on steel had an almost musical quality. He hurried away from the spur and worked his way in the dark through the industrial detritus – the scrap wood and old ties and abandoned work shacks – towards the boarded-up boathouse up the shore from the terminal he had just wrecked.

The terminal's operations had already been strictly curtailed by the shortcomings of its ancient machinery, and it was a safe guess that no one would authorize repairs of such a marginal operation in the face of the steel and labour shortages. Such a safe guess that he'd already rented this boathouse from an amazed but grateful owner. With the terminal out of action, it would be as private a spot as existed anywhere on the New York waterfront.

This boathouse would be his emergency repair station; the only thing he couldn't do inside the *Normandie* was haul the *Seehund* if it had to be repaired. Air, electricity, and a cloak of opaque water were his inside the *Normandie*, but neither room to make repairs nor privacy guaranteed to keep the boat on the surface very long. Thus, this remote boathouse – private enough to work on the boat, though not as secure in the long run as the secret cave in the *Normandie*'s stern.

A tongue of narrow-gauge rails protruded from the river side of the boathouse and descended a short, marshy bank to the river – a small shipway, primarily designed for yachts, but big enough to handle a *Seehund* of fifty feet.

The Otter hoped never to see this repair building again, never to have to make repairs, hoped the *Seehund* would arrive in perfect working order. But a four-thousand-mile journey by sea was a long trip for any machine, and the *Seehund* was bound to take a battering; nor did he trust that everyone who worked on the *Seehund* would do his job perfectly.

The *Normandie* lay directly across the river from the repair station, floodlighted tonight despite the city dim-out because the salvors were pouring concrete around the clock to seal the giant watertight bulkheads they'd constructed inside the gutted shell of the cavernous first-class dining room. Even as the bulkheading was completed, patching the hull was in full operation. Soon they'd be shoring her decks, then setting up to pump her – both massive jobs, but he knew, having seen them hew to their schedules for close to a year now, both within the Americans' capability. If Uncle Willy didn't send the *Seehund* soon, his chosen Trojan horse would sail away.

The guard at the Hoboken Ship Yard remembered him. 'Nice to see you, Mr Gates. Heard you left your uncle's firm.'

'For a while.'

'Here on business?' he asked, scanning Gates's now out-of-date navy pass.

'Where's the *John Potter*?'

'Liberty ship?'

'Yes.'

'Jeez, there's so many of them you can't keep track. I'll look it up.' He directed Gates to one of the newly built ways where the yard was turning out freighters. Several were under construction at once, in progressive stages of completion, like an automobile assembly line. Gates found the man he was looking for, welding deck plates on the next ship to be launched.

'Mike Nash?'

'Yeah?' Nash looked at Gates's coat and suit and turned off his electric arc welding machine. 'Take a break,' he told his helper.

'I'm Steven Gates.'

'Yeah. I got your letter. Then I never heard from you.'

'Do you mind if we talk about the *Normandie*?'

'Just let's make it quick.'

Gates asked Nash if he had realized that the helpers had removed their shields while he was still burning through the steel stanchion in the grand salon.

'I knew that Armstrong had, but I thought the other guy was still there.'

'Larson?'

'Yeah. The redhead.'

'And you didn't realize that Larson had also walked away?'

'I really didn't, mister. I mean, a guy doesn't just walk away from a cutting torch.'

'But you had two guys walk away.'

'Larson told Armstrong that he'd finish up with me. The cut was almost done.'

'So why did he walk away?'

'I don't know, mister.'

'Did you ask him?'

'The DA asked him.'

'He told the DA he thought you were done.'

'I didn't tell him to go.'

'Did you realize you were burning next to kapok?'

'Mister, it was crazy that day. Hauling the outfit here, hauling the outfit there. Cut this, cut that, orders changing. I did what I was told. They said cut the stanchions, I cut the stanchions.'

'You met this helper Larson – the redhead – for the first time that morning?'

'I met him in the afternoon. We just worked in the lounge cutting them damned stanchions.'

'Was he any good?'

'He knew what he was doing. He straightened Armstrong out a couple of times. I says to myself, the guy's good, wonder why he's just a helper. You know? By the time we reached the fourth stanchion, he had Armstrong doing exactly what he told him to do. Fine with me, made the job easier. Armstrong was green and pretty dumb, and I was spending half my time straightening him out. No, this guy Larson was okay.'

'Do you think the whole thing was an accident?'

Nash sighed deeply and rubbed his eyes. His breath hung

white in the cold air. He looked at Gates, looked out over the Hudson River at the spiky Manhattan skyscrapers and shook his head. 'Do you know how many times I asked myself that? Listen, when Mr Hogan got done chewing me out that night, he told me the real fault was the life jackets shouldn't of been there. Now that's the DA himself.'

'Do you know where Larson lives?'

'Someplace over in Yorkville. I read it in one of the reports.'

'You read the reports?'

Nash looked at him as if he hadn't heard. 'The damned ship was a mess. Half the guys were like Armstrong. First time on the job — any job. And where the hell was the fire watch?'

'But you're an old hand,' said Gates. 'Why'd you burn when there wasn't a fire watch? You know you're supposed to have firemen with hoses or extinguishers standing by.'

'I did what I was *told*.'

Gates put his hands in his pockets, thanked him for his time, and walked away.

'Gates.'

He turned.

Nash gestured at the Liberty ship with his arc welder. 'You want to know why I'm welding this tinker toy?'

'Why?'

'I don't use a burner no more.'

Jimmy Armstrong, Nash's regular helper, had disappeared from the Bayonne tenement he'd given as his address at the congressional hearings. Owing money to the other apprentices he had shared the flat with, he hadn't left a forwarding address. Gates got luckier with the temporary helper whose address he found in the congressional *Normandie* hearing report. Larson lived in a divided-up brownstone mansion in the three-hundred block of East Seventy-eighth Street. His landlady was hauling a cart of groceries up the steep front steps. Gates gave her a hand, commiserated what a cold winter it was, then asked if Larson was in.

'He's away.'

'Holiday?'

'I don't know.'

'When did he leave?'

'Four weeks ago.'

'That's a long vacation,' thinking at the same time that if he hadn't got involved diving he would have found Larson here.

'He's been away quite a lot lately.'

'On a shipfitter's pay?'

'I don't know about that, but they make a lot of money, don't they? Always pays his rent on time, which is more than I can say for some people around here.'

'Do you mean you didn't know that he's a shipfitter?'

'He *said* he worked sometimes in the navy yard. I don't know what he did there. But I'll tell you one thing, he had awfully clean hands for a shipfitter.'

'When's he due back?'

'I thought he'd be back last week. The rent was due then and he never missed it, except the time he was robbed. Are you a friend of his or something?'

'Robbed? He was robbed?'

'It was terrible. He was beaten so badly. It took weeks for the bruises to go away. But later he paid the rent he'd missed. I told him there was no rush, but he paid it all back real soon. I don't know how he did it.'

'What do you mean?'

'He couldn't work for weeks. He had to heal.'

'When was he robbed?'

'Oh, last winter. Around Christmas. I remember it was after Pearl Harbor because I thought what an awful thing for one American to do that to another American when the Japs had just attacked. I mean, we ought to stick together.'

Gates recalled faint yellowish blotches on the shield man's face as he walked away a second ahead of the flames.

'I'd like to leave my name and address for Mr Larson when he comes back. I'd like to talk to him.' He gave the landlady his business card which he'd taken to carrying again. 'If you could give this to Mr Larson.'

She held his card at arm's length, squinting. 'Naval architect? What should I tell Mr Larson you want to talk about?'

Gates hesitated. But if Larson were a saboteur he'd know anyway as soon as she told him he had been asking questions. 'About the *Normandie* fire.'

'Oh, that. Everybody came around about *that*, last year.'

24

At the Abwehr overseas radio station on the outskirts of Hamburg, Admiral Canaris stood over the radioman he'd chosen to transmit a message to the Otter. When the radioman had finished with the Morse key he clapped his hands over his earphones and listened intently. At last he removed them, smiling.

'He's got it, Herr Admiral.'

Canaris hurried out of the house into the cold north German dawn. Across the street a forest of receiving antennae stood in the meadow. *He* did not have it. Would that it were that simple. The message was only through the first part of the infuriating maze the Otter had set up to protect himself. Most agents were content with a single radio. The Otter had three. None of which he operated himself. Three, Canaris reflected ruefully, that he knew of. Two transmitters and a third separate receiver.

It was still midnight in another meadow 4,500 miles away in Connecticut, where the receiver's antenna was concealed in the barren top of an eighty-foot tulip tree so tall and so straight that the line it cut against the starry winter sky looked man-made. The meadow, deep inside a rural estate and screened by thick hemlock, was less than ten miles from Long Island Sound, but the land rose quickly here and it was four hundred feet above sea level, so the signal from Hamburg came in loud and clear.

The antenna wire ran underground from the base of the tree into a horse barn and up to a clean, spare office above the tackroom. The office smelled of hay, and when he removed the earphones, the aesthetic-looking old man operating the powerful receiver could hear the ancient sounds of large animals sighing contentedly. Less satisfying was the noise of automobile traffic on the Merritt Parkway.

When the forest-green Duesenberg with Connecticut licence plates rounded the corner of West One-hundred-fifteenth Street and Seventh Avenue, the other girls roused Casey from her thoughts. It took a moment because she'd bought a half-pint of Southern Comfort after her last trick and had a good buzz on.

'You're up, Casey.'

'Casey's at the bat.'

'I just *love* that automobile. Want a pinch hitter, honeychile?'

Casey unbuttoned her coat to show her legs and sauntered to the kerb. She made it look like she wasn't hurrying, but she was sure to get there before the car. There was a chauffeur in his own separate part up-front, but she opened the back door herself. By the time she shut it the car was rolling again. The passenger compartment had velvet seats and velvet curtains drawn across the windows. It was warm and the old guy who smelled of horses sat there like a king, with his fly open.

She saw a ten-dollar bill on the seat and five twenties. Ten for the frenching. The hundred meant he had another message. At first, he'd come only with a message. But when they'd begun to taper off after Pearl Harbor, he'd started showing up just for the french. Either way it was a good deal for her.

Casey knelt wordlessly on the thick rug as the car glided into Harlem. Sometimes when she got high she wondered a little about the message. The man who'd set it up in the beginning told her she'd get killed if she ever told anybody. She'd finally decided that the people with the messages were pulling a fast one on the numbers game – somehow the old guy found out the next day's number ahead of time and passed it on to somebody at Miz Sally's. If she was right then somebody in the mob was cheating somebody else in the mob. And about that she didn't want to know any more, thank you.

When she'd finished him he poured her a drink from the little bar that popped out of the seat, then sat there, a vein throbbing in his temple until the car dropped her back at the Market. She worked a few more tricks – a car with a couple of soldiers and a hotel with a fat guy who couldn't make it. Towards morning she wandered up to Sugar Hill and slipped in the kitchen door at Miz Sally's.

'Well, look what the cat dragged in. You had breakfast, chile?'

'Nothin' I could sink my teeth in.'

The old cook howled with laughter and threw a handful of chicken wings in a skillet. 'Don't you beat all. When you gonna get off the street and come work for Miz Sally?'

Casey's brown eyes hardened. 'Ah don't like girls. 'Specially fat old lady girls like Miz Sally.'

'She tole me I wasn't supposed to let you in here no more.'

'When's the last time she squeezed her big behind through that kitchen door?'

The cook laughed again. 'Want some coffee?'

'Yeah. Back in a second.'

'Where you going, gal?'

'I got to use the ladies'.'

'Not out front. Miz Sally sees you she'll have a fit.'

'I'll be careful. I don't want to see her neither.'

This late Miz Sally was usually in bed with her twins, but not tonight. The joint was jumping and Casey stole a glimpse down the long hall. Miz Sally was sitting on her white satin sofa with the twins curled up at her feet. Some of the other girls were downstairs dancing. A bunch of Park Avenue swells were drinking and laughing with Miz Sally. They'd brought a couple of classy white women. Slumming.

Casey got into the bathroom unseen. She locked the door, got rid of the message, and sneaked back to the kitchen, where the cook was suddenly busy carving roast beef sandwiches and brewing fresh coffee for the special party out front.

Gates couldn't believe they'd ended up here.

It had been one of those evenings that built in stages of mutual acquaintance that were more likely in a small, inbred John O'Hara-type town. In its way, Manhattan wasn't so different, at least at some level. He and Cordi had gone to the theatre and seen *My Sister Eileen*, then to the Rainbow Room for supper and dancing to Leo Reisman's sedate orchestra. Cordi agreed the room was 'pretty', but when Gates realized she wasn't enjoying it they left early. Cordi had telephoned her 'studio' to make sure she didn't have to work early in the morning, and then expressed a sudden desire to see the Stork Club.

The Stork Club wasn't Gates's favourite place, being too promotionally exclusive, and this had to be the night that the man at the velvet rope didn't recognize him. They were standing on the sidewalk, wondering what to do, when Rik van Slough spilled loudly out of a cab with Charlie and Kay.

Van Slough was delighted when he saw Cordi, bowed and kissed her hand. She had asked Gates about Rik van Slough a number of times since the Strattons' Christmas party, mentioning that she'd like to see him again, but Gates had held off, and now, seeing Rik in his top hat, cape and stick and his golden hair and confident smile, he knew why.

Van Slough started turning the Stork Club upside down to please her. The rope fell before Mr van Slough, sir, and within seconds they had a huge centre table, waiters running for champagne as if to douse a fire, and cigarette girls passing out six-inch cigars.

Cordi said, 'Steven tells me you're going to own New York. It certainly looks as if you've got a good start.'

Rik laughed.

A stream of people stopped to greet van Slough and sent drinks to the table. Gates thought that many looked like movie gangsters and recently elevated shipfitters, and discovered he was right as Charlie leaned over Kay and supplied a running commentary.

'I met that one when he was beating up strikers for five dollars a night. The yo-yo before him was on Home Relief until the navy started building piers on Staten Island.'

'Be quiet,' Kay said.

'War's a great leveller, sweetheart.'

A man came over from the bar and said, 'Hello, Steven,' and Gates looked up from Cordi and saw Jim Tweed. He introduced Tweed to Cordi and Rik. Charlie was hostile, and Kay was coolly polite, but van Slough insisted that Tweed join them. 'Any landlord of Steven Gates is a friend of mine,' he said expansively. 'Especially a policeman.'

The Otter was glad of his chance to meet Tweed. Uncle Willy had relayed information right after Pearl Harbor that a number of New York City cops were secretly employed by the Office of Naval Intelligence. Tweed, with the sabotage squad, could be one of them.

'Waving to the waiter to refill Tweed's glass, he leaned close and threw his arm over the back of Tweed's chair. 'Quite a town since the war, isn't it?'

'It was quite a town *before* the war, Mr van Slough. You should have seen it.'

'Rik. Call me Rik. I saw some of it, but only after '39. Tell me something.'

'Sure.'

'Don't, if you are not supposed to. I don't mean to pry into police business, but I was wondering . . . what do the police do about the draft?'

'Same thing you do. Get an occupational deferment. Essential work.'

'I have trouble getting men to work for me, even with the deferment. They're still enlisting.'

'A lot of people feel strongly about the war.'

The Otter then called for a fresh bottle. 'Charlie? What kind of basic training did they give you in the Abraham Lincoln Brigade?'

Charlie looked at him, a little surprised and a little annoyed. He shrugged. 'Mostly taught us how to duck.'

'You didn't cross the Pyrenees in wintertime ducking. How'd they make you tough, Charlie?'

'Can it, Rik.'

'Charlie,' said Kay. 'Rik's just asking.'

'*Sorry*. There was more enthusiasm than training. I saw Spanish peasants going at machine-gun nests, standing straight up and holding their left fists clenched over their heads. That's how they showed revolutionaries on the recruiting posters. Those boys wanted to do it right.'

'Fighting is crazy,' said the Otter, still holding his glass. He peered into it, and when the conversations resumed again he turned to Tweed and said in a low voice. 'That's an amazing story about Charlie escaping over the mountains.'

'Sure is,' Tweed agreed.

'Hard to believe a man could cross those mountains wounded, without any help.' He raised his voice slightly to make sure that Cordi Grey had heard, as well as Tweed. One of them might carry a suspicion of Charlie back to their bosses. It would not hurt to shift some suspicion to Charlie in case Gates, who was *still* investigating the sabotage of the *Normandie* after the diving school hiatus, got too close and he had to kill him instead of using him as a shield. Collins, with his checkered, unconventional background and natural inclination to go against established authority, just might be fashioned into a replacement shield of sorts if Gates had to be killed.

And Gates was still coming at him. Larson had panicked on the telephone when he learned that Gates had been snooping around what he had thought was a safehouse.

The Otter had ordered him to stay out of New York, which meant he was no longer available for small chores. The arsonist had sounded relieved. He had gone ahead and married the soldier's widow and seemed content to bury himself in the aircraft factory near his wife's home. Once again, Gates had unknowingly chipped away at him.

When the Stork Club closed, van Slough had grabbed the bill. 'I know a place uptown we can get a drink all night.' They piled into a cab and headed up to Harlem.

To Gates's horror it turned out to be Miz Sally's, the same Sugar Hill whorehouse Rik had taken him to the previous spring. Miz Sally – a shiny black mountain of a woman – greeted Rik like an old friend, but after quickly taking in Cordi she acted as if Gates were there for the first time. Cordi and Kay got big smiles, which wavered slightly when she made Tweed for a cop. He'd muttered, 'I'm just out with my friends,' and turned his hand palm down, as if demonstrating he hadn't come for a pay-off.

The parlour was low-lighted and furnished with thick rugs and overstuffed couches and loveseats. A dignified and powerful-looking man tended a small bar in the corner and carried their drinks on a silver tray. The walls were hung with large, gilt-framed oil paintings. A young black man in glasses, who looked like a music student and was, played softly on a baby grand.

Couples were dancing – well-dressed white men and light-skinned black girls. Miz Sally motioned them to seats and settled on her thronelike white satin couch, a pair of soft, kittenish and very beautiful lookalike girls at her feet. Rik van Slough talked nonstop, interrupted by waves of laughter from Miz Sally. Charlie observed the room glumly. Tweed drank and said nothing.

'What were you doing at the Stork Club?' Gates asked Tweed quietly while the others were talking.

'Cops not allowed?'

'No – I didn't mean that. I was just wondering.'

'As a matter of fact I had to talk to a guy and he named the spot. I was just leaving when I saw you and figured it would be a good chance to meet van Slough, which I've been wanting to do.'

'How come?'

Tweed gave Gates his flattest look. 'In my business it pays to know the bigshots.'

The Otter reached under the lid of the toilet tank and untaped his message. The message was short. He broke it in his head – a date, a name, and a position – and flushed the paper down the toilet.

Uncle Willy was sending a *Seehund* with an operator named Ponte. The Otter straightened his tie in the mirror. An Italian. Ponte and the *Seehund* would arrive thirty miles off New York on the last day of June.

Three months. Time enough to lodge the submarine inside the *Normandie* before they began pumping her in August. But a long time to wait in New York while Gates nosed around and the British kept hunting.

25

'*Heil spaghetti! Heil spaghetti! Heil spaghetti!*' rose above a din of drunken shouts and laughter. A hundred U-boat officers were celebrating survival in a hotel bar in Lorient on the west coast of Brittany, but the mocking cry drew their attention with a promise of something new. The accordion player stopped fingering his wheezing instrument, and all eyes shifted expectantly towards the door.

Standing there was a short, stocky Italian submarine officer, muffled to his chin in a long coat and scarf.

'Hey, Hans?' called out the German who had spotted him.

'*Ja*, Fritz,' answered his companion, balancing a French girl on his lap.

'What's the best anchor in the world?'

'I don't know, Fritz. What's the best anchor in the world?'

'An Italian submarine on the attack.'

The whole room burst into laughter. The Italian peered about, searching. Fritz lurched to his feet.

'What do you want here?'

'I am looking for German officer,' the Italian replied in halting German.

'Why don't you check the line at your mother's door?'

It took a moment for the language to sink in. When it did the Italian flushed and slipped out of his greatcoat as lithely as if it were a cape. He was a head shorter than Fritz and had incongruously long arms, which dangled from his enormously broad shoulders. His appearance drew more laughter, though his rank was captain and medals glittered on his chest.

He stepped closer to the German, scooped him up in his

oddly long arms, lifted him to his shoulder like a circus performer, whirled twice in a full circle, and threw him over the bar.

He glanced around at the rest of the Germans, and for a long moment the loudest sound in the building was the crunch of broken glass as the German floundered behind the bar. Then someone laughed and the accordion player resumed his music and with it the shouts and laughter.

The Italian dragged his coat over his shoulders, glanced around once more and walked out. A good performance.

A U-boat captain strolled out after him, caught him on the dark street. 'Captain Ponte?'

'Captain von Harling?'

'I was led to believe,' the German said angrily, 'that my boat had been recalled from its cruise for a mission as *secret* as it was important.'

'And I was led to believe that I had more to fear from the French underground than my German allies.'

'Do you have a message for me?'

'The boat is finished. It left Hamburg by train this morning. Are the brackets ready?'

'My boat's in dry dock now,' von Harling said unhappily. 'Your engineer is doing the electric work.'

'He is a German?' asked Ponte.

'Yes. An old U-boat man. Seems good at it.'

They stood, awkward and silent. The sea was near, pungent in the night. The U-boat captain asked, 'Would you like to come in again for a drink? They won't bother you further.'

'No. In Hamburg they put me in a barracks while I trained to operate the little boat. Where are the women?'

'There is a house up the road for officers. Off to the right. Here, I will show you.'

Ponte's face took on a sudden, bright smile. His dark eyes and white teeth seemed to gleam. 'Thank you, my friend.'

Gates inched along in forty feet of black water, feeling for an open porthole. The mud was deep – still more than

334

a foot despite the pumping – and still soupy so that his hands and knees sank to the hard skin of the ship.

He found the port the hard way. His leading hand plunged through the opening, deep into the soupy mud, and he fell face forward on his helmet, smashing his nose against the useless glass eye. The telephone crackled in his ear.

'Hey, Junior?'

'What?'

'Find the port?'

'Yeah, with my face.'

'What are you blaming me for?'

'Shut up and send me down a hose.'

Gates waited in the dark, fighting the ever-present impulse to shoot for the surface and stay there, and wondering what he was doing with himself. He felt dead-ended. He couldn't find Armstrong. And Larson, the shield man who'd told Armstrong to move *his* shield – his best suspect – still hadn't come back to his rooming house.

'Heads up! Water hose coming at you. Sliding right down your line . . . ten feet, twenty feet, thirty. Ought to be parting your hair in a second.'

Gates positioned the iron-weighted hose with the slow motions that were becoming second nature as he developed a new, almost languid sense of time and grew accustomed to the stately pace dictated by the water's relentless drag.

'Give me pressure, Charlie.'

The hose convulsed and jerked rigid as a steel pry bar. Fighting to keep it from flying out of his hands, Gates aimed the nozzle down and blasted the mud out of the open port with the high-pressure water jet. He gouged a deep hole in the mud, dispersing clouds of silt he couldn't see.

'Shut it off!'

He knelt and inspected the port with his hands.

'Tooker patch!'

Charlie lowered the wood-and-steel hinged patch on a line. Gates removed its strong back and folded the patch in half, shoved it through the round port and opened it outside the hull like an umbrella. Pulling the patch tight against its rubber gasket, he laid the strong back across the inside of the port and screwed the patch to it with turnbuckles. Charlie lowered two bags of cement to strengthen the patch and told Gates it was time to come up.

He surfaced out of the deep water into the mad clatter of air machines driving power tools, compressors feeding the other divers, and chains roaring through winchs, out of the black dark into the white glare of a hundred naked work lamps.

Feeling light-headed, he wondered if he could talk Cordi into going dancing tonight.

When Cordi, Mark and Duncan filed into the back room at the Meurice, Weatherburn sat waiting, his eyes on the long, thin pearl-handled knife in his hands. It looked like a clasp knife as he shuffled it back and forth, but then he shot out his right hand and a long sliver of a blade leaped out and locked with a sharp click.

'Rather something, isn't it?'

'Is that a gravity knife?' asked Duncan.

'Switchblade,' Weatherburn said. 'Versatile little implement . . . All right, we're here. Now. We're getting both nearer to, and further from, Herr Otter.

'On the positive side, if you can call it that, we've pretty much gutted the list of suspects, with the help of BSC and the FBI, unknowing, of course. We've damned few names left, I rather like the look of Gates, but Cordi can't seem to pin anything on him. I also like van Slough, a rather unsavoury sort, heavily involved in the black market, it would seem. I've never thought much of Collins as a suspect, but now we get some new, albeit vague, information about his disappearance in Spain when he was separated from his unit of the International Brigade. It's possible he was either captured by the Germans or went over to them voluntarily. At any rate it would help explain how a wounded man got over the Pyrenees in wintertime. Something to keep looking into – '

'I think Collins is a very credible suspect,' Cordi said. 'And I still think van Slough is, too.'

'But he said the Dutch name. You were there. You gave him the test.'

'I know.'

'Are you suggesting he taught himself to say it? Because if you are I've been told that it's virtually impossible for a German adult to pronounce it.'

'He was rather smug,' said Cordi. 'It's been bothering me, but that's what it was. He was pleased with himself. As though he had won a contest. He's a very arrogant man and his arrogance came through.'

'Women's intuition?'

'Is my intuition suspect because I'm female?'

'Of course not, dear, though you might agree that a display of arrogance is odd behaviour for a spy.'

'Or a good cover.'

'Granted.'

'Or even a characteristic of an agent who's done as well as the Otter has. You told me yourself, this is not a man who sneaks about in the shadows.'

'Quite. I am, however, particularly interested in this Collins information – *and* in your feeling about van Slough. It's been occurring to me that we could be looking for more than one man. A group perhaps. We're still waiting for that New Guinea coastwatcher to confirm van Slough. And we're checking with International Brigaders about Collins. And you, Cordi, can consider it while you work on Mr Gates.'

'I'm not getting much from Mr Gates . . . '

'Perhaps there isn't anything to get,' Mark said.

'Or *perhaps* Cordi isn't going about it the right way,' Weatherburn said. 'Speaking of things female.'

'What is that supposed to mean?' She knew, of course.

'You've been going about New York City with him for months and he still hasn't told you what he was doing at the trucking concern, or even what he testified to at the Office of Naval Intelligence.'

'But we *know* what he told ONI because ONI told us when you asked. He said he opened the doors and later they were closed.'

'Don't you see, that's the point. The doors that trapped the hose water and contributed to the *Normandie* capsizing *were* closed. Doesn't it occur to you that Gates could have been the one who closed them?'

'I don't know.'

'And that Gates testified just in case someone saw him? So he could say he was not closing them but opening them? Isn't that possible?'

Cordi's thoughts were spinning. What Weatherburn said wasn't all that likely, perhaps. But none of his points was impossible. Inwardly she cringed when she realized that Weatherburn wasn't through, he had more against Steven.

'But it's not only the doors. Gates and Collins attacked the dispatcher at T and C Trucking. The fellow escaped, and what happened that very night? Again someone tried to kill him — and nearly us in the process. I haven't forgotten that evening. Have you?'

'No.'

'And what is Gates's purpose,' Weatherburn continued, needling her, 'in pretending to be a common labourer on the *Normandie*. What is he doing there? Who is he contacting? Why is Collins with him? What are these trips Gates makes around the port at odd times? Who is he talking to in those offices he visits? Who does he meet in the shipyards? Gates is a cipher, Cordi. And you haven't found the key.'

'There *are* other suspects.'

'Your responsibility is Gates,' he snapped back. 'Leave

the other suspects to me.' He glared at her a moment, then continued in a gentler tone. 'Mark and Duncan and I are re-examining our list of names on the chance that BSC or the FBI have mistakenly cleared one of them. We are still monitoring the Otter's radio frequency. We're in close touch with the Americans . . . closer than I like, but those are my orders and I obey them, make no mistake about it. And Mark is still waiting for the coastwatcher to double-check van Slough. But do I *still* have to remind you of what the Otter has done to us in the past? In Europe, in England and now here in New York. He is smart, ingenious. And he knows as well as we how crucial the Port of New York is to England. To winning the war . . . trouble is, New York is not our port. It belongs to strangers.' He shook his head. 'Do you know that even though the Americans have been our allies for more than a year the Coast Guard still boards British merchant vessels docked in Hoboken to warn our sailors to travel in groups on leave? Otherwise the German-Americans in Hoboken will beat them up in the streets. The same sailors who run the U-boat gauntlet. We're serving among strangers, Cordi. We're at war in a foreign land.'

'All the more reason to keep a clear head and not leap on the obvious.'

'Well put, young lady. But in the meantime let's just keep an *open* eye on Mr Gates, and see what happens next . . .'

26

Charlie Collins said, 'For Chrissake,' as the turbulence swirled around the wooden ladder eight feet below the diving stage between C and D decks. The steel chamber, lighted by bare bulbs in wire mesh, echoed the sounds of water, tools and men's voices.

Charlie told Marty, Gates's relief tender, to go to lunch. 'I'll tend him myself.'

'Marty's fine. We've been working together all month.'

Charlie shook his head. 'You have a rising tide headed upstream and a flooded river coming down and I'm not going home to tell my wife that her brother drowned shoring up C deck while I was playing foreman for Rik van Slough. Watch your tail. There must be a hell of a reverse flow down a few feet.'

'You're telling me? Look at Rik's line.'

The current was snapping van Slough's line like a whip as his tender pulled him up. When he got out, Rik said, 'Getting nasty down there.' His gaze fell on Charlie, who was rigging Gates's lines. 'Where's Marty?'

'I'm tending Steven till the water eases up.'

Van Slough looked annoyed. 'What did you come down here for?'

'Guy wants to know if you're through with that air compressor in the mooring compartment.'

'I'll take care of it. Tell him to see me. As a matter of fact, I want that compressor bolted down.'

'What for?'

'I don't want anyone borrowing it.'

The Otter saw a unique opportunity in the Hudson River's

late spring flood. Not a single man had died on this job, yet. But the current swirling angrily around the ship's frames today was a killer and no one could question what happened to Gates in conditions like these. He'd already shifted a good deal of suspicion towards Charlie, and when the time came for what the Americans called a fall guy, the big Irishman would do. And Gates would be dead.

'Let's go,' he ordered his tender.

'I thought you were takin' a break.'

'Not now. Work to be done. I'll take that timber. The big one.'

Gates eyed the water racing like a mill stream with a tree fallen in, rippling and eddying in fierce chaos, speckled with sewage, the surface swift and churning, pocked by deep whirlpools, and leaping white and frothy up the deck frames that impeded its flow.

'Sure you want to do this?' Charlie asked.

'It won't be so bad with a helmet, Mr Tender, or do I hold my breath till Marty comes back?'

Charlie plunked it over Gates's head and locked the ring with a quarter-turn. 'Hello in there,' he rasped over the telephone, giving the brass a playful rap, but Gates was already feeling the tension that preceded submersion in the black water and was through joking.

'Let's go, Charlie.' He understood why the older commercial divers preferred rope signals to telephones. You didn't always want to talk, even to your tender, particularly when you were working by feel. You had to be alone with your sense of touch. He shuffled to the ladder, backed down the rungs, shoved off when he was up to his shoulders and kicked and swam against the current. It was much stronger than usual and if Charlie weren't walking along the diving platform heaving his lines he'd have been swept backwards the breadth of the fallen ship.

Charlie positioned him under a massive timber which

dangled from chain falls. Gates caught hold as it was lowered to the water, wrapped an arm around it, released some air from his suit, reducing his buoyancy, and sank.

Lengths of railroad track weighting the wood dragged it down thirty feet. Gates's brass-shod boots struck a work platform and he spoke into the helmet phone. 'Okay, Charlie.' The timber stopped descending and began to spin as the current caught one end.

Working by touch and memory, Gates manhandled the timber into the latticework they were constructing between C and D decks to shore C against water pressure that would increase when pumping began. Crisscrossing girders formed a bridge which transmitted the weight of the unsupported C deck to the stronger D deck by way of a forest of stanchions.

He oriented himself in the blackness by locating the last stanchion he'd placed the day before. Close by he located the next seating with his hands, pushed one end of the weighted timber into it and started to work his way along it to place the other end. The current shifted abruptly. He'd been leaning into the flow to hold his position, and the reversal sent him tumbling.

Charlie must have felt it because the line fetched up short and dragged him back to the timber. His helmet clanged dully where the brass met the wood.

'Easy, Charlie. Don't kill me!'

'Sorry, Junior. All hell's breaking loose in the water. You want to come up?'

'No! Just take it easy, for God's sake.'

'What?'

'I said take it easy.'

'I can't hear.' Charlie's voice came thinly. And then the phone went dead.

Gates tugged his signal line for Charlie to take him up. Whatever had damaged the phone, he wanted it fixed. The signal rope, looped around his wrist, pulled against something hard. Fighting panic, Gates started pulling himself along the line to find where it had fouled.

His air felt thin.

Imagination. He dragged himself against the current, inching his way along the line.

There were other divers nearby, but without the phone to relay through their tenders, he couldn't find them. The deep blackness began to pound him, as if it had physical dimension. His face prickled and his breath came short and just as fear threatened to destroy him a powerful euphoria released the fear.

He let go the line and let the current take him where it would. There was magic in the current, sorcery in the flow. A spell, a black spell. The river was racing. The ship was still. But the current passed the hull as it had before she burned. The current tossed him suddenly into a stanchion. His helmet rang and his arm hurt where the timber smashed into his canvas suit.

With the pain came fear, and the murky realization that he was hallucinating. His air had been cut off. He was being poisoned by carbon dioxide building up in his suit.

'Charlie.'

He gripped the lifeline and started frantically pulling. He fought his way against the current, gasping huge breaths to find some small amount of oxygen, and struggling to maintain his sanity against the flood of weird pictures forming in his mind. The hull . . . the hull racing . . . it was black before the war . . .

Anger burned the pictures, seared them from his brain. He kept pulling his line, pulling to the point where it had fouled, driven by the same anger that had drawn him to the wreck, drawn him to the salvage; like the weights that dragged him underwater. He yanked the lead weight lanyard and they fell away and he rose swiftly, out of control, but rising.

The fouled lifeline ripped out of his hands. In his panic

and confusion he had ceased to vent exhaust and the suit had begun to blow up, increasing his buoyancy, floating him to the surface. He started to lean against the valve, but the thought moved sluggishly through his oxygen-starved brain that he shouldn't.

He was rising swiftly. He would make it to the top.

Something yanked his helmet and he flipped upside down and stayed there, and as the blood rushed into his brain it jolted him with one last insight before he blacked out . . . the fouled line had fetched up short. It was holding his head down and his feet up and he would hang upside down like a balloon until he breathed the last breath of oxygen. How close to the surface had he come? How far beneath the water were his heavily-weighted shoes? His knees had bent from the weight. He straightened them with all his might and tried to kick to attract attention. He concentrated all his effort on straightening his legs. The fear was gone. In its place was regret . . . that he'd never see Cordi . . . or the *Normandie*.

'Rik!' The helmet phone sounded like tinfoil being crumpled.

'Who's that, Charlie?' said the Otter.

'Come up. Steven's lost.'

'What?' Of course he was lost. He was meant to be.

'Come up. His line's fouled. You should be near him.'

'I'll find him.'

The Otter moved slowly through the dark water, towards the weighted timber he had dropped on Gates's line to crush it. He'd wait a minute more before he would free the line and bring it up only to find it too late for Gates, but holding the kinked armoured line to show them all how Gates had died.

He heard panic on the diving phone. His own tender yelling and Charlie Collins's voice bellowing orders. He found the line and felt for the timber. He could hear Collins in the background.

'No!' yelled the Otter's tender. 'Don't do it!'

'What is it?' said the Otter. 'What did Charlie do?'

On the surface, Charlie Collins dragged an underwater gas cutting torch to the edge of the diving stage. He hauled frantically on the gas lines, heaping slack around his feet. Gates's boot broke surface again, vanished.

'Open them bottles,' he yelled. 'Gimme a lighter.'

An apprentice ran to the gas bottles and spun their valves. A tender jumped onto the stage, flicking a flint strike-a-light, and directed the sparks to the torch's nozzle as Charlie screwed it open. Flame roared. Charlie honed it down and jumped into the water.

Kicking and stroking with his free hand, he swam towards the disturbance that marked Gates's boot, sucked in a deep breath, grabbed Gates's foot and dived into the opaque water, dragging himself under his diving suit, feeling for the sheathed cable that tethered Gates's helmet . . . down until a dense mass of bubbles rising from the submerged cutting torch was all that showed on the surface.

Below, the Otter raged for information. What was happening? What had gone wrong? *What is Charlie doing?*

'Collins spotted Gates's feet,' the telephone rattled back. 'He jumped in with a burner.'

Forty feet down, his exhaust echoing hollowly in the silence, he might as well be a mile away. How could he stop Charlie from down here? He found Gates's line. It was shaking. He wrapped both hands around it, gathered his weight and pulled. If he could shake Charlie loose, the Irishman would have to go up for air. If he could pull Gates further under – the line suddenly cascaded around him in the dark like a collapsing snake.

Charlie had done it. The damned fool had cut Gates's lifeline. Now, with the other jumping in to help with ropes and hoists, he'd be pulling Gates out of the water.

The fool. He could have got killed. Or was *he* the fool for failing to consider that Charlie would do anything for Gates?

'He's got him,' the Otter's tender yelled.

'How is Gates?'

'I don't know. Looks like he's out cold.'

'Bring me up.' Gates was a lucky man to have a protector like Charlie. Only Uncle Willy would have done the same for him . . .

Charlie Collins lay prone on the diving stage, dripping wet and spitting water. Gates lay beside him, helmet off, a hoisting chain still wrapped around his chest. The tenders and other divers were grouped around, yelling at each other to give them air. A first aid team came running.

'He's breathing!'

They broke ammonia nodules under Gates's nose. He sat up slowly, brushing them away and mumbling that he was fine while they peppered him with questions and listened to his heart with a stethoscope.

Charlie Collins sat up too, spat more water and reached for Gates with both hands.

'I'm fine . . . I'm fine . . . '

Charlie gripped his shoulders for a long moment, his face working. Gates grabbed the stub of lifeline sticking out of his helmet where Charlie had cut it.

'You made a mess of my suit.'

Charlie hauled him to his feet and shook him. 'Goddam it, Junior, how many times do I got to tell you to come up head first?'

The Otter telephoned police headquarters at Centre Street.

'This here's a message for Lieutenant James Tweed, Sabotage.'

'I'll switch you to Lieutenant Tweed,' the operator replied.

'You switch anything and I'm hanging up. You tell Tweed that there's a guy named Jimmy Armstrong gone to live at 87 River Street, Union City.'

'You want to leave a name?' asked the police operator, but the Otter had hung up. His rage had dissipated. Fate had saved Gates as much as Charlie Collins. Fate meant there was a reason. Gates was meant to be his shield. But if he was going to use him as a shield, it was time to add to the case against him.

27

He went out to his tug moored at the end of the *Normandie* and slept beside the telephone. He'd rigged a phone line for Van Slough Salvage right onto the boat. The salvage job was run first class; no time-saver was too good or too expensive for its contractors. Gates called early in the morning with a story about a doctor visit to see if he'd hurt his lungs in the accident.

The Otter cranked up *Hollandia* and headed for Jersey.

'Will you hate me if I cancel our breakfast?'

'Is Rik making you work early?'

'No. Something's come up.'

'What?' Cordi asked.

Gates hesitated, then said lamely, 'I'll tell you about it some other time.'

Gates hung up and read Tweed's note again:

'I got a tip that Armstrong went home to live with his old lady. 87 River Street, Union City, Jersey. The tip's anonymous so don't count on too much. Tweed.'

'Mark.' Cordi burst into his room. He sat up, pulling the sheet around his muscular waist, rubbing his eyes with the other hand.

'He's off to something . . . he broke our breakfast date. Get dressed, I'll get the car.'

Next to Jimmy Armstrong's house was a barren Victory garden protected by a fence of rusty bedsprings. The apprentice's mother was seeding cold frames, which were glassed with old window sashes. She directed Gates to a desolate automobile dump on a run-down stretch of the Weehawken shore, not far from Rik van Slough's scrapyard. Gates wished he had rented a car, but a meandering string of trolleys eventually got him there late in the morning. The scrapyard contained fewer junked cars than blackened twisted girders. Apparently with the automobile shortage, the yard specialized in scrap metal taken from buildings razed by fire.

Towering above the flat, low river shore was a tall scrap crane with a magnetic lift. The crane stood at rest, the magnetic lift laying on a heap of short lengths of steel. Between the crane and a pile of bent I beams that Jimmy Armstrong was cutting into pieces was an empty gondola on a rail spur.

Armstrong was young and chubby, no more than a teenager, with a petulant mouth screwed up in concentration as he tried to force the flame through the thick steel faster than it could cut. Gates did not remember him from the *Normandie*, which wasn't surprising . . . the kid looked so ordinary. Armstrong was working alone, crouched in the lee of the gondola. Beyond the car, gusts of wind whistled through the latticework of the tall, silent crane.

After Armstrong noticed him and pushed up his goggles and shut off the outfit, Gates handed him his card and asked abruptly, 'Why did you take your spark shield away before Nash was done burning?'

Armstrong read his card and made sure the other side was blank. 'I don't have to talk to you.'

'Did Larson tell you to go away?'

'What if he did?'

'I just want to know why you moved your spark shield before Nash was done cutting.'

'You can't blame the whole fire on me, mister.'

'I'm not blaming you, Jimmy. You didn't put the life jackets there, did you?'

'*Course* I didn't.'

Gates hunkered down beside him.

'So who's blaming you?'

'So how come I'm fired and working in a scrapyard? Tell me that.'

'I'm just asking you,' said Gates, glancing around the desolate yard. No wonder the kid felt screwed.

'I told 'em already. I thought Nash was done burning. I thought he'd finished cutting. Somebody said, give 'em a hand carrying out the stanchion, so I figured it was cut and I got up to help the chain gang carry it out and then all hell broke loose.'

'Who told you to give a hand with the stanchion?'

'Jesus, I don't know. I thought it was Nash, but he says he didn't, so I guess it was Larson.'

'Well, who did you take your orders from?'

'Nash. I was his helper. I don't know, Larson kept telling me to do this, do that.'

'Why did you do it?'

'It wasn't like he was bossing me around or nothing. He just seemed to know the right moves, you know? I didn't care, I thought he was helping me. You know how when you meet a guy in a union? An organizer? They got a line of talk. They make you feel good. By the time they get around to asking for your vote, you like 'em already. You know?'

Gates nodded. He'd seen Charlie Collins operate. 'I know. Listen, have you seen Larson?'

'I ain't seen him since the hearings.'

Gates nodded, thanked him and walked away, thinking that Larson sounded more and more interesting, and wondering if he could ask Tweed to help track him down.

He telephoned Tweed at his office at Centre Street.

Tweed was sympathetic, but busy. 'How dumb is Armstrong?'

'Dumb enough for Larson to push him around like the foreman said.'

350

'Sounds like maybe you're getting someplace. If you can find Larson . . . '

Armstrong watched Gates pick his way out of the scrapyard. He started to relight his cutting torch, then figured since he'd stopped already and the boss was out on the truck he might as well eat lunch early. He opened his pail and spread out the sandwiches and hard-boiled eggs his mother had packed for him. A shadow fell on the plank he was using for a table. He looked up. Too much . . . a beautiful girl was smiling at him. She had soft reddish hair, wore a long belted coat and slacks. A big guy was standing behind her but she did all the talking.

She asked if he was Jimmy Armstrong. He nodded. A girl like that had never looked him straight in the eye in his life. She looked like a girl in the movies. She asked who he'd been talking to. Tongue-tied, he bridged the space between them by extending Gates's card.

Armstrong was vaguely aware now of hearing the scrap crane start up. Which meant the boss was back and if he saw him from the control cab he'd yell at him for starting lunch early. Quickly he scooped his meal into his pail and snapped it shut. He'd tell the boss that the big guy said he was a cop and he had to talk.

'What did Gates want?' asked the girl. The wind from the river was blowing towards the crane. She didn't seem to notice it, though it was only fifty feet away, but the big guy did. He glanced at it lifting a heap of I-beam chunks to the gondola, then looked back at him, waiting for his answer. He told the girl that Gates was asking about the fire on the *Normandie*.

'What sort of questions?'

'Gates said – '

He felt a shadow cross his face and heard the distinct *click* as the electricity went off and the lifting magnet dropped its load. He looked up in astonishment. The crane had reached beyond the car. It was falling on them – chunks of I-beam like bricks growing big in the sky. The big guy started to move but he was too slow. The girl pushed the guy backwards. Somebody once told him that girls had faster reflexes than men. It was Armstrong's last thought.

'The Otter was within fifty feet of you. You didn't see him. And then you let him get away – '

'Mark was unconscious, and the boy was still alive. I was so stunned I just did the natural thing and tried to stop his bleeding.'

'Unsuccessfully.'

'I admit I was stunned.' That was putting it mildly. One second she was talking to the boy, the next the metal was falling from the sky. Had it been a trap? Or had the Otter seen them with Armstrong and feared the boy knew something? . . . Steven had been there minutes before. He'd had plenty of time to double back and climb onto the crane. She'd been so damned anxious to have the boy clear him with some innocent explanation that she blundered like a novice. She was damned lucky to be alive.

'I'm sorry, sir,' Cordi said, shaking her head.

'Good God, girl, we almost had him.'

Mark St George lowered his fingers from the bandage above his throbbing eyes. 'Beg your pardon, sir. But he almost had us.'

Gates telephoned Larson's landlady from the hall phone in his rooming house.

'Oh, Mr Gates, I've been meaning to write you a letter – '

'Is he back?'

'Well, no, he's not. But I'd slipped a note with your address under his door, and your message, so I gave it to Mr Larson's friend when he came back for his things and then I thought maybe I should tell you. So you'd know this person has your name.'

'What friend?'

'I don't know his name, but Mr Larson has gone to California. He's going to be a riveter in the Kaiser yards. You know, building the Liberty ships.'

'When did he go?'

'Some time last week, his friend said. Mr Larson got a sudden offer. So his friend came by with the back rent and took his things. He's going to send them to California. He left an extra week's rent because Mr Larson hadn't given notice. I thought that was nice.'

'Did he say how long he'd be in California?'

'No, but it sounded like he's going to stay. There's a lot of work out there – '

'Wait a minute . . . did you say Larson said he was going to work as a *riveter*?'

'Yes.'

'Are you sure? Not a welder?'

'He said riveter. I told you, he said there's lots of work on the Liberty ships.'

'Are you sure you don't remember his friend's name?'

'I . . . I don't remember. I don't recall that he said it. He just told me what I told you and gave me the money and took Mr Larson's things.'

'And you gave him my address?'

'I hope that's all right.'

'Sure, thank you. I guess I'll be hearing from Mr Larson pretty soon.'

'If you do, Mr Gates, please thank him for me. I mean, for paying the extra rent.'

Gates said he would and hung up. He paced the hall for a while, then knocked on Tweed's door. Tweed opened it, holding a newspaper.

'Sorry if Armstrong was a bum steer. Still don't know who sent the tip. What's up?'

The kitchen had an enamel table across from the wall with the stove, sink and refrigerator, and looped over its single chair was Tweed's gun in a holster and shoulder harness. He saw Gates looking at it. 'What's up? I haven't seen you since our night at Miz Sally's. The old broad's a corker, isn't she?'

Gates told him what Larson's landlady had said.

Tweed shrugged. 'Well, if he comes after you then you're onto something. If he doesn't, you know the whole thing's in your head.'

'I think I'm a little worried – '

'Don't worry. If anybody with a machine gun asks for you I'll say you're out.'

'You don't think this is serious?'

'I'm going to look into Larson.'

'I don't think you'll find him. I'm going out to get someone I know to check out the Kaiser yards, but I don't think we'll find him there either.'

'Why not?'

'Kaiser's building Liberty ships. They weld them. It's a major factor in their speed. They weld big prefabricated sections. They don't rivet individual plates.'

'They use any rivets?'

'A few. But it's not the process. The friend she gave my name to specifically said Larson was going to be a riveter. I don't believe it.'

'That's pretty interesting,' Tweed said, and then the telephone rang. 'Excuse me.'

'Tweed,' he said, pulling the receiver into the kitchen for privacy. He was on the phone a while and when he came back he said, 'How'd you like to take a ride over to Jersey?'

'What for?'

'Weehawken cops want to talk to you.'

'What about? What are you talking about?' Tweed was watching him intently.

'What did you do after you saw Armstrong?'

'Got on a trolley and came back to New York.'

'Anybody see you?'

'The trolley conductor.'

'Anybody else?'

'I don't know. Somebody on the ferry . . . what's this about?'

'Armstrong got killed, right around the time you saw him. Crushed under a load of iron. His boss found him in the yard when he came back.'

'And you think *I* did that?'

'To tell you the truth, the Weehawken cops are the ones who'll need convincing.'

'Wait. Before I got on the trolley I ducked into a bar and telephoned you. I looked at my watch. It was exactly a quarter to twelve.'

'That should help. Get your coat.'

'Should I bring a lawyer?'

'They'll take a sight more kindly to me than a lawyer. Get your coat. I've already called for a car.'

'Who do you think killed Armstrong?'

'Maybe somebody who was afraid he'd talk.'

'You mean he was in on the fire?'

'*If* it was intentional, maybe he was. Or maybe somebody was trying to set you up for a fall . . . Get your coat. Let's not keep these guys waiting.'

'I've got to find Larson.'

'First you got to go to Weehawken.'

The next morning, after a long night with the Weehawken police department — a night which would probably still be going on if Tweed had not repeatedly gone in to bat for him — Gates ran for a phone in his coffee break and called the navy office that ran security checks on Prince and Gates's new draughtsmen and asked for an officer he'd dealt with in the past. The man was still at his post, which was odd . . . everyone seemed to be moving around since the war.

'Trying to run down a fellow we might want to hire as a foreman. I hear he went to California. His name is Hank Larson. I heard he was working for Kaiser. No, I don't know which yard. We'd appreciate . . . yes, I know you don't run an employment service. On the other hand, somebody sent my uncle a couple of tickets to the Yankees' opener and . . . good, thanks, I'll call you tomorrow.'

He called a ticket agent and had two box seats sent to the security officer. The next day he called back. No Hank Larson was known at any of the Kaiser yards.

28

On the fifty-ninth night, when the VII C U-boat surfaced to charge her batteries and make speed in the dark, Captain Giuseppe Ponte rejoiced at the lively odour of fish and weed. They had crossed the mid-ocean desert. The great depths were astern and the American continent loomed near.

Ponte filled his lungs with the rich smells. The North Atlantic was too big an ocean for his taste, and the U-boat had crossed it so slowly, submerged in daylight except for a short stretch in the middle out of range of enemy aircraft. For more than a month its waters had been as cold and dead as the starry sky, and he had longed for his Mediterranean, embraced warmly by land so that birds and fishes lived on all of it. Not barbarous like this cold ocean and its German masters.

The signs in the lobby directory and on the frosted-glass door of the offices themselves still read 'Prince and Gates'. Inside, there were changes.

Several dozen extra drawing tables had been shoe-horned into the bullpen along the walls furthest from the windows and lighted by new hanging fixtures. It was almost seven o'clock on a Friday evening, but thirty or forty draughtsmen were still at work.

'Hey, where do you think you're going?'

A stout young man in thick glasses was watching from his drawing table. Gates didn't recognize him. Nor did he know most of the others who looked up.

'I'm Steven Gates. This used to be my office.'

'Oh. Sorry.'

'That's okay. Sorry to interrupt.' He waved to an engineer who'd worked for his uncle for years, then entered his office and closed the door.

He turned on his light and stood at his drawing table. The last piece he'd been working on, a four-inch gun tub, was still taped to the board. He took out some fresh paper, picked up a pencil and started sketching aimlessly, trying to catch the flow of thought in lines and numbers.

He worked easily and slowly, letting the ideas run and forcing himself to stay detached and uncommitted so he wouldn't block the flow. When the windows were reflecting black night a drawing began to take shape – an aspect of a hull which grew rapidly in quick strokes. He walked sightlessly around his office, went back for a fresh look. He laughed out loud. It was a very beautiful hull, and Vladimir Yourkevitch had drawn one very similar ten years ago. The *Normandie*. Would he ever break with it?

He sat down again and mused over the hull, then drew a quick side view of her splendid profile. Or how it would look when she was upright again, shorn to the straight line of her promenade deck.

With luck she'd be raised by late summer. He tapped his finger on the paper, picked up his pencil and began designing a new superstructure in swift strokes.

'Steven – '

Richard Prince stood with one hand on the knob, his face guarded.

'Hello, Uncle Richard.'

'What are you doing here?'

'I got a funny idea. Kind of a different way of looking at things. Something tells me I should study water more and hulls less.'

Prince looked at him sharply. 'What do you mean?'

'I'm not sure yet, but I don't think we've gone very far beyond the problems of stress. We design our hulls to be strong enough to bear the loads and stresses of weight, pressure, buoyancy, vibration and wave impact.'

358

'Those happen to be real problems – '

'Sure. But we're steaming at *twice* the speed we did fifty years ago, and we sure as hell haven't doubled our knowledge of speed. You can build the engines, but who knows what's really going on under the hull at thirty-five knots?'

'We tank test models – '

'If only we could see directly the way the water flows past the hull. Submerge a motion picture camera, or something – I'll bet you we'll design new propellers that make the ones we're using now look primitive – what are you looking at?'

'I didn't know salvage divers cared so much about engineering.'

'Neither did I.'

Prince threw an arm around Gates's shoulder. He hugged him, then stepped back, embarrassed.

'Have you had dinner?'

'Wait. Look at this.'

'The *Normandie*?'

'I was playing around with these flow ideas and look what the pencil drew all by itself. Embarrassing as hell – here, look at this.' He flipped the drawing aside. 'She's going to need a new superstructure to become a trooper.'

'Two-stacker?'

'Why not? Simpler. We'd have to build her fast.'

'That you would.' Prince fingered the sketch. 'What's this hanging off the stern?'

'Lido decks. Like the Italian ships.'

'On the North Atlantic? What for?'

'I saw the *Queen Mary* with a huge load of German prisoners last week. They were jammed topside like sardines. Our troops could use a lot more deck space to walk around and get some fresh air. They don't care if it's cold. Better than being cooped up belowdecks for five days. See, they overhang the hull aft like a carrier's flight deck.'

'Very nice. Very nice.'

'Uncle Richard . . . who should I see about doing the trooper design for the *Normandie*?'

'I'll introduce you when your sketches are presentable. But, Steven, don't set your heart on it.'

'Does Gibbs have it?'

'Not that I know of. It's just – they may not use her.'

'What? Why?'

'Who knows how badly she's deteriorated? I hear that both port motors are ruined.'

'She'll turn twenty-five knots with only two. That's still fast enough.'

'But they might decide to use the time and material to build more Liberty ships. We're losing a lot more of them than liners. There's no point in transporting soldiers to a front we can't supply.'

Prince explained as they walked through the darkened bullpen. 'Just when I thought we'd beaten the U-boats with the radar and our air umbrella the Nazis tore the convoys apart again. March was the worst month of the war. April and May were better, but not by much.'

'What's the answer?'

'More ships. Which brings us to you. I'm at my wits' end, son. Can you help me?'

'I'll change to the swing shift on the ship and work here in the day.'

'When will you sleep?'

'From midnight to six. That's enough.'

'Do you want to come home to live?'

Gates thought about it. 'I'd like to, but I'd waste too much time travelling crosstown. Where I am now I'm only a few minutes from the ship to my room.'

Prince nodded, hesitated, then said, 'Steven, I have to say something about your father – '

'It's okay.'

'I'm sorry I said what I said. About the boiler room.'

'I guess I always suspected.'

'Try to remember that a lot of decent people got caught up in that speculative craze. It was a reaction to the war, or some damned thing. All I know is, everything seemed so simple until the Crash.'

'How come you didn't get caught?'

'I got my satisfaction, excitement, building ships. That's what most people did it for. Excitement. That's how I escaped. I already had my excitement in my work. I couldn't wait to get to the drawing board in the morning . . . '

'By the way,' Gates said. 'I don't think I ever thanked you for calling Captain Tooker.'

'What do you mean?'

'Didn't you call Captain Tooker and ask him to put me in the diving school?'

'No. I would have, if you'd asked . . . though God help me if your mother had found out. . . but I didn't.'

'That's strange . . . I wonder who did?' What the hell was going on? Why would somebody other than Uncle Richard do him such a favour without telling him? What would they gain? Well . . . the training had taken him out of action for a while. People like Commander Ober at ONI who didn't want him poking around must have been pleased by the quiet . . .

29

'I'm going to put this bluntly,' Weatherburn said. 'You're a damned attractive woman. It seems to me you could do a better job of getting Gates to open up.'

Duncan stiffened. Mark's face went blank. And Cordi looked at Weatherburn, who was toying with his switchblade, to see if she had heard right.

He looked right back at her. 'You heard me.'

'I *heard* you, but I'm not sure I believe you could mean – '

'Of course you do.'

'You want me to sleep with Gates? I thought that sort of thing went out with the Zimmermann Telegram.'

'You know damned well it hasn't, but I didn't say that. I do, however, expect you to figure out what has to be done and do it – '

Cordi stood up. 'Listen to me. If you have your heart set on getting Steven Gates in bed with somebody to learn more about him, I'm sure that you can get some girl from BSC who's a specialist at that sort of thing. I'm not, and I don't intend to be.'

'May I remind you that there's a war on and people are making sacrifices all the time, and of more than their precious virtue.'

'May I remind you that I've lost my share in this war.' Cordi ran her hands through her hair. 'It doesn't have a damned thing to do with virtue, anyhow, but it would be a mistake with Gates. It wouldn't *work*. You can maybe try that sort of thing with someone like van Slough, but it won't work with Gates.'

'Why not?'

'In his way he's as naive about women as anyone I've ever met — '

Weatherburn fidgeted with the knife, snapping the blade and clicking it shut. 'You haven't told me your real reason, have you?'

Cordi looked at him, surprised. 'Reason for what?' She knew full well that they both knew ... 'You're right, I haven't told you the *whole* reason.'

'Which is?'

'It doesn't matter. And it's nothing you would understand.'

Weatherburn didn't press it, instead presented his evidence in a relentless drone ... 'The fire at the truckyard, Cordi. The doors closed on the ship. Van Slough managing that Dutch pronunciation test. Gates's trips to England. And now Armstrong murdered in front of your eyes, only moments after you followed Gates to the scrapyard. What do you need? Gates to walk in here with a gun?'

'I told you, I'm not convinced by the Dutch test.' It was all she could find to say.

'This just came from London,' Mark said. 'They've exchanged messages with the coastwatcher in New Guinea. He reports that van Slough was a salvage diver in Shanghai, just like he said, before the Japanese took the city in '37. Left Djakarta, where he was born, in '38 for New York. France briefly in 1939, and was on his way back to New York when Cordi met him on the *Normandie*. Made a trip to Sweden after hostilities broke out and stayed a while arranging scrap metal contracts and then back to New York.'

Cordi's heart sank. She'd been holding onto the hope that Mark's information from the Orient would indict van Slough and thereby clear Steven. Now what could she say when Weatherburn threw the trucking fire at her, the doors, the trips to England, the murder of the boy, Armstrong? Worse, what could she think?

Weatherburn looked at her. 'So much for Cordi's favourite suspect.'

She refused to give him the satisfaction. 'That's too bad for van Slough.'

'How so?'

'Now he won't get a girl from BSC.'

They turned off Canal into Mott Street. Cordi took Gates's arm, which she squeezed so tight that he looked questioningly at her.

'Mr Weatherburn warned me to be careful in Chinatown.'

Gates laughed. 'My mother used to warn Kay about white slavers down here. And me about Tong wars. Tweed says it's the safest precinct in town.'

Restaurant and shop doors were open to the street, flavouring the spring air with ginger, cooked meat, fresh vegetables, hung fowl and burnt incense. The narrow sidewalks were jammed, shared by chinese shopping with string bags and uniformed soldiers and sailors jostling along in boisterous, gawking packs.

Cordi kept holding his arm. 'A beautiful day.'

'Hungry?'

'Not yet.'

The stepped into the street to get by a crowd of Chinese men who were clustered around a storefront and exclaiming over the long yellow sheets of paper that were taped to the windows and covered with columns of bright red characters.

'What do you think they're doing?' asked Cordi.

'Reading the war news from China.'

'How do you know that?'

'Charlie told me.'

'Ah, the brilliant clod.'

'He's all right,' Gates said. 'You two ought to declare a truce. He can't help being Irish and you can't help being what you are.'

'What's that?'

Gates stopped and turned and faced her for the pleasure of seeing her eyes. 'Lovely.'

Cordi smiled slowly and gripped his arm. 'Oh, my God, is that the wrong arm?'

'It's the other.'

'Still hurt?'

'Not much.'

'I suppose on the basis of Charlie cutting your hose I should declare a truce with him. Was he this way before the Spanish War?'

'I guess he's a little calmer, now that you mention it.'

They passed a storefront burial society. Charlie had told him that the war had halted the traffic of burial boxes back to China. Somewhere in Chinatown a warehouse bulged with the miniature coffins in which they transported cremated remains.

'Steven?'

'What?'

'Do you miss your work?'

'Funny you'd ask. I had a sort of revelation in the middle of the accident when the current flipped me over and I saw that I'd do better to study water flows than hulls. All of a sudden I started thinking about design again. That's the reason I went back to Uncle Richard. And he needed help.'

'I was wondering what you'd do when the salvage is finished . . . will it be over soon?'

'Couple of months, with luck. I haven't really thought about what I'm going to do . . . I guess I'll just work with Uncle Richard and try to land some work on the refit . . . Let me ask *you* something. Do you know anyone in British Intelligence?'

'How would I know such people?'

'I know you meet a lot of people in your work. You're always interviewing somebody important.'

'I might know them, but wouldn't know if I did. They certainly wouldn't tell me . . . why do you ask?'

'Do you ever come across any rumours about the *Normandie?*'

'There was a lot of talk at the time. I gathered the inquiries found it accidental. Isn't that why you're working on the salvage?'

'What do you mean?' He looked at her curiously, and Cordi knew she'd made a dangerous slip. She said, 'I don't know . . . Charlie once mentioned that you'd been angry over the accident reports, and that's why you left your uncle.'

'Charlie? He does have a big mouth . . . Yes, I don't believe the reports. I've been looking around, talking to people.'

'Is that your big secret?' Cordi tried to sound casual.

'If you want to call it that.' Gates sounded annoyed. 'No big deal.'

'Have you found anything?'

Gates looked at her again and wondered if he should tell her he'd found a guy who got a load of girders dropped on his head because he was talking to him . . . or about a truckyard that burned down to the ground after he was there . . . or should he tell her that the Weehawken cops admitted to Tweed that Armstrong had already got in trouble for using the crane when the boss was away, and maybe it *was* an accident, that maybe the owner of the scrapyard was at the controls and was afraid to admit it? Should he tell her about the doors in the *Normandie* nobody but him thought were important? Or the man he saw in the *Normandie*'s stack? Or about Larson, who seemed to have disappeared? Should he tell her that he was the only person he knew who believed that the *Normandie* was sabotaged – including Charlie and Uncle Richard and Commander Ober and even Tweed – and after a year of getting nowhere that maybe he was nuts?

'No,' he said, 'I'm dead-ended,' and took her hand firmly to close the subject.

And Cordi thought, as she felt his strong fingers close around hers, that if he was the Otter, and he had killed Armstrong, then he saw her with Armstrong and tried to kill her too. If he wasn't the Otter, then he might not know that Armstrong was killed right after they spoke . . . 'Steven, did you read about that crane accident over in New Jersey?'

'The kid who was killed? Yes . . . '

'When I read something like that I worry about you having another accident on your job. It's such dangerous work – '

'Don't. And it's a lot safer than getting shot at by Germans.'

'What do you suppose went wrong with the crane?'

'I didn't read the story that carefully.'

She felt she knew him well enough by now to at least know when he was uncomfortable . . . Clearly he didn't want to talk about the crane. His shoulders were hunching up a little, tightening, and the little round burn-scar on his cheek had reddened slightly.

She pushed. 'It sounded so terrible – '

Gates pulled her to him.

'What is it?' But he looked away and held her without a word and buried his face in her hair until people on the sidewalk were staring. She didn't know what to do. Had she really upset him? Or was he just trying to shut her up? Or . . . could his conflict be like hers? Could he be the Otter, and feel something for her at the same time . . .?

'Steven, people are looking.'

Gradually he seemed to relax, though still holding her.

'Just hungry,' he mumbled, nibbling at her neck, then letting her go with a laugh.

After lunch they walked downtown through the Saturday afternoon quiet of the City Hall district, then down Broadway into the empty canyons of the Wall Street area, stopping occasionally in small bars for a beer, and getting a bit high in the hot sun.

Once when they stood in the middle of a cross street, empty in four directions and lined by sidewalks equally deserted, Cordi kissed him suddenly on the mouth, then broke away, smiling. Weatherburn, damn him, should be pleased.

They rested at the Fraunces Tavern bar and had cocktails, then walked to the Battery to watch the sunset. The promenade was crowded with tourists and soldiers and sailors, and the harbour seemed filled to capacity by freighters and anchored warships.

'What are those little boats?' Cordi asked as they leaned on the railing. Several small cabin boats were lined against the seawall, and as they watched, another boat docked at the end of the line, while a sailor and a pretty girl holding hands boarded the boat at the front.

'Statue of Liberty sightseeing.'

'But doesn't that great excursion boat go there?' She pointed at the Statue of Liberty ferry, moored for the night.

Gates grinned. 'These offer a private viewing.'

'What's so amusing?'

'Watch them a moment.'

Cordi watched. The first boat putted away from the wall. A couple boarded the next, and it too headed into the harbour, bobbing on the chop. Another docked and a couple disembarked, flushed and smiling.

'Oh . . . I see what you mean.'

'Have *you* ever seen the Statue of Liberty?'

'I remember it quite clearly, when you showed it to me from the *Normandie*.'

'I forgot,' Gates said, thinking how odd it was that they'd never re-created the single moment of intimacy they'd shared the night they first danced in that heartbeat between peace and war.

'Steven?'

'What?' He turned away from the water. He hadn't the faintest notion what she was thinking, her eyes had become so empty. It was eerie, but then he decided it had to be because she was looking into the sun.

'It's been a long time,' she said. 'I think I'd rather like to see it again . . . up close.'

They walked to the first boat.

He held her hand as they stepped onto a deck scuffed and splintered by a constant assault of leather-soled shoes. The boatman took his money and started the engine. Vibrating, the boat lurched away from the seawall while Gates and Cordi went into the cabin and closed the door. It was warm and dingy, nearly filled by a large divan covered with blankets. Curtains hid the ports, admitting slivers of light when they swayed as the boat rocked.

'Will the man tell us when it's time to come out and see the statue?' Cordi asked, sitting on the edge of the divan and smoothing the blankets around her.

'I seriously doubt it,' Gates said. 'I think it's up to us to keep track.'

'Would you like the first watch?'

'I think he'll circle Bedloe Island a couple of times. That should give us a clue.'

'You sound familiar with the process.'

'Wally told me.' He was still leaning against the door.

'Well, here we are.'

'A moment of truth, as they say . . . '

Not yet, she thought. She patted the blanket.

Gates sat beside her and took her hand. It felt cool, but after a moment's hesitation she curled her fingers around his. The boat hit a wake and rocked violently.

'Oh God . . . what if I get seasick —?'

He kissed her mouth, and Cordi's hand rose to his hair as she kissed him back. He was almost trembling with the softness of her mouth and the taste of her, when she broke away.

'I can't do this, I'm sorry but — '

'What's wrong?'

'I'm not sure . . . '

'We've been dating for months. I'm twenty-seven, you're twenty-eight – '

'Seven.'

'Sorry. And I'm a man and you're a woman and I'm crazy about you and you seem to be able to stand me . . . and I think something must be wrong.'

Something had to be wrong, of course, so she invented something which was about ten per cent true. But the explanation got out of hand. 'Do you remember when we met on the *Normandie* and I told you about a man who came to my dressing room and offered me a job with the BBC?'

'I remember . . . Alec, wasn't it? A perfect voice for the microphone, you said.'

'Well, we were very close and after the war started I went back to Geneva. He ran the BBC newsroom there. We were together through the winter – during what the Americans called the phony war. Well, it wasn't. I didn't know about it, but Alec was approached by someone in the Foreign Office and asked to turn our facilities into a secret transmitter for British agents. Switzerland was neutral. Alec was just an ordinary journalist, but of course he agreed. What he didn't know was that the Nazis had broken virtually every British ring in Europe during the so-called phony war. A German agent tricked him into betraying some of the people he'd serviced with the radio, and when Alec realized what was happening and tried to stop them, they shot him to death in the street. I've had a hard time getting over that . . . '

Cordi looked up at him. The story had got away from her and she'd told it all, except about the end, when Weatherburn had saved her, and the real reason why she couldn't allow herself to sleep with him. The reason that had nothing to do with Alec . . . Steven reached gently for her hand.

'The boatman's about to get the shock of his life. No action.'

370

Cordi allowed herself to laugh. 'We might as well enjoy the view. How do I look?'

'Lovely.' He opened the door and they climbed out, holding hands. What the boatman thought was unknowable because he was squinting into the sunset. The Statue of Liberty was a dark silhouette, growing large as they drew near, and a breeze from the water took the warmth from the dying June day. Cordi shivered. When Gates put his arm around her, she moved away.

'Tell me something,' she said. 'Do you really find me attractive?'

'Do you have to ask?'

'I mean you haven't . . . insisted.'

Gates looked back towards the Battery, then down at her. 'I'm not sure . . . I was so happy to see you again. I don't want to push my luck . . . Whatever happens with you will happen.'

It sounded very convincing . . . she wanted to believe it . . . 'What did you expect when you rang me up in London?' she asked abruptly. It occurred to her that just as she and Mark and Duncan had been instructed to make American friends, he could have been told to cultivate her. But to take it easy, not risk losing the contact . . .

'I wanted to see you. A lady who worked for the BBC, I figured, would know her way around.' He smiled when he said it. 'Say, look at *that* – the *Mary*.'

She was steaming up from the Narrows, slowly, trailed by a half-dozen tugs that looked as if they were pulling the dusk after her. The boatman speeded up to get back to the Battery ahead of her awesome wake. As she passed the Battery she was backlighted by the glowing remnants of the sunset. Her decks were thronged. Gates borrowed glasses from the boatman, scanned her, then handed them to Cordi. There didn't seem to be a single square foot that wasn't occupied by a man in a rumpled, faded khaki uniform.

'German prisoners,' she said. 'They must be the ones

Monty beat in North Africa.' Gates, she noted, said nothing. He was watching the *Mary* intently, and she wondered if it was the sight of one of his beloved liners that enthralled him so, or the humiliating spectacle of his side's defeat.

'Soon now,' Lieutenant Erich Kroner told Grandzau. 'Soon you will see.' Kroner was blind but he had heard how the Luftwaffe had bombed New York and he had primed Grandzau to describe the ruin as their prison ship sailed up the Hudson.

Kroner had been blinded and captured one night in North Africa as his sand-yellow Panzer III(J) Special ploughed across the moonlit desert, at the head of a short ghostly column of the Fifteenth Panzer Division – *Panzerarmee*, Afrika Korps. A veteran of Poland and France, the years in the desert had burned the young tank commander hard and lean, his sun-blackened face bony, hawkish, spare as an Arab's, his brain tuned acutely to survive. His first defeat had been dealt by his last sight on earth – a new American Sherman tank that shrugged off a hit from the Panzer's .88 and returned fire just as Kroner had pressed his face to the view-slit to give his driver new orders. There'd been a sudden, loud noise that still echoed in his mind, and everything he saw turned a terrible white.

It stayed white for weeks, first in the American field hospital and then in the desert prison camp. After a while it began to turn red. Grandzau, the mechanic who'd pulled him from the burning Panzer seconds before the ammunition exploded, stayed with him as the red slowly, inexorably darkened. His sight was black now – lighted by occasional dazzling flashes – and Grandzau's thick, calloused hand held Kroner's whenever they moved.

From the prison camp they'd travelled for weeks in trucks, and boarded a giant ship. Some of the German prisoners said it was the British *Queen Mary*, but Kroner didn't believe them. Berlin radio had reported her sunk last year when Rommel still ruled North Africa.

Ten thousand prisoners of war were crammed into her for eight days as she sped from North Africa, every man waiting for a German raider to swoop down and, unknowingly, sink her. The guards wouldn't say where they were bound for, but Rommel's desert fighters watched the sun and the stars and knew that their course had been laid for the American slave labour camps, repeatedly described by their indoctrination courses.

On the eighth morning, this morning, Erich had heard the other prisoners talking excitedly. A guard had admitted they were landing in New York City, the great American port which they'd been told had been bombed even more than London. He felt the engines slowing.

'What do you see? Are any skyscrapers standing?'

'I see a giant woman standing in the water,' Grandzau answered slowly. 'It's a green statue.'

'Still? The buildings. Look to the right, Grandzau. Right, from the woman. Are any of the buildings still standing?' He'd seen the city as a boy. Around him, the other prisoners stopped talking and the deck grew very quiet.

'What do you see? *Tell me.*'

'It's beautiful,' Grandzau said in little more than a whisper.

'Destroyed?' Kroner was delighted, even as he prayed that the Bund had evacuated his father and mother to the relative safety of Peekskill, up the Hudson. 'All of it?'

'No,' Grandzau said. The spired skyline was pink in the sunset. 'It is beautiful.'

'But the bombs?'

'No bombs, Erich. No bombs.'

Grandzau was stunned by the tears suddenly coming from Erick Kroner's blasted eyes. He patted his shoulder and mumbled over and over, 'Don't cry, Erich. Don't *cry.*'

'Where's the guard?' Kroner said. 'Bring a guard, Grandzau. *Guard.*'

A Royal Marine shouldered through the quiet prisoners, a short billy dangling from his burly arm. 'What's going on?'

'Are you guard?' Kroner asked in the pidgin English he'd learned in the prison camps.

'I'm bloody well no damned Nazi. You blind or someth – Oh, I'm sorry.'

'I want to see my father,' Kroner said, tears visible in his sightless eyes.

The marine patted his shoulder as clumsily as Grandzau had and shared a look with the fat German mechanic. 'So, I suspect, do we all, mate.'

30

The water shallowed every night after Giuseppe Ponte
smelled the land, and the waves gradually changed shape,
losing the smooth rise-and-fall symmetry characteristic of
the neatly spaced Atlantic rollers and assuming a sharp,
serrated and increasingly chaotic chop that made the
submarine pitch and roll and corkscrew so violently when
it surfaced at night that many of the German sailors,
including Ponte's engineer, were seasick.

The boat was heavily burdened, carrying as she did her
full complement of torpedoes and anti-aircraft ammunition
as well as a full crew to fight in the American shipping
lanes after her delivery mission was performed. The crew
understandably resented the miniature, which hung under
the U-boat's hull, flooded and attached by the fore and
aft brackets. It added eight feet to the U-boat's draught
and complicated its manoeuvres. Trimming the U-boat
required constant, painstaking work by the controlman
whenever she flooded or blew her ballast tanks, or ran
at periscope depth.

Ponte thought the miniature actually stabilized the U-
boat in heavy seas, but tensions were so high that he
didn't venture his opinion. The already brutally crowded
boat was jammed further by the addition of Ponte and his
engineer. They shared a forward bunk with two torpedomen,
which meant he had six hours to sleep and no place to
spend the other eighteen. No matter what cranny he
wedged himself into, standing or crouching, a sailor or
cook or engineer was always asking him to move. For
eight weeks Ponte did nothing but wait and move. Except
at night.

At night von Harling allowed him up on the rolling deck to exercise. Ponte's German engineer preferred helping out in the U-boat's motor room, servicing the electrics while the diesels ran. Ponte concentrated on staying in condition. Afterward, while Ponte rested, he and von Harling would talk, leaning on the rails of the conning tower, watching the black night.

The Italian frogman and the German U-boat captain had discovered a common language in English. Ponte had learned his as a boy diving for coins to amuse British tourists on the Amalfi Riviera. Von Harling had gone to school at Charterhouse when his father was posted to England as the Kaiser's representative of the *Kriegsmarine* before World War I drove them home.

Ponte talked about underwater exploits in the Mediterranean, his miniature submarine attacks against the British harbours at Gibraltar and Alexandria. Not bravery, he said, just a game of skill. But the night that the radio brought news of the Axis defeat in North Africa, the Italian turned morose. Would the Allies invade Italy?

Two weeks later, when Admiral Dönitz ordered the U-boats to break off their wolf-pack attacks on the convoys and retire west of the Azores because of disastrous losses, it was von Harling who turned dour.

About Ponte's mission, they did not speak. von Harling knew only what he had to and nothing about the Otter or the plan to sink the *Queen Mary*. It did not make him happy that he had to wait to rescue Ponte and Canaris's agent and return them safe to Germany.

'Will you wait for me, my friend?' Ponte teased. 'Or will I spend the rest of the war in New York?'

'I'll wait,' von Harling said gloomily.

Ponte understood the German's mood. When they'd left France the U-boats were winning the battle of the Atlantic, but in the time it had taken to creep across the ocean, Allied aircraft and radar had reversed matters. Poor von Harling had his head full commanding a fifty-man crew and worrying about distant admirals at the other end of the radio. Better a little *Seehund*, Ponte thought, and a man's own skills, to command.

Twice a week, throughout the crossing, Ponte inspected the diving gear and disassembled, cleaned and reassembled the mouthpiece, hoses and valves of the self-contained underwater breathing apparatus. He worried that acrid fumes from the diesel engines and the battery acids would cause his rubber fins and face mask to disintegrate, so twice a week he soaped and rinsed them in sea water in the reeking head.

And then, finally, the U-boat was off New York – thirty miles to the south-east in a quiet slot between the European and coastal convoy lanes. Ponte dived that night with a powerful light and inspected the miniature. It had grown a beard of sea grass, but the electrical switches, motors and pumps were sound.

They hid on the bottom for four days – they had arrived early for the rendezvous with Admiral Canaris's agent. Ponte scraped the sea grass from the miniature, exiting the U-boat through an empty torpedo tube, and revelling in the opportunity to restore his body in the depths. At night von Harling surfaced cautiously, with only the conning tower emerging, to run the diesels and clear the air. He allowed no one up but the look-outs with night glasses.

Late in the evening of the fifth day – the day of rendezvous with the agent's boat – they crept to the surface on electrics. Ponte and his engineer put on their rubber suits and breathing gear. Von Harling scanned the sea and sky again and again through the periscopes. No sign of the agent's boat. But it was still daylight. Another few minutes until the agent would appear on the horizon and his U-boat would be free of the *Seehund*.

Suddenly shouting erupted in the control room.

A trim tank valve had refused to shut. Air was pouring into the tank, lifting the bow, canting the U-boat at a steep angle. von Harling ordered the forward ballast tank flooded, then countermanded his order. There was a danger in submerging with the malfunctioning trim tank. There was also danger on the surface. He'd seen none of them by the light of the setting sun, but this close to New York he knew the defences had to be all about. The Americans had organized their fishing fleets as long-range observers and equipped the boats with radios. There were aircraft, observation planes and rescue patrols. They were manned, according to U-boat Command and his friend Admiral Canaris, by reservists. But he was off the main sea routes and the sun was dying a red death in the skyscope. It would be dark in ten minutes.

'Prepare to surface.' The look-outs and anti-aircraft gun crew crowded around the conning tower ladder, poised to spring out the hatch.

'It's not dark yet,' his chief said.

'I know,' muttered von Harling, his eyes on the skyscope.

'It's too dangerous.'

'And what do we do with the *Seehund* if we're stuck on the bottom fixing that valve when the agent comes to the rendezvous? Take it back to Germany?'

The chief's answer was short and vulgar. Von Harling shook his head. '*Surface.*'

Air hissed, stinging the ears. The steel was thrown back. Before the first man was out, blinding red sunlight poured into the tower like burning oil.

'Look at that!' Wally Stratton yelled.

'Where?' Then the pilot saw it too. 'Jesus Christ! What's he doing there?'

'We better tell the skipper,' Mel said.

Manned by its weekend volunteer crew, their two-hundred-and-fifty-foot navy K-2 blimp floated close to the water, tethered to a conical canvas bag which acted like a sea anchor holding a yacht's bow into a gale. It didn't exactly moor the patrol blimp, but it did a fair job of keeping her near one place if the wind didn't blow too strong.

They had lowered the sea anchor so the crew could rest and eat supper while waiting for stragglers from a mauled, widely-scattered convoy they'd been escorting all day to the safety of New York. No stragglers had appeared when they finished eating so the skipper decided to head back to Long Island. The sun was setting. Without radar, which rumour promised they'd have soon, they'd see nothing at night.

Then the anchor winch had jammed, and the skipper, who'd replaced the Annapolis man six months ago, went back to the stern to help the riggers. And it was then that Wally Stratton looked down and saw a submarine break water right in front of the blimp's shadow.

The sub came up bow first, parting the water from below like a whale Wally had once seen with his mother from the deck of the boat en route to Bermuda. He was sitting in the cockpit in the skipper's seat beside the pilot. His friend Mel, the high-school history teacher, was leaning over his shoulder. The cook was cleaning the pantry, the engineers were helping the riggers. The radioman, having signed off with the naval air station on Rockaway, was tuning in WNEW music for the trip home.

The submarine rose high in the water, much more angular than a whale, and bristling with anti-aircraft guns. It looked dark grey and reflected dull red highlights from the sunset. The bow tapered to a thin wedge.

'That's a U-boat,' the pilot yelled. With the engines quietly idling, his voice carried easily to the rear of the gondola.

'Can it,' the skipper called back. The pilot was a known practical joker and the skipper, who owned an Oldsmobile agency in Hempstead, was in a black mood over the jammed winch.

'It's American,' said Wally. 'Got to be ours – '

'It's a *U-boat*, for Chrissake. Skipper, get up here, I ain't kidding.'

The captain came forward. Wally trained binoculars on the submarine's conning tower. Encircled by handrails and studded with the anti-aircraft guns, it looked a little like a castle turret. He tried to match it to the photos and silhouettes pasted to the hangar walls back in Rockaway. At this angle and with the sun, it was hard to tell.

'My God,' the skipper said, shouldering between them. 'It's a U-boat, like I said.'

'But what's he doing up in daylight, so close to New York?'

'He surfaced bow first,' Wally said. 'Maybe he's damaged.'

'Okay, battle stations, but nobody shoots till we see who he really is.' He nudged the pilot. 'Listen, move us right over him, we may want to drop a couple of depth charges.'

Wally saw a hatch pop open in the conning tower. 'They're coming out –'

'Get ready to cut that line, McClosky,' the skipper shouted towards the stern. 'But not till I tell you. Stratton, take over McClosky's gun.'

The pilot nudged his throttles and the engines revved, straining the blimp against the sea tether. Wally dropped into the seat behind the forward .50 calibre machine gun and trained it on the sub. A man in a black beret climbed out of the hatch, followed quickly by others. They had to be Americans. The hats, though . . . maybe British. He certainly wouldn't fire yet. In seconds the sailors had swarmed on top of the conning tower, scanning the sea and sky with long binoculars.

At first they missed the blimp in the glare of the setting sun. But when the huge shadow moved over the submarine, the look-outs whirled around, shielding their eyes. A half-dozen sailors poured out of the hatch and clambered over the anti-aircraft guns, wheeling the thin barrels upward.

'Germans,' the skipper yelled. 'It's a U-boat for sure. Fire, Stratton. *Fire, fire, damn it . . .*'

Wally triggered the .50 and the machine gun broke into a roar that drowned out the aircraft engines and filled the forward compartment with flying shell casings and a blue haze of cordite. On the sea, so close below, bullet geysers leapt out of the water and raced across the submarine's deck in bursts of splinters. It was the first time Wally had fired the weapon with intent to kill and he found his mind compartmentalizing, one part leading the geysers towards the conning tower, another remarking on the fact that the sleek steel boat had wooden decks, realizing they gave better footing for the gun crews, a holdover from the early days of the war when they still sank merchantmen on the surface to conserve torpedoes.

The machine gun shook and bucked in Wally's hands as he pivoted it on its mount, firing in long bursts. Sailors were pouring from the U-boat's main hatch now, and Wally stared in disbelief as they crumpled up and fell in the stream of his bullets. Some sprawled, some dropped like stones, one – wearing something on his back – pinwheeled across the deck, arms and legs flailing, and plummeted towards the water, only to smash into a ballast-tank casing when the wallowing boat heaved one side out of the water as a swell fell away.

Ponte was bracketed by a pair of .50 calibre machine-gun bullets. The first seared a hot ridge across his chest, causing blood to spill from a ragged tear in his rubber diving suit, and killed his engineer. The second hit his right-hand air tank a glancing blow, ricocheted across his shoulder, numbing his arm and hurling him off the splintered deck into the water.

He landed hard against the starboard ballast tank, hit his head and blacked out. The frigid water shocked him back to consciousness. The roar of the guns was unceasing and the water seemed to boil with bullets. He bit down instinctively on his mouthpiece, fumbled the tank valve open, and sank into the quiet Atlantic.

Deep in his best element, his instincts took charge. He swam away from the dark shape of the wallowing submarine. He swam until he was alone. Then, as pain began to throb through his chest and arm and shoulder and head, he began to think. He was some thirty miles from land, enemy land, and too badly hurt to swim, even with the scuba.

The U-boat was finished. Von Harling dead in the first fusillade, her trim tank jammed, she might last the night, might even defeat the air ship, but she'd never make it back to Germany. In the morning a flotilla of destroyers would seek her out and depth-charge her to pieces. If her surviving crew didn't scuttle her first. Von Harling had ordered charges set while they lay waiting.

What would the Otter do when he saw the battle on the way to the rendezvous? Would he save him? He'd never see a single diver at night. But he might see the miniature submarine. Ponte rose cautiously to the surface. The cold numbed his pain. He had swum two hundred yards from the U-boat. The blimp was still moving over it, raining down machine-gun fire.

It was night in the east; day waned in the west.

The Otter searched the dark horizon. He was alone at sea, thirty miles from New York, towing a laden barge. Astern of the tow, monstrous thunderheads rose to snuff out the half-set sun. Ahead, where he scanned the dark, a handful of early stars began to burn feebly behind thickening clouds.

He was ready for the *Seehund*, rigid with anticipation, legs taut on the rolling pilothouse deck, fists white on *Hollandia*'s helm except when he let go to hammer at the already wide-open throttle. Everything was ready. He had widened the *Normandie* lair's secret entrance, had piped in air, water and electricity, and prepared food and clothes and a cover for the man Uncle Willy had sent with the *Seehund*. Somewhere ahead a sleek raider was breaking surface in the dark, an entire U-boat and crew waiting for him.

Anticipation compressed the future into quick images . . . towing the *Seehund* under the barge through the submarine gates, past the patrols, slipping the miniature submarine into its lair in the *Normandie*, close to its victim's berth, launching torpedoes, and then escape as the *Queen Mary* toppled on her side, her naked propellers snatching at the sky, her stacks venting steam with a dying roar —

Ahead, the night suddenly flashed orange and white. For a moment he thought it was lightning, but the thunderheads were astern, still over land. Did he hear, or did he imagine an explosion rolling over the water? He cut the engine to hear better. A chill inched through his chest. There was a crackling, like a distant brushfire, a sound so unlike the sea that it could only be guns.

He shoved his throttle wide open.

'You got 'em, Wally!'

'Get ready to drop them bombs,' yelled the skipper. 'Cut that anchor line, goddamn it.'

In seconds four more German sailors went to the anti-aircraft guns, kicking and pushing the bodies of the first crew aside, and pivoted their guns towards the blimp. Wally sprayed the conning tower with a long burst. When he released the trigger he could hear nothing but an echo of his gun. He stared down at what he had done. It was incredible, but by merely pointing the machine gun and pulling the trigger he'd killed the entire gun crew before they could aim their weapons. They'd fallen like targets on the navy range, but he was sure that he hadn't really aimed. Just pulled the trigger.

He glanced the length of the swaying gondola. The tail- and mid-gunners were pounding away, shell casings flying like brass fans. Mel was firing the midships gun. Wally was astonished by the teacher's expression. He had often stopped at his Queens apartment after patrol. They'd sit half the night, drinking coffee, Mel with a cat on his lap and talking about past centuries. Now he was pouring fire onto the submarine, his thin frame shuddering from the recoil, his lips drawn tight. The riggers were slashing at the thick anchor line with a butcher knife from the pantry. The cook stood by with a fire axe, but there wasn't room to swing. Then the tail gun jammed.

The gunner, a grey-haired insurance executive from Larchmont, frantically tugged the belt. The riggers finished cutting the anchor line and started cranking open the bomb bay, which was in a separate compartment beneath the gondola. The skipper came running to the cockpit, shouting. The pilot stared at the sea ahead, his hands white-knuckled on the helm.

The blimp was swiftly nearing the U-boat now, coming lower and closer, and Wally wondered why the sub didn't dive. Couldn't they see the bomb bay opening? A forward hatch popped open near its long deck gun and a half-dozen sailors boiled out. The blimp gunners opened up again, sweeping the U-boat with wild fire, but the Germans slogged through it. Two fell. The survivors tried to elevate the deck gun high enough to fire at the blimp.

The blimp's stern machine gun jammed again. And the blimp was turning slightly, carrying the midships gun which was on the port side out of sight. Wally watched his bullets race across the water and into the deck gun crew. They collapsed and lay still, and again someone shouted congratulations, but Wally was staring in disbelief as another group of German soldiers ran to the gun where others lay grotesquely sprawled. The compartments in his mind began breaking up and he thought he could see where his bullets had smashed their arms and legs and he wondered what made them so brave.

'Look out,' shouted the pilot. 'Fire, Stratton. *Fire.*'

Again and again the U-boat crew tried and failed to reach their weapons. The air ship loomed over them like rolling fog, drifting closer and firing fitfully. Exhausted by pain and cold, Ponte trod water with his rubber fins. He saw a wounded seaman drag himself into the sheltered top of the conning tower. Another followed, and together they began to unlimber the rapid-firing *flak vierling*.

If the seasoned German gunners succeeded in getting that weapon into a firing position, then both the submarine and the air ship were finished. His only chance, he decided, was to try to rescue the little *Seehund* and hope the Otter found him. He took a bearing on the U-boat with his wrist compass, bit down on his mouthpiece and dived.

'Fire, Wally. *Fire.*'

The stern .50, unjammed again, had opened up and Wally was watching the wild fire scrambling the sea, yards from the U-boat. Then he saw what the pilot was yelling about. A new crew had reached the anti-aircraft guns on the conning tower while he'd been shooting at the deck gunners. Four barrels, long and needle-slim, turned skyward. He swung his weapon back, but he was too late. Flame lanced from the German guns.

The cabin exploded in flying rubble, and the entire ship shuddered to the concussion of the shell hits. Three men near him were thrown up against the ceiling. Their bodies crashed back to the deck, torn, bleeding, their faces smears.

Wally homed in on the conning tower and fired, vaguely aware that it was his own voice he heard bellowing out rage and fear. His bullets speckled the water, but somehow he couldn't make the killing stream bear on the German gunners. They unleashed another burst at the blimp.

The shells tore through the cabin near him. He heard screams and saw the skipper flung from the cockpit, which was spouting flame. The skipper's clothes were burning but he didn't seem to notice as he shambled towards the stern. A wounded rigger tackled the skipper, dragged him down to the deck and beat at the flames. Another struggled awkwardly with a fire extinguisher.

Wally kept firing until the wind blew the blimp over the U-boat, blocking his field of fire. He ran back to midships and found Mel dying. Almost delicately Wally pulled him off the machine gun, crouched in his bloody seat, and got the U-boat in his sights. Now the sun was blinding him, as it had the German lookouts. He squinted into the red glare and tried to distinguish the high mass of the conning tower against the scarlet sea.

Ponte swam fast and deep, propelling himself solely by his fins, one hand to the wound on his chest, the other on the compass in front of his eyes. The water was getting dark, with a blood-red tinge overhead from the setting sun.

The U-boat appeared at the limits of his underwater horizon, marked by the white froth of the sea sliding up and down her submerged sides. Ponte swam under it, down to fifty feet, and found his *Seehund*, held under the U-boat's keel by two brackets. To release the *Seehund* Ponte had to crank open the hinged forward bracket and disconnect the electrical feed cable which had conducted electricity from the U-boat's generators to periodically charge the *Seehund*'s batteries during the long Atlantic crossing.

He cast the beam of his diving light on the forward bracket, found the crank he had left in place the night before and began turning it. The steel brackets transmitted the kick of the U-boat's anti-aircraft guns . . . it felt as though the Germans had opened up with everything they had, and Ponte wondered, through the pain of his chest wound, whether the Americans on the blimp realized the intense desperation that fuelled the German gunners' bravery.

Slowly the bracket hinged away from the *Seehund*'s nose, until suddenly the fifty-foot miniature submarine was drifting free of its mother, tethered only by the heavy electrical feed cable. She started sinking, pulled down by a slight negative buoyancy. Ponte tried to disconnect the electric cable, but the short length had already fetched up tightly, putting such a strain on the connection that Ponte couldn't work it loose with his hands. He gave up quickly . . . any minute the blimp would drop depth charges . . .

Entering the *Seehund* by its wet-dry hatch, Ponte pumped out the water and crawled into the cockpit where he took the helm and played his hands over the controls – the hydroplane and compressed-air wheels, the ballast and trim-tank valve levers, the electric-motor and torpedo-firing switches. There was room here for two men; the rest of the fifty-foot boat was filled with her batteries and her four torpedoes. He switched the motor to half-speed reverse. The *Seehund* pulled against the electric cable, trembling. Ponte went to full reverse. The cable snapped, and the *Seehund* fled the stricken U-boat.

Wally fired blindly, fired until his machine gun had devoured its ammunition. He couldn't see if he had hit anything, but when his weapon was at last silent, the anti-aircraft guns below had stopped raking the gondola.

Where were the depth charges?

He saw the bombardier, dead, and the skipper burned and moaning and holding his face, the gunners dead, and the riggers. The cook, the short order man from Horn and Hardart, had a bloody arm, but he was standing.

'Crank the bay,' Wally said. 'We gotta drop the bombs before we blow past. I'll try to hold her.'

'They're all dead,' the cook said.

Wally shoved him towards the bomb-bay crank and ran forward. The sea looked closer. The blimp was sinking. It occurred to him that all the shells that had ripped through the gondola had pierced the gasbag as well. He yanked a fire extinguisher out of a dead man's hands, sprayed the flames in the cockpit and vaulted himself into the pilot's chair.

The controls were shot away. There was no way to turn the rudder or move the elevators. He finally realized that the engines had stopped. The blimp was adrift, the wind holding it above the U-boat. Wally slid down into the bombardier's nest, excited by this sudden strange ability to act decisively. He found the release lever and saw that the sub was directly under them. He pulled the bomb lever, hoping the cook had opened the doors, and hoping the depth charges were set shallow.

The blimp lurched as if it had been hit again, but he knew it was because the explosives had lightened her load by several hundred pounds. The wind was turning the blimp. He climbed out of the cockpit and joined the cook at the stern viewing-windows. A hail of fire from the sub shattered the glass and dropped the cook in a bloody heap.

Wally stepped over the body, thinking he was the last one alive, and watched the U-boat through the broken windows. The blimp was close to the water now, losing altitude fast. The sub was less than fifty feet away. A depth charge exploded under it, rocketing a huge geyser out of the sea, throwing men from the deck, heeling the sub on its side. Wally caught a glimpse of a huge steel fixture hanging down from the keel and wondered what it was. Then the second depth charge burst, a deep explosion followed and the U-boat reared out of the water and broke in half.

'Jesus,' Wally said to the dead cook. 'We did it.'

As the stern section floated away from the bow and began to sink, a lone German sailor walked slowly to the deck gun. With eerie deliberation he pivoted the big cannon and aimed it at the blimp. Waves broke over the deck and tugged at his knees.

The walls of the gondola were buckling, causing electric sparks to glint and chatter where torn wiring rubbed bare metal. The radio, which the first hail of bullets had silenced, suddenly came on again – music, loud in the dying quiet, static-muddled but clear enough for Wally to hear the familiar words ... 'Blue skies, smiling on me ... blue skies, do I see.'

He stood riveted in the stern of the cabin, gazing into the eyes of the German sailor who was staring down the cannon barrel as the sea came up to meet the blimp.

Book III

31

The Otter steered towards the flashes on the sea. They blazed intermittently for a few moments as the tug, tethered by the barge, strained to cover the distance. There was a sudden bright light, brighter by far than the rest, and then the flashes were gone, as abruptly and mysteriously as they'd begun. He checked his compass.

Dead on course for the rendezvous.

He covered several miles with deepening apprehension. Proof came in the form of a sudden impact against the tug's hull and a resounding clang as the eight-foot propeller struck something solid. The boat gave a sickening shudder but kept going. He yanked back the throttle and turned on the overhead spotlight, which had been installed atop the pilothouse courtesy of the US Navy because he had enlisted the tug as a member craft of the volunteer Inshore Patrol. He rotated the light with a hand crank on the ceiling. The beam slid through the night, highlighting wreckage in a hard, white moving circle.

A blimp's gasbag, big as a ball field, sprawled like a flattened tent. The cloth undulated on the swell and was peaked in placed by air pockets trapped under it. German life jackets drifted around its ragged perimeter. Tied in some of them were bodies – torn, battered, burned.

The tugboat's soft prow parted a cluster of broken wood – the U-boat's deck grating, he guessed. So much for the thin hope that she was hiding on the bottom. She was down there all right. Permanently. What disgusting twist of luck had protected the *Seehund* across the entire span of the Atlantic Ocean only to let an air patrol spot the U-boat in the last mile? Pounding the helm with a tightly clenched fist, he commenced a slow circuit of the battle area.

A light flashed suddenly on the water, beyond the gasbag several hundred yards into the night. Instantly the Otter killed his spot and the sea turned black. The light blinked again. Morse Vs – dot dot dot dash – the Vs that homed a radio signal to Hamburg? Or an American airman blinking victory Vs?

He watched the light for a long while, anxiously scanning the darkness, searching the points of the compass until he was satisfied he was alone with the wreckage and the signal. He steered past it, circling less out of wariness than the need for sea room to stop the barge. But as the tug deadened in the water, he reached for the throttle . . . in case the light belonged to an enemy . . . and prepared to ram.

He waited until the tug had drifted very close to the blinking light and turned on the spot. Fifty feet ahead, in the brilliant glare, a man appeared to be standing on the water. The tug inched closer, the spotlight revealing more. He stood on a flat wet shiny steel deck, inches above the waves.

The Otter continued to watch from inside the pilothouse, caution at war with hope, until he was near enough to see the man's tightly fitting rubberized canvas suit, the air tanks on his back, the fish-shaped *salmone* lead weights and the rubber bag in front which would contain a calcium solution to absorb carbon dioxide so that no bubble trail would give away the presence of the frogman. He would be invisible, using that closed-circuit rebreathing device, the most modern diving outfit in the world.

Hope soared through the Otter. The frogman was not standing on wreckage. The *Seehund* had survived. It lay beneath the diver's feet, sleek and steady, riding assuredly on the swell.

The Otter turned off the spot, turned on the white masthead light, and stepped out of the pilothouse for a closer look as the tug drifted alongside. There was something wrong with the diver. He had a wound across his shoulder. The Otter's relief began to crumble. He was in no position to treat casualties.

The diver spoke now. He had a light Italian accent . . . 'I am Captain Giuseppe Ponte, Herr Otter. The admiral sends regards.'

'What if I'm not who you think I am?' the Otter said. 'What if I'm a navy patrol?'

Ponte shrugged. 'Whoever you are, Herr Otter, Giuseppe Ponte is a long way from home.'

'Is the boat damaged?'

'I don't know. I rescued her before the explosion. She seemed to behave properly.'

The Otter tossed him a line and readied a second.

'Make fast fore and aft.'

'*Grazie.*'

In spite of the bloody tear in his rubber diving suit and exhaustion in his face, Ponte scampered over the wet decks and secured the lines.

'Flood your tanks,' the Otter called out.

Ponte returned to the cockpit. Green light showed from inside a shallow hatch. 'At what depth do you want her?'

'Ten feet. Under the barge.' He tried to see how Ponte manipulated the controls. The fifty-foot *Seehund* settled beneath the waves, and the Otter reached down and pulled Ponte on board the tug. Ponte mumbled '*Grazie*' again, swayed, and fell against him. He smelled of U-boat, blood and the sea.

'Gates, wake up. Somebody's on the phone for you.'

Gates stumbled out of his room, rubbing his eyes. The mechanic who lived down the hall pointed disgustedly at the pay phone. He was barefoot and shirtless and holding his trousers up with one hand.

'Thanks . . . what time is it?'

'Middle of the goddamned night,' the mechanic said,

slamming his door and yelling through it. 'Tell her to *write* next time.'

'Cordi?'

'Hello?'

'Steven, it's mother. I'm at the Strattons'.' Vera Gates's voice was strained. 'Wally's air patrol hasn't come back yet.'

'What? What time is it?'

'Midnight. Can you come over here, Steven? Aunt Louise is a wreck and Wallace could use another man to talk to.'

'Ten minutes.'

He dressed quickly and ran into the street, thinking that a late blimp wasn't as serious as a late plane. The thing would probably float for hours after it ran out of fuel. And if it dropped to the water the gondola would at least float for a while if they managed to get out from under the gasbag.

It was raining hard. The sky was flickering as thunder rolled in the distance. He had to walk to Ninth Avenue for a cab.

'Park and Fifty-sixth. Step on it.'

His mother was hovering behind the Strattons' butler. Gates gave him his hat and coat. She took his hands and led him to the library.

'Where are the girls?' he asked her.

'Both away. I'm glad I was home when Louise called.'

As they entered the room Wally's mother came forward. 'Steven . . .'

Gates embraced her. 'Everything's going to be fine, Aunt Louise. It's not as if he's overseas . . . they'll find him in the morning – '

'That's exactly what I have been saying.' Wallace Sr, crossed the room and shook Gates's hand. 'Probably just a simple engine failure – '

'But they have a radio. Wally told me they just got one.'

'It might have broken or it might need the engine to operate, dear. Don't worry.' He looked at Gates and Gates saw that despite his calm assurances there was deep fear in his eyes. 'The navy's doing everything they can,' Wallace said. 'But they can't really search until daybreak. They tell me they have a destroyer out with radar. Do you think they might find it that way?'

'It'll certainly help,' Gates said, thinking that big as it was the blimp didn't have enough metal on it to make much of a radar target . . . 'Aunt Louise,' Gates said, 'he's in the safest craft there is. Even if the engine fails it'll still fly. He's probably blown off course.'

'What about the storm tonight?' The wind, audible even there in the library, had been fierce on the street.

'The rain has stopped,' Wallace said.

'I heard thunder. If he were hit by lightning the blimp would explode like the *Hindenburg* – '

'No, no, Aunt Louise.' Gates explained that Wally's much smaller air ship was filled with helium instead of the volatile hydrogen that had burned at Lakehurst before the war. Wallace Stratton picked up the telephone and called 'a fellow I know at the navy.'

As Gates listened he realized the 'fellow' was the Secretary of the Navy and that Wallace had spoken with him several times already and the news was no different. He hung the phone up with a heavy shrug. 'They can't search at night. They've ships out but nothing can happen until dawn, unless we get very lucky. Steven, you don't have to stay – '

Louise grabbed Gates's hand. 'Just for a moment, Steven.'

'I'll stay all night, Aunt Louise. It's okay.'

'Thank you . . . Vera, you look tired,' she said to Gates's mother.

'I'm fine, Louise, I'll make some tea.'

Wallace had made another phone call. He replaced the receiver on the phone and gave his wife a tired smile. 'How unwieldy is that ship in this wind, Steven?'

Gates answered carefully. 'With an airspeed of about fifty, she's not capable of pushing into a strong headwind.'

'But the wind's out of the east.'

'Now it is,' Gates said. 'But it was westerly most of the night and evening. If anything, it's pushing them back to shore now. Probably find him in a cow pasture in Jersey tomorrow morning. Sleeping in a haystack.'

'Well,' Mrs Stratton said, 'Wally's one boy who can sleep through almost anything.'

Gates smiled, said nothing.

Intermittently turning his attention from the broken sea, the Otter watched Ponte sleep. He was a tough-looking man, about half the Otter's weight and only a few inches taller than five feet but with massive shoulders roped with muscle that bulged through his diving suit. His face was almost childlike – except for his sensual mouth – and when the storm thundered and the discharge pealed across the raging sea he moaned in his sleep and curled into a foetal position, his black rubber swimming fins extending naturally from his muscular legs like the cleft tail of a sinuous fish.

The Otter had bandaged Ponte's chest and shoulder, but couldn't tell in the dark, rolling pilothouse how badly he was wounded. There was no way to care for him . . . of course, he couldn't be taken to a hospital. The Otter considered tying some chain scrap iron to Ponte's arms and legs and dropping him over the side before he reached the Ambrose Channel.

The Otter switched on the big spotlight and inspected the sea, looking for a calm patch large enough to let him tie the wheel for a few seconds. The sea looked ugly and the chop was shortening, turning more violent as they neared land. He saw a flat area where the ground swell had momentarily planed the chop and steered for it. He looped a rope around one of the steering spokes, and knelt down to strangle Ponte . . .

Could he bring the *Seehund* into the harbour himself? Yes. It was already under the barge. Could he teach himself to run it and maintain it? Yes, again. He was an engineer. A machine was a machine. Could he hide it inside the *Normandie* himself? A single man could. It was designed, obviously, to be piloted by one. But could he handle the *Seehund* skilfully enough to survive the Hudson currents rampaging around the fallen *Normandie* when he tried to hide the boat the first time?

Too risky. One slip and he'd wreck it for sure.

Nor could he risk keeping it under the barge for days of practice. Not when the navy found the wrecked blimp and started probing the shallow ocean floor for the cause of the crash.

The Italian was watching him, his dark eyes reflecting the back-glow of the spotlight. '*Grazie. Grazie*, my friend.'

Dumbfounded, the Otter stared back as the Italian sat up and ran his fingers over his chest and shoulder, tracing the long gash with the practical knowledge of a man who had been wounded often.

The boat lurched dangerously. The Otter stood up and felt for the wheel as a tremendous thunderclap pealed across the water. He turned off the spot and resumed steering. Incredibly, the Italian pulled himself to his feet, stood beside him and gazed out the wheelhouse windows. Sheet lightning exploded above the riled sea, obliterating every shadow, painting the foamy crests and deep valleys stark, brutally white.

'Beautiful,' Ponte said, his rolling accent firing the English word with heartfelt meaning.

The Otter stared at him. 'How do you feel?'

'Alive, thanks to you.'

'I couldn't tell how badly you were hurt.'

'Flesh. Not bone. I can breathe. It hurts, but in pain is life. I will not complain – ' he smiled and the Otter's compass light glittered on his eyes and teeth ' – too much.'

'What happened back there?'

'Von Harling . . . the captain . . . surfaced while it was still day. The forward trim tanks jammed open. The air ship was waiting.'

'Did you see any survivors?' If the battle were known about in New York, the Harbour Entrance Control posts would scrutinize every inbound vessel for German survivors.

'No, my friend. Only me. And my little boat.'

And my little boat. Ponte was a bit strange, suffering shock, of course. He was watching the Otter now with trusting eyes. The Otter spoke without looking away from the waves, the breaking tops of which glistened despite the dark.

'Are you well enough to operate the *Seehund*?'

'Yes.'

'How are you going to run your boat without a crew?'

'I am the crew.'

The Otter glanced sideways. Despite his wound, Ponte was standing straighter. 'She is a beautiful boat,' he added. 'Beautiful.'

'Is it armed?'

'Certainly. She was loaded with her torpedoes already aboard.'

'How many?'

'Four. In their tubes.'

'Is it damaged?'

'She responded when I rode her away from her mother.'

'If it is damaged, can you fix it?'

Ponte spread his palms. 'The German crewman was my engineer.'

That meant Larson, if the boat needed work, and that meant that three men, instead of two, would know that the *Seehund* existed. '*Why did you leave the engineer?*'

Ponte's face set hard. He was no longer childlike. He seemed a man with a very short fuse. Not a man to be bullied or pushed around like Kroner or De Villeneuve. He looked set to ignore his wound and if necessary fight it out in the rolling wheelhouse. The Otter had already decided he needed Ponte. He held back his anger.

Captain Tooker was flanked by a navy diver – attired as Gates was, down to the heavy brass boots – and a full lieutenant, decked out in a beribboned uniform. Tooker was slouched behind his desk with his hands in his pockets. There was no doubt, though, who was boss.

'Gates, right?'

'Yes, captain.'

Tooker jerked his thumb at the lieutenant. 'Lieutenant Graham wants to borrow some of my divers for a special job. I told him you might be the right man, but it's open sea work and I know you haven't done any of that. Want to give it a try?'

'I'd rather stay on the *Normandie*, sir.'

'It's just for a day, right, lieutenant?'

'Yes, sir. Petty Officer Royce is rated Diver First Class, Mr Gates. He'll look out for you.'

The other diver nodded.

'I don't mind for a day or two,' Gates said. 'But I don't understand what you want me for. First class means demolition and ranger stuff and I'm barely capable of finding my way back to the top.'

'It's a piece of cake,' Royce said. 'Eighty feet. Clear water.'

'You happen to be a naval architect,' Tooker said. 'In fact, the only one anywhere nearby who is also a qualified diver, which is why I thought Lieutenant Graham could use you.'

'That's right,' Graham said.

'And you've got top secret clearance, which the other civilian divers don't. I'll fix it with your boss. Van Slough, right?'

'What's this about?'

Tooker took his hands out of his pockets. 'They can't tell you until you say yes.'

The seas were still running heavily when the Otter reached the Ambrose Channel a few hours after daylight and

Harbour Entrance Control's roving launches were sheltering behind the net-gate vessels – huge, anchored barges tended by a navy tug. The moored launches were bouncing wildly and the Coast Guardsmen watching him approach the gate were having a hard time steadying their binoculars.

He steered a straight course right down the middle of the two-thousand-foot mouth of the net gates, fearing at any second the sharp *boom* of a heave-to cannon – the signal to stop and be boarded for inspection.

His guise for the rendezvous was multi-layered. Operating under his main van Slough cover, he had procured forgeries from the Jersey mob to document the tugboat's false name. As payment, he was transporting a thousand sacks of stolen Colombian coffee in the barge, but the racketeers would never know that the man they thought was a war profiteer had taken the best of the bargain.

The forged documents would pass normal inspection if he was boarded. But in the event that some overeager ensign made a double check by radio, the contents of the barge constituted a second – although desperate – defence. Smuggling coffee for the black market – a surely more manageable crime than espionage, and one for which the accused's lawyer could post bail – was at least a credible explanation for attempting to sneak past Harbour Entrance Control post with forged papers. With luck, he'd escape before they found Ponte and the *Seehund*, but it would, of course, surely be the death of his attack on the *Queen Mary*.

Boom.

The wind blew the sound of the heave-to cannon so that it sounded very near. He picked up his binoculars and saw them struggling to untie the roving patrol launch. They started towards him, rolling hard in the cruel chop. The Otter throttled back and allowed *Hollandia* to drift. In seconds the tug was rolling as violently as the launch. He stepped out of the wheelhouse, gripping the handrails around the upper deck, and checked that the false nameplates and the counterfeit funnel letters were in place. Then he waited as they slowly crossed the thousand feet of water between the tug and the gate vessels.

At hailing distance he called out, 'What's wrong?'

'Permission to come aboard.'

They were coming anyway. He climbed down to the low, wet stern and handed his forged papers to the first ensign aboard. The sailors looked seasick and thoroughly disgusted to have been dragged away from the relative comfort of the gate barge. They were glowering and obviously in sympathy with the tug captain. Everyone knew what a nuisance the submarine nets posed to busy small-craft operators.

'Where you from?' the ensign demanded.

'Philly. You got problems reading, lieutenant? It's right there in my papers. It's also on the stern. Philly with a *Ph*.'

'You a wise guy?'

'I got an engineer below with a busted arm and I been at the wheel all night and I really want to find a pier and a cup of coffee.' Had he pushed too hard? What would he do if the ensign asked to see the engineer? 'Sorry, lieutenant, but it's been a hell of a tow.'

The ensign slapped the papers back in his hand.

'Go get your coffee . . .'

The Otter towed his barge to a Hoboken dock, where he delivered the mob's coffee. Ponte came up cautiously on the offshore side while the stevedores unloaded the sacks. He had left his tanks in the submarine and stripped off his rubber suit, face mask and fins. The Otter threw a blanket over his shoulders and hustled him into the galley below the pilothouse. His teeth were chattering. The Otter fed him hot coffee and fried eggs and while he ate explained what would happen that night.

Ponte listened without comment, but his eyes grew wide at the sight of the New York skyline across the river.

Gates said yes, he would make the secret dive with the navy team if he could return the next day to the *Normandie* salvage work, but they were on the Atlantic in a fast light cabin launch that roller-coasted up and down the ocean hills and valleys before they told him what it was about . . . they were diving, they said, to inspect a Nazi U-boat sunk the night before by a navy blimp.

'Wait a minute, what happened to the blimp?'

'No survivors – what's the matter, Gates?'

He mumbled out the connection. Royce asked if he wanted to skip the dive. Gates shook his head, regretting too late each of Wally's calls he hadn't returned.

'Why was a U-boat in so close?'

No answer made sense of Wally's death, but the other divers from the *Normandie* went at it wholeheartedly.

'Good pickin's,' said one. 'Hundred ships a day in and out of New York.'

'Against two hundred planes and destroyers?' said the second diver. 'Nobody's taking a sub through that. Not when they can rip up convoys in the middle of the ocean.'

'Finding convoys is harder than ripping them up. Naw, he came in close looking for an easy shot.'

'Could have been putting rangers ashore,' Royce said.

The navy divers nodded, respectfully. It was the first time Gates had seen navy divers respect anything. Royce was in another class and they all knew it.

Gates turned away and looked down at the water boiling away from the launch's stern. Wally had been an innocent. Like the *Normandie*. Definitely unsuited for war.

Gates had been working up design sketches for her new life as a two-stack troop carrier, but misgivings were holding him back, gnawing at him. Unsuited. No matter how carefully he designed and redesigned for the safety and comfort of the soldiers and the conversion back to peacetime use that he hoped would follow – if there ever were peacetime again – he couldn't bring himself to alter one frivolous accoutrement of the *Normandie*.

She hadn't a chance in combat. The French had put all her electric motors – without which the giant boilers and turbines and dynamos were useless – in one room. A single lucky torpedo or drifting mine or well-directed cannon shot that breached that motor room would stop her dead in the water. And it wasn't hard to imagine the horrific sight of the stricken liner wallowing in mid-Atlantic while fifteen thousand helpless soldiers awaited a leisurely Nazi *coup de grâce*.

'There they are,' called Royce.

Gates shielded his eyes from the sun and spotted a distant clump of small craft. Nearing the site, they could make out a couple of launches – requisitioned pleasure yachts like theirs – and a navy tug and a barge with a crane and deckhouse. On the horizon a navy destroyer prowled.

'There's the gasbag,' Royce said. The huge grey cloth sprawled over the sea, undulating on the swells. 'We'll dive from the barge.' A diving platform was affixed to one side, low to the water, with waves splashing on it. An air compressor chugged on the barge, surrounded by a half-dozen tenders who were readying helmets and an underwater cutting torch to burn open the smashed gondola.

Gates looked into the blue water, brilliant in the bright sun, and wondered if they had found Wally's body yet. He didn't want to go into the water if they hadn't. The launch slowed and nudged against the barge and the crew moored it. Royce led them onto the barge and down to the diving platform. Waves were breaking over the edges of the gasbag, as if the sea was eating it . . .

It was cold, much colder than the Hudson.

A wet chill seeped through his canvas twill diving suit and the pressure building at the lower depths forced the cold through his long wool underwear and drove it to his bones, but what Gates noticed most was the clarity of the water. Compared to diving on the *Normandie*, it was like watching a sunny day through a clean window.

Royce, descending beside him, was clearly visible down

to twenty feet. His shape was apparent to forty. At fifty they turned on their diving lamps. The powerful beams probed stiffly through the water – long, green shafts of eerie light. Overhead he could hear the launches growling as they circled the area.

At eighty feet – twenty feet deeper than Gates had ever dived – they touched bottom in a cloud of fine sand.

Gates's tender relayed by telephone Royce's description of what they were seeing. 'Royce says the gondola is to your right and the sub is to your left. He says look out for the trench. The conning tower section is close to the edge of it.'

Royce tapped his arm and signalled to follow him. The other divers, including two who'd been resting on the barge from the first search dives, reached bottom and started towards the gondola. Gates caught a vague glimpse of its riddled side in their lights. He turned away. Royce's light was scrabbling at a dark and distant shadow. Gates followed him towards the shadow, plodding over the sandy floor which sloped and tilted like wind-shaped dunes.

The shark nose of the U-boat was tipped on its side as if one of the great killer fish had set up an ambush. Royce led him around the wreckage, communicating with hand signals and tender-relayed telephone messages. The sea floor was littered with debris, some pieces as small as a brick, others large enough to identify – a compressor, a diesel motor, a trim plane, a torn body under a jagged plate.

They passed close to the bow section, a piece nearly twenty feet long, then came on the high conning tower – miraculously upright, looming overhead like a castle. Gates played his light over the conning tower, traced the sand aft, which was heaped with bits of metal, and spoke to his tender.

'Ask Royce where's the stern.'

'Royce says he doesn't know. He says it could have fallen down the trench.'

'How deep is it?'

Chart shows four hundred feet. You're standing on a kind of cliff.'

'Tell Royce he can look for the stern without me.'

The tender laughed. 'Good thinking . . . He wants to know what part you want to see first.'

'Conning tower.'

They trudged closer, playing their beams over the dark steel. Royce tapped his arm and pointed with his light. The Germans had kept score by painting ship silhouettes on the armour plate. Gates counted ten freighters and a destroyer. Above them in more white paint was a stylized trident, the boat's insignia.

Gates looked back in the direction of the gondola, but they were too far to see the other divers' lights. He moved closer and worked his light along the edge where the steel plate had separated when the boat broke apart. He inspected the outer hull and the pressure hull. The forward separation had been caused by an internal explosion, whereas on the aft end the steel was caved inward as if by a bomb.

The conning tower section – the midships part of the sub – standing all alone reminded Gates of the new Liberty ship construction methods by which separate parts of the ship were welded together. From keel to periscope the section consisted of three layers – fuel and ballast tanks on the bottom, the control room in the middle and the upper conning tower itself, topped by the open bridge. From the tanks that were seeping oil to the bridge, its height looked about twenty-five feet.

Gates stopped nudging his helmet exhaust valve, keeping more air in his suit and increasing his buoyancy, and floated slowly upward, with Royce following, holding his line to protect it from the metal edges. He stopped at the middle control room and swam into it, stood on the deck and cast his light about the shambles. Checking that Royce still had his hoses, he moved forward and stood on the brink of the broken deck. He retraced his steps and floated up to the conning tower level, playing his light over the boat's ribs, which seemed intact.

A death face leaped at him like a fanging snake. He fell backwards, dropping his light, kicking away from the horror. Royce grabbed him from behind and held him fast in his powerful hands.

'Easy,' shouted the tender. 'Take it easy. Royce says it's just a body.'

Gates fought to keep from getting sick in his helmet.

'You okay?' asked the voice in his ears.

'Jesus, the guy was floating right there.'

'Royce says do you want to come up?'

Gates tried to control his breathing. 'No.' He tapped Royce's hands to make him let go and worked further into the shattered control room. The body drifted into his lamp beam again, its clothing snagged on ragged steel. Gates tried to ignore it and the thought that a day ago this little room had resounded from the engine beat while a living crew operated live controls.

'Royce wants to know what you think.'

'Tell him this whole chunk ought to hold together.'

'Okay . . . he wants you to check the bow.'

Gates followed him out the gaping hole they had entered, picking up Royce's hose as he came to its slack and guiding it past protrusions as Royce had guided his on the way in. They stepped off the conning tower deck and floated down to the ocean floor and made their way the fifty feet across the battle-spilled sand to the bow section, which on closer inspection turned out to be little more than a half-shell. The explosion that had torn the front thirty feet from the rest of the boat had gutted the bow. All that remained was the deck and the port side down to the keel. The starboard side was gone, as if sheared off by a long knife.

Gates stood still and looked around, trying to piece together what had happened. 'Tell Royce,' he said to the tender, 'that the torpedoes stored between the control room and here must have blown all at once. Up here there's a torpedo still in the tube, but the starboard must have blown too.'

Gates traced the damage with his light. The port-side plating was crazed like old china. 'Tell Royce they'll need a basket for this piece.'

The steel shifted suddenly underfoot. A crack in the deck widened. 'Back,' shouted Gates. 'Tell him to move back.'

Royce was already retreating – half-swimming – exiting gently as a floating leaf. Gates pushed off and floated and Royce pulled him out by his lines.

Outside, they warily circled the bow fragment. Gates saw something that looked out of place and stepped under the overhanging deck. Royce trapped his arm and motioned him out, pointing at the section that looked like it might collapse, but Gates knelt and crawled under the piece, trying to get a closer look at a large steel hooklike protuberance that stuck out from the keel and would have hung straight down when the boat was upright.

It was about four feet long – massively built, with a diameter of six inches. He pushed Royce away and continued to puzzle over the odd structure. Then he saw a broken piece of cable dangling behind the hook. Accustomed to close work on the *Normandie*, he gave little thought to his next move but flattened himself on his belly and slithered under the bow, reaching for the cable. His telephone erupted angrily.

'Royce says get your tail out of there, kid. Right now.'

'One second,' Gates said. 'Tell Royce there's something damn strange here.'

He grabbed the cable and tugged. It was fast. Through his glove it seemed to feel sheathed by something. Not naked steel but coated with rubber or canvas, or both, like his lifeline. It felt solid beneath the coating and stiff, as if the two-inch-thick cable were solid steel or copper under its coat. Unable to budge it, he dropped the cable and passed his glove over the hook. Shining his light on it with the other hand, he saw that the hook end was actually a massive hinged fitting, with a hole for what looked like a gigantic allen wrench. How it functioned, he couldn't guess, but it was unlike any fitting he had ever seen or heard of on a submarine.

33

He thought about it all the way to the surface.

'There's some ONI boys and a couple of sub experts come aboard while we were down,' Royce said. 'We got to talk to them.'

Gates followed Royce into the deckhouse, where a half-dozen officers were gathered around the table. Lieutenant Graham made the introductions.

Leading the ONI contingent was Lieutenant Commander Ober, whose epaulettes now identified him as Commander Ober. He and Gates exchanged stiffly courteous greetings, barely softened by what Ober considered Gates's sarcasm in congratulating him on his latest promotion. Royce noticed the byplay and grinned, forcing Gates to work hard to keep a straight face. Every diver he knew considered naval officers as a comical subspecies.

He and Royce described and sketched the U-boat's position. He thought the conning tower section could be raised intact, provided the navy could locate a big enough lifting crane, but the rest of the boat would have to be gathered piece by piece.

'It looks like a junkyard down there,' Royce said.

'Did you find any code books?' Ober asked.

'The other guys are looking for them now, but that's mighty fine sand,' Royce told him. 'Maybe you'll get lucky. Sir.'

Gates sketched some interior views.

'There,' said one of Ober's men. 'The control room. Did you see a cipher machine? Might have looked like a typewriter.'

'No,' Royce said. 'No typewriters.'

'A *cipher* machine. Not a typewriter. Just looks like one.'

'How about you, Gates?' Ober had taken over.

'No. But we saw something strange on the bow.' He quickly sketched the hook and cable hanging from the keel. 'The technical men will look that over,' Ober said. 'We have some coming up from Panama. Now think hard about that cipher machine. We hear all kinds of stories about their ciphers.'

'Sorry,' Gates said. 'But I do think this hook thing is kind of interesting – '

'Some sort of anchor, probably,' said one of the sub experts. 'We'll check it out. Now I have some identifying silhouettes here. I want you to look them over and tell me which kind of boat she was.'

As he began to unfurl his material Gates said, 'She was a Type VII C.'

'Like this?'

'That's her,' Royce said. 'Only she had a lot more AA stuff on the bridge.'

'You sure she wasn't one of these?' He unfurled a picture of a thicker version of the VII C. 'Krauts call her a *Milch Kuh*. Fuel tanker and supplies. Extra fish.'

'No,' Gates said. 'Not that big . . . That cable was coated with rubber. I don't think it was an anchor line.'

'What were her numbers?' Ober asked.

'I didn't see any,' Royce said.

'Nothing on the conning tower?'

'Tonnage sunk,' Royce said. 'Bastards said they got a destroyer.'

'She had a trident insignia,' Gates said. 'Like this.'

They glanced at his line drawing.

'But no numbers? Not even on the bow?'

'None.'

The ONI men looked at each other.

'The hook had a hinge on the end,' Gates said.

'We'll look it over.'

'And a big hole, like for an allen wrench. Maybe to open

414

and close it.' Ober nodded vaguely and left the table to confer with the sub experts. The door opened.

'Gates?' It was Lieutenant Graham. 'When these gentlemen are through with you, would you like to identify your friend?'

'What?'

'He's not too bad. His face, anyway.'

'I don't think so.'

'He had a friend on the blimp,' Graham told the others. 'You'd be saving his family the trouble,' Graham said.

Gates nodded, inwardly shuddering.

Graham led him out of the cabin. They had arranged the bodies in a launch, and the sailors were waiting to cast off. 'Stratton's papers were on his body so we figured it's him,' Graham said. He lifted the blanket revealing only Wally's face, though Gates couldn't help noticing that there seemed very little of his body left under the blanket.

His face was drawn in a tight mask. Gates thought it was important to remember to tell Wally's family that his last expression on earth was one of courageous determination. Some might once have said that was out of character. Including Gates. They were proved wrong, too late.

'Cordi, it's Gates. He's downstairs,' Mark said. 'In the hotel. Shall I invite him up for a cup of tea?'

They were in the back room. Cordi was wearing earphones while she listened to wire recordings of shortwave messages intercepted by the American coastal monitoring stations, listening to wire after wire for the Otter's fist. He had never called De Villeneuve again, and Weatherburn kept insisting that even the most self-sufficient, taciturn German agent eventually had to communicate through their Hamburg shortwave radio station.

She took off the headphones and shoved into the desk a revolver she had been cleaning while she listened. 'Very funny, Mark.'

415

Mark had already hung up the telephone. 'I told the desk to tell him you'd be down. He's in the bar.'

There was a small bar off the lobby – a cocktail lounge and restaurant, dark as a cave. Steven was sitting on a barstool, his head down. He didn't notice her until she had sat down beside him.

'Are you all right?'

It was too dark to see much of his expression. His voice was tight. 'Thanks for coming down. I'm sorry I couldn't call. I was upset. Wally's been killed.'

'What?'

'The blimp went down.'

'How?'

'The storm last night. They found it this morning. No survivors.'

She slipped her arm over his shoulder. 'I'm very sorry.'

'Guess I've been lucky so far. Wally's my first war victim. First person I've known well who bought it – want a drink?'

'No, thank you.'

'I'm going to blow the top of my head off with a double martini in his memory. Sure you won't join me?'

'I'll join you.'

A barman stepped out of the shadows, and Gates ordered. 'You know, Wally was right. It *is* a simple drink. You don't have to say rocks or no rocks, or what glass, or any of that. You say martini, you mean gin, vermouth, thank you . . . Wally made a fetish of such things. Don't bruise the gin and – ' He banged the bar. 'Had to go and get himself killed. Stupid drunk . . . '

'Drink didn't kill him.'

'Neither did the storm.'

'What?'

Gates looked at her. He slid quickly off the back of the stool. 'I'm sorry. I can't stay, I'm beat. Thanks for coming down. I got to get out of here.' He brushed her cheek with his lips and hurried out.

Cordi called after him but he kept going. She sat down again and stared at the two full glasses beading on the bar. She hadn't realized until now how much she held back, afraid of who he might be, but today whoever or whatever else he was, he seemed honestly wounded, and she hadn't been able to do a thing to help. She'd listened, detached, as if his voice were coming out of the radio.

Upstairs, Weatherburn was waiting eagerly.

'Just popped in for a chat, did he? What the devil did he say he wanted?'

Cordi looked up at him bleakly. 'His best friend was killed.'

'Really? Did the friend happen to be Wallace Stratton Jr?'

'How did you know?'

Weatherburn ignored her question. 'Did he tell you how he died?'

'He was flying with the volunteer naval air patrol. His blimp went down. How did you know?'

'Did he tell you how it went down?'

'In a storm – well, matter of fact . . . he was a little vague about that . . . ' She thought back. That was when he ran out. 'First he said the blimp crashed in a storm. Later, I made some remark that drinking hadn't killed Wally. And Gates said, "Neither did the storm." But he was very upset, I don't think too much significance should be put on it – '

'Is that a fact?'

'What are you getting at?'

'I'm *getting* at the fact that the Office of Naval Intelligence is treating that crash top secret. Whatever happened out there, the Americans aren't talking. And it's too hush-hush for an ordinary crash. Something's going on.'

'How did you find out?'

'Man I know at military intelligence got wind of it. But the navy doesn't talk to the army, so all I know is there's a considerable flap and I can't learn a thing more without going to the Old Man at BSC and persuading him to twist some arms. I don't even know if he can find out. They've really clammed up . . . so Gates knew one of the crew?'

'He'd actually gone up in it. Wally Stratton took him along for the ride.'

'What do we know about Stratton?'

Cordi sat down and ran her hands back through her hair. 'Rich old New York stock. Public service. He was with the shipping board. Father does special missions – privately – for the State Department. Old friends of Gates's family.'

'Politics?'

'Republican, I'd assume. I was at their Christmas party. He turned rather beet red when someone offered a toast to President Roosevelt.'

'Rather like toasting Lloyd George among our sort of people.'

Cordi didn't smile. Weatherburn's sort of people were not typically her sort. 'I would *not* call the Stratton family candidates for the "genteel circle" theory, if that's what you're driving at.'

'You say young Wallace drank?'

'Yes. If he wasn't an alcoholic he was apparently on the way. A rather sad, gentle, harmless fool – '

'Have you any idea how many seemingly harmless fools who appear to drink too much are employed by secret intelligence services?'

'I suppose quite a few.'

'Wouldn't the Otter employ such types?'

'Forgive me, but I just don't see Stratton that way – '

'I am *merely* trying to make sense of what's going on – or isn't going on. For example, where the hell is the Otter?'

'Perhaps he's gone home.'

'Or maybe he's just busy getting ready for something. How are you getting on with those intercept wires?'

'It's clutching at straws.'

'Until he moves, that's all we've got left. Ever hunted tiger?'

'No, sir,' Cordi said, mystified. He'd been telling stories a good deal lately, recalling the past as some sort of antidote to the frustration over the Otter – which was driving them all crazy. Sometimes the stories had a point. 'Have *you* hunted tiger?'

'Once, in India. Cane applied to the right pair of buttocks had produced the ringleaders of a communist cell, so the local rajah invited me along on a tiger hunt as a sort of thank you.' He paused for her reaction.

Cordi was still upset about not being able to help Steven. She snapped, 'Are you baiting me, sir?'

'Not at all. Just reminding you that this game can turn rather tough. At any rate, for three nights we crouched above a game path in a blind twenty feet up a tree – a Bengal tiger can leap that high without thinking about it, and I can assure you that one remains extremely alert regardless of conditions, which were appalling – ruddy blind buzzing with bloodthirsty mosquitoes and every other damned Asian insect you could imagine. Hot and sticky till it rained cold and wet, night after night, straining into the dark, praying some viper hadn't slithered up the tree, hoping to see the cat before he saw us. Well, after we shot him it occurred to me that the tiger had had a much better time of it than we'd had those three days we lay in ambush. The pressure is on the hunter, Cordi. The Otter is going about his business, putting together his plans, whatever they are, and all we can do is wait, and, as you say, clutch at straws. It's not a pleasant time. It's also a dangerous time . . . if you're not alert, or miscalculate out of boredom, that may be the moment the damned beast will pounce.'

Gates came abruptly awake at midnight, sat straight up in bed and scrambled for the light switch, a drawing pad and a pencil. The crook in the hanging fixture he had called a hook had faced aft.

Facing what? Perhaps a second 'hook' pointing forward? Brackets?

He pencilled in the effect on the keel of a hastily sketched submarine. Clearly, with two such hanging fixtures, brackets or clamps, the U-boat had been carrying something.

He got into his trousers, searched his pockets for change and ran barefoot to the hall pay phone. The Office of Naval Intelligence was listed in the Manhattan directory. Gates asked to speak to Commander Ober.

'He's gone home, sir. Twenty-two hundred.'

Ober had reluctantly given Gates his home number when Gates had first pushed forward his suspicions about the *Normandie* fire. He got a sleepy hello on the seventh ring.

'Commander Ober?'

'Who the . . . yes? Who is this?'

'Steven Gates.'

'What the hell time is it? Damn it, Gates, it's midnight.'

'Sorry, sir. Those hooks . . . that hook on the keel of the sub.'

Ober's voice came awake. 'This is not a scrambled phone, Gates.'

'A what?'

'We don't have scramblers on our telephones, Gates. Anybody could be listening in.'

'Oh. Sorry. Can you meet me? I have to tell you something that – '

'It'll keep until morning.'

'I'll come to your place – '

'Eight o'clock. My office.'

The phone went dead. Gates called back. 'I'll call all night, Ober. This is important.'

'All right, all *right*.' He gave Gates his address – a house in Murray Hill.

'This had better be good,' Ober said. He wore a silk dressing gown and didn't invite Gates in past the foyer.

'That hook?'

'Yes, I *know*.'

'It's not a hook. It's a clamp. There must have been a

420

second one aft. A pair of clamps for carrying something. *The U-boat was carrying something.'*

Ober smiled. 'We're way ahead of you, Gates. We already found the second bracket in the trench. Thanks for nothing.'

Gates felt his mouth drop.

'Anything else, Gates?' Ober was opening the door and indicating the street.

'What do you think it was carrying?'

'That's easy. We sank all their milk cows, so the krauts are trying another way to extend their transocean patrols. The U-boat was carrying extra fuel.'

'Fuel?'

'Yes, of course. Auxiliary tanks, like a plane. They burned it on the crossing, then jettisoned the tanks and went into action all topped-out. The bastards could have hung around a month if your friend's blimp hadn't spotted them.'

'What about the cable hanging down?' asked Gates, but Commander Ober had already shut the door in his face.

The Otter replaced the tug's false name boards with *Hollandia*'s and uncovered the white VSS on either side of her stack. At midnight he towed the *Seehund* with Ponte in it under the now-empty barge upriver from Hoboken and across the Hudson to the *Normandie*.

The wreck was ablaze with floodlights and was swarming with workmen despite the late hour as they moved into the final stages of the salvage effort and prepared to pump. The salvors were dismantling no-longer-needed scaffolds, and cranes were lowering the excess wood and steel to barges waiting in the slip alongside her vertical promenade deck.

But no one was working in the stern mooring compartment; Van Slough Salvage had broken records clearing that huge windowed cave of debris and the general contractor still held that operation up before laggard subcontractors as a prime example of the fast, quality work expected on the *Normandie*. As for the light, the opaque water reflected it like a mirror and absolutely nothing could be seen which was submerged more than an inch; pilings seemed to stand on the surface, rather than emerge from below.

The Otter manoeuvred his barge into the row waiting to be loaded with scaffolding. Then he returned *Hollandia* to her customary mooring at the fallen ship's stern, just at the edge of the floodlights' spill. He sipped a cup of coffee in the tug's wheelhouse, trading greetings and friendly insults with the tug captains entering and leaving the slip; the old steam boaters always referred to the sparkling *Hollandia* as a yacht, knowing that van Slough would counter with complaints that they were dirtying the air with their smoke. All the while, Ponte scouted the *Seehund*'s lair inside the *Normandie*; his rebreathing device was remarkable and the Otter could only guess when the frogman had entered the mooring compartment, inspected the underwater cavern and swum back to the barge . . . no air-bubble trail disturbed the sewage and detritus swirling on the play of tide and river.

Ponte left the *Seehund* under the barge, exiting by the wet-dry underwater-access compartment, and dived deep to avoid the small tugs and launches which were crisscrossing the slip alongside the capsized *Normandie*. The water, as the Otter had warned, was completely opaque. He put his hand over the face mask and still could not see his fingers.

The Otter had drawn him charts, showing where the liner lay and where, approximately, he would stop the barge, and where Ponte would find the *Normandie*'s stern mooring compartment. He'd even drawn the layout of the lair inside, but Ponte preferred to inspect it with his own hands before he tried to fit the *Seehund* inside. Agents with big plans, he had discovered, were sometimes overly optimistic about physical detail.

He dived to the mud at the bottom of the slip, found the *Normandie*'s promenade deck rising out of it like a wall and traced the liner back to the mooring compartment. As the Otter had said, the windows were huge. Ponte uncoiled a measuring line he had cut to the height of the *Seehund* and stretched it over an opening. Too low. He worked his way up, and found another, the one the Otter had told him about, the one where he had cut away a strut. Ponte found the cut and measured. High enough. The width, though, was close. Wide enough, he thought, but tight . . .

He swam inside and rose cautiously to the surface.

The huge cathedral-like room was empty. Dark, with just enough light spill to find the electric and air lines the Otter had prepared. Ponte floated, silently, gazing about the space, listening to the lapping water echo. Nearby, in another world, a crane engine chugged and tugs whined and snorted in the slip. He even heard workmen laughing. But here was a lair as remote and mysterious as a cave beneath the reef, the sort of cave a diver swam into never sure what creature would be found living there . . .

He dived underwater and swam out of the *Normandie*; into the slip, back to the *Seehund*. Untying it from the bottom of the barge, he entered the submarine, turned it around and crept along the bottom of the slip, slowly retracing his path back to the entrance the Otter had widened.

Twice he got out of the boat to check his position and to ascertain the fit. He felt the rim of the opening with his gloves until he knew the clearances intimately. A strong tidal flow gripped the boat several times, and lower down a river current nipped at his legs. The harbour at Hamburg had been like this, fed by a river full of jokes.

At last, when he was sure he knew the space, he nudged the *Seehund*'s nose through the opening, and drove her home. Into the *Normandie*.

The Otter waited, looking intently at the waters around the ship's stern – they roiled cloudily in the pale light as if blades were churning beneath the opaque surface. A tug and a launch passed each other going in and out of the slip. Their wakes splashed against the *Normandie*, obscuring the *Seehund*'s hint of its passage, while the din of an air compressor perched on the overturned flank smothered the sounds of their engines.

The Otter entered the ship and walked sure-footed!y along dark catwalks checking repeatedly to be sure he was alone, and entered the aft mooring compartment by climbing over the after-most watertight timber bulkhead. Moving deep into darkness, he found where he had hidden air, water and electrical lines and uncoiled a thick, insulated electrical cable that he had tapped into the salvors' electrical system. He crouched on a wood platform at the water's edge, squinting into the semi-darkness, waiting for Ponte to surface, and thinking about escape.

The river lapped and echoed in the huge dark cavern. Heavy machinery rumbled nearby, sending vibrations through the bare steel plates. He thought he heard a scraping sound, as if the *Seehund* had rubbed against the side of the entrance. The sound repeated, but he couldn't tell whether it was the submarine or the hundreds of machines pulsing in the wreck. He waited, sharply reminded of his dependence on the Italian, and worrying about radioing Uncle Willy. He hated the risk of using the radio. But there could be no escape without another U-boat to pick them up.

'*Herr Otter.*'

He started. Ponte's hoarse cry came from deep shadow less than five feet from where he crouched. The Italian had emerged from the water as silently as a reptile.

'*Herr Otter?*' he whispered again. 'Our little boat is safe.'

34

'Cordi,' asked Weatherburn. 'Do you ride?'

'Yes, sir.'

'How would you like to come away with me for the weekend?'

'I beg your pardon, sir?' She almost batted her eyelashes, quickly decided he'd miss the humour of it.

'I'm invited to a Connecticut hunt. The BSC monitors located another clandestine receiver several months ago. They've been listening like little robins since De Villeneuve's proved to be such a disappointment, but nothing new. I've been ordered to trace the messages and their content. The invitation is legitimate, arranged through friends of a friend. Our host thinks I'm a London businessman in New York with his secretary. We'll pretend for his sake. Country weekend, separate rooms and all that, the only difference being I *won't* tiptoe across the hall when the house is asleep.'

'I have a date with Gates —'

'Cancel it. Give him something to worry about.'

When they stopped to rest the horses on a ridge that overlooked the Merritt Parkway, Weatherburn pulled his breeches leg out of his boot and showed his host a bright red bruise, an almost perfect circle on the pale skin inside his knee.

'Look here, Blanchard. Ten years off a horse, but I still remembered my knees.'

Blanchard, a tall and lean old man who sat his horse ramrod-straight, nodded approval. Weatherburn was in his element, and they'd hit it off well, so well that when the rest of his weekend guests were leaving after Sunday lunch, Blanchard had invited him to spend another night, and this morning they'd set out alone for an early ride.

Weatherburn stuffed the breeches back into his boot and uttered a self-satisfied sound in the back of his throat.

'Riding master at Sandhurst used to drum it into us. "Your horse's brains are in his ribs."'

Blanchard nodded vaguely. Something had distracted him. His eyes fixed on the parkway. The twin concrete roadbeds were connected by a wide, elm-shaded street to a nearby village of white clapboard houses set around a manicured green. Leaves and grass were at a lustrous early summer peak, but nearer the parkway was the evidence of recent destruction. The double row of elms stopped abruptly, where they'd been cut down for the new road.

'Hear that?'

Weatherburn looked down the steep slope. 'The cars?'

'Yes, damn it. Cars.' Blanchard raised a quivering arm and swept it across the low hills. 'Roosevelt destroyed the hunt country with his socialist roads. Slashed our lands like a butcher knife. It's been one thing after another since the Market crashed. Taxes, home relief, alliances with the *Russians*, now this damned fool war and the inflated wages that had to follow.'

'Oh, yes,' said Weatherburn.

Blanchard clenched a bony fist in his saddle and his horse moved uneasily. 'You can't hire a decent stableboy any more, much less a trained groom.'

'We've had similar problems in England since the last war,' Weatherburn said in some genuine sympathy. 'Perhaps when this one's over things will straighten out.'

'Maybe for you. But they've already done our people in over here. Look down there. Not one house on that village green is occupied by its rightful family. All taken by *New York* people. Writers, advertising people, radio producers – *actors*, for God's sake – and their nervous wives shrilling at one another in the market and kissing

426

in public. They come on that road. By God, this was good country before FDR and his crowd built that road.'

'I must say I found it a bit odd driving out here. No sense of being anywhere. No towns, just miles and miles of lawn and stubby little trees.'

'I don't permit my driver to use it,' said Blanchard. 'He takes the Boston Post Road the entire way to New York.'

Weatherburn stroked his horse's neck, casually asked, 'Do you go into New York often?'

'No.'

Though he had quite a taste and a genuine flair for deception, Weatherburn was a man of action, trained as an army officer to make up his mind on the spot and act. And years of intelligence work hadn't entirely convinced him that patience was a virtue. He'd been patient all weekend, probing Blanchard for some way to make him talk, but this was the first hard information Blanchard had volunteered. A voice clamoured in Weatherburn's brain to go slowly, but another voice said *push*.

'When you do go . . .'

The old man looked at him, and now the British agent looked squarely back at him.

'Yes?'

'When you do go to New York, to whom do you carry the German radio messages?'

A look passed over Blanchard's face. Terrified, thought Weatherburn. He'll talk.

Blanchard lashed out suddenly with a heavy hunting crop. Weatherburn ducked, but the whip grazed his horse's ears and it reared. Blanchard raked his spurs across his horse's flanks and bolted. By the time Weatherburn had his horse under control the old man was galloping down the hillside, glued upright to his mount like a Prussian cavalry officer. Weatherburn tightened his aching knees and pounded after him.

Blanchard, of course, had nowhere to go. He was already

427

home, and as he attained the level ground near the parkway he saw Cordi Grey come out of the woods, binoculars dangling from her neck. Three men appeared on horses, and a black car pulled off the parkway onto the shoulder. Several men got out. Weatherburn galloped up behind him.

'Give it up, Blanchard. You won't be hurt, I assure you – '

Blanchard wheeled his horse. He saw a gap in the line of men and urged the animal towards it.

'No,' Cordi shouted. 'Look out for the road – '

But Blanchard had already seen the road and seen the pair of sedans – one passing the other at forty miles an hour. He spoke to the horse. The animal bounded over the grass and hit the road at a dead run, its iron shoes striking sparks on the concrete. The cars slid into it on screaming tyres.

'How did it happen?' demanded the voice on the telephone.

'Bloody fool killed himself. As much as committed suicide.'

'What did you do to him?'

'I didn't *do* anything to him. He bolted. I've told you the rest.' Weatherburn leaned against the walls of the pay phone booth and brushed earth from his riding breeches.

The voice said, 'And what about our friends at ONI?'

'They've probably tapped this telephone. *We* discovered the radio; why the bloody hell we had to bring them in on it I don't know. And at risk to my group. I still say the Otter could be in ONI. We don't know.'

'Forget that. What do you intend to do now?'

'Well, I've sent our lot back to New York and I'm letting your ONI *colleagues* deal with the local constabulary.'

'And what about you?'

'Blanchard let on that he made occasional trips to New York. We already know that the only telephone calls he made were to invite guests up here and to speak with his

Wall Street brokers. Nor has the post office found any mail that wasn't legitimate. I think he made the drops himself.'

'What do you suggest?'

'Move,' said Weatherburn. 'The man who set the conduit up is probably the man who gets the messages.'

'How do you intend to move?'

'I'm going to have a chat with Blanchard's chauffeur.'

Blanchard's chauffeur looked up hopefully when Weatherburn walked into his room above the garage without knocking. Hope faded when he saw that the new intruder recognized the man sitting on his armchair, though it was clear they didn't like each other.

Commander Percy Ober stood up. He was wearing a dark business suit that bulged, despite the good tailoring, where he wore a navy .45 automatic. He was angry, but determinedly calm. 'What are you doing here?'

'I could ask the same.' Why, when they didn't even know what the Otter's target was, did they have to deal with such upstarts?

'Would you mind waiting downstairs?'

Weatherburn sat on the end of the chauffeur's narrow bed. 'Yes, I would. Apparently we've come to similar conclusions.' He turned to the chauffeur, who was seated on a stool and twisting his hands. 'What's your name?'

'Putnam, sir.'

'Well, Putnam, you're in the shit for sure.'

'I've already told him why,' Ober said.

Weatherburn turned to Ober. 'Would you care to step outside a moment? I'd like to talk to you. Putnam, you stay were you are.'

Outside on the stairs Weatherburn started to speak but Ober cut him off. 'More hinges on this matter than just tracing a radio link. A successful conclusion to a venture between BSC and ONI would lead to further cooperation.'

Weatherburn gave him a flat look. 'It would be nice

for the Office of Naval Intelligence. BSC has already demonstrated its cooperative inclinations by helping out with the OSS. You and the FBI are another matter.'

Ober reddened and started to answer. Weatherburn cut him off. 'Leave me out of it, I'm not in a policy-making position – '

'Okay,' Ober said stiffly. 'I will leave you out.' He turned to go back into the room.

'What do you mean by that?'

'I mean I'm taking charge of this myself. After I get through explaining to Putnam what will happen to him for transporting German radio messages – which, incidentally, he had no idea he was doing – then I'll give him a chance to get off the hook by taking me to the drop.'

'I'd been considering the same thing,' Weatherburn said. He felt his left eyelid start ticking.

Ober smiled. 'I've arranged for several cars to shadow the limousine. One of them ought to have room for you.'

'Of all the bloody cheek. We've taught you everything you know. If it wasn't for us you'd be hanging from Nazi gallows – '

'What do you want? Gratitude?'

Weatherburn turned away to hide his rage. Right now what he wanted was Ober's hide. Almost as much as he lusted for the Otter's.

35

The Otter peered through the dirty windows of Kroner's shop. It was closing time and the streets of Yorkville were filled with workmen heading home for supper. A man in overalls with a lunch pail came out carrying a radio under his arm. The Otter turned away so the man could not remember his face. Inside, the balding German Bundist bent over his workbench like a tonsured monk, tinkering in the failing daylight.

The Otter backed into the shop and slipped the stocking over his head. Kroner looked up, smiling hopefully until the Otter pulled the shade and turned around with a face of bulging silk. Kroner stood up and retreated a backward step to the curtain that shielded the rear room. There he stopped and, folding his arms over his worn apron, said firmly, 'No.'

'No *what*, Herr Kroner?'

'I'm through. No more radio.'

The Otter needed to radio for a U-boat pick-up, but he adhered to the basic procedures that Uncle Willy had taught him for operating safely in enemy territory. *The test is how you conduct yourself when you are desperate.* He was desperate. Without escape. With the burden of a second agent dependent on him and whom he was dependent on.

He had carefully, methodically scouted the street from a rooftop before venturing into Kroner's shop. The British or the FBI were likely the reason the trombone player had disappeared from the RCA Building, and possibly the reason for the man he had sighted outside De Villeneuve's the night of the air-raid drill. Only when he was sure that

431

Kroner's shop looked clear had he entered it. He hadn't expected rebellion.

'Aren't you forgetting a certain tank officer's career? Not to mention his life?'

'His life?' He yanked open the rear-room curtain.

The desert had a way of drying a man. It was more than sun and windburn, but a rapid desiccation that left skin with the appearance of being a disconnected outer layer that moved separately from the flesh. As impossible as it seemed, the man in dark glasses hunched over a workbench in Kroner's back room had to be his son, *Panzerarmee* veteran Lieutenant Erich Kroner.

A radio vacuum tube and a pair of needle-nose pliers looked absurdly delicate in young Kroner's big, leathery hands. His whole body shook with frustration as he tried to fit the tube into a socket. Suddenly he cocked his head towards the curtain, as if he'd been concentrating so hard that he had not heard the beginning of their conversation.

'*Vater?*' he called in a tentative voice. '*Ist das* you?'

'Speak English,' said Kroner. 'Everything in English.'

'*Ja*, father. Who ist dere?'

Kroner sighed. 'Just a bill collector. He's been paid.' He smiled tightly at the Otter. 'I didn't believe what the newspapers said had happened to our Afrika Korps, but Erich tells me it is true. Outgunned, outsupplied, even outfought. The boy told his guards about me, that I was here in New York. The prison camps were bulging, and he was too much trouble to take care of. So they were happy to give him back to me.'

Even with Kroner's Bundist past? The Otter wondered.

'It was all lies,' Kroner said. 'We couldn't beat the whole world – '

'You can't win if you don't fight – '

'We've already lost,' Kroner said bitterly.

The Otter pushed him aside. '*Achtung, Lieutenant Kroner.*'

Young Kroner jumped as if burned.

'Lieutenant Kroner, please tell your father to do his duty

432

as a German citizen.' He raised a hand, threatening to hit the elder Kroner if he said anything.

The young man actually now burst out in sobs.

'He's blind,' said his father. 'Now please get out of our shop.'

The Otter locked the door.

'Where did you move the radio?'

'I smashed it.'

'Where are the pieces?'

Kroner said nothing. The Otter took his neck in one hand and squeezed. Hearing his father's strangled sound, Erich felt around the workbench and moved towards the Otter. The Otter knocked him down with his other hand, surprised how light, frail, the man was. He eased the pressure on Kroner's neck. *Where are the pieces?* Young Erich lay motionless on the floor.

'In the garbage. They're gone.'

The Otter yanked him around and pointed at the shelves. 'Give me the parts for a shortwave radio.'

'I don't have them all here. Shortwaves are illegal – '

'I *know* that. Give me what you have.' He let him go and pushed him at the shelf. 'Hurry. Or I'll kill the boy.'

Kroner believed him. He pawed through the radio parts, heaping them on the counter. 'That's all I have,' he said in despair. 'It's not enough to build a radio. Perhaps with time I could find – '

The Otter crushed his neck and shoved the radio parts into a suitcase he found in Kroner's basement. He had no intention of building a radio, but Steven Gates was in his thoughts . . . if conditions got any worse he'd have a use for this bagful of incriminating evidence.

It was only at the Eighty-sixth IRT station, two levels down on the express platform, that it occurred to him that, of course, Kroner must have offered something to get his son released from the prison camp.

He dropped the suitcase beside a bench, moved quickly away from it and looked around. As if on cue two men in coats and hats trotted down the steps, glanced up and down the platform. A train had pulled out as the Otter arrived. The platform was almost empty on the downtown side. Had they staked out the shop and gone in it after he'd left?

The men were heading for him. He glanced over his shoulder. No one behind him. And no stairs in that direction. They closed quickly, moving apart. One showed a badge. The other kept his hands in his pockets.

'Federal Bureau of Investigation. May we see some identification, please?'

'FBI?' the Otter smiled. 'What, are you kidding?'

'Would you step this way, please?'

'Why?'

'We'd like to talk to you a moment.'

The Otter fought to keep himself from running. Hit them both and run into the subway tunnel? Seven blocks to the next station. Emergency exits along the way. No. Uncle Willy had taught him, *Never deepen the trap*. He shrugged and spread his empty hands wide. 'Sure.'

They moved close on either side and walked him to a painted tin door near the end of the platform, opened it with a key and ushered him into what turned out to be a janitor's storage room, small and square, neatly kept, with pipes overhead, painted cinder-block walls, cartons of toilet paper and urinal disinfectant and a row of mops and pails at one end. They closed the door and drew guns.

'Turn around and put your hands on the wall.'

'Hey, what is this?' He noticed they were very tight. Nervous. They'd probably seen Kroner, and now they knew they were looking for a killer. He turned around and placed his hands on the cinder blocks, which were cool and smoothed by the paint. They searched him thoroughly and took his wallet.

'Turn around.'

One was leafing through his wallet. Both seemed relieved

that they had found him unarmed. The one with the wallet pocketed his gun. 'Nothing in here but cash.'

'That's all I have,' the Otter said quietly.

'What's your name?'

'Now, wait a minute,' said the Otter, pretending anger but lowering his voice still further, forcing them to lean closer to hear. *Distract them*, Uncle Willy had said.

'Name and address,' said the one with the gun. 'Here, or downtown. It's all the same to us.'

'My name,' he murmured, grabbed the backs of their necks in either hand and smashed their heads together. One hit his jaw and staggered, but the other squirmed to one side and took the blow on the forehead. He dived under the Otter's big arms and smashed hard punches into his ribs that drove the air from his lungs. He clubbed downward with his clasped hands, drove the agent hard to the floor, but the other had recovered and was raising his gun.

The Otter kicked him down, but he landed rolling and still holding the gun. The Otter kicked again, missed. The agent levelled the gun at him and climbed to one knee.

'*Hold it.*'

The Otter raised his hands, kicked again, ducked. There was nothing left to do. The agent fired. The shot whined off a pipe just above the Otter's head, but the Otter was already falling on him, crushing him in his arms, squeezing. The Otter tightened his grip until the man's spine parted with a wet-sounding snap.

The Otter rolled off, found the dying man's partner unconscious. He strangled him, then ran, stopping to pick up his hat and retrieve his wallet, and again to grab up the suitcase of radio parts he had left on the subway platform. Conditions were already worse.

The change-clerk on the upper level was peering curiously at the stairs from his booth. The Otter hurried past this booth, collar turned up, hat low. On the street he realized that the token-seller must have given the FBI agents the key to the maintenance room. Too late to go back and do anything about him. He started to hail a cab, checked his hail and ran for a bus. Enough mistakes.

He wondered, as he had at times before, if he should have taken the risk of setting up his own radio years ago. But then, as now, a high-power shortwave transmitter fairly shouted agent . . . the prohibited equipment was undeniable evidence of intent to communicate with the enemy. And signals were too easily traced. So even though he had kept his transmissions short and infrequent, he had further reduced the danger by using Kroner and De Villeneuve as shields. The radiomen took the up-front risks, or had, until the Kroner shield had turned against him. He should have thought about the son . . . everyone knew German prisoners of war were being sent to North America. He should have thought of the possibility of Kroner's son being among them when Rommel was defeated. The temptation for Kroner must have been enormous when the boy made contact. Information in exchange for his son. His blinded son . . . And what had really happened to De Villeneuve? Was he still there? Were they watching him? Did he still have his radio?

The Otter hurried to his West Side safehouse to change into clothes harmonious with De Villeneuve's wealthy neighbourhood. He left the radio parts in the suitcase in the safehouse, took a cab crosstown to Fifty-third Street and started down Park Avenue wearing a dark suit, a pearl-grey fedora and topcoat. He blended inconspicuously with the residents coming home from cocktails or heading out for a late dinner in the nearby clubs and restaurants. But he was wary . . . still mindful of the débâcle at Kroner's and he noted uneasily the contrast civilian clothes made with the remarkable number of uniforms on men and women of all ages. The Americans had mobilized with the enthusiasm he had predicted to Uncle Willy back in 1939, and if he were not able to leave New York soon, he decided it would be wise to add a military disguise to his repertoire.

He walked slowly from Fifty-third down to Forty-seventh and up again. He retraced his route several times, changing sides of the broad, divided avenue as he studied De Villeneuve's apartment building. Nothing had gone right since the submarine had arrived and he had no reason to believe that the change in his fortunes would stop at the Frenchman's door.

Again, he passed the building and again he saw nothing unusual, though he felt that one of the white-gloved doormen glanced at him curiously. Noticing he'd passed by twice before?

There were two back ways into De Villeneuve's apartment, and he was dressed for neither. Nor did he want to barge in the service door on a kitchen full of cooks and maids serving one of the Frenchman's parties.

He walked a block east to Lexington Avenue and bought sunglasses, gauze and medical tape in an all-night drugstore. He went in the Lexington Avenue entrance of the Waldorf and then into a small, unattended men's room downstairs, where he affixed a white bandage over his nose and one cheek and put on the sunglasses.

He exited the hotel on the Park Avenue side, walked down to De Villeneuve's building and told the doorman he was expected. De Villeneuve still lived there. Not arrested. Now he had to worry that he'd been turned. One man telephoned the apartment and when De Villeneuve answered, the other took him to the elevator.

The elevator man closed the scissors gate of gleaming brass and turned the operating wheel with white-gloved hands. The walls were burnished wood – walnut. The car hummed quietly and smelled of fine furniture wax. The elevator man ushered him into the Frenchman's foyer, stepped quickly back into his car, closed the door and descended.

The Otter looked about the lavish foyer. De Villeneuve had done things right. What a cover. An ornate umbrella stand caught his eye; it was of highly polished brass and it stood guard at the elevator door, sprouting a bouquet of walking sticks and umbrella handles of silver, ivory and gold. It was highly doubtful, the Otter thought, that De Villeneuve had ever been rained on in all his years in New York.

It was about time that he was.

Mark St George was in charge at the Meurice while Weatherburn extended his stay in Connecticut. There'd been a flurry of confused signals. Something had gone wrong up there. Then the Frenchman, De Villeneuve, telephoned in a panic. The Otter was downstairs in his building. The doorman had announced a 'Mr Potter'.

Mark gave Duncan orders to track down Weatherburn, then follow with whatever heavies he could round up from Weatherburn's pool. He slipped a revolver into his belt and went out alone. He thought of trying to find Cordi but there wasn't time. His hastily belted trenchcoat flapped around his legs as he ran for a cab to De Villeneuve's. The shadow from his hat barely hid the glint of excitement in his eyes. Getting closer. Close.

The apartment felt empty, and if the doorman had not just spoken to De Villeneuve on the intercom the Otter would have thought he wasn't home. He removed the dark glasses and white bandage he'd pasted on to confuse the doorman and elevator operator and took off his hat. This would be the first time the Frenchman had ever seen his face.

And the last.

De Villeneuve shuffled in wearing a silk robe and slippers. He had aged since the last time the Otter had watched him leave the apartment. He glanced at the Otter, then looked away. 'Good evening.' He reached for the Otter's coat with unsteady hands.

'What's wrong?'

'Nothing. It's strange. I've never seen your face, yet I

438

knew it was you. Can I presume this is your last visit? Is that why you show me your face?'

'You will transmit for me, this time.'

'Ah . . . are you afraid they recognize your fist?'

'Exactly. I'll hold the coat.'

De Villeneuve stepped back, clinging to the garment, and said heartily, 'Don't be silly. You can't drag your coat through my home. I'll leave it here.' He spread it over a chair. 'Shall we go to the radio or would you like a sherry first?'

The Otter whisked it off the chair, draped it over his arm and clamped his hands around the Frenchman's throat. He drew him closer, squeezing firmly.

De Villeneuve clawed at his wrists. The Otter shook him. 'What is going on here? Where is the girl?'

De Villeneuve barely managed to gasp out that she was gone.

'Where?'

'To her family . . . she left me – '

The Otter relaxed his hands. De Villeneuve backed away, swallowing tentatively. 'You hurt me – '

'The radio.' It was an order.

Carrying his coat, he followed the Frenchman to the library and watched him slide the shelves that opened the alcove. De Villeneuve smoothed his silver hair and began fiddling with the telegraph key.

'Turn on the transmitter. Warm the tubes.'

De Villeneuve fumbled for the switch and turned it on. He was taking too long to connect the key. The Otter turned to the door, ready to run for it.

'What is your message?' De Villeneuve asked, sending a string of Vs and nodding at a gold fountain pen and a pad of expensive laid bond beside the radio. The Otter enciphered quickly. It was a simple message. 'Send a U-boat immediately. Not from Germany. No time. Send a boat already on patrol.'

Mark St George glided into the room behind him, his

439

footsteps muffled in the deep carpet. His gun was still in his belt. This one had to be taken alive. Halfway through the door, Mark stopped. The German looked like a reporter hunched over his notes. In his haste to take him before Weatherburn arrived, he realized he had come in too soon. Better to give him a chance to send his message so Duncan's machine could record it. He started to back out.

The Frenchman looked up and recognized him. Relief showed in his lined face. The Otter noted it, whirled towards the door, dropped the pad, and exploded into action.

Mark was paralysed for an instant by the realization that he had seen this man before . . . that he was *Rik van Slough*. And then the Otter was on top of him, dealing out sledge-hammer blows. He fell back, bought time by twisting through the door, bounced off the corridor wall and launched a right fist with all his weight behind it. He connected solidly with the Otter's jaw and was rewarded by a satisfying gasp of pain. Landing a second punch, he snapped the Otter's head back and felt him stagger. Still no need for his gun.

He directed a third, the finishing blow. But the Otter slipped the punch with a twist of his head and neck that was as fast as it was professional. Mark shifted his weight, swung again. He hadn't seen a move that good since he'd fought for the heavyweight championship of the home fleet. He landed a hard right-cross. The Otter took the blow, swung back. Mark sidestepped it and started a left counter.

Pain burst wide and deep through his whole right side. He staggered, knees buckling. How could anyone feint that fast and hit that hard at the same time? The Otter had landed a terrible left into his ribs. First he thought he'd been double-crossed by De Villeneuve, but as he fell, reaching for his revolver, he saw the Frenchman gaping in surprise from across the room.

The gun . . . his vision was fading. *Don't be proud, don't take any more chances with this one.* He tried to get the gun out of his belt. Too heavy. He tried a deep breath to steady himself. It was no use — his splintered ribs were sliding in and out of his lung.

The Otter finished him with a second blow.

'Come on,' he called to De Villeneuve.

The Frenchman shrank back from him. The Otter went across the bedroom and took his arm. 'You can't stay here, your cover's blown.'

The Frenchman wasn't sure which cover he meant.

He dragged him out and down the hall towards the kitchen, but before he got there he pulled him into a small pantry with a frosted-glass window. He closed and locked the door.

'What are you doing?'

'Be quiet. They have the doors covered.'

'We can't stay here . . . '

The Otter climbed onto the narrow windowsill and opened the doors of the highest cabinet. He reached further in and pulled out a tightly coiled length of thin rope.

The Frenchman watched him tie it to a riser pipe.

'That window is painted shut.' Anything to divert the Otter . . .

The Otter removed the shims that jammed it, and it slid open on a grey airshaft. A brick wall stood six feet opposite. The Otter lowered the rope into the air shaft.

'Come here.'

'It's seventeen storeys – '

'Do you prefer to hang? Move.'

Footsteps sounded past the pantry. A man shouted.

'*No*,' said the Frenchman, backing away. 'In here, *ici, ici* . . . ' He clawed at the doorknob.

The Otter came to him. 'I installed a good lock on that door when I left the rope. Apparently your new friends didn't notice . . . How did they turn you?'

'A trick . . . with a girl – '

'Who tricked you?'

'The English – '

'A redhead?'

'Lighter than red, a very beautiful girl – '

Cordi Grey. He rabbit punched De Villeneuve, caught him before he fell and shoved him out the narrow window. Then he followed him down the air shaft, using the rope . . .

Cordi Grey had turned the Frenchman. Which meant they'd been after him even longer than he'd thought. Well, he had Mr Steven Gates to give them.

He had one transmitter left. His most remote. The crazy old man in Connecticut. He had never transmitted from it, only received messages relayed to Miz Sally's on Sugar Hill. He hurried down Park Avenue to Grand Central and bought a ticket for the last train to Westport.

He cleaned up in the men's room and let the attendant brush his suit, which had suffered in the descent down De Villeneuve's air shaft. He headed for his train, but before he could board he saw the morning papers' bulldog editions.

Blanchard had been politically active in the 1930s, subsidizing right-wing organizations that had espoused return at all costs to so-called true American values. That and the spectacular way he had died made Blanchard's death big news. There was a picture on the front page of the *Daily News* and a headline: RICH NAZI ANGEL GALLOPS TO DEATH.

The Otter went into the subway, took the shuttle across to Times Square and the A train to One-hundred-tenth Street. Even if Blanchard's death *was* a riding accident, the estate would be swarming with police, family, lawyers and reporters. If they hadn't found the radio yet, they soon would.

Now he was completely cut off from Uncle Willy, with no way to signal for a second U-boat to meet the *Seehund*. And he had a much more immediate problem. When they found the radio, they would trace the message route. And it would

442

lead straight to the Otter's main cover if they got to Casey before he did. The police and the FBI would take Miz Sally's apart and come away with a guest list. Worse, in hiring Casey he had felt it necessary to personally look for a girl tough enough to survive a long time in the flesh market. She knew his face. And she would remember him because he had gone back to her again and again.

At One-hundred-tenth he hailed a taxicab to search for Casey.

'The Market.' Everyone knew where that was and what it was for, and the driver warned, 'You ain't doing it in my cab.'

'Not unless you want to help.'

'No, thanks,' the driver said, swinging onto Seventh and heading up the broad, divided avenue. 'I like mine white.' The Otter scanned the streetwalkers parading along the hot sidewalk. Casey's usual haunt was on the downtown side, but he couldn't see much of that past all the buses.

'Turn around at a Hundred-and-fifteenth.'

'If you don't make up your mind damn soon you're going to pay more on the meter than for the girl – hey, look at that car. I ain't seen one of those babies in years. That's a Duesenberg.'

The long green limousine was heading downtown and as it passed, the Otter spotted its Connecticut licence plate. The Duesenberg glided in the opposite direction, trailed, the Otter realized a moment later, by several black cars filled with men carefully watching.

'Look at 'em run the light,' the cabbie said. 'Guess if you're that rich you can do what you want.'

'I'll get out here.' The Otter tossed him a bill.

'Hey, you want change?' the driver called after him, but he was gone after the Duesenberg, weaving between cars and buses, moving fast for a man that big, vanishing into the dark.

'Casey's at the bat.'

Casey did a little fast shuffle for the girls and headed for the kerb. Two tricks already and here came the big green Duesenberg gliding into the Market.

The night was hot, the air sticky. The girls were down to sheer skirts and sleeveless blouses. Casey reached the kerb ahead of the car, did another foot riff for the girls and called out, 'High and inside.'

'Look out for his spitball, Casey.'

The car stopped. She opened the door, hopped in, shut the door. Halfway to her knees, she froze. There was no money on the seat. Nor was the old man who smelled of horses in the car. In his place was a slick-looking guy with a gun bulging inside a black suit. The mob must have been tipped to the old guy's numbers scam.

Casey reached for the door.

He grabbed her wrist and the car started to roll.

'Let me out, mister. I ain't done nothin'.'

'Take it easy, miss. I'm Commander Ober of Naval Intelligence and you're in a lot of trouble if you don't answer a few questions.'

Casey pulled her razor from her bag.

Ober's face went red. His eyes were fixed on her blade. The car was picking up speed. He reached inside his jacket. Casey tried to free her wrist but he was too strong.

'Let me *go* – '

She saw the thick barrel of a .45. The gun snagged, but the man ripped it loose. Casey slashed at the gun. Her blade sliced a long white line that angled across the back of Ober's hand and into his fingers. He watched as the line filled with blood.

Casey pushed the door open against the car's rush of wind. The street flew beneath her. She jumped. The car flashed past, and she was running and slipping and trying to make her feet go as fast as the ground and failing and falling on her hands and knees . . .

Her palms stung and the skin was scraped from her knees. A car screeched up behind her. She flung herself towards the gutter, but it had already stopped. Men in dark suits, and she realized with a burst of fear that got her to her feet and had her running in spite of the pain that they had been following the green car, probably were on the same side as the guy she'd cut.

They called out to her to stop. She ran harder, back towards the Market. They went after her. She saw the other girls and their pimps and some soldiers cruising.

'Stop her,' one of the men called out. The soldiers watched curiously, but the pimps shoved their girls off the street, into doorways and waiting cars. In seconds she was alone, except for the men behind and the soldiers in front. The soldiers spread out, as if thinking they'd try to stop her. She raced into a side street. The soldiers trotted after her.

She called out for someone to help her. A group of black men were drinking on a stoop on the other side of the street, half a block ahead. They stood up slowly, watching.

She looked back. The soldiers were gaining, and behind them the white men in suits. She ran into the middle of the street, towards the black men on the stoop. They didn't move. She turned towards an alley she knew, a place she took a busted trick on a really bad night. She slewed into the alley, screaming now. Which seemed to galvanize the men on the stoop. When she looked back she saw them tangling with the soldiers. A white man shouted nigger and by the time the men in suits reached the stoop, steel was flashing in the street lights.

She ran through the alley to the back door of a bar and into the ladies', where she dabbed cold water on her skinned knees and cried because she hurt like hell and never in her life felt so alone and scared. She tried to think. She was in bad trouble and nobody could get her out of it. Even if she was working for Miz Sally, she'd be on her own. No one messed with the mob.

She stepped out of the ladies' and started out of the bar. There was a crowd of people by the front door, peering into the street.

'Don't you go out there, girl,' the bartender said. 'There's people fighting.'

She heard police sirens. Down the street, flames were jumping from a car.

'Baby, that's no fight,' somebody said. 'That's a riot.'

'I got to get out of here.' She headed again for the back door. Halfway there a hand reached for her from one of the booths.

'I'll help you, Casey,' the Otter said. 'They're after me too.'

He'd run after the Duesenberg, then followed the agents chasing her, waiting for his chance. He had skirted the street fighting that broke out in her wake – schooled in urban warfare in Vienna, Madrid and Barcelona, this was child's play – and followed her down the alley and into this bar, where he'd ordered a Scotch and milk and taken a booth where he could watch the door to the ladies' room while she cleaned up.

'The mob?' she asked warily. 'They're after you, too?'

He nodded. Relief softened the fear in her face as she slid into the booth opposite him, but she still clutched at the tabletop with her long brown fingers. She'd broken several nails when she fell. 'I got to get on a train. I got to get out of town.'

'I'll take you to a train,' the Otter said.

'I need money.'

'How much, Casey?'

'A hundred bucks. I'll do anything you want.'

The Otter nodded. He had managed. Won. Even though he was cut off from Uncle Willy, and from rescue . . . his radios all destroyed . . . the enemy still hadn't caught him. And in less than a single day he had eliminated the threat of Kroner, of the two FBI agents, of De Villeneuve and the British agent. And soon Casey, his only 'vice'. He deserved a little celebration. A final 'vice'.

'Yes,' he said to her. 'Yes. That first.'

Duncan Haig led Weatherburn to Mark St George. He found the boy dead pale and breathing raggedly in short, shallow gasps that made his whole body start with pain. An English doctor knelt beside him, listening to his heart with a stethoscope and feeling his pulse.

'Is he all right?' Weatherburn asked.

'Something caved in his rib cage.'

Weatherburn glanced around for the weapon, and said to Duncan, 'What happened?'

'He told me to contact you, then round up help. He went ahead alone.'

'Why alone? Why did you let him do that?'

'He was the boss – '

'Oh, my God . . . '

'Sir,' the doctor said, 'he's trying to say something.'

As Mark tried to speak a red bubble formed on his lips. He took a shuddering breath.

'What? What did you say?' The doctor's ear was at his lips . . .

The doctor removed his stethoscope and laid Mark's hand on the floor. 'I'm afraid he's dead, sir.'

'I simply can't understand why anyone, regardless of colour or creed, would riot while their country is at war.' Richard Prince looked around the breakfast table. 'Charlie, can you explain it?'

Charlie Collins put down his paper. 'Everyone's being rationed, Uncle Richard, but it sure as hell doesn't look that way to blacks when soldiers and private citizens come up to Harlem flashing money and looking high on the hog.'

'Well, it's no reason to start attacking soldiers.'

Gates walked in just then, yawning.

'What are you doing up so early?'

447

'Rik called. He wants me to work on the tug.'

'I thought you were taking a day off. Isn't that why you're sleeping over? To get some rest?'

Gates poured coffee at the sideboard. 'The Lord of the Stern Empire arrived back from Washington last night, having probably negotiated statehood for his scrapyard, and discovered that somebody he'd rented *Hollandia* to had used the propeller to dice submerged objects. He can't wait for a free marine way to haul her, so he asked me to dive with him to fix her in the slip.'

'He could get somebody else,' Prince said.

'Who? Every diver in New York is working the *Normandie*. We're almost done patching. They're installing the pumps.'

The morning after Mark's funeral, Weatherburn called Cordi Grey to his apartment in the Hampshire House. She found him sitting in a dark room with the shades drawn, opening and shutting his switchblade. He hadn't shaved. His face bristled with stubble. His tweeds were rumpled. His eyes were very cold.

'Are you all right?'

'I'd like to put Gates in a quiet cellar and screw it out of him.'

'But if Gates is who you most suspect,' she said coldly, 'the others will go underground the moment you take him.'

Weatherburn lit a cigarette with unsteady, yellowed hands. 'They won't know I have him until it's too late. It won't take long with Gates.'

'But you'll risk everything to question him. At the least, they'll hide. At worst, you'll force their hand and make them do what they are planning before you can find out what it is.'

He stood up abruptly, brushing at his jacket. There was earth on his sleeves and Cordi had the odd feeling he had slept outdoors. He'd hung back after the funeral and hadn't returned to the city in any of their cars.

'We've lost a golden opportunity. The Otter has failed twice in a single day to transmit a message to Germany. If the damned FBI had told us about his other radio we'd at least have been better prepared at the Frenchman's.'

'What is *wrong* with them?' asked Cordi. And then, looking at Weatherburn, she realized that his group was disintegrating. The Otter, it seemed, had beaten them.

'Who knows?' Weatherburn snapped. 'I've just left a meeting where I was accused by different members of two different American intelligence services of being, first, soft on communists, and *then* a colonial imperialist undermining our Soviet ally. They have no goals beyond defeating the Germans.'

'Sir' – Cordi had heard all this before – 'what do you think the Otter was trying to transmit?'

Weatherburn ignored her.

Cordi shouted, '*What* was the Otter transmitting, damn it?'

'He's in some kind of trouble,' muttered Weatherburn. 'He rarely contacts Canaris . . . now all of a sudden he's trying like his life depends on it . . . '

'What sort of trouble?'

Weatherburn opened his eyes wide. 'If nothing breaks in a few days I'm going to ignore the consequences and *ask*. May even forget I'm a bloody English gentleman . . . '

The cave – half-water, half-air – in the stern of the *Normandie* murmured with machine sounds and tide flow, but the *Seehund* was silent, invisible just below the surface. Ponte boarded it in his diving suit, brought it up, and dewatered the cockpit. The Otter disconnected the electrical lead, climbed in, and lay down behind the helm, which was on the folding periscope's eyepiece and within reach of the ballast and trim controls, the motor switches and torpedo course-setters and firing-triggers.

They lay on their bellies, side by side. The Otter closed the hatch, let water into the ballast tanks, submerging the boat, and started to ease it out of the *Normandie*. The *Seehund* ran with an almost silent electric hum, but the cockpit resounded loudly from the cutting, metallic rumble above of ship screws on the surface, the thrashing of tug propellers and the whine of heavy machinery.

The Otter eased the boat towards the surface while Ponte readied the periscope. He took a quick look around to make sure nothing was coming at them. The *Normandie* lay a hundred yards away, swarming with workmen. Tugs and lighters moved in and out of the slip.

He took the boat down to thirty feet, deep enough to pass under tugs and barges. He stayed close to shore to avoid the deep draught ships in midchannel. It was not a foolproof strategy. The previous week on one of their practice runs they'd hit something a glancing blow and it was only by the grace of whatever god still smiled on the Axis that they hadn't crushed the thin hull and drowned in the muck or caused some zealous Coast Guard volunteer to investigate the noise with a depth charge. Tonight, remembering, they listened intently for the rumble of approaching screws.

The boat grew quiet after a while, a sign that there were no moving ships in the area. The Otter partially blew the ballast tank, raising the boat, and manipulated the trim-tank controls to stabilize her as she nudged the surface. Ponte reached over to help with the periscope, but the Otter was there ahead of him, pumping the hydraulic crank with one hand, playing the trim wheels with the other and securing the helm with his chin the way he'd seen Ponte do.

The periscope now locked into place on the fifth pump. It had a good night range. The Otter scanned the surface. He had strayed nearer to a main channel than he'd meant to, which was why running at periscope depth was better than deep running, especially at night when the risk of detection was relatively small.

He sighted a heavy cruiser making for the Narrows and sped after it. It was ploughing along at eight knots, casting a harsh, dark shadow against the moonlit sky. He caught up with it quickly and switched the electric motor down to half-speed.

Ponte spoke for the first time.

'Where are we going?'

'Gravesend Bay.'

'What is there?'

The Otter smiled at him in the pale green light shining from the amperage, air-pressure and depth gauges, and the calibrated face of the bobbing compass.

'A surprise.'

The Otter felt exhilarated by the swift, secret passage through the dense harbour, and watched the ship ahead through the periscope. She looked like a *Minneapolis* class, with nine eight-inch guns on the three main turrets. He envisioned her bridge – all smug order, dark and remote. Could they begin to imagine that four torpedoes armed with one and a half tons of dynamite were trailing their wake two hundred yards astern? The temptation was enormous. His fingers moved towards the torpedo switches.

He followed the cruiser for half an hour, then abruptly overtook it and raced past. Ponte stirred nervously. At this speed the periscope was leaving a fine plume of spray that would reflect the moonlight like a prism. The Otter tripped the remaining power switch and ran the submarine at its battery-draining top speed.

He stopped short of the open harbour gate, circled swiftly and made for Gravesend, his eyes fast on the periscope as he turned it to and fro. To hit something at this speed would be fatal.

'The batteries,' murmured Ponte.

Reluctantly, the Otter reduced speed. There were limits, but for moments in this machine the limits seemed unessential. Tonight was the best yet. He had blended with the submarine and commanded it. He was ready.

The ammunition carriers exiled to Gravesend Bay were moored much further apart than the shifts of wind and tide required of normal freighters. Riding tight spans between double anchors and swinging within a radius equal to their own length, they shunned each other as avidly as the rest of the harbour shunned them. The Otter chose a big one, which stood black at the end of the moon's path like the blade of a long-handled broadaxe.

He centred it in the periscope's cross hairs and stopped the electric motor. When the submarine had drifted to a halt, he took a bearing on the ammunition carrier.

'Bearing forty-seven degrees,' he said. He looked away from the periscope and turned a torpedo course-setting knob. Crammed into the stern of the twenty-three-foot-long torpedo were gyroscopes which would now alter the torpedo's course up to ninety degrees to put it on the course the Otter had set.

'That's a stern tube,' said Ponte.

'I know.' He made another setting. 'Depth five feet.'

Ponte nodded. 'But only if your target is an ammunition ship do you set so shallow.'

'I know.' The Otter moved a switch beside the course-setter. 'Ready to fire. The tube door is open.'

'Very good,' Ponte said. 'You have prepared your port-side stern tube to fire on a course of oh-forty-seven degrees at a depth of five feet. Excellent. Disarm it, and try another target.'

The Otter glanced out of the periscope and reached for the trigger switch.

Ponte clamped a powerful hand around his wrist. '*What are you doing?*'

The Otter calmly returned his startled gaze. His size put him at a distinct disadvantage in the cramped space.

'I am going to sink it.'

'Are you crazy?'

'How else can I test the torpedoes?'

'But then they will know we are here. We will achieve nothing but a couple of sunken freighters when they have thousands.'

'Who knows why an ammunition ship explodes?'

'*No.*'

'It is *necessary*,' the Otter said.

'Why?'

'Did the U-boat get off a signal before it sank?'

'Of course not.'

'Have you raised any U-boats on this radio?'

'You know I have not.'

'Have I made radio contact with Hamburg?'

'No.'

'How can we escape if I don't contact Admiral Canaris?'

'What are you talking about?'

'Look.' The Otter twisted aside and pointed at the periscope. Ponte leaned over and looked into the viewer.

'So?'

'What do you see?'

'Ammunition ship.'

453

'It will make quite a bang, will it not?'

'It is not worth it — '

'It is a message,' said the Otter. 'A message to the admiral. He will hear it, and understand.'

Or at least so the Otter hoped.

Ponte was still doubtful.

'It's our only chance,' the Otter told him. 'The admiral doesn't even know you made it here. This will tell him.'

'If he is listening.'

'One way or another, in a day or a week at most, the news of an ammunition ship exploding in New York will reach the chief of the Abwehr.'

'But how will he know what it means?'

'He will guess.'

'How?'

'Because he will *want* to. He will hope. He will at least send another U-boat, hoping we will sink the *Queen Mary*, hoping we will escape.'

'How can you be so sure?' said Ponte.

'Because Germany needs its heroes,' the Otter said. 'And because the admiral needs proof that the victory was his.'

Ponte let go of his wrist. The Otter turned the submarine around, and aimed the stern tubes at Gravesend Bay.

The chief petty officer at the US Naval Signal Station at Atlantic Beach on Far Rockaway watched a bouncing fluxmeter recording pen over the shoulder of a navy signalman. It appeared that something quite small was crossing one of the Harbour Entrance Control post's magnetic indicator loops which recorded ship movements on the east side of the Lower Bay.

A runner came into the room. 'Still nothing visual, chief. You want me to call Fort Wad?'

The chief had been at Atlantic Beach a long time. He unfolded a dog-eared Long Island Railroad schedule.

'What time is it?'

'Oh-two-hundred.'

'Funny,' he said, running his finger down the schedule, 'no trains.'

The railroad's electric track paralleled a mile of the tailcable along Atlantic Beach and the passing trains played havoc with the fluxmeter readings. He called Fort Wadsworth himself and asked with little enthusiasm if the sono-radio buoys were picking up an unidentified movement south of Gravesend Bay.

The sono-radio buoys were moored a thousand yards inside the magnetic loops, and late at night when the traffic was light like this they worked fairly well because propeller chatter was not too heavy, provided they had not been run down by a ship, which happened regularly, or dragged away by the ice in the winter, or their batteries hadn't gone on the fritz or their antennae hadn't broken off. He wasn't surprised when Fort Wadsworth, which sat at the Narrows on Staten Island, reported that their radios had not received anything unusual from the buoys.

He strolled outside with binoculars and joined the seamen on watch. Far down the Rockaway beaches the moon lighted the Lower Bay. A big cruiser was ploughing seaward and other ships were moving in and out of the Ambrose Channel. The moon was so bright that he could distinguish the gate vessels at the open submarine net and the dark faraway dots of hundreds of freighters riding at anchor from Sandy Hook to Raritan Bay.

On a hunch he called Fort Tilden and asked the army bonehead who answered if their hydrophone squawk boxes had picked up any unusual sounds. The audio receivers hadn't, which wasn't surprising. The last time they'd tried to calibrate that system an ash can dropped on the shoals of the False Hook was recorded way back at the Narrows and the army couldn't decide whether the depth charge had detonated in the Atlantic or inside the Brooklyn-Battery Tunnel.

He went back out for another look at the moonlit bay.

The torpedo slipped from its tube with a hiss of compressed air, and the submarine's stern leaped out of the water, throwing the Otter forward against the helm. Ponte reached over and calmly opened the stern ballast and trim valves. The tanks filled with water. The submarine settled on an even keel and the Otter chided himself for not remembering that the sudden exit of a three-thousand-pound torpedo had to be counterbalanced.

'Thirty seconds,' said Ponte.

At the half-mile range the torpedo would hit in less than a minute. The Otter braced for the explosion and found the target in the periscope. The moon hung behind the anchored ammunition ship and cast a sparkling line from it to the *Seehund* – a glittering path down which the torpedo was hurtling. The Otter fancied he could see its wake, sparkling like fish scales.

'Forty-five seconds.'

'I see it!' the Otter said. 'I can see the torpedo.'

'Impossible. You can't'

It porpoised suddenly out of the water, glistening, leaping and falling, almost airborne in the cold moonlight.

And then it vanished.

'I saw it again. Something's thrown it off course.' There was motion in the right-hand side of the periscope field. A ship was moving into the dark anchorage, as if preparing to moor itself near the target ship.

'What's that sound?' Ponte asked abruptly.

The Otter was still trying to locate the erratic torpedo track in the periscope again and hadn't noticed, until Ponte asked, the loud rumble of screws *behind* the submarine. He turned the *Seehund* around, a full one hundred and eighty degrees and looked for the source.

'Capital ship,' he said. 'Big cruiser.'

'Where is the torpedo?' There was an unusual strained

quality to Ponte's voice. The Otter was confused. All he knew was that the torpedo had turned away from the target and had not yet exploded.

'Take the controls.'

Instantly, as he had done often while teaching the Otter to operate the boat, Ponte looked into the periscope, which hung down between them, reached across and took command of the controls. The Otter didn't relinquish control lightly, but this *Seehund* was still in better hands with Ponte. Ponte turned the boat and looked into the periscope.

The Otter heard a new sound over the rumble of the cruiser passing behind them. A whine, high-pitched, insistent and growing louder.

Ponte spoke without taking his eyes from the periscope. His hands were busy on the *Seehund*'s controls. 'It is pursuing us, my friend.'

'What?'

'The torpedo . . . it is running wild, attracted to our sound – '

'*Our sound?*'

'Or the sound of the ship behind us. We can either hide here and hope it doesn't hit, or we can run and hope our running sounds don't bring it chasing after us.'

'*Run,*' the Otter said.

'Yes, my friend.' The *Seehund* heeled sharply. Behind it, a dull keening began to resonate through the water as the rumble of the cruiser's screws – which had attracted the torpedo in the first place – faded now as the ship steamed away from the area.

Ponte played the helm. The *Seehund* responded, changed course again, but the sound of the torpedo grew louder, screaming now, loud, almost on top of the *Seehund*.

'It's catching up . . . '

Ponte's face was set. The Otter realized the Italian was deathly afraid.

'Last chance, my friend. All we can do is try to dodge. She is too fast for our little boat.'

Ponte put the *Seehund* into a graceful turn, cracked the ballast and trim tanks a hair and eased her into an elegant dive. Levelling at thirty feet near the bottom of the channel, he hurled the boat into a ninety degree turn and stopped the propeller.

The Otter was thrown against the side of the cockpit. The sound of the torpedo was louder; he flinched reflexively as it hurtled past like a subway in a dark tunnel.

Out on the bay the chief saw the merchantman's running lights closing on the point of Coney Island. The ship was making for Gravesend Bay, which meant she was an ammunition carrier since no other vessels were allowed to anchor there. Her lights disappeared, bow to stern, as she slipped behind the land jut. He started back into the instrument bunker when the sky suddenly lighted white as the sun on hard snow.

All the ships before his eyes, and all the land, the buildings of Brooklyn, the hills and church steeples of Staten Island, stood sharply visible. The sky turned black again, and the sound of the explosion rolled loud and hollow across the water. Flaming debris flew into the air behind Coney Island, burning out before it fell, like fireworks.

It took him an instant to realize that the ammunition ship had blown up as it entered the anchorage. It took another instant to really believe it, and a third to figure out how.

Sailors boiled out of the bunker, yelling astonishment.

'What happened?'

'A goddamned army mine busted loose.'

'Wha'd it hit?'

'Ammo ship, that's goddamn what.'

'You mean them signals we got was from a drifting mine?'

'Goddamned army. Senior service, *my ass*.'

The shock wave tumbled the *Seehund* backwards and rolled it on its side. The Otter turned on all the motor switches

458

with a single swipe of his big hand, trying to regain control. The boat shuddered, rooted in the heaving water.

'The propeller is cavitating,' Ponte explained calmly, reaching over to slow the motors and turn the helm. 'You must start her gently or the propeller cuts a hole in the water and the hole fills with air.' The propeller slowed, took hold of the water and the boat levelled out at periscope depth.

The Otter brushed Ponte's hands off the controls and found Gravesend in the periscope. He couldn't find his bearings at first. When he had, he turned to Ponte with death in his voice.

'What happened? Why did it come after us?'

Perspiration rolled down Ponte's forehead, into his eyes. He blinked it away.

'I did exactly as you taught me,' the Otter said. 'It hit the moving ship, after it missed us. What did you mean by sound? What went wrong?'

'The torpedoes are fitted with acoustical heads – '

'*Acoustical?*'

'Attracted by sound. The *noise* of the ship.'

'In a harbour? What's to stop it from bypassing the *Queen Mary* for the Weehawken ferry?'

'Nothing, my friend,' Ponte replied miserably. 'It is made for the silence of the sea. It seems they loaded the wrong torpedoes. Or perhaps these were all they had at Hamburg. Conditions at the boatworks were strained. The admiral seemed – '

'Change the others,' the Otter snapped. 'Make them explode on contact. Cut out the acoustical guidance.'

'I cannot,' said Ponte. 'It was the engineer that knew how.'

'He's dead.'

'Yes, my friend.'

'You should have saved him, damn you.' Rage was tearing through him. Damn Uncle Willy for sending the wrong torpedoes. Damn the engineer for getting killed. Damn Ponte for letting him die. He felt his control going. He felt the deepest rage of all that he had allowed this to happen to himself. He had put himself in the care of fools.

37

'You making a no-helmet dive, Junior?'

Gates was sitting on the diving platform inside the fallen *Normandie* above a watertight compartment near the stern. He was thinking, however, about the cable he had seen dangling from the forward clamp under the German U-boat's bow. What *had* been the purpose of the cable? There was a reason for every object on a ship – especially on a U-boat. They'd carry nothing extra on the four-thousand-mile voyage from Germany. So why had they carried the cable? What had the Germans intended? How had it served the extra fuel tank that hung between the clamps – if Ober was right about it being a tank at all. But Gates knew that if he could figure out what the rubber-coated cable had been used for, he'd have a clearer idea what the U-boat had really been carrying –

Charlie grabbed him under his arms and pretended to wrestle him into the water, interrupting his thoughts.

'Knock if off!' Van Slough came along the diving platform at a fast walk. 'Come on, you guys. We got to put six more suctions down there. Get in the water, Steven. Charlie, put his helmet on. One diver left topside, and *he's* mine. *Gott.*' He grabbed his own helmet and raised it over his head.

'Take it easy, Rik, you'll bust a gut.'

'*Ja, you* take it easy.' Take it very easy, Mr Gates.

To cool him down, Gates asked, 'Hey, Rik, who's the funny little guy with the long arms?'

'What funny little guy?'

'The new diver. He's working in compartment sixteen.'

'Oh, him. Giuseppe. He's Italian.'

'No kidding. But where'd he come from?' Charlie asked.

'Italy, I suppose.'

'Italy's part of the enemy, Rik. In case you hadn't noticed.'

'I mean originally ... he's been here a long time. He worked for the Italian Line and stayed in New York when the war started.'

'How you know that?'

'He told me. He speaks English better than I do. I offered him a job.'

'Is he going to take it?'

'No. He's with Cennamo Salvage. Those Italians stick together ... All right, let's go to work, men.'

Charlie Collins tended Gates and Marty tended van Slough. The riggers, specialists at the dangerous work of manhandling tons of steel machinery into small dark places, ignored van Slough and worked at their own pace, placing the pumps on hinged platforms which could be levelled by slacking off on chain falls when the *Normandie* rotated and began to stand up and float.

Flexible steel pipes were run up through the starboard ports to exhaust the pump's gasoline engines. The discharges exited through the vertical promenade deck, down which the pumped water would spill into the slip.

Gates picked up his helmet. 'Throw me in again, Charlie. Before the Flying Dutchman has the world's first underwater heatstroke.'

The patching and rigging work was going on along the full thousand-foot length of the *Normandie*'s hull. Every few minutes a pump engine would roar to life and a test discharge would spew out of the ship creamy white, then stop as suddenly as it had begun, like a storm cloud that threatened to rain and never did.

In preparation for her eventual movement, cranes were hoisting the shantytown of work sheds off her high flank, along with excess catwalks and structures that wouldn't stand the strain of rotating from the horizontal to the vertical. A single structure was erected on the vertical deck, fastened by hinges – a command bridge for Captain Tooker, rigged, like the pumps, to remain horizontal as the capsized ship tried to rise.

The barges that housed the machine shop and the carpenters and the supply buildings and the company site office, and even Monte Carlo, the lunchroom-gambling barge, were warped further away from the *Normandie*.

When Gates came up at his next break, van Slough was finally resting on the diving platform, wearily drinking coffee.

'Rik says he's not coming to Vera's party,' said Charlie.

'I'm too busy. Who knows what may come up for me to handle that night? Emergencies . . . '

'But you already said you would come,' Gates said. 'My mother's counting on it. You're beat anyway, you could use the rest.'

'I'll try. Okay, Marty, let's go. Maybe Steven will join me in the water when his behind gets tired.'

'I'll join you when I can breathe again,' said Gates, fingering a length of cable that the riggers had dropped. It was a habit he'd developed – comparing wires, steel lines, and cables of all sorts to the rubber-coated cable on the sunken U-boat. He could not get it out of his mind and had even placed calls to Commander Ober to ask if they had raised the bow piece of the U-boat. Ober hadn't returned his calls, but neither of the navy divers who had been shanghaied for the job were back, so maybe they were still trying.

As near as he could recall the feeling through his thick diving glove, the cable on the U-boat hadn't been as stiff as a wire hawser or the heavy one-inch stays they'd been rigging to support the parts of the *Normandie*'s superstructure which they hadn't been able to cut in the deep mud, but which would rupture dangerously as the ship rotated. Nor had the cable been as flexible as a diving hose or the winch lines the riggers used to hoist the pumps aboard.

462

Gates made one more dive than he should have and finished the shift in a semi-daze, angry at himself for allowing van Slough to bully him into pushing it too hard. He wandered out on the gangways and into Monte Carlo for coffee. He was threading his way through the crap games when a pair of dice skittered off a table and bounced on the deck. He rescued one of the dice an instant before a huge crane operator lumbering by with a sandwich could crush it under his boot.

'What do they say, buddy?' yelled the man who'd thrown.

'Don't count off the table,' shouted another.

'Five spot,' said Gates.

'What about the other one?'

'Rolled under the stove.'

'Oh for chrissake, we forgot to tell Pickert craps ain't bowling.'

The entire game trooped over to look for it, but Gates was already down on his hands and knees trying to get his hand behind the electric range somebody had rescued from the *Normandie* and installed on the gambling barge to heat coffee for all-night games.

'Gangway.'

Gates rocked back on his heels while the craps players pulled the heavy range away from the bulkhead. 'Okay.' He reached in and felt around. A tug captain leaned over the top of the stove and peered down.

'There it is, sitting right behind the pigtail.'

Gates moved the thick electric cable and picked up the dice.

'What does it say?'

'It don't count off the table!'

'It's a four,' declared the tug captain. 'And it does count. That's nine and I made my point – hey, buddy, pick it up.'

But Gates had dropped the dice so that he could hold the pigtail. He twisted the short length between the stove and the bulkhead.

'I'm not ready to blow the plant, if that's why you're here.'

The Otter was not surprised. Larson had got comfortable. He'd put on weight. His bright red hair was neatly slicked back and he wore a pressed shirt and slacks. The Otter gazed down a grassy path between two widely spaced rows of weeping beech trees. 'I have a new job for you.'

Larson ran his hand through his hair. 'But I'm right in the middle of this one.'

'This is more important. Five thousand dollars now and ten thousand more in a month.'

Larson came down the porch steps. 'What do you want? Another fire?'

'No. And I will tell you no more until you agree.'

'That is a lot of money . . . When?'

'Right now.'

Larson glanced down the road where his wife had gone. 'For how long?'

'A few days. Pack a bag. And bring your tools.'

'New York?'

'What does it matter?' The Otter was fed up.

'If it's New York, I got to dye my hair.'

Larson loosened a long, low whistle and shook his head in disbelief as he circled the *Seehund*, which lay on a wheeled cradle on the tracks inside the Otter's boathouse on the Weehawken shore. Ponte leaned against the submarine, patting its steel skin and grinning. The Otter watched them both, his broad face set tight.

'Does this thing *work*?

'That's not your concern. I brought you here to re-arm the torpedoes.'

Larson whistled again. 'Where did you get it?'

'Can you do it?' the Otter asked. 'And can you bypass the acoustical guidance?' He hated needing Larson. The redhead was the sort who sensed need and exploited it.

The problem was the Otter knew of no one as good as Larson.

'Can you set the warheads to explode on contact only?'

Larson put down his beautifully crafted wooden tool box. 'Sure . . . what are you going to shoot at?'

Before the Otter could reply, Ponte said quietly, 'Contact is contact. It does not matter what target.'

'Just curious.'

It was then that the Otter decided this would be Larson's last job.

They inched the first torpedo out of its tube with a twenty-ton jack. When the small screw device had pushed the torpedo to its limit, a little more than a foot, they tightened a steel collar around the exposed warhead and hauled the huge cylinder the rest of the way out of the tube until it was hanging in chains from the overhead sliding hoist formerly used to remove and install marine engines.

The Otter eyed the torpedo while Larson and Ponte opened its gyro compartment and stripped the nose off the warhead. It was huge, twenty-three feet long, nearly half the length of the *Seehund*, and almost two feet thick. The smooth, greased cylinder had a rounded nose and tapered aft to a tail festooned with hydroplanes, rudders and a shielded propeller. It was, the Otter thought, as the work proceeded and he began to relax, quite a beautiful thing to behold.

'Can you do it?' he asked.

Larson didn't look up. 'Your people make 'em a little different than we do,' he muttered. 'I gotta figure out how different or Jersey's gonna be a big hole in the ground.'

The torpedo was the standard weapon launched by German U-boats, although it was powered by electric batteries instead of the more common compressed air. At least, he thought grimly, Uncle Willy had simplified matters to that extent. It was charged with the same electricity as the *Seehund*.

The tug captain yelled a warning. 'Watch it, buddy. That's two-hundred-twenty volts. It'll weld you to the bulkhead.'

'It's insulated,' Gates said softly.

'Yeah, well, don't tempt it.'

'It's got a rubber coating,' Gates said, shaking his head in private amazement. 'In case it gets wet behind the stove. That's it . . . It's an insulated electric cable – '

'You want to hand me the dice?'

The Otter gathered his emergency escape money.

He went to the West Side rooming house and dug up the money under a cobblestone in the landlady's backyard. He went to the tenement west of midtown and removed cash from a mattress. He went to a rented office in a warehouse near the Fulton Fish Market, which he rarely used, and took money from a locked desk. And he went to the Harlem apartment and removed the cash he had hidden in a wall behind an electrical outlet.

Next he drove to eastern Long Island, where Hank Larson lived in an old South Shore town of comfortable frame mansions with his new wife. He'd moved up to a supervisor's job at the Grumman aircraft plant. His house was freshly painted and the lawn, which was being mowed by a handyman, was flat and broad and extended to a canal where a cabin boat, a narrow inlet runner with shiny brass fittings and varnished mahogany, gleamed at his dock.

The army officer's widow Larson had married must have been well-heeled even before the insurance. The Otter waited until she'd bicycled off towards the village. Gas rationing was apparent here, and the Otter's car – with a full tank of black market gasoline – was one of only two on the street. Larson came out on the porch. He looked surprised to see him, and a little wary. But he was, as usual, blunt.

The warhead occupied the first six feet of the cylinder and contained eight hundred pounds of dynamite. The torpedo was self-propelled and self-contained – a miniature submarine in essence – but the complexities of cramming its motor batteries, gyroscopes and depth regulators into the small space left by the dynamite made it a mechanical nightmare, nearly comparable to stuffing the workings of a railroad locomotive into an automobile.

Larson stepped back, kneading his neck muscles. He paced around the boathouse, flinging his arms about like an athlete loosening up. He whistled as he had earlier. 'I can't believe I'm doing this.'

'Why?' asked the Otter.

'I don't know. Setting fires is one thing. This is more like a real war. I mean this thing is a warship.'

'It is a good little boat,' said Ponte.

Larson gave him a flat look. 'Yeah.'

'How much longer do you need?' asked the Otter.

'I'll tell you when I'm done.'

'Where did you learn to do this?' asked Ponte.

Larson gave the smiling Italian another look. *'Popular Mechanics.'*

'What is that?'

'Forget it – the Germans sent over an explosives guy before the war. Seemed like a good thing to learn. Mr Otter here got me a job at Electric Boat for a while. And then in an aircraft plant.'

'We have two more torpedoes,' said the Otter. 'Let's get moving.'

'You seem very skilful,' Ponte said.

'Americans got a knack with machines . . . you know something, Mr Otter, I think maybe my fee oughta be tripled. Once for each torpedo.'

The Otter nodded. 'I think you're right.'

He turned away. Killing was like clearing a field of stones – necessary to plough and plant. But there was the occasional stone a man was extremely satisfied to see out of the ground and stacked on the wall. Larson was such a stone.

They stayed overnight in the boathouse. The next day, when Larson had finished converting the third and last torpedo, the Otter told him to remove a few ounces of dynamite from its warhead. He wrapped the explosive in foil and put it in the suitcase he had taken from Kroner's shop . . . the suitcase he had used to carry off the shortwave radio parts. Nearly time now for their delivery, along with the dynamite, to their new owner . . . Mr Steven Gates . . .

After they had sealed the torpedo and returned it to its tube in the *Seehund*, Larson said 'I'd be damned careful after you arm these babies. Like your friend said, contact detonators don't care what they contact.'

The Otter took him into the miniature's cockpit.

'Arm them.'

'You just turn tnem switches.'

'I'd like to see you do it.'

Larson wet his lips. 'You don't trust my work?'

'I am more interested in how much you trust it.'

Larson shrugged and turned the first arming switch. The arming light glowed green. He turned the second and third.

'See?'

'Very good. Let's get her back in the water.'

'You need me?' Larson asked. 'I wouldn't mind going home.'

'Yes, I do. Go take a look in that suitcase.'

Larson walked across the boathouse to where the Otter had left the suitcase and opened it and looked inside. 'What's this supposed to be?'

'Shortwave radio transmitter-receiver.'

'Are you kidding?'

'I want you to fix it for me.'

'You're missing a few parts.'

'There's plenty there,' the Otter assured him.

'For what?'

468

The Otter joined him and picked up the foil package. 'A gift wrapper for this.'

'Very funny. Okay, I'll need a little electric battery and a blasting cap.'

The Otter handed him a battery and Ponte tossed him a blasting cap. Larson caught it gingerly.

'Where'd you get this?'

'The hardware store,' Ponte said. He was not smiling.

At nightfall they opened the barn doors and trundled the cradle down the gently sloping rails into the water. Larson watched Ponte ease the boat off the cradle and whistled a final time as the *Seehund* disappeared silently into the Hudson River.

Across the river, Steven Gates strode along a catwalk, his eyes roaming the *Normandie*. The fallen hull was stripped clean, cleared at last to essentials, and sealed. The salvors had made her a vessel again – a watertight container ready to be pumped dry – shored and strengthened for the stresses of her imminent rise. She was mere days from her new launching, her slow, inch-by-inch journey up out of the mud which would begin when the pumps began to empty her. Gates knew he should be proud. He had been part of it. But he was still angry – more angry that she'd been destroyed in the first place than proud that he had helped salvage her.

And the thought of the electric cable he'd seen on the U-boat kept gnawing at him. Now he knew that whatever it was that the U-boat's unusual brackets had held had used electricity. Vast amounts of electricity, because a cable that thick and short could carry a considerable load. Electricity meant machinery. Some large machine suspended between the two brackets? At least forty or fifty feet long? What kind of machine?

An auxiliary power source for the U-boat? A generator of some sort? Extra batteries? An electric motor to make

469

the U-boat faster . . . a second electric motor and propeller to increase the U-boat's speed underwater? That was possible.

But why hadn't they found it? Or had it fallen into the sea trench like the stern section? Perhaps something experimental . . . that would explain why the U-boat had had no numbers on the conning tower. Top secret. But why risk an experiment in American waters? . . . Or should he ask, why *bring* an experiment to American waters? . . .

'I had a toast planned for our celebration,' Richard Prince said, rising at the head of the candlelit table. 'But the news on the radio demands a grateful prayer first. Mussolini has been overthrown, thank God. Let's pray that the Italians make peace before the Germans take Rome.'

Prince, Gates, Charlie and van Slough were wearing dinner jackets. Kay, Vera Gates and Cordi Grey were in long dresses, and for the moment Gates had the feeling he was years back, before the war. His uncle nodded to him. 'So much for *Il Duce*. Now a toast.' Prince raised his glass. 'Controlled pumping is about to begin on the *SS Normandie*, thanks to Rik and Charlie and my bullheaded, obstinate nephew Steven, who stuck with her against all advice from all sides, particularly mine. Congratulations.'

'The three thousand other guys helped a little,' said Charlie.

'Mostly they were in the way,' said van Slough winningly.

Gates said, 'Sorry it took so long.'

'How much longer?'

'She'll rotate slowly. A couple of weeks if we don't run into any hitches.'

'Will you please explain one more time how you're going to lift it up?' Cordi said when they'd lowered their glasses.

'She'll lift herself up,' Gates said, 'as we pump her out. She'll slowly rotate until she's upright.'

'How?'

'We've made her into a ship again by sealing her, so when she's pumped dry she has to float.'

'But why won't she just float on her side?' asked Kay. 'What's going to make her stand up?'

'That's what *I'm* asking,' said Cordi.

'Because by pumping the water out we will lower her centre of gravity to a point *below* her metacentre. With a positive metacentric value, she has to stand up.'

'Why?'

'Because, damn it, an upright ship has a positive metacentre. The higher the metacentre is above the centre of gravity, the more stable she is and the quicker she'll come back from a roll and the less likely she is to turn over in the first place. The *Normandie* has a high metacentre, which is why we know she'll stand up.'

'Cordi,' said Vera Gates, 'it's impossible to understand this.'

'Actually,' said Cordi, 'I looked all this up in the encyclopaedia, and I think I *do* know what Steven is talking about. This metacentric height – the distance between the centre of gravity and the intersection of a vertical line through the centre of buoyancy when the hull is level and when it's inclined – is just a convenient way of measuring stability. No applause, but thank you.'

'You've got it,' Prince said. 'The *Normandie* will stand when her centre of gravity is lowered by decreasing her weight by pumping the water out of her hull. Don't let Steven bulldoze you with his jargon.'

'I'm not bulldozing her,' Gates said, adding in a good-humoured mutter, 'The encyclopaedia? You mean I didn't have to go to school?'

'I doubt you could bulldoze her,' his mother said.

'You're welcome to keep trying,' Cordi told him with a quiet smile.

'Speaking of bulldozers,' Kay Collins said, 'I have another toast, and news – no, mother, I'm not pregnant.

After all – ' and she grinned at Charlie '– I'm married to a child and don't want another.' She raised her glass. 'Good luck to Captain Charles Collins, US Army.'

'What? You joined up?' Steven said.

Charlie grinned and Gates saw that Uncle Richard and Rik already knew. 'I decided I'd better, and I confess, Uncle Richard pulled a string and I got a commission. Sorry . . . hope I can live up to it.'

Vera Gates looked worried. 'You were a major in that Spanish Civil War,' she said distractedly.

'I told you, Vera. That was a battlefield commission.'

'Don't deny the honour.'

'Everybody else was dead.'

'What made you decide to enlist?' Cordi asked.

Charlie grinned at her, covering up what Gates knew had to be extremely complex emotions about his decision. 'Well, the amateurs are dragging things out. I figured it was time to turn this war around – '

Cordi said, 'But wasn't the army – ouch!'

Turn around . . . Gates had reached for her hand under the table when Charlie's phrase hit him, and closed his hand convulsively on hers . . . 'Sorry,' he mumbled. *Turn around* . . . he'd got it *backwards*. The machinery in the U-boat's brackets didn't serve the U-boat. *Turn it around,* stupid . . . it was the U-boat that served the machinery . . . he'd been right in the beginning. The U-boat had carried something, transported something run by electricity. Something detachable – because the hook or clamp he'd seen on the U-boat's keel hadn't been damaged, not broken, merely opened. Detachable. Something too small to cross the Atlantic into American waters alone. Something connected to an outside source of electricity – the U-boat – until it was detached. Then what? Batteries? Batteries that would have to be recharged after a short time by an outside source again? The U-boat? But any generator would do if it were powerful enough, and the machine was mobile – which it would have to be

472

if it were detached from the mother sub – *a harbour sub* . . .?

Gates stood up, unaware that they were staring at him, unaware that he had begun to speak his thought aloud . . . 'Right here in New York Harbour? Could it possibly . . . be an electrically powered miniature submarine . . .?'

38

'A joke?' the Otter laughed.

'What are you talking about, Steven?' his mother asked.

The Otter glanced around the table, gauging reactions.

'You *are* joking,' the Otter said.

'No joke. It could have escaped from the sub that Wally – ' He caught himself and stepped away from the table. 'Excuse me. Uncle Richard, I have to talk to you.'

Prince got up and followed with mumbled excuses. The Otter exchanged mystified glances with the others, and listened as their footsteps stopped and the library door shut firmly . . . How had Gates connected the blimp with the U-boat? The navy had borrowed him the next day. Had they dived to the wreckage? All right, maybe they did, but how did Gates get to the conclusion that the U-boat had delivered the *Seehund*?

He glanced at Cordi Grey, who clearly was desperate to get out of the dining room and call her superiors. She could barely contain herself. The Otter smiled at her. Sorry, little lady. We're going to sit this one out together. He could see a pulse in the cleft of her beautiful throat.

His own heart had also jolted into high gear and was staying there. What would Gates do? Begin a search? He forced another smile at Cordi, wondering behind it . . . how big a search?

'What the devil are you talking about?' Prince asked in the library.

'Wally's blimp wasn't lost in a storm. It got shot down in a fight with a Nazi sub. I know because I was sent down

474

for an evaluation of the sub. It looked like it could have been carrying something about fifty feet long under the keel suspended from a pair of clamps. In their so-called wisdom ONI decided it was a reserve fuel tank for crossing the ocean.'

Prince nodded. 'Sounds reasonable.'

'Except that hanging down from the clamp was a thick electric cable. About two or three times heavier than a kitchen stove's pigtail. How much juice would that carry?'

Prince shrugged. 'Enough to power a trolley, at least, if it wasn't too long.'

'It wasn't. How about enough power to charge the batteries of, say, a fifty-foot electric submarine?'

'Incredible.'

'Possible?'

'I guess . . . '

'I think the miniature got away from the mother sub before the attack.'

'The blimp and the sub destroyed each other?'

'Completely. Poor old Wally died a hero. And nobody'll know until the war's over because ONI is drooling over the idea of raising a Nazi sub without the Nazis knowing. Code books.'

'What shall – '

'We have to search the harbour. *Right now*.'

Prince rubbed his mouth. 'I'm not sure of the best way to go about this.'

'The Coast Guard has responsibility for the defence of the port, and they're under the navy in wartime. Let's go to the navy.'

'Convincing the navy might be difficult. I'm not sure at what level to try.'

'Call the Secretary of the Navy. Start at the top.'

'Well . . . our contact is business, not strategy – where are you going?'

Gates was already out the door. 'Wally's father,' he said

as he turned down the hall. 'He has a right to know, and he can put on the pressure.'

'It certainly clears him in my mind,' Cordi was saying.

'Completely?' asked Weatherburn.

Until Charlie Collins had announced his enlistment – his commission secured with the help of Richard Prince – Weatherburn had had Duncan poring over Charlie's background, interviewing New York police and beaming to England for more information on his Dublin and Cambridge years. Tonight, despite Steven's talk about the miniature submarine and the efforts he'd made to start a search, Weatherburn was still pushing Cordi at Gates, as if he were still a prime suspect.

'Completely cleared,' she answered firmly. 'He's surely made a good case for the midget submarine being in New York – according to your own sources at ONI – and he took his information directly to the Secretary of the Navy. What more – ?'

'Why did he go over their heads?'

'Because his business is dealing with the navy and he knows how to get things done. He would have used Wallace Stratton Sr, I should guess.'

'And that clears him?'

'Sir, we owe it to Steven – to Gates – that a major search of New York Harbour is being launched at daybreak.'

Weatherburn gave her a chilly smile. 'Do you mind if we restrain our expressions of gratitude until we see if they *find* it, dear?'

Gates stood beside a youthful-looking rear admiral who was addressing a group of navy, Coast Guard and civil air pilots in the back of a hangar an hour before dawn.

'It's not going to do any good to panic the population with rumours of German subs nosing around their ferries, so the sub itself is on a need-to-know basis. The police and Coast Guard boatmen and the civil defence volunteers have been told that some fifty-foot steel tanks of explosive chemicals broke loose from a merchantman in the night and are floating just beneath the surface wherever the tides have taken them. If they see it, they're told to report it immediately and don't touch.'

The briefest moment of quiet laughter rippled the tense atmosphere. No one was as qualified as the pilots to judge the gigantic proportions of the task ahead of them.

'You men have to know, of course. Those of your planes that can are carrying depth charges and you're instructed to use them. Those of you who don't have them should use your radio to instruct us where to send a plane that does have depth charges. There's ninety-two thousand acres of harbour out there, gentlemen. Good luck. The K-2 blimps will take off now. The rest of you get up at first light.

Gates cadged a ride on a PBY at dawn and taxied across the water past an airfield crowded with an assortment of light- and medium-sized planes while a squadron of PBYs lined up behind his flying boat.

It was a high-winged, two-engine plane that afforded wide vistas of the water below. Someone had painted, 'the Hottest Tail in Town' on its fuselage, but it flew, in fact, at the appropriately slow pace of a search craft. The flying boat's radio operator checked in regularly with the Third District's intelligence office, Section B-8 – Coastal Information – which had established a communication network including North Atlantic Naval Coastal Frontier and Eastern Sea Frontier as well as units of the army and army air force, Coast Guard, FBI, and state, county and municipal police.

What looked like a well-organized, though rarely used, system was in place and functioning smoothly, but by noon Gates began to worry. Only from the air was the vastness of New York Harbour truly apparent.

The port sprawled across seven major bays, sixty anchorages and countless coves and inlets. There were piers and docks for thousands of barges, scows, lighters, car floats, freighters and warships under which a fifty-foot submarine could hide.

'Best chance of spotting him is when he's moving,' called the pilot who invited him into the co-pilot seat whenever the second man took a break. 'Sometimes you can see the anchor on a mooring from up here when the tides come in clean.'

'What if he's under something?'

'That's what the boats are looking for.'

All morning Gates had watched the little launches probing the inlets and piers, but he knew from experience that you couldn't see much from the pitching deck of a small boat.

'Tell you one thing,' said the pilot. 'I'm glad we're the ones with the ash cans. How'd you like to meet a U-boat with a boat hook in your hands?'

He stood the PBY on its wing and plummeted to the water like newsreels Gates had seen of Stuka dive bombers. He spotted the long dull shape, lighter than the water, then Raritan Bay came up at a frightening speed.

The pilot hauled back on his yoke and the plane levelled out about a hundred feet above the waves. 'Sorry. False alarm. Sand bank. Remember that spot.'

'Why?'

'Oysters. They're illegal to take, but they won't hurt you if you know the right spots where the water's still clean. I grew up on Staten Island.'

'How did you learn to speak Italian so well?' asked Ponte.

The Otter's Italian was indistinguishable in accent or syntax from a slum dweller's of the North and he knew, immediately, what Ponte was leading up to. He'd been waiting for it.

The fall of Mussolini was a big topic of conversation at the salvage job, and, of course, in the papers. The fate of the Italian dictator and the question of what Germany would

478

do had so preoccupied the population that it must have made it easier for the authorities to squelch rumours about their search for the *Seehund*. He wondered how the Italian frogman was going to react. Ponte had started circumspectly.

'I learned my Italian in Milano,' the Otter answered. 'My mother was half-German, half-Italian. We lived in Milan and in Italian communities in Vienna and Switzerland. With the exiles.'

'And your father?' asked Ponte, still circling around the difficult subject.

'A German spy.'

Ponte nodded. 'You have heard about the *coup d'état*?'

'It's in the newspapers,' the Otter said. 'If you can believe them.'

'Today it seems the German army has occupied the Alpine passes.'

The Otter looked him directly in the eye. 'To protect Italy.'

Ponte looked away, shrugged.

Four days after they started, the navy called off the air search of New York Harbour. The rear admiral who had commanded it sent Gates and his uncle a note.

I'd rather we looked and didn't find it, than didn't look and find it. Good luck. Yours in victory.

'I like that man,' said Prince.

'I'd like him better if he'd look longer.'

'They've done all they can from the air. If it's there, the police will have to find it. Are you going around with Tweed?'

'If the invitation still holds.'

'Don't complain about it,' Tweed said, 'Four days is a long time to fly aeroplanes. It's not like there's a lot of gas. We'll find it if it's there. Come on down to the office.'

The 'office' was in the Police Building on Centre Street. Tweed introduced Gates to his captain, then showed him a map of New York Harbour. 'It's not as bad as it looks.'

'It's got six hundred and fifty miles of shoreline,' Gates said.

'We can rule out most of it. Nobody's going to hide a miniature sub in the East River, for instance, not with those currents, which also rules out this area from the Long Island Sound to Hell Gates. There's no target in those waters worth the effort. So we're talking about the Hudson and the Upper and Lower Bays.'

'How far up the Hudson?'

'That's a problem,' Tweed agreed. 'On the other hand, we've got local police checking every dock and anchorage on both shores as high up as the Tappan Zee. Tough to hide out in hick towns anyway. There's bound to be some old coot saying, "There didn't used to be a sub in that old trout hole".'

'What about Newark Bay? And the Hackensack?'

'What kind of targets is he going to find there? Sure, I know, you think he's got a long range with all those batteries, but you have to consider his physical limits too. Can he afford to ride around for five hours in the New Jersey shallows before he even gets to where the real action is?'

'What do you think he'll shoot at?'

'I'd ride up to the Bayonne Annex and sink a few aircraft carriers,' Tweed said.

'That's what Rik said. Charlie thinks he'll go for a troop ship.'

Tweed said, 'First we have to find him. I vote for under a pier. We've got men checking all of them. And the Coast Guard is following up.'

'How about shipways along the shore? Could he pull it up into a barn?'

'We're checking every boathouse in the city. Come on, we'll get a boat.'

Gates was accustomed to Jim Tweed as a sometimes remote, sometimes friendly landlord who sat around drinking beer in his shirt-sleeves, and was surprised by the respect shown Tweed by uniformed and plainclothes police officers. After a crew of grizzled sergeants saluted smartly on the way to the garage, Gates said, 'I didn't realize you were a lieutenant.'

'Got it last year.'

'Were you a lieutenant when you came looking for Charlie?'

'Not yet. You know how it is, things move fast in wartime.'

A police chauffeur drove them to the Docks Department Building at the Battery which housed the marine precinct. They boarded a waiting motor launch, which took them up the Hudson, stopping at each pier for a quick word with the police or Coast Guardsmen on watch. No one had seen the missing tanks of chemicals they'd been ordered to look for.

'Almost ready to raise her?' Tweed asked as the launch passed the fallen *Normandie*. The salvors had removed both the starboard propellers. Only their shafts remained and Gates felt the old anger go through him, still hot and consuming as the fire that destroyed her.

'Almost.'

'Bulkheads holding?' Tweed had tried to keep up with the progress of the salvage.

'So far.' They were testing the patches and the bulkheads daily by pumping the water a foot or two lower, one compartment at a time to vary the pressure.

At the Seventy-ninth Street boat basin they turned across and started down the Jersey shore, weaving through thick concentrations of freighters riding at emergency anchorages for convoy assignment.

'It could be sitting under one of them,' Gates said.

'I wouldn't want to be. Look at the current and the tides. Forget it. We have enough docks to worry about. Seven hundred and fifty, at last count.'

'How many boats do you have out?'

481

'The whole department has men on anything that floats. This is too much for just my squad.'

'What do you think of the idea of hiding the sub in a shipyard?'

'There's at least forty shipyards,' Tweed said. 'But they're too busy. Too many people around. Of course, they're noisy, which might help him sneak out. Think the sub makes much noise?'

'With electric drive? It's pretty silent.'

'Then I don't see why he'd want to be around a yard, but we're checking. They're crawling with Coast Guard.'

Crossing the river below Bayonne, they passed an excursion boat coming home to the Battery from Coney Island. The decks were packed with men in straw hats and white shirts and women wearing light-coloured cotton print dresses that the warm sea breeze blew around their legs. People waved and Tweed waved back. 'Hard to believe there's a war on.'

'There must be more we can do,' said Gates.

'I'm staying out till it's dark. Want to keep going?'

'Sure. My last day. I have to be back on the *Normandie* tomorrow.'

'Did you work last night?' Tweed asked.

'Yes.'

'Sleep?'

'Later.'

They circled the Battery and up the East River three-quarters of a mile to the Brooklyn Bridge, then down the Brooklyn shore, stopping as before at each pier to talk to the police and servicemen guarding them, and continuing through the Buttermilk Channel between Governor's Island and Brooklyn Heights, circling through the Atlantic and Erie Basins.

'I hope to hell he's not in here,' Tweed said, in that huge man-made harbour, 'but I don't think he'd risk hiding among so many people. I don't know. Say, maybe it never survived the fight with the blimp.'

Gates looked at him. All afternoon he'd been in the dumps while Tweed was optimistic. He felt suddenly like a diver who'd been flipped upside down by a reverse current. Now at least he was able to believe again, even as he scanned the miles of piers in the fading light. 'We'll find it. Damn it, we've got to.'

The Otter knew they'd never find the *Seehund* in the *Normandie*.

But Larson was another matter. What if the search led to Larson? It was too dangerous to go back and move him. *Assume the worst will happen*, Uncle Willy cautioned. *And act accordingly. Prepare for the worst*. And the worst had happened. The blimp had attacked the U-boat. The *Seehund* engineer had been killed. Uncle Willy had sent the wrong torpedoes, acoustical instead of contact. He'd had to haul the boat into the repair shed, had to hire Larson to fix the torpedoes – crisis after crisis, he had anticipated and handled correctly . . . consider the radios . . . he'd got through anyhow, he was confident of it. Uncle Willy must have heard of the ammunition ship blowing up in New York Harbour – then one miscalculation . . . the boathouse had seemed as safe a place as any to leave Larson's body; no one would have found it if Gates hadn't somehow deduced the *Seehund*'s existence and started the search. Now they might, and if they did they would come down on him from every direction.

If he hadn't been prepared with a last defence he might have decided to kill Gates out of pure hatred for him for starting the search; but he had heeded Uncle Willy's warning, learned his lessons well and prepared for the worst. Gates's punishment for trying to destroy the Otter would be his own destruction.

All the pieces were ready now, in place for him to use Gates as his shield for his last defence. All but one – Glenn Walsh. And Walsh was waiting, anxious, even desperate, to be tapped for the most vital service a minor clerk would ever be privileged to perform for the Otter, for Adolf Hitler, for the Third Reich.

Police and Coast Guard launches were crisscrossing the river, hunting the *Seehund*. It was time. He called Walsh at Third District supply and gave him a pay phone number to call back. When he hung up he was surprised to see he had left a wet handprint on the black receiver. He hurried to another phone six blocks away, and dialled. Walsh answered.

The Otter said, 'It is time to alert the authorities that you are a forger. You had better hide.'

There was a long silence. Always wary, the Otter listened for clicks that might mean a tap, a trace. Two minutes and he would be gone. But Walsh had only been thinking – reconsidering? He said, finally, 'I understand.'

'I will contact you at your safehouse in a few days. No more.'

Silence again. The Otter waited. 'What's wrong?' The radio parts alone would not suffice. Not without Walsh's contribution, a contribution the Otter could only ask of a fanatic. Of course, that was it . . . the true believer . . . the Otter had forgotten to play his part . . . He pressed the mouthpiece to his lips and whispered, '*Heil Hitler*.'

'*Heil Hitler*,' Walsh responded, and meant it. 'Who will I accuse?'

'Gates.'

'How?'

'How, and when, I will tell you when the time comes. Go to your safehouse.

The Otter hung up and hurried away. He hoped, now, that he was truly prepared for the worst. If the searchers found Larson now, he had the means – an accusation, an illegal shortwave . . . and an explosive – to distract the enemy by placing Gates's meddling neck in a British noose.

39

Admiral Canaris observed Grossadmiral Dönitz's habits. The U-boat admiral spent most of his time in Berlin since Hitler had sacked Raeder and appointed Dönit commander-in-chief of the entire Germany navy – a victory for the U-boat admiral which had to be tempered, Canaris assumed, by the hard fact that the surface fleet Dönitz had inherited with control of the *Kriegsmarine* was more liability than asset these days when the British navy, the Royal Air Force and the Norwegian underground were competing to send the bottled-up ships to the bottom of the fjords.

Canaris waited his chance, then cornered Dönitz in a Berlin restaurant where Dönitz occasionally escaped to a solitary late breakfast. No one recognized the diminutive chief of the Abwehr in his shabby greatcoat, not even Dönitz when he first looked up from his newspaper, annoyed by the intrusion.

'Good morning.'

'You?' Dönitz's thin lips tightened.

'I will be brief, Grossadmiral,' Canaris said, sitting opposite.

'What do you want?'

'I want to share a victory with you.'

'What sort of victory?'

'What sort of victory is there but a victory that bestows honour from below and gratitude from above?'

Dönitz said nothing. The silence lengthened. Finally Canaris spoke again.

'You, of course, are so highly regarded these days that your gratitude from above comes directly from the Führer.'

'What do you want?'

'I want your help. In exchange, I will share the honour and the gratitude.'

'What kind of help?'

'I have placed a miniature submarine in the Port of New York.'

Dönitz stared. 'I don't believe you.'

'It's mission is to sink the *Queen Mary* bearing an American regiment.'

'I don't believe you.'

'My agent will do it in such a way as to block the harbour.'

'I said I don't believe you.'

The shadows in Canaris's sunken cheeks deepened. 'Has Captain von Harling reported recently?'

Dönitz tried to hide his surprise, and failed. 'Von Harling's boat does not reply to our signals.'

'He is lost,' Canaris said. 'One of your best.'

'How do you know he is lost?'

'Von Harling ferried my miniature to New York.'

'He *what*?'

'A personal favour, Grossadmiral. Von Harling is my loss as well as yours. A good man.'

Dönitz turned dark red. 'You subverted one of my boats for a *spy mission*?'

'What did you expect me to do? Ask permission?'

'You'll pay for this – '

'Pay? You should pay me, Grossadmiral. If you pick up my men after they sink the *Queen Mary* we will present them jointly to the Führer.'

'I don't need your help to talk to Hitler. I am as close to the Führer as any officer – '

'Any officer? Or any officer except army officers on the eastern front? This victory will take his mind off Russia.'

Dönitz countered with another cold silence.

Canaris's expression never changed as he said, 'Grossadmiral, you lost forty U-boats in June and seventeen in May. The convoys are mauling you. You've surrendered the Atlantic.'

'In March my boats sank more tonnage than any month in the war – '

'How long can you tell Hitler about March? The Allies have outwitted you, Grossadmiral. They are using brand-new 1943 aircraft, radar, asdic and destroyers against your 1935 submarines.'

'There are new boats – '

'In production? Not yet. You need the commitment of the entire Reich to build your new boats. Which means you need the Führer's enthusiastic support. Germany needs a victory. And Germany needs heroes. We will present both.'

Dönitz clenched his fists and half-rose from his chair. '*We* will do nothing, you miserable little upstart. Get out of here.'

'I saved you from Raeder's plan. If I had admitted to Hitler that I could supply weather reports from New York, he would have let Admiral Raeder attack. I saved you. You owe me for that.'

'I owe nothing. *Get out.*'

Canaris looked up. His eyes were totally without guile. '*He's my son.*'

'What? Who? You have daughters.'

'I had a child by an Italian girl during the last war.'

Dönitz's lean face twisted with disdain.

'I took care of him,' Canaris said. 'Money. Schools. I visited often. And when I travelled in Spain and Holland – building your boats – I took them with me. We told him I was his uncle. I promised his mother I'd leave my wife for them. But I love my wife. And my girls. I couldn't. You're right about me. I was a coward then. But when the Austrians executed his mother, I told him the truth.' He stopped talking.

Intrigued in spite of himself, Dönitz asked, 'Why did the Austrians execute his mother?'

'She was a go-between in the Dollfuss attack in '34. She carried messages between the chancellery and our embassy.'

'So you told the boy he had a father, after all. Not Uncle Willy, but Papa Willy.'

'I took him away. He was nineteen years old. His mother had been a fanatic and I knew that the enemies she had made would kill him.'

'Why?'

'How many of the early firebrands are still alive in the Nazi party? Röhm had already been shot in Germany and the same sort of . . . clearance . . . was bound to happen in Austria once the party came out of hiding. Politics seem to work that way. Röhm in our party, Trotsky with the Soviets. The first wave are too radical for the second. So I took my son east while I set up the *Etappendienst* – to protect him.'

'Conveniently protecting him from your wife at the same time, I presume.'

Canaris looked at him. 'Please don't presume too much, Grossadmiral. I had had a plan for the boy since he was a child. Our setting up the raider-supply bases together was both a continuation of his schooling, which I had supervised personally, and a test. I succeeded.'

'At what?'

'He is a magnificent German. He is strong as a bull, a big man – his mother was half-German, her father a strapping fellow, not a runt like me. He has a quick and brilliant mind. He is a business genius. We actually showed profits on some of the dummy corporations we set up around the South Atlantic and Indian Ocean. He is cunning. A good engineer. And a fighter. Schmeling owed me a favour. I had them spar. My son might have killed Max if I'd let him.'

'All that, and you made him a spy?'

Canaris missed the irony in Dönitz's voice. '*Yes*. I created the *perfect* spy. I taught him *everything*. And by the time war came he was ready . . . more ready than I. I hesitated – my way, as you already know – but he pushed ahead boldly.' Canaris's voice changed, lost its fervour and took on a note of regret. 'He is very ambitious. I don't know how he will fare in Germany. I may have to send him out again. He had a difficult childhood, because of me. When he was sixteen, when his mother was still alive, he tried to enlist in the *Kriegsmarine*. Wanted to be a sailor like his Uncle Willy. They rejected him on psychological grounds. He is impelled to be accepted by others, even to be liked, yet at the same time abnormally suspicious of others. Useful attributes in a spy, at once complementing and counterbalancing each other . . . but not good for much else.'

Dönitz nodded. So the little spymaster had not missed the irony after all. He asked, 'And your son is the agent in New York?'

'He is code-named Otter. He is a German hero. I beg you, please don't abandon him.'

Dönitz stared at the figures walking past the curtained windows. They were distorted by the wire mesh recently installed between the glass and the cloth. There'd been some surprisingly ferocious air raids against Berlin lately; not the wholesale destruction suffered by Hamburg, but enough to suggest that city life was going to deteriorate and that the smug Berliners were about to begin sharing the miseries suffered by men at the front. Abruptly, he signalled, and two waiters hurried to the table.

'Bring Admiral Canaris a cup of coffee.'

When it sat steaming before him and Canaris had loosened his scarf, Dönitz asked, 'I presume von Harling was to rendezvous near New York.'

'Fifty miles.'

'It is possible that I might be able to put a boat in that neighbourhood in a few weeks – '

'A few weeks will be too late,' said Canaris. 'The *Queen Mary* was sighted off Ireland the day before yesterday, westbound. If she keeps to the schedule she's been sailing all summer, my Otter will sink her next week.'

40

At one in the morning on August fourth, the salvors started ninety salvage pumps in unison. The *Normandie* resounded with the roar of their engines, and a blue cloud of gasoline exhaust gathered swiftly in the lights mounted on the piers and the ship's high side. They clamoured into the dawn and through the day as thick white gushes of water poured from her promenade deck hatches and spilled back into the river.

Steven Gates and van Slough were stationed near the stern. They dived repeatedly, as did divers up and down the length of the ship, to tend the air and water jets installed in the large patches. The jets, it was hoped, would break the mud suction that threatened to hold the *Normandie* on the bottom.

Throughout the day of pumping, Gates and van Slough dived to fasten additional wire stays to sections of the boat deck and promenade bulkheads, which had been, too deeply buried in the mud to cut away, to prevent them from tearing loose and rupturing the *Normandie*'s structure when she began to rise. The benchmark that hung from her bow like a giant ruler still measured no vertical movement, no sign that she had moved despite the day of pumping. No sign she would ever move.

The slip was oddly quiet with the pump engines still, and the sounds of men carried far as diving tenders called back and forth and instructions were relayed to the ironworkers fastening the dry ends of the stays high on the starboard side. Tightening turnbuckles, they took up the slack.

A foreman came down the line shouting, 'Everybody out of the pool. Bring 'em up!'

'We're not done,' said van Slough.

'*Queen Mary*'s coming in. Everybody out of the water. Before Her Highness throws you the hell out.'

The *Queen Mary* eased into her berth. Up and down the *Normandie* the salvage men paused to watch.

Gates studied her solemn progress.

He could hear the shrill police whistle the docking pilot blew to signal the tugs as she crept in the last few yards, and then the shouts of the longshoremen warping her into the pier.

So slow.

Pier 90 blocked all but her stacks and mast, which loomed ghostly behind the corona of the floodlights. Soon the tugs filed away back into the river, and the salvors could hear the *Queen Mary*'s gangways banging down, followed immediately by the thunder of thousands of boots.

'More kraut prisoners,' said Charlie. 'We're going to have enough of them pretty soon to start our own Germany.'

It took ten minutes to negotiate the wooden catwalks to the gangway in the centre of the ship and out the pier, which was crowded with homeward-bound workmen and stragglers for the next shift. A pile-up around the front door slowed things further.

'What the hell is blocking that door?'

A knot of workmen was impeding the flow just outside the pier.

'Come on, Junior.' Charlie shouldered through and Gates hurried along in his wake. 'I should have known,' he growled suddenly. 'See you, Junior. I don't think we'll be having dinner tonight.'

'What? Why?'

'See for yourself.'

Charlie moved along, and Gates saw Cordi Grey surrounded by a mob of wisecracking workmen. She wore a raincoat and a beret, and the floodlights sparkled on her auburn hair.

'Excuse me . . . ' Gates pushed towards her.

She was smiling distractedly, straining on tiptoe to watch the door.

'Excuse me,' Gates said, then taking a note from Charlie's book, '*Gangway.*'

Cordi saw him and waved and then surprised him by wrapping her arms around his neck and kissing him lightly on the mouth, which provoked a ragged cheer from her admirers and cries of 'Next.'

'What are you doing here?' Gates asked.

'Looking for a diver friend.'

'Mind if I wait with you?'

Cordi jabbed her knuckles into his work shirt. 'Buy an underpaid working girl dinner?'

'Sure. I better go home and change first. You look *delicious*.'

'Thank you.' She put her hand through his arm as they crossed under the highway and walked towards Forty-sixth.

'I have to talk to you.'

'Sounds serious.'

Cordi nodded, said nothing more. When they reached the rooming house, Gates said, 'Come on up?'

She followed him wordlessly up the front steps, through the shabby foyer and up the creaking stairs to the third floor. When he opened his door she asked, 'Don't you lock your door?'

'My landlord's a cop.' He turned on a light. 'You can sit on the bed or you can sit on the bed. I traded space for my armchair for a drawing table – like to turn your back while I get dressed or just enjoy the show?'

Cordi was unusually subdued. 'I suppose it's better if I turn my back.'

'Want something to read?'

'No, we can talk.' She sat on the bed, her back to him.

'What about?'

'It's rather a difficult subject.'

Gates opened his wardrobe and isolated a suit and a clean shirt, stripped off his trousers ... and glanced at Cordi. Her back was rigid, her coat heaped around her like petals.

'Let me guess,' Gates said. 'You're pregnant on account of we held hands in the subway.'

Cordi said nothing.

'Sorry.'

She turned around, face sombre, then burst into laughter.

'What's so damned funny?'

'What are you *wearing*?'

'Long underwear. Haven't you ever seen long underwear?'

'Yes. On my grandfather. What are you dressed like that for? It's summer.'

'It happens to get damned cold underwater.'

'Do all the divers wear that?'

'Yes. Now turn around if you don't want to see something even funnier.'

Their eyes held for a moment and she turned around again. 'I have to tell you something,' she said after a short silence.

'What?'

'It's a long story.'

'Okay.'

'You're not going to like it.'

'It's a hell of a build-up ... come on, tell me.'

She shook her head. Her hands clenched on the bedspread.

Gates took a step towards her, stopped.

'Cordi, we're pretty close ... friends. I've told you a good deal and you've told me – '

'Not true things,' she said, turning to face him now.

'You said you wouldn't look,' Gates said. 'I wouldn't have taken off the funny underwear.'

Cordi stared openly at him. 'You're fine,' she whispered. 'So strong – '

'*That* would get a laugh from the musclemen on the job.'

'No, you're really . . . ' She turned her back again.

'Maybe we should get dinner delivered . . . while you tell me what you want to tell me. What do you mean, not true things?'

'Like I've been seeing you under orders from British Intelligence.'

Gates laughed nervously. '*What?*'

'I was assigned to investigate you.'

The hurt rushed through him. And anger. 'Why?'

'You were suspected of being a German saboteur, or at least of supporting one.'

'That's crazy. And you came to tell me – what are you an agent or something? What about your so-called BBC job?'

'You've been cleared. At least so far as I'm concerned you cleared yourself with the search for the midget sub – '

'Oh really? Well, nobody found it. Maybe I was putting them on. You came to me to – '

'I've not even been authorized to tell you this – '

'A *spy* . . .? Oh, for God's sake . . . wonderful . . . so that explains my fatal charms.'

Cordi continued to stare at the wall. 'I don't blame you for your anger, Steven, but – '

'Wait a minute. What am I complaining about? Maybe if I *act* like a good little spy you'll have to keep on seeing me . . . By the way, what was I supposed to be doing?'

She answered in a flat voice. 'We've been trailing a Nazi agent for years. He hurt us in Switzerland. And in Lisbon and London. And then he came to New York. Where he's hurt us . . . you too . . . very badly. He's code named the Otter.'

'But *me*? For God's sake, Cordi – '

'You just have no idea how New York looks to us. Britain's lifeblood flows through this city. Our food. Our weapons. The soldiers you send us. Your ships. But it's all

494

in the hands of, well, strangers . . . This is Britain's most important port, too. And who is here? German-Americans. Irish-Americans. Isolationist Americans. All enemies of Britain. It wasn't so far-fetched to be suspicious . . .'

When she became silent Gates's mind ran alone for a while.

'When this Otter hurt you in Switzerland, you meant your friend Alec, didn't you?'

'Yes. And my brother . . . his convoy was sabotaged from here . . . it was very hard not to be suspicious. Not to hate, even . . .'

'Are you supposed to tell me all this?'

'No. The people I work with are extremely . . . secretive, for obvious reasons.'

'Suspicious, you mean.'

'The Otter is still here. And no one has found that submarine. There *is* a war on, Steven.'

'You connect this Otter and the submarine?'

'If there is a submarine, it certainly would be his.'

'If?'

'I mean, we haven't found it . . . but knowing the Otter's capabilities, we're terrified that he's about to launch some major attack.'

'What?'

'We don't know.'

'But the submarine – '

'Steven, I've told you all I know. We're in the dark. No one . . . including you, *knows* there's a submarine. Your logic was convincing, but the evidence . . . well, it *could* still be anything.'

He was still recovering from the shock . . . and the *Normandie*, never far from his mind, made him ask, 'Do you think this Otter character might have sabotaged the *Normandie*?'

Cordi shrugged. 'All we ever came up with on that were rumours. We don't know. He could have . . .'

'I saw him,' Gates said.

'*What?*' She faced him, but now her eyes stayed fixed on his. 'What does he *look* like? What do you mean – '

Gates told her about the man in the stack, and she was instantly disappointed. 'You couldn't have seen his face at such a distance.'

'I still know it was him. The son of a bitch was watching, watching what he had done. I've kept looking for him ever since . . . that man watching the destruction of the most beautiful ship that ever put to sea – '

'And your actions, as you looked for him, helped make us suspicious . . . can you forgive me?'

Gates sat down on the bed beside her. The cheap, tufted bedspread reminded him he was still nude, but in the context of what she'd just told him it didn't seem to matter.

'Would you have seen me, without orders?'

'You mean if we'd just met? Like on the *Normandie* . . . Well, I can tell you that it wasn't the worst assignment in the world. Except in a way it was – '

'Wait a minute. Aren't gorgeous women spies supposed to sleep with the enemy to get their secrets? What was wrong with me?'

Cordi sat cross-legged on the bed. She touched his face. 'They told me to sleep with you. I refused – '

'Why, damn it?'

'Because I think I love you.'

'Not very professional.'

Cordi pressed her fingers to his lips. 'Listen to me. I'm very serious. I do love you. I was deceiving you, and I didn't want to start that way.'

Gates kissed her fingers. 'How about starting this way?'

'Do you forgive me?'

'For refusing orders? No.'

'I'm serious, Steven.'

'How the hell are we going to win the war if spies won't follow orders?' He traced the line of her throat down her blouse to her breast.

496

She put her hand on his. 'Please. Seriously. Forgive me . . . '

'Not only do I forgive you, I intend to mail an anonymous contribution to your superior officer for bringing us together again. I forgive you. And I love you, very much. Even if you are a not-so-hot dancer. And even if . . . much worse . . . you have a lot more clothes on than I do.'

'Not here,' said Cordi.

Gates looked around the room. 'Kind of dreary. Tough getting into a good hotel without luggage.'

'Not a hotel.'

'Your place?'

'I don't think so.'

'How about – '

'I want you to take me to that little boat.'

'What?'

'I want to see the Statue of Liberty. After all, before this day is out I'm going to be *very* American . . . '

41

The next morning of August fifth, the water inside the *Normandie* was fifteen feet lower than the water in the Hudson. The salvors stopped the pumps and waited to see how she responded to the rising tide.

'Breakfast, Junior?'

'I'll stay on her,' Gates said. 'I think she's almost ready to float.'

'Want something?'

'Coffee and anything you can carry.'

'I got to call Kay,' Charlie said. 'I forgot what she looks like.'

Gates had started work at three o'clock, an hour after he had finally kissed Cordi goodnight, and he was blind-tired, and very happy. He lay back in the morning sun and tried to sleep. He'd spoken to Tweed after he'd taken Cordi home. Tweed sounded encouraged. Brooklyn and Manhattan were clean and Coast Guard volunteers were searching every dock, warehouse and pier on the Jersey side as well as Staten Island. Still riding on the euphoria of what had happened with Cordi, Gates accepted Tweed's optimism.

He watched a tug bully a cluster of carfloats towards the Thirtieth Street railroad yards, and sat up with a sudden idea. Could the Otter have maybe hidden the submarine under a barge . . .? Barges were long enough. He sank back.

A barge wouldn't do. The submarine needed electricity, huge amounts of it to charge its batteries. What source? A big generator? Or a Consolidated Edison main? Neither of which you'd find under a floating barge. He dozed off, still puzzling about electricity and dreaming of Cordi . . .

Across a stretch of intimidatingly rough and marshy ground was a big old boathouse. The sun was hot, the air so muggy they could hardly see Manhattan. Both members of the auxiliary volunteer Coast Guard search team were perspiring. They were middle-aged – Fred an office manager, Don a diesel mechanic – and each had a son in the service.

Fred wanted to knock off after they'd finished searching the wrecked carfloat terminal, but Don thought about his son in Sicily and insisted they finish the area they'd been assigned to. Fred argued. Don went alone. He slogged across the marsh and looked in the water around the rusted way rails. No missing tank. But rumour had it that it was something more important than a chemical tank. Why else would thousands of guys be combing the waterfront for a week? He walked up the slanting rails, slid the sagging door open a crack, and stepped into the dark boathouse. He turned on his flashlight and, though he recoiled from what he saw, he was proud he had come.

'I'm Lieutenant Tweed.' He was shaking hands with the uniformed navy officer. 'New York Police Department. Sabotage Squad.'

'Commander Ober.' Ober looked soft, but he had the smart, ambitious look that Tweed called hotshot eyes. Ober sized up Tweed and said, 'You're a little out of your territory, aren't you, lieutenant?'

'I heard you'd turned up a body. Anything to do with the submarine?'

'Possibly,' Ober replied without enthusiasm. 'You're welcome to look around if the Weehawken police have no objections.'

'We've met,' said Tweed, making a point of waving at a Jersey detective he knew who was crouching beside the

499

rusted rails of the boatway that ran up the middle of the boathouse. 'This place been used recently?'

'I don't think so,' Ober said.

'Who's the body?'

'There was no identification on it. We're checking the fingerprints, and I've called in our forensic specialists.'

'Excuse me. I think I'll say hello to my friend over there.'

Tweed walked across the boathouse, ignoring both the body, which was under a blanket, and the clusters of navy and government agents conversing in low tones. He squatted beside the Jersey detective. 'What have you got?'

'I was wondering if this here track's been used lately.'

Tweed ran his finger along the rusty rail. He'd been wondering too, and the crown looked and felt slightly smoother than the edges. 'Looks like it might have. Maybe once or twice.'

'That's what I was wondering. The ONI boys started having kittens when they found the cradle down in the water. Wonder why?'

'I kind of doubt ONI's going to tell us.' Most cops, including this one, were not in on the real reason for the search. He asked, 'When'd the joint close down?'

'After Pearl. They was on their last legs, hauling yachts. No more yachts. The whole area's gone to hell. They had a fire next door and then the old carfloat terminal got wrecked by a runaway.'

'The coal car?' asked Tweed. 'Last winter?'

'That's the one.'

'What'd you find out about that?'

'The railroad says it was impossible. What the insurance boys call an act of God. So either they're lying to cover themselves, or somebody set it up. Try proving it.'

'How about the fire?' asked Tweed.

'Arson. Perpetrators unknown.'

'So who's the stiff?'

'Nobody I know.'

'Was he dumped here?'

'Coulda been.'

'Shot?'

'Slugged. Busted his neck. Want to see him?'

The Jersey detective rose on creaking knees. 'Guy woulda stayed here till he was a skeleton if we hadn't been on this damned hunt all over the place. Coast Guard auxiliaries found him. That's how ONI found out about it.'

Tweed waited while he pulled back the blanket, revealing the bloated face.

'Dead about a week, I'd say,' said the Jersey detective.

Tweed agreed. The Jersey detective was a good cop, but he was automatically deferential because Tweed was from New York. It made no sense, but it was true.

'You find him right here?'

'Right here. Lying on the track like he'd fallen on it, you know? Busted neck. Maybe a busted jaw. Looks like he got hit by a sledge.'

'Looks that way.' He knelt beside the body for a closer look at the face.

'Funny-looking hair,' said the Jersey detective.

Tweed thought so too. 'Let me borrow your light.' He shone it on the dark brown hair and inspected the scalp where the hair parted, then rose, his cheek ticking. This looked much better than the maybes and possibles of a rusty boatway.

'His hair's dyed.'

'You sure?'

'The roots are lighter.' The lab would confirm with micro-chemical tests whether it had been dyed with salts of bismuth or lead, or permanganate of potassium, pyrogallic acid, silver nitrate or henna, but there was a quicker way.

'Give me a hand with his pants.'

'Maybe you want to ask the navy?'

'Maybe I don't.'

The Jersey detective grinned back conspiratorially. 'I better do it.' He pulled back the blanket. The man's hands were greasy, his nails black. The detective unbuckled his belt, unzipped the fly and opened boxer shorts, exposing the pubic hair.

'Well, I'll be damned. A gen-u-ine redhead.'

Orders came down again from Captain Tooker's hinged control bridge: all hands turn to installing more stays; uncut portions of the superstructure were still threatening to rupture when the ship started to rise from the mud. The divers worked through the night.

When they broke for breakfast, van Slough and Gates and Charlie and Marty walked to the nearest bar that served food. Armed Coast Guardsmen made them walk on the other side of Twelfth Avenue as they passed the *Queen Mary*. Trucks and provisioning lighters were converging on the troop carrier's slip from the pier and the river, and the way she was venting steam told Gates she was keeping her pressure up and would be sailing soon – likely on tomorrow's dawn tide after loading her soldiers all night. The excess steam burst from her stacks and dissolved in seconds in the hot morning sky, roaring as loudly as the salvage pumps which had started again on the *Normandie*. He was so exhausted that he hardly thought of the submarine while they ate. Cordi was out when he called her studio. The Meurice telephone was off limits for lovers' talk.

On the way back a Coast Guard ensign and two armed guardsmen intercepted them on the catwalk. Van Slough stopped dead, so suddenly that Gates bumped into him. The ensign and his two men blocked the narrow, wooden way. 'Are you Steven Gates?'

'Yeah?'

'You're supposed to call this number. Use my phone.'

'What's up?' Rik said.

'I don't know.' Gates turned the paper over. 'It's from Jim Tweed.'

'I'll wait for you.'

Gates asked for the number and a police operator transferred him to a radio-phone connection.

'Tweed.'

'Jim? Gates. You called.'

'I got something to show you.'.

'You found the sub – ?'

'Larson.'

'You're kidding.'

'I think it's him. He's dead. I want you to identify him. Police launch will pick you up at the slip. Tell the Coast Guard guy to take you there.'

Van Slough was talking to the Coast Guard officer.

'He says you're supposed to take me down the slip for the police launch,' Gates said.

'Okay. See you, Mr van Slough. Nice meeting you, sir.'

'Where are you going, Steven?'

'Tweed says he wants to show me something.'

'What?'

Gates hesitated. 'I'm not sure. I'll tell you later. I guess in about an hour or two.'

'Oh? Well . . . make it quick. This ship's about to start rising.' Time, the Otter thought, was running out for everybody . . .

The Otter watched the police launch skirt the torrents gushing from the *Normandie* and break out onto the river at high speed. Gates stood in the stern – razor-slim and peering into the wind. The launch beelined straight across the Hudson to the boathouse.

Gates and his goddamn search . . . The worst *had* happened.

They had obviously found Larson's body while looking for the *Seehund*, and someone – Tweed, probably – had remembered that Gates had been looking for the red-headed Larson. Now they'd redouble their efforts to find the *Seehund*. He should have killed Gates, never mind his eventual usefulness.

He made for the nearest telephone.

It was too late to kill Gates. But it was exactly the right time to use him . . . He issued instructions to Glenn Walsh.

The clerk pretended he wasn't excited. He repeated the Otter's orders in clipped phrases, ending, 'Weatherburn, Hotel Meurice, 145 West Fifty-eight.'

The Otter returned Walsh's inevitable heartfelt *'Heil,'* and hailed a cab to his own safehouse west of Times Square. He picked up the shortwave parts and walked to Tweed's house, up the stairs to Gates's room, and through the unlocked door . . . Twenty-five minutes after he had called Walsh, he was back at the *Normandie.*

Now, he hoped, it would no longer matter that they found Larson. They'd stop searching tonight . . . when they learned that Gates had been arrested. And by dawn, the *Queen Mary* would be on the bottom of the Ambrose Channel.

Gates walked down the rails and stood in the open boathouse doors, which framed the Manhattan skyline across the Hudson. The *Normandie* lay opposite, like one of the skyscrapers fallen. Beside her the *Queen Mary* loomed grey, barely visible, her hull garlanded by the oil barges and provisioning lighters.

Tweed followed.

'You're sure that's Larson?'

'I'm sure.' He was thinking that this was the final dead end, the last possible connection cut between him and the man who had destroyed the *Normandie.*

'His face is kind of . . . distorted,' Tweed pointed out.

Gates turned to him. 'Yes, it's bloated, but I'm still positive he's the man I saw move his shield just before the fire. The one who told Armstrong to leave first.'

'Okay. So now try to figure out what he was doing here.'

'Hauling the submarine,' Gates said. 'Right up these tracks to hide it.'

'Not enough electricity here,' said Tweed.

'How about a portable generator on a truck?'

'No sign of any truck, but the rails look like maybe somebody used the way.'

'So maybe it was just for repairs.'

'That's what I've been thinking,' Tweed said. 'Sure makes it seem worth it to keep searching. I already talked to my captain, he's waiting for confirmation, but I think he's ready to pull men from every squad in New York.'

At the moment Gates almost didn't care. The long days and nights of diving and the frustration of finally finding Larson dead had drained him. Even the possible connection between the miniature submarine and the saboteur who had destroyed the *Normandie* didn't excite him as it should have . . . All he could think of was that now it seemed he would never find her destroyer. Well, damn it, at least he could go back to working on her rebirth . . .

Back on the *Normandie*, Gates drove to install another stay, and dived immediately after with a gang of divers stuffing sawdust into a leak. Then all pumps were stopped again, to wait for the tide.

Gates collapsed on a catwalk and fell asleep in the sun. He had been thinking about the dead Larson, but it was Cordi who wandered through his dreams. They embraced as they had while the cabin boat had rocked from side to side.

He awakened with a start and sat up, feeling the catwalk with his hands. Charlie and Rik were coming back along the catwalk carrying paper bags. But that wasn't what had awakened him. He glanced down at the slip. He'd slept about an hour, judging by the height the tide had climbed the pilings.

Charlie and Rik stopped. Behind them, the skyline moved a hair. Across the slip, behind Pier 90, the *Queen Mary*'s three stacks trembled against the blue sky.

Gates stared, slowly climbing to his feet. Again it happened. The Manhattan buildings gave a spasmodic shiver, as if they'd swayed in their spaces. Around him divers and ironworkers, riggers and tenders touched the catwalks disbelievingly. Some stood up with their arms out like tightrope walkers. A cheer burst all along the thousand feet of the *Normandie* and echoed between the piers.

'*She's rolling*,' Gates yelled. '*She's afloat.*'

42

The *Normandie* seesawed across a tiny arc while the tide completed its rise. Still more in the mud than out, her stern was virtually afloat and she was moving on water for the first time since she had burned.

At noon the engineers on the hinged control bridge stopped her by flooding compartments a couple of feet so that the divers could inspect how their patches and bulkheads and shorings had held. The order came down to install more stays and to pack sawdust into a leak in compartment sixteen. They dived until late in the evening.

'Cordi?'

When the studio phone rang, she and Duncan had been using an engineer's booth at the BBC studio in Rockefeller Center to listen to radio intercept recordings that Weatherburn had borrowed from British Security Coordination. Duncan had answered it. Now, as he cradled the telephone, he had a puzzled expression on his face. He stood up, put his hands on his hips, his stocky body planted like a fireplug.

'Cordi? Where does Gates live?'

'They have a townhouse on East Fifty-fourth.'

'No, I mean that policeman's rooming house.'

'. . . Four thirty-two West Forty-sixth . . .'

'That's what I thought.'

'Why?'

'Weatherburn says to meet him at that address.'

'It seems we've finally got our break.' Weatherburn was clearly excited.

'How so?' Cordi asked warily, eyeing Steven's window from Weatherburn's car. It was getting dark, but Steven's lights weren't on.

'One of the Otter's men came to me.'

'What?' Duncan asked. '*Came* to you?'

'He was a plant in a US Navy office. The navy got onto his forgeries and he fled. He's been hiding for a few days and he got to thinking he'd end up better with us than the Americans. The Otter knew about us at the Meurice – for obvious reasons,' he added, with an angry look at Cordi. 'And he'd told this agent. So the agent came around and offered information in exchange for leniency. He didn't know much – the Otter obviously plays it close to the chest – but he gave me *this* address as the Otter's safehouse.'

'*Steven*'s address?'

'Including his room number.'

'How could this be a safehouse? A flat in a New York City policeman's house?'

'Why don't we drop in and have a look?'

Weatherburn went first and Cordi trailed behind him, up the stairs she'd gone with Steven two days before to tell him who she was. Weatherburn had a gun in his hand. Tweed, the policeman, wasn't at home. Weatherburn didn't care. He was heading for Steven's room. He stopped to scan the hall. She stopped, and Duncan nearly bumped into her. She felt calm, sure that whatever this was about it had nothing to do with Steven. No point in arguing. Let Weatherburn find out for himself.

Weatherburn fished in his pocket, came out with a set of spring steel picks. 'He doesn't lock his door,' Cordi said quietly.

'How do you know that?'

'He told me.'

Weatherburn looked at her. 'Convenient.'

The hall was clear. They walked down it and into Steven's apartment, Weatherburn first. This was crazy.

They were intruding. Steven was out, as she had said he would be, diving on the *Normandie*. Weatherburn poked under the bed, looked around his drawing table and opened the wardrobe. She was struck again that it was a monastic room, spare and clean, like his drawing board.

'Duncan!'

Duncan peered in. 'It's an *Afus*.'

'What?' Cordi said. 'That's impossible.' She pushed past Weatherburn and stared at the radio components in a suitcase on the floor of Steven's wardrobe. 'It's only parts.'

'He's lost four radios,' Weatherburn retorted. 'He's building a new one.'

'No – '

'Perhaps Gates needs a shortwave transmitter-receiver to listen to baseball games.'

'No. It can't be – '

'Why don't we see what else he's got? Duncan, pull that out of there and we'll take it with us.'

Cordi followed him numbly across the room. Weatherburn picked up a set of house keys. 'Want to bet five pounds these open the Frenchman's apartment?'

Duncan said, 'Jesus Christ, it's a bomb,' and a brilliant flash threw his body like a shadow across the bed.

Pumping resumed at nightfall. Gates and van Slough dived with water- and air-jet hoses and joined a mob of divers shuffling in the dark at the bottom of the slip, trying to break the mud's hold on the remnant sections they had shored up with stays. They worked until midnight, when the divers and salvage supervisors conferred and agreed that the mud suction had no hold on the *Normandie*.

Rik van Slough said he was going to catch some sleep and headed out to his tug at the end of the pier. Gates headed for shore. He was blind tired, but he thought he'd call Cordi for a nightcap. Maybe more. Maybe. The pumps were thundering the length of the hull, and the catwalks had assumed a peculiar slant, the *Normandie* having risen a few degrees.

He noticed that the night was turning darker, overcast. Patches of fog were forming on the water, blowing in from the sea, gathering around the floodlit *Normandie* and the darker *Queen Mary*. He looked from one to the other, the fallen *Normandie* rising, the *Mary* loading, venting steam from the stacks that rose above her pier as thousands of soldiers were herded aboard.

Like the *Normandie*, the *Mary*'s speed was her sole defence. The Otter had attacked the *Normandie* where she could not move to defend herself, at dockside in the harbour. The *Queen* was safe on the high seas at thirty-one knots, and safe in a protected anchorage like Gourock, Scotland, where she would deliver her soldiers.

But New York was not a safe harbour. Not any more . . . And somehow in that instant, recalling how *slowly*, how *ponderously* and above all how *vulnerably* the huge liner manoeuvred in the harbour, Gates thought he knew the Otter's target.

His exhaustion lifted like a curtain. The logic was perfect, almost too perfect, even if he lacked proof. If there was a submarine in the harbour, he believed the target had to be the *Queen Mary*. Tweed. He had to tell Tweed. He ran out of the pier, heading for a pay phone, rummaging for a nickel in his pocket. His mind was racing crazily. If he could only slow down he might even figure out where the Otter had hidden his submarine . . .

Cordi Grey was standing in the shadows at the pier entrance. He could tell it to her . . . tell her British agent colleagues . . . She was wearing a beret and her long, belted trenchcoat, and as she moved into the light, opening her arms to him, he thought he had never seen her so beautiful.

'*Steven.*'

Gates embraced her, bent to kiss her. Her lips were ice.

He felt something hard in his stomach, looked down – and saw her gun.

'What the – ?'

Cordi said, 'If you get past me, they'll kill you.'

Her eyes went to the black Packard with a high-priority E gas-rationing sticker on the windshield and several figures inside. Gates said 'What?' again, and Cordi said, 'I almost hope you try.'

43

Two men got out of the car, took hold of him from either side and hustled him into the back seat. A third was driving. The door slammed and the car screeched away from the kerb into a U-turn under the highway. Gates strained to catch a glimpse of Cordi. One of them squeezed a nerve in his elbow. Pain went through his arm. He tried to get loose.

'Easy, Mr Gates. It's all over.'

'What's going on?'

An upper-class English accent. 'We thought you'd tell us. Actually.'

'I don't know what the *hell* you're talking about.' He twisted around and looked out of the back window for Cordi, but she was gone. 'Where are we going?'

They settled back, still holding his elbows, and said nothing more. One was young, bull-necked and solid. The other, the man who had spoken, was older, with bushy ginger eyebrows and moustache. He smelled of cigarette smoke and drummed his fingers on his knees as the car sped uptown. They passed a police car. Gates's sudden hope died when he realized they didn't worry about the cop.

Still in the prowl car's sight, the driver put the Packard into a tyre-squealing turn onto a side street. The Packard shot across to Eleventh Avenue, went north again and into a side street that ended at the New York Central's Sixtieth Street freight yard, pulling up to a warehouse entrance. A corrugated steel door slid up electrically and lowered behind the car as soon as it drove into the building.

'What's this?'

They pulled him out of the car and down a bank of stone stairs into a deep cellar that smelled of the river. A door slammed shut heavily at the top of the stairs. There were other men in the room, standing in the shadows along the walls, and two chairs, one under a light. The ginger-moustached man took the chair in the dark. The others forced Gates into the other and handcuffed his hands and feet to it.

'All right, Mr Gates. We have a number of questions we would like answered.' His accent was more sharply defined than Cordi's.

Gates squinted into the light, a bare bulb hanging from a beamed ceiling, and tried to see his face. The others had melted into the shadows.

'Listen carefully. Your answers will determine if you walk out of here alive.'

Gates turned his head as far as he could into the darkness. 'What *is* this? Who are you?' He turned back to the man he couldn't see. For some reason the handcuffs were especially terrifying.

'Exactly our question, Mr Gates.'

'I *still* don't know what you're talking about. What this craziness is all about — '

'We'll start with the radio.'

'What radio?'

A man stepped into the pool of light, laid a large corrugated cardboard box on the floor and opened it. In it was a burnt and broken suitcase and a jumble of what looked like smashed radio components. The pieces were singed and stained. Gates recognized a tuning device and chassis studded with glass and bent wire filaments — all that remained of its vacuum tubes.

'Familiar?' asked the voice.

'No.'

'These are the remains of your shortwave transmitter, Mr Gates. The dark stains are the blood of a man who saved our lives by throwing his body on your bomb.'

512

'*Bomb?* What bomb?'

'Mr Gates, a young man saved my life and Miss Grey's.
I warn you – '

'Look, I don't understand – '

'We found it in your room on Forty-sixth Street.'

'What?'

'Where were you going to erect your antenna?'

'There's been a crazy mistake.' Apparently Cordi wasn't
convinced earlier; they still suspected him. But *bomb* . . .?

'I'm afraid not. Miss Grey confirmed it was your room.'

'That's crazy.'

'She expressed the same thought until Mr Walsh got in
touch a short time later.'

The bull-necked man stepped into the light, his big
hand clamped around Glenn Walsh's spindly arm. Gates
recognized the clerk he had seen at the navy supply office
on Church Street, the one who'd patiently explained that
T and C Trucking might have taken the shipment Gates had
claimed he was looking for. Walsh was wearing a drab grey
shirt and pants. His face was pasty white as he blinked in
the light.

'That's him,' said Walsh. 'The guy I told you about.'

'The man you know as Herr Otter?'

'That's him.'

'You weren't entirely certain about his picture.'

'I know his voice. And I know him now. That's him.'

'What?' Gates heard himself shouting. 'Sure I know that
man, he's a navy clerk – '

'And he knows you, Mr Gates. Mr Walsh was caught
forging his superior officer's signature on a shipment of
sugar he was diverting to the black market. This evening
he decided he might get off more lightly by talking to me
before the FBI caught up with him. Under questioning he
admitted he worked for a German agent known to him as
Herr Otter. We persuaded him that it would be in his best
interests to tell what he knew. And that included your
radio and your address.'

513

'That's crazy, it isn't mine – '

'I wasn't exactly surprised,' said a man in the shadows. 'We've been watching you for a long time, Mr Gates. Your activities are a trifle odd for a naval architect – even a salvage diver.'

'What activities?'

'The ransacking, assault and subsequent burning of T and C Trucking.'

'What?'

'The lunches and telephone conversations with US Navy personnel you have no legitimate business with. The meetings with others who were at the fire on the *Normandie*, culminating in the murder this week of the man Larson. Not to mention what happened to Armstrong – you do remember Armstrong, short, rather flattened fellow? Did Canaris pick you out in '39? We know that you were in London that summer . . .'

'All those things you're talking about are . . . look, I've been trying to find out what happened on the *Normandie*. I believed the fire was sabotage. I thought that Larson tricked Armstrong into removing his spark shield too soon – '

'Have you told anyone about your suspicions?'

'Damn right. I told ONI.'

'And what did they say?'

'They said I was crazy.'

'Like a fox, Mr Gates. You cleared the way to contact your subagents by pretending to investigate. A very nice cover. Clever. You were free to move about issuing new orders and disciplining people like Armstrong and Larson – '

'That's ridiculous, someone has set me up – '

The door opened, shut, and Gates thought he smelled Cordi's perfume.

'Understand something,' the voice in the dark said. 'I don't care a damn that you're a murderer. That's beside the point for us now. I'm not even about to report you to the police. But I do want to know where your submarine

514

is. Bad enough to make you want to tell us – you know the game.'

Gates nearly laughed. 'The submarine? I *started* the hunt for the submarine.' He shrugged excitedly until the handcuffs brought him up short, cutting his wrist.

The man with the ginger moustache stepped out of the shadows and hit him hard in the face with his open hand. 'You're a cheeky little bastard. You made a balls-up of ONI's investigation by going over their heads and persuading your political contacts to institute that ridiculous search – knowing your submarine was so well-hidden it wouldn't be found. Isn't that right, Cordi?'

'Yes, sir,' she answered back from the dark.

'Wrong. It's still out there someplace,' Gates said. 'And the *Queen Mary* is sailing tonight.'

'The *Queen Mary*?'

'I can't prove it, but I believe she's the target – '

'How do you happen to know when she sails?'

'I saw the *Marie Moran* at Pier 90 just before you grabbed me. She's the *Mary's* number one tug. You really don't have to be a big-time spy in New York to know that.'

His interrogator hit him again. Gates recoiled, fought to keep control. The first blow had surprised him. This one hurt.

'I . . . we've been set up, you crazy bastards . . . *Some-body's going to sink that ship while we're sitting here.*'

Cordi braced for the next blow. Weatherburn would hit him again . . . Steven was launching a classic counterattack to deflect a line of questioning – insulting Weatherburn and raising a phony issue at the same time. Cordi's attention switched to the radio parts in the suitcase at Steven's feet.

Gates cried out, and Weatherburn pressed the advantage, whipping a long switchblade knife out of his jacket and shooting out the blade with a sharp *click*.

'You're crazy,' Gates said, his voice unsteady now as he tried to draw away, turn as far as the cuffs would allow him. 'Cordi? Are you there? Tell him, for God's sake, that he's *wrong* – '

'I wish I could, Steven.'

Her voice was empty. Gates sagged in the chair. The switchblade flickered. The man holding it said, 'All right, we've heard a few lies and a few half-truths, and we've come to an agreement that the *Queen Mary* is in danger.'

'Then you know!'

'I concluded that some time ago. If there was a submarine, what else better to sink than the biggest target containing the most lives? Funny, Gates, you told everyone how sure you were that there was a submarine, knowing how well it was hidden, but never once mentioned the *Queen*, not until we sat you down for this little chat. One wonders what else . . . well, we've worked our way back to the meat of the matter, Mr Gates. Herr Otter. Whoever the hell you are. One simple question. *Where is that submarine?*'

Gates could not take his eyes off the knife. *'I don't know.'*

'This will be your last chance – '

'I don't *know*. Cordi, please – '

'I'll have Cordi leave if necessary. Expect nothing from her.'

'I'm not your enemy,' Gates tonelessly repeated. 'Just please believe me.'

Cordi had to steel herself against the thought that everyone in the cellar knew the rules of interrogation except Steven. Except that the Otter *would* know . . .

The knife cast dots of light against the walls.

'Cordi,' Weatherburn said. 'I think you'd better leave.'

She started up the dark steps, her heels clicking on the stone.

Weatherburn showed Gates the point of the knife and slowly brought it close, circling towards his left ear.

'Where is the submarine?' he asked, inserting the tip inside Gates's ear and probing into the aural canal.

Gates pulled abruptly against the handcuffs, against the knife threatening the depths of his ear.

'Mr Gates, this is no time to stop talking.'

The tip of the knife touched his eardrum.

'I don't *know*, I don't know – '

He jerked against the handcuffs, twisted away from the knife and lunged around in the chair, calling out, 'Cordi, please, just make him listen for a minute, damn it . . . all I know is the U-boat dropped a sub. I don't know if it even made in into the harbour – ahh . . . '

Weatherburn had pushed the knife into the skin behind his ear; the pain shot through his skull. 'Turn around, Mr Gates, and let's resume our conversation.' He pressed harder, and Gates screamed.

Weatherburn then straightened up and hit him open-handed with a full swing that snapped Gates's head back and knocked him and the chair over. The other men scooped the chair up and set it back under the light. Blood was running from Gates's mouth. His eyes were fixed on the knife.

Weatherburn leaned close and placed the point back into Gates's ear. 'Before I put your eardrum out, I want you to listen to one last sound. The sound of my voice explaining why I know that you're lying. You will remember it when we get to your remaining ear, and the truth. Are you listening to me?'

'I'm listening,' Gates whispered. 'What difference does it make?' He started violently as the cold steel brushed the soft skin inside.

44

'Listen, and find out the difference, Mr Gates,' breathed Weatherburn, leaning closer and tensing to thrust. 'Our *Queen Mary* sails from the Cunard-White Star pier at dawn. I will do *anything* to stop you and yours from drowning fifteen thousand Allied soldiers and destroying the finest ship in the world.'

Gates's mouth set, the burn scar on his cheek seemed to turn an angry red. 'The finest ship in the world, damn you, has been on the bottom of the Hudson River for eighteen months and is finally trying to come back to life. Her successor is still berthed on a drawing table. Yours is a lousy third – *my God, that could be where it is* . . . everything fits . . . the place . . . the electrical power source . . . *it's in the Normandie, has to be* . . . '

'*What* is in the *Normandie*?'

'The submarine, it's hidden in the *Normandie* – '

'Really? Where, precisely, Mr Gates?'

'I don't *know*, for chrissake. They'd have to open up one of the compartments. But how the hell would they get around the divers – wait, compartment sixteen was leaking . . . there's an Italian guy there, a new diver. I wonder – ah . . . '

Weatherburn had hit him backhanded across the nose. 'Why do I think you're stalling me, Mr Gates?'

'Are you *crazy*? I'm trying to tell you where it is. Plenty of electricity and compressed air. Marine gear . . . It's so noisy you'd never hear a sub.'

'I don't believe you.'

'At least go look for it, prove I'm lying before you kill all of us – '

'And waste two days in the process,' Weatherburn said. 'Too cute, Mr Gates. We'll blunder around an eighty-thousand-ton capsized liner for a couple of days while the *Queen Mary* sails at dawn. It won't wash and you know it – '

'I'll take you there, I'll *help* you – '

'Yes!' Cordi said abruptly. 'We'll get the salvors to help.' She'd come back.

'Shut up!' Weatherburn told her.

'But I think he may be right – '

'I thought you'd left, Cordi. Please do. Now.'

'Sir, what do we have to lose?'

Weatherburn inserted the knife inside Gates's ear. 'How stupid can you think we are? Cordi, how stupid can *you* be?'

The steel was cold again, pricking at the drum. Gates tried to pull away, but Weatherburn followed him with the point this time, kept following until Gates had strained to the limit of the handcuffs. If he jerked his head, moved a quarter-inch, the knife point would split the tympanic membrane.

Cordi called from the stairs. 'I just don't understand what is wrong with at least looking there? He *could* have been set up – '

'There are three thousand men working on the wreck, you silly woman. How many are his agents? Who do we tip off when we march him aboard? What do they do? Launch their attack immediately is what they do. Signal the submarine to come out from where it's hidden and torpedo the *Queen Mary*. While we're rooting around the *Normandie* for his fairy tales – get her out of here,' and he turned back to Gates.

A light flared overhead, illuminating the stone cellar.

Weatherburn jumped back with the knife. The others, deprived of their shadows, reached for their guns.

'*Don't.*'

Gates twisted towards the sound of her voice.

She was crouched behind the balustrade on the top step of the cellar stairs, her back to the door, her gun resting solidly on the railing. The men traded quick looks.

'I won't take chances against three of you,' Cordi said. 'I'll have to shoot. Raise your hands.'

The two who had been in the shadows lifted their hands slowly, looking at Weatherburn, who still held the knife, and spread apart with small, quiet movements.

'Stop,' Cordi told them quietly. 'Stay exactly where you are.'

'Are you out of your mind, Cordi?'

'Drop the knife, sir. Drop it. Then remove your gun butt-first from your shoulder holster and put it on the floor and unlock Steven.'

'You won't shoot me,' Weatherburn said.

'I'll try and aim for your shoulder, sir. But I haven't fired one of these in a while, so I will cut it rather close. Drop it.'

Weatherburn dropped the knife.

'Now the gun.'

He removed his gun with two fingers and laid it on the cement.

'And theirs.'

Weatherburn approached each and removed his gun in the same manner.

'Unlock him.'

Weatherburn knelt and unlocked Gates's feet. As he released his wrists he said, 'Neither of you will survive this, I guarantee. I'll have you stopped in an hour. Cordi, don't you see he's going to kill you so he can go to the submarine? Why are you doing this?'

'Because I think he's right. He knows the *Normandie*. He knows this port. And he knows where that submarine is hidden.'

'You're a naive fool. You want to believe that because you've gone soft on him.'

Her eyes flickered for an instant at Gates, who was standing up and tentatively rubbing his wrists. 'Yes, I've done that. But that's not the point . . . he can save the *Mary* . . . and if you won't give him a chance, I will.'

'He'll kill you, Cordi.'

'Pick up their guns, Steven. And the knife. Quickly.' Was she right? Maybe not. But damn it, she'd have to take the chance.

Gates picked up the three guns and the knife and carried them up the stairs. He gave her a look of astonished admiration, which made her feel a thoroughly unprofessional jolt of pride. It was all Weatherburn needed.

He was halfway to his other gun before she even saw him move. Cordi fired. The bullet burst a puff of concrete from the cellar floor, inches from Weatherburn's outthrust hand. He rose slowly, shaking his head in frustration. 'Keep going,' Cordi ordered Gates. 'Start the car and open the outside door.'

She stayed where she was, sheltered by the balustrade, watching them, knowing that the two assistants were out of it without their guns but that Weatherburn still was not. He eyed her almost sadly.

'I told you once, Cordi, that you lacked the natural duplicity to survive behind enemy lines.'

'Did you have to torture him?'

'Authenticity, my dear. I intended to let him go and report back – or return to – the people around him so I could see who jumped which way. We don't know the size of the Otter's ring. And now we have nothing, thanks to your misguided – it's my own fault. I should have picked Gates up myself.'

The car horn sounded.

'We can still stop him,' Weatherburn said. 'And with no blot on your copybook.'

Cordi backed towards the door.

'You're a monster – '

'Of course. Takes one to fight one. Poor Cordi. You've

521

stepped in it for sure. What will you do for the rest of the war?'

'What will you do *after* it?' she asked, backing out of the cellar and jamming the door with a tyre iron by wedging the hubcap pry over the saddle, the way he had taught her.

'I'm going to the ship!'

'We can't keep this car. He'll put the police on us.'

'How can he do that?' Gates was turning onto West End Avenue, where tendrils of Hudson River mist uncoiled in the headlights.

'He'll tell them you killed that man in the boathouse and that we're armed and dangerous.'

'Tweed won't believe that.'

'He'll go miles over Tweed's head. Flag that cab down.'

Gates signalled the cab, pulled up behind it and ran with her.

'What's the matter with your car?' asked the driver.

'Out of gas.'

'Want a garage?'

'No,' said Cordi. 'Mayflower Hotel.'

'Wait!' She held him back as he tried to flag another cab in front of the hotel.

When their cab had pulled away and was hidden by a bus she took Gates's arm and steered him around the corner and across Sixteenth Street to Broadway. 'Now we get a cab.'

They took that one to the Pennsylvania Hotel at Seventh Avenue and Thirty-third, went in one side of the big lobby, out another and got another cab.

'We have to get to the *Normandie*,' Gates whispered.

Cordi leaned close, pretending to kiss him. 'They've put plainclothesmen all around the *Queen Mary*. And riflemen on the piers. We can't just walk aboard.'

'By boat,' Gates said.

'What boat?'

'Tweed. A police boat.'

'No, you can't trust anybody. Not now.'

'The Statue of Liberty boat.'

'Yes!'

They changed cabs again and at Sheridan Square caught the IRT local, which was filled with servicemen and their dates heading downtown by subway for a late-night ride on the Staten Island ferry.

'Let him get underway before we tell him,' Cordi said. 'Just pay and get in the boat.'

The boatman apparently recognized them. Gates stifled his panic, paid and joined Cordi in the cabin. 'I think he remembers us.'

'I should think so,' she said as the boat chugged away from the Battery.

Moments later they stepped out of the cabin, Cordi's hair blowing in the damp wind.

'How much to run us up to Pier 88?'

'I don't go there.'

'I know. How much for a special trip?'

'You really want to go?'

'Yes. It's very important.'

'Fifty bucks. Why don't you take a cab from the Battery? Be there in twenty minutes.'

Gates pulled out his money clip and counted. 'I have thirty-three.'

'I have nine,' said Cordi.

'I want fifty.'

Cordi fished deeper into the handbag she'd pulled from her raincoat. 'And a half a book of tin coupons?'

'Tin?'

'Cans,' snapped Gates. 'Blue coupons.'

The boatman inspected the dates in Cordi's ration book with his flashlight, stuffed the rations in his pocket, turned his boat upriver.

'How you plan to climb up on the pier from my boat?'

'There are plenty of barges in the slip,' Gates said. He looked at his watch and the rising tide. It was near the highwater mark on the piers they were slowly passing, near slack, when the inflowing tide and the outflowing tide and the outflowing river would neutralize each other and the *Queen Mary* would back out of her slip.

45

Giuseppe Ponte gazed at the floodlit *Queen Mary* from his niche inside the *Normandie*'s stern mooring compartment and began slowly removing his mask and lead weights. The *Seehund* nestled low in the oily water, and wavelets echoed against the cavern's walls like loose links of steel chain as the Otter heaved on a line to pull the boat alongside the diving stage so they could board for the attack. Ponte had been quiet all night, and the Otter had let him be. Men prepared to fight in different ways. He got the boat positioned and snubbed the line. When he looked up, Ponte was pulling off his fins.

'What are you doing?' The frogman's gear was heaped around him on the stage.

Ponte moved towards the Otter, across the diving stage, his long arms and huge shoulders swinging easily. The Otter looked down at him. 'You are going to try to stop me?'

'I *will* stop you,' Ponte said, 'We gain nothing by destroying the ship, nothing by killing those men. It is over. For my country ... for me ... for you ... '

'Get out of my way.' He spoke only to fill space, to buy seconds, to distract. He had worried about Ponte ever since *Il Duce*, Mussolini, had surrendered –

Ponte darted inside the Otter's grasp and kneed his groin. The Otter doubled up, startled by the sheer speed of the attack, staggered by the pain. Ponte cupped his own large hands and drove them down on the back of the Otter's neck.

The Otter kept his footing. He dodged Ponte's knee, which was driving up at his face, straightened up and reached again. But the Italian had already slipped away. In the spill of light from the *Queen Mary*, his teeth shone in a sudden, deadly grin.

'You are clumsy, my friend.'

'Can't this thing go any faster?'

'My customers aren't usually in a rush.'

'Where will we look?' Cordi asked, drawing him back to the stern, out of earshot of the boatman. 'Weatherburn was right. It's enormous. What can we rule out?'

He recalled standing in the doorway of the abandoned boathouse, looking across the river where the sterns of the *Normandie* and the *Mary* lay side by side, one climbing back to life, the other waiting to die.

'I don't know. The entire ship is sealed bottle-tight for pumping. Wait. Except one place. The Stern Empire.'

'The what?'

'It's one of Rik's areas. It's got huge windows, open. We cleared it out, but we didn't seal it. There's a submerged area at least ten-by-forty-by-sixty feet – '

'Rik could even be the Otter . . . We've suspected him all along.'

'I don't think much of your suspect list, but it's the only open part of the ship . . . '

Ponte came at him again, leaping, grabbed a pipe overhead and swung like a trapeze artist, kicking the Otter in the face. It snapped his head back, knocked him down. Ponte dropped from the pipe, kicking.

The Otter took the blows, absorbed them and struck back. Ponte was already skipping away, but the Otter connected with his ankle, and the Italian fell backward with a startled gasp. The Otter surged up from the stage. Ponte scrambled away from him, favouring the injured foot, yet still dancing lightly, his eyes gleaming.

The Otter lunged at him, trying to press the advantage, suddenly kicked out at him. Ponte floated out of range and swung one of his long arms. A length of steel cable was in his hand. The heavy braided wire wrapped around the Otter's face. He thought his head had exploded. He clawed at the fiery welt. Ponte swung again. The cable smashed his ear.

The Otter pushed through the agony, stepped inside Ponte's next swing and launched a long, hard jab straight from his chest. Ponte catapulted backwards, his nose gushing blood. The Otter stalked him. Ponte pulled the knife from his leg sheath and went into a crouch, the knife in one hand, the cable in the other.

The Otter reached into the heap of the frogman gear and came up with the *salmone*. Dangling the garland of lead weights, he advanced and straightened up to his full height.

'Fighters have a saying over here. A good big man will always beat a good little man. You're a very good little man, Captain Ponte.'

Faint grey light was collecting in the Manhattan cross streets when the wreck of the *Normandie* hove into view. From a distance the ship looked as if she had rotated higher in the night, and it was almost possible to imagine that it was she – and not the *Queen Mary* – straining to sail on the tide, but the illusion crumbled as the boat drew nearer.

Hollandia was moored at the edge of the floodlight spill, riding jauntily on the wakes kicked up by a half a dozen small boats patrolling the water around the *Queen Mary*. The VSS shone white on her sleek, low diesel stack. A barge and gangway connected her to the *Normandie*'s stern.

'Rik's here,' Gates said.

Cordi opened her bag and clicked off the safety on her gun.

'Take it easy. If he's not the Otter . . . and I'm not convinced he is . . . he can tend for me when I dive into the mooring compartment.'

527

Cordi kept her hand inside her bag. Then she saw the *Queen Mary*'s stern, which stuck out into the river beyond the pier. '*Look* at all of them.'

Gates looked and was stunned by the enormousness of the human load the liner was preparing to carry.

Thousands of American soldiers were belowdecks, he knew, crammed into tiers of standee bunks – ten men in cabins built for two – but thousands more had crowded onto the *Queen Mary*'s terraced stern decks – a solid mass of men, motionless in a moment of quiet apprehension. The express liner thundered a long, shivery blast on her whistle. They clapped their hands to their ears and the mass rippled like a ripe meadow in the wind.

'There?' Cordi pointed at the row of huge, sightless black eyes – the giant, glassless ports that circled the *Normandie*'s half-submerged stern.

'Got to be,' said Gates. The *Normandie* had risen to a seventy-degree angle. She was moving, rocking across an arc of several feet – no longer tentatively but with the stately beat of a sleeping heart.

'Drop us on that tug.'

The boatman was alternately gripping the wheel and the throttle. 'I don't know if I can get by the patrol boats, mister.'

'If you can't, I'm taking my money back.'

'Okay, okay.' He veered towards van Slough's tug, shooting nervous glances at the patrol-boat lights crisscrossing the river behind the *Mary*. Sailors were perched on their bows, cradling Thompson submachine guns.

'You got to jump . . . go!'

In his confusion, he hit the tug hard. The cabin boat splintered its forepeak with a loud bang. Gates grabbed Cordi's hand and jumped over the round steel gunnel. The boat bounced off and raced away.

'*Rik! Rik!* . . . Where the hell is he?' He ran through the tug, Cordi at his heels. Rik wasn't in the pilothouse, nor in the galley, his sleeping cabin or the engine room.

He jumped onto the barge and ran up the gangway to the catwalk on the *Normandie*'s promenade deck. The catwalk was slanted oddly, turning cock-eyed as the ship rotated. Cordi kept right behind him.

'Is that Charlie?'

Charlie was coming along at a fast pace, with a length of staying wire dangling from his hand. When he recognized Gates he called, 'Was that you just got on Rik's boat?'

'They hid the sub in the mooring compartment. They're going to torpedo the *Queen Mary*.'

'What?'

'Come on, tend me. I'm going to dive.'

'Easy, let's just take a look first.'

They ran into a shaftway and down a lower corridor, past a startled pair of pump operators who gaped at the unlikely sight of a woman on the wreck. Crouching, they went down the low, side-turned corridor to the final, aftmost bulkhead. Gates climbed over it and pulled Cordi after him. Charlie threw his bulk over the timbers and landed beside them on the work platform. The floodlights shone through the gaping windows, lighting the water.

Air bubbles were rising beside the thick, insulated electrical cable that came out of a hole in the bulkhead and disappeared into the water.

'The feed for the batteries,' Gates said quietly. 'It's here.'

They hauled it onto the work platform in dripping, foul-smelling coils. It fetched up tightly after twenty feet. 'Heave, Junior,' They pulled harder. Cordi called out.

Gates and Charlie crouched beside her. They'd pulled up a man clad in a shiny, black rubber suit.

Charlie lifted him to the platform and turned him onto the tanks. His eyes were bulging. The electrical cable was twisted tightly around his neck.

'The new diver amidships,' said Charlie. 'The Italian guy.'

Gates tore off his jacket, shirt and work boots, and snatched up the length of staying cable that Charlie had dropped. He poised at the edge of the platform.

'What's the idea, Junior? The guy's dead.'

'Whoever killed him's got the submarine. I'm going to wrap this around the prop before he gets away.'

He jumped into the water feet-first. Ten feet down, he struck something solid. He felt for it in the black water, his eyes squeezed shut, his lungs pounding dully, ran his hands over its thick, oval head. When he located two immense indentations that had to be torpedo tubes, he knew, at last, he'd found the Otter's submarine.

This was the bow. He tried to pull himself aft to sabotage the propeller, but he was out of air. He shot to the surface, swam back to where the huge windows curved into the water, and dived again with the staying wire, located the submarine again and began searching for the propeller.

The smooth hull started moving. Water surged. The hull slipped through his hands, moving backwards, gaining speed. Gates lashed out with the wire, trying to snag something, anything that would stop it, but it kept going. He heard a loud scraping of steel against steel, and then it was gone, loose in the harbour.

46

The *Queen Mary* blew a deep, resounding blast on her whistle. Echoing between the piers, rebounding from the buildings on Twelfth Avenue and thundering back through the *Normandie*'s steel caverns, the resonant bone-shivering blast smothered the sounds of the salvage pumps and the patrol boats scurrying in the dark. To Gates's ear it was a violent, doom-stricken noise – the fury of the cold sea exploding in the hot boilers of a sinking ship. She blew again and again – three blasts commencing her voyage.

'The tug!'

He ran out of the aft mooring compartment with Charlie and Cordi pounding after him. On the catwalk, the salvage workers were watching the *Mary*'s three funnels slide slowly behind Pier 90. Within the lightspill, steam tugs with tall, narrow stacks strained against the *Mary*'s stern hawsers, pulling her into the river.

Gates ran to the end of the catwalk and down the gangway to the barge *Hollandia* was moored to. He untied the bow line and hurled it onto the tug. He was heading for the stern line when Cordi and Charlie caught up.

'What the hell are you doing?'

'He has to raise a periscope to shoot. I'll ram him – '

'Forget it, let the navy do it.'

Gates looked at the *Mary* sliding from her pier. 'By the time I convince them to, she'll be on the bottom.'

'The patrol boats'll stop him.'

'Not here. They're looking in the wrong place.'

He loosened *Hollandia*'s stern line and tossed it onto her deck. The river held the tug tightly against the barge. He climbed into her stern and saw Weatherburn and two heavy-set men in trenchcoats hurrying aft on the catwalk. They spotted him and broke into a run.

'Charlie, stop them – '

'Who are they?'

'English Intelligence . . . crazy hoods . . . ' shouted Gates, scrambling up the ladder to the pilothouse.

'English?'

Cordi took out her pistol. She looked up at Gates, who was reaching for *Hollandia*'s controls, then at the catwalk. Weatherburn was twenty feet from the gangway to the barge. 'They're much tougher than hoods, Charlie.'

Charlie Collins gave her a tight smile, acknowledging her conflict. 'Put it away . . . I'd enjoy taking care of them . . . '

With a scream and a *whoosh* the compressed-air starter kicked over *Hollandia*'s diesel. Charlie bounded across the barge and started up the gangway to the catwalk. Cordi jumped onto the tug. Weatherburn pulled a gun out of his coat. Charlie kicked it from his hand in a blur of motion and knocked him into the water with a long left hook. The others were immediately on him with a flurry of kicks and punches that drove him to the boards of the gangway he was fighting to block.

Gates engaged the electric drive, and as the tug rubbed away from the barge he put the big helm hard over and steered into a broad turn downriver.

'Where are you going?' Cordi called out at him.

The *Queen Mary* continued backing ponderously into the river, but Gates held his course and *Hollandia* vanished into the mist.

'Attention!' The order boomed into every corner of the *Queen Mary* from the public address system as the liner completed her turn and started slowly down the river. 'All personnel will stand to attention!'

The fifteen thousand soldiers who'd been primed for this moment stood silently in their assigned places. They'd been told that the ship was so heavily laden that the inches clearance between her keel and the Lincoln Tunnel tubes would be lost if the crowds aboard moved enough to make her heel. Slowly she slid downriver, her decks, cabins and public rooms silent while they waited.

'At ease!'

Fifteen thousand men started talking at once.

Few had been to sea.

Many had never seen the ocean except in the movies.

It was generally agreed that the *Queen Mary* was an American ship. Anything this big would have to be. No one was sure why the crew was English, but the most obvious suggestion was that the limeys supplied the sailors in return for the GIs they needed to beat the Nazis.

As for the aircraft buzzing around their troop ship and the circle of little patrol boats, it was as good a send-off as any, especially since it was too dark and foggy to see the famous Manhattan skyscrapers.

Gates ran the tug at top speed. When he reached the Lower Bay, he tied the wheel and spread out a chart.

'He'll go for maximum damage – try to drown every man aboard *and* block the harbour.'

'But why did you go past the Narrows?' Cordi asked.

'The channel is actually much narrower here.' On the chart he traced the Ambrose Channel seaward to their present position five miles south of the Verrazano Narrows. 'The channel is only seven hundred feet wide in this narrow area here between East Bank and the Romer Shoals. If he sinks her here, the *Mary* will block the Port of New York like a cork in a bottle.'

Another tug loomed out of the dark mist and Gates pulled one of the overhead whistle cords strung across the ceiling. *Hollandia* shrieked, and the other boat shrieked back and disappeared quickly astern, leaving *Hollandia* alone again.

'West Bank is too shallow,' Gates said. 'You can stand on parts of it. He needs at least ten feet, as much as us. So we'll look on the Romer Shoals.'

'You're gambling a lot on a guess.'

'No guess. He built the best fire possible on the *Normandie*. It was a perfect attack. This is the perfect place to attack the *Queen Mary*.'

He swung *Hollandia*'s wheel and steered out of the channel onto the Romer Shoals. Cordi took the binoculars outside onto the narrow deck that ringed the wheelhouse, and Gates opened the windows to see better and so he and Cordi could hear each other. He searched forward and to the left; Cordi took the right.

They crossed the shoals twice and crossed them twice again, steering through patches of thick fog, through which they could see nothing, and then across clear spaces only slightly streaked with mist.

Cordi lowered the binoculars to rest her eyes. Suddenly she stiffened, rubbed her eyes, and looked again.

'*Steven.*'

Gates steered in the direction Cordi was pointing. He had guessed right about the Otter's plan – there, less than a hundred yards ahead, was the black iron stalk of a periscope. At first Gates thought it was moving because it was trailing a sharp V-wake, but then he realized that the apparent wake was caused by the tide, which had turned and begun flowing out of the harbour. The Otter's submarine was actually standing still, hovering just below the surface, while he watched the Ambrose Channel and waited to aim and fire his torpedoes by periscope view.

Gates heard himself thinking the most ancient of sea-fighting commands, one he'd never imagined he would ever hear or utter – *stand by to ram*. He shoved *Hollandia*'s throttle wide open and shouted to Cordi, 'Hang on, we're going to ram him.'

The tugboat's propeller bit deep and seawater began stampeding past her massive bow.

The Otter focused his periscope on the Verrazano Narrows five miles up the channel from where he lay on the shoals in the *Seehund*, but his calm evaporated and his pulse began stirring when a dark shape formed within the mist that wreathed the distant Narrows. He pressed hard against the periscope eyepiece – the *Queen Mary*'s smoke. It had to be. Accelerating to half-speed, she would be in torpedo range in fifteen minutes . . . He was so absorbed in his first sight of the liner that he did not notice the faint vibrations which had begun to drum on the *Seehund*'s skin. The water was resounding loudly before he actually registered what he was hearing. *Behind?*

He spun the periscope around and looked back.

The high, shaggy bow of a harbour tug bulged out of the mist and bore down on him at high speed, its pilot surely unaware of the submerged *Seehund* in his path and apparently blind to its periscope thrust out of the waves. A hundred feet from collision, the front of the tugboat, clad in the traditional hemp bumper, looked enormous, but the Otter was already feeling for the *Seehund*'s motor switches before he recognized, with shock, the stubby diesel-electric exhaust stack and the sleek, low wheelhouse that belonged to his own *Hollandia*.

For an instant, he couldn't quite make a connection. Then he saw . . . Cordi Grey on the wheelhouse deck, her auburn hair blowing in the wind, and *Gates*, with his damned jaw set and both hands on the wheel. How had the English woman managed to save Gates from Weatherburn? One thing was certain, they weren't bearing down on him by accident. They had seen his periscope – and they were out to kill him.

The Otter's first impulse was to launch a torpedo – the

one left in the stern. But they were too close, so close that the explosion of eight hundred pounds of dynamite would obliterate the *Seehund* as thoroughly as the tug.

He swept the motor switches full open. The *Seehund* shook but didn't move. *Cavitating*, he remembered from Ponte. He cut back to half-power and the *Seehund* slid obediently into motion. He could hear the tugboat's propeller thrashing, gaining on him. There wasn't enough depth over the shoals to dive, and he knew he didn't have Ponte's skill at quick manoeuvring. He could only run. He switched the motor to full speed – it was too late.

The *Seehund* leaped ahead, first under its own power, and then a moment later was smashed forward by the tremendous impact of the charging tugboat.

Gates aimed for the periscope, but the tugboat hit the hull of the submarine first ... he caught a glimpse of an indistinct dark shape just beneath the waves at the moment of impact.

'Got him.'

But the periscope lunged ahead, then submerged and disappeared without a trace. Gates shouted back, dumbfounded.

'What happened?' They looked, but the choppy water was as empty as a dead face.

Gates knew he had hit the submarine square with his bow, but that was it, that was all that happened ... the soft hemp bumper draped over the front of the tugboat to protect what the tug pushed had cushioned the impact.

'The bumper's too soft, we just shoved him – '

Gates searched the water, painstakingly scanning the Lower Bay sector by sector. To the south were the running lights of the patrol boat picket line along the submarine nets at the mouth of the harbour. To the east, the Ambrose Channel was speckled with dark ships near the submarine gates, and empty and mist-shrouded here. To the west were the shoals. North, the *Queen Mary*'s smoke and funnels were visible in the first morning light.

No damage, the Otter concluded . . . other than a negligible stiffness in the rudders, the *Seehund* was running perfectly. He had put distance underwater between the *Seehund* and the point where Gates had rammed him with the shaggy hemp bumper, and he no longer could even hear the tugboat.

Still, he opened the stern torpedo door, in case Gates got lucky and spotted him and tried to move at him again. He raised his periscope to look for the *Queen Mary*. The dark spot he'd seen at the Narrows was closer, and much more distinct – funnels and smoke, with a strong hint of tremendous bulk beneath. In five minutes he would be able to take a torpedo bearing.

Gates steered towards the Ambrose Channel.

'Where are you going?'

'Deep water. He'll dive into deeper water to get away from us.'

'No. He's a hunter. He's going for his shot. From the side, the way he planned. From the shoal.'

'But he has to get away from us,' Gates argued. 'He's running – '

'He's a hunter. Steven. I *know* a hunter.'

Gates was trying to steady his breathing. He looked at Cordi. Her lips were drawn tight. She was a hunter too. He'd put all his hopes into ramming the submarine. That it had survived had, at least momentarily, stunned him. But Cordi was just warming up for the fight.

He steered back to the shoals, as she'd said he should, and almost immediately they sighted the terse black line of the Otter's periscope.

The Otter didn't hear Gates, but he turned his periscope

away from the mist-shrouded form of the approaching liner and scanned the area behind the submerged *Seehund*, just to be careful. And he saw *Hollandia* trundling out of the fog, bow-on and headed his way. Gates and Cordi had spotted his periscope again, but if they thought they were going to spoil his shot, they were very damn mistaken. He had more than enough room for a torpedo shot this time and he could spare the torpedo – gladly – because his two bow torpedoes, or even one, were sufficient to sink the troop-loaded ship speeding down the channel.

He circled until the *Seehund*'s stern was aimed in the direction of the tugboat and, with a pleasurable sense of finishing up properly, took a bearing on the tug through the periscope, set the torpedo to that course – and fired.

Cordi was following the periscope with the binoculars when she saw it cut a sudden half-circle in the water. 'He's manoeuvring . . . he turned . . . I think he sees us – '

'I'll ram him sideways this time,' Gates called out. 'I'll try to get him with the whole hull.'

To see better, Cordi hoisted herself up onto the roof of the wheelhouse. The tugboat was rolling in the choppy waves as she stood up and clung to the firefighting water nozzle Rik van Slough had installed on the roof.

From that higher perspective Cordi could see the torpedo track as it started in the vicinity of the periscope, then cut towards the tugboat – straight and bright as a reflecting dotted white highway line.

Inside the wheelhouse below her, Gates was watching the Otter's periscope. Beyond the black stalk loomed the *Queen Mary*, her smokestacks and superstructure growing large as the first rays of the morning sun lighted her tops and burned through the thinning mist – '*Torpedo* . . .' Cordi's voice exploded in his ear.

A moment later Gates saw the track too – pointing an angry finger at them, just below the waves and incredibly fast. In seconds, it seemed, it was so near that Gates could see the torpedo itself, a thick and long black cylinder, fatter than a telephone pole, breaking surface slightly as it closed at thirty knots . . .

It looked as big as the tugboat . . . The engineer's side of Gates's mind instructed him that if the Otter's torpedo was armed with an acoustical or magnetic detonator, he and Cordi were already dead. If the warhead had a contact detonator, they had five seconds.

A quicker part of his mind had started him swinging the tug's wheel on Cordi's warning. *Hollandia* turned her long flank to the torpedo, dangerously increasing her exposure in the time it took to turn. The tugboat heeled sharply. Cordi clung to the fire nozzle, almost hypnotized by the sight of the white line that never wavered, never turned – still an angry white finger pointing at the tug.

Hollandia completed her turn and slowly – too slowly, it seemed – started out of the path of the fierce black cylinder. With bare inches separating the two, the torpedo tore across *Hollandia*'s wake . . . and disappeared in the direction of Sandy Hook.

Gates let out his breath. *Contact detonator*.

Cordi scrambled down from the roof and burst into the wheelhouse. '*Look* – '

The submarine's long, narrow stern had popped out of the water two hundred yards from the tug. It seemed stuck there at a steep angle, bobbing and lurching like a lopsided channel buoy, exposing its twin rudders and shielded propeller spinning in the mist.

'Get him Steven. *Get* him . . . '

The Otter slammed face-first into the helm of the sharply angled *Seehund*. Cursing himself for forgetting Ponte's instructions, he punched at the ballast control levers. Again, he had failed to compensate for the sudden extra buoyancy when he fired the torpedo. The bow felt as though it was in the sand, and who knew how much of the stern was sticking out of the water? Blood poured down his nose. His eyes were tearing ... the instrument panel a blur of shiny switches and green dials.

He heard the tug pounding the water behind him.

He pawed at the levers, found the right one at last and filled the forward ballast and trim tanks. Slowly, maddeningly slowly, the *Seehund* regained equilibrium and settled under the water. Gates was near. The tugboat sounded much louder, almost on top of him. He tilted the *Seehund*'s planes and raced the motor to dive away from the tug's high-pitched dynamo whine and the quick-threshing beat, beat, beat of its eight-foot screw.

The *Seehund* descended rapidly under full power, but there was not enough water on the shoals. The boat grounded and lunged ahead, hitting again and again with bone-jarring thuds that threatened to detonate the bow torpedoes, then caromed off the harbour bottom as the Otter blew ballast, and lifted to the surface, climbing out of control ...

The sub's stern slid under the waves seconds before Gates reached it, but a moment later the periscope appeared again dead ahead of the charging tugboat. *Hollandia* rammed it. But this time Gates put the wheel hard over the instant before colliding.

The manoeuvre slammed the tugboat sideways into the submerged submarine. *Hollandia*'s steel bottom smacked the sub's full length with a hollow, underwater *clang*, followed by muffled screams of metal ripping metal as the tugboat scraped past.

The sub blew air and foam like a whale, and its dark shape vanished beneath the waves ...

Hollandia staggered away from the impact. A ring of bubbles in a swirl of empty water marked the spot where they had struck the submarine, but it had vanished. Gates saw no wreckage, nothing, in fact, but the *Queen Mary* well into the Lower Bay, the lights of her harbour escorts trailing far behind her as she sped down the channel into the Otter's torpedo range.

Blinded, the *Seehund* lay on the bottom of the bay while the Otter assessed the damage. He was scraped and bruised and painfully battered, and had so much trouble moving his left arm that he assumed a bone was cracked. Water was trickling into the cockpit from three leaks he could see; where else the fifty-foot boat had been breached, he could only guess, but the torpedo-arming lights would not light.

The diving planes on the side Gates had hit felt very stiff, barely movable at all. The forward torpedo door on that side would not open – jammed shut in the crash. Fortunately, the other would, not that it would do much good . . . the worst damage of all was to the periscope.

He had already tried it at the surface, but it wouldn't budge. The eyepiece showed nothing and the water was leaking in around the periscope's seal. The periscope had been up when the tugboat hit and it was surely smashed. Underwater the *Seehund* was now blind.

The Otter felt the *Queen Mary*'s quadruple screws begin vibrating the water around the thin-skinned *Seehund*. She must be within three miles . . . He turned on the motor. The boat inched ahead in the sand. The motion gave him hope.

Could he still attack? If so . . . only on the surface, like a torpedo-boat. But a very slow torpedo-boat, too badly damaged to make speed, too cumbersome for fancy manoeuvring. A surface attack meant surrendering all the advantages of a submarine. The risk of detection before he could launch his torpedo was huge, particularly with Gates blundering around in *Hollandia*. But he had no choice. Underwater, the *Seehund* was dead blind.

Could he sink the liner with only one torpedo? He knew he could. The *Queen Mary* was no armoured battleship, just a thin-skinned liner.

But could he fire even that one torpedo? The arming indicator refused to turn on. No green light. He tried the torpedo-arming switch. Still no light. Well, that could be just a minor electrical failure. He had to try. He had to try to climb to the surface and stay up long enough to clock an accurate estimate of the *Queen Mary*'s speed and to take a bearing. He tried the arming switch once more. Still no light. Forget it, just a broken wire . . . nothing serious . . .

The Otter threw his weight against the stiff hydroplane wheels. The *Seehund* rose sluggishly from the sandy bottom. He blew more ballast, and she broke surface, wallowing low in the choppy waves. He opened the hatch and desperately looked around for Gates. *Hollandia* was circling in the distance, dogging the area of their last collision, too far away to notice the low, wave-washed hull of the damaged *Seehund*. And the weather was on the Otter's side, too, not Gates's. Although the sky continued to grow light in the east and north, the cold mist was still clinging close to the water, cloaking the *Seehund*.

The periscope lay flattened and mangled on the deck, a damning accusation of how wrong he had been about Gates – *forget* Gates . . . The Otter was back in control, ready for his attack. He'd shaken the tug and stabilized the *Seehund*. Gates hadn't done too much damage. The propeller, or its shaft, felt bent, the boat was shaking as he moved it towards a thicker fog patch to hide in, it was slowed considerably, but the leaks didn't seem serious and he could still make the rendezvous at sea with the replacement U-boat that Ponte had raised on the radio last night. Yes, Uncle Willy had delivered.

And now so would he.

He knelt in the cockpit, steering the boat with his knees, leaned his elbows on the rim of the hatch, favouring his injured left arm, and readied his compass to take a bearing on the *Queen Mary*, which was speeding down the misty Ambrose Channel like the wind.

Hollandia pounded along at her full twelve knots, rolling

and pitching as she drove her shaggy bow through the chop. The wind was rising, clearing the fog but making the water rougher.

At Cordi's repeated urging Gates swept deeper and deeper onto the shoals while she scanned the water with the binoculars for the telltale periscope in case the *Seehund* had survived. Gates still worried that if the Otter had survived he would hide in the depths of the channel, but Cordi insisted she knew a hunter.

And again, she was right.

'He's come up,' Cordi shouted suddenly, pointing across the shoals, and Gates was astonished to see not the periscope but the entire submarine wallowing on the surface, nearly a half-mile away, and aimed straight at the Ambrose Channel.

Gates threw the helm and steered for it. The submarine was a low, flat boat about fifty feet long, slightly smaller than the tug, but with the frightening, alien appearance of any surfaced submarine, a look of stealth that admitted no purpose but destruction.

The conning tower put Gates in mind of the Civil War *Monitor*'s centrally-mounted round gun turret, but as *Hollandia* cut the distance between them, he realized it was neither turret nor tower, but a low cockpit hatch from which a man was intently watching the channel.

The Otter.

Cordi got him in her binoculars.

He was hunched in the open cockpit, only his head and shoulders and arms showing, manipulating a hand-held instrument he was pointing at the *Queen Mary*.

'He's taking a bearing.'

'We must have messed up his periscope. That's why he's on the surface.'

Cordi took her gun out of her bag.

'If he gets a bearing, we're too late,' Gates said. 'He can fire at that range the moment he sees her, and before we get to him.'

And in the Ambrose Channel, the *Queen Mary*'s profile formed up solidly in the strengthening light.

The Otter calculated the *Queen Mary*'s bearing relative to his position. He estimated her speed at twenty knots and her range at two miles. He set the torpedo for a course which would take it ahead of the liner's present position, lead her like a fowler shooting a bird.

Gates had spotted him at last, had wheeled the tug in a smart turn and was charging again, but this time Gates was too late. The wind bore a faint popping noise to his ears – pistol fire . . . Cordi Grey was shooting at him, but way out of range. He had out-manoeuvred both of them . . .

He reached down into the *Seehund* for the levers to flood the ballast tanks to compensate for the torpedo's exit the moment the hiss of compressed air told him it had launched. A wave broke on the long deck, splashing his face with cold, clear water. Salt delicious on his lips, stinging the welts on his face where Ponte had hit him.

The *Queen Mary* steamed into range. She was all his . . .

The Otter glanced back at the tugboat. He could see Gates's slim figure tense behind the wheel, and Cordi beside him, firing her pistol again and again. The Otter tossed them a mock salute, and triggered his torpedo.

Nothing happened. No hiss. No sudden lurch. He tried again, flipping the trigger switch up and down, up and down. The torpedo wouldn't fire. *Gates* . . . the damage from Gates's ramming was more than he'd wanted to admit . . . the *Seehund* could not even launch one torpedo. The arming light which wouldn't light hadn't lied. Steven Gates had wrecked his *Seehund*, ruined his attack.

Everything he saw turned a hazy red – the *Queen Mary*, the wave-chopped bay, *Hollandia* drawing nearer, Gates and Cordi Grey. He would wait for them to come close and he would kill them with his bare hands. He would pretend to surrender and kill them with his bare hands. He would get aboard the tug and kill –

I didn't send you to New York to kill Gates, Uncle Willy said. All Gates wanted was to save the *Queen Mary*. It meant more to him and that ridiculous Cordi than their lives, or they would not be out here duelling with Uncle Willy's Otter.

Fine. Because there was another way to sink the *Queen Mary* . . . a simple, foolproof way, a personal delivery. He would miss the rendezvous with the waiting U-boat, but to go home to Uncle Willy a failed man . . . that would be a worse death, a death of the spirit. A betrayal of the man who had given him life . . . who had created his life . . .

He ducked inside the *Seehund*, pulled the hatch cover shut and dived into water that vibrated loudly with the sound of the *Queen Mary* drawing closer in the channel, and with the propeller beat of Gates's tugboat circling futilely above.

'Where is he?'

Gates pounded *Hollandia*'s wheel in frustration as he circled the area where the submarine had dived. Where it had been floating on the surface, aiming at the *Queen Mary*, there was now nothing but empty waves.

Cordi scanned the water between the point the submarine had dived and the racing *Queen Mary*. She saw no sign of a torpedo, no repeat of the angry white line the Otter had loosed at them.

'No torpedo track.'

'Maybe we scared him under before he could shoot,' Gates said, not really believing his own words as he scanned the shoals.

'I doubt that.'

'Then wrecked him so he can't fire. Probably barely afloat.' He glanced away from the shoals towards the channel where the *Queen Mary* was drawing near.

'Steven. *Look* . . .'

The Otter's submarine had broken surface in the middle of the Ambrose Channel. Cordi found it in the binoculars, its flat decks awash, rolling ponderously, but when the chop kicked its stern high she also saw its propeller turning.

The submarine's hatch popped open and the Otter thrust out his head, arms and shoulders, kneeling as he had the first time he surfaced. He looked back over his shoulder at the tugboat, and before he faced the *Queen Mary* again Cordi got a clear look at his face in the binoculars.

'*Van Slough. It's Rik.*'

Gates couldn't believe it. He had attributed Cordi's suspicions of van Slough to the same back-to-the-wall British paranoia that had made *him* look suspicious. 'We worked together for a year . . . he could have killed me anytime he wanted . . . why didn't he . . .?' Gates spun the brass rim wheel and drove the tug after Rik . . . faces, phrases tumbling through his mind . . . Walsh, the grey little navy clerk, T and C Trucking's being thick with the mob . . . the characters slapping him around in the truckyard . . . Jimmy Armstrong killed by the scrap crane . . . diving school, 'a couple of calls from your bigshot friends helped' . . . the radio equipment and explosives planted in his room . . . Weatherburn measuring his fear down the length of his knife . . . '*The son of a bitch set me up —* '

'He's moving,' Cordi said, still watching in the binoculars. 'Is he taking a bearing again?'

'No . . . he's not using an instrument . . . He's just leaning on the hatch and moving up the channel.'

Gates looked at the *Queen Mary*, pounding closer. Less than two miles separated the speeding troop ship and the Otter's submarine. And they were on a collision course. No bearing. The Otter hadn't fired before when he had the chance . . . because the tug had damaged the submarine too badly. The Otter . . . Rik . . . had *contact* torpedoes. A suicide attack?

'*Oh no, no, goddamn you . . .*'

'What's he doing?'

'He can't fire, he's going to try to hit the *Queen Mary* with those goddamn contact torpedoes.'

'He'll blow himself up along with the ship – '

'Not if I get to him first.' Gates slammed the throttle wide open and went after him.

As he knelt in the cockpit, the Otter's head was less than three feet above the waves breaking over his battered decks, making the *Queen Mary* look impossibly tall. She was driving towards him, growing wider in his eye every second. High above the slab-sided V of her great bows were the dark windows of her bridge – black squares set amid her misty grey profile. He doubted whether the officers on the bridge could see him; though the dawn had become more light than dark, the mists still coiled around the *Seehund*. But even if they could see him the ship was going too fast to stop and had no room to turn, no way to avoid his final attack.

Deep down ... a small voice of fear ... could he somehow scuttle the *Seehund*, slip back into New York, go on being good old jovial Rik van Slough? And immediately there came the answer ... Rik van Slough did not exist without the Otter.

He looked back once. Gates had again spotted the *Seehund* and was coming after him. Let him come ... the tugboat was too far away to stop the Otter from detonating his torpedoes against the *Queen Mary*.

The *Queen Mary* burst from one of the patches of grey mist that checkered the Lower Bay – a great stacked mountain tearing down the Ambrose Channel with a creamy white wave at her bow and slabs of dark smoke pouring from her funnels, flattening astern in the wind of her passage.

'Steven, what are you doing?'

Gates was turning the tugboat towards the submarine. 'She'll kill herself on his torpedoes. Contact detonators.

The torpedoes will explode if the *Mary* hits the sub – we've got to push the sub out of her way – '

'*Can* we?'

'We've got the power, if we can catch up, and a good bumper on the bow. She can do it if I can handle her.'

Cordi raised her eyes to the *Mary*'s towering stem. It was so close that the liner's bow wake was visible as two distinct waves, thick and creamy as snow-covered banks split by a swift-running brook. 'Steven, there isn't time – '

'Got to try, he'll sink her – '

'Why doesn't she turn?'

'She can't see him and there's no room anyway.'

The Otter looked over his shoulder.

The submarine's speed quickened, and it changed course to an angle that would intercept the liner. Gates turned with it. Cordi took a fresh clip from her coat and slapped it into her pistol. They could see the Otter, see Rik, hunched over his helm steering towards a suicidal triumph, but the range was longer than before and three shots went wild.

The tugboat was faster than the damaged submarine. The distance between them shortened, but even at two hundred feet Rik's head and shoulders were an impossible target for a handgun on a pitching boat. Cordi missed again.

Now, this close, there was suddenly a familiar set to the Otter's shoulders – van Slough's shoulders – a calculating, deliberate and contained stance that Gates had seen once before . . . No, he had never noticed it on Rik; when the Otter was Rik he was somehow a different man. But now Gates saw the same arrogant observer he had seen at the fire – the man in the stack – and Gates knew, suddenly and completely beyond doubt, that the Otter, Rik van Slough, was the same man who had watched from the *Normandie*'s afterstack, gazing with satisfaction on the beautiful ship he had defiled.

And defiled again . . .

A vision took cold flame in Gates's eye, a memory of light and music when the *Normandie* put to sea on a summer night in '39, before the war, before the Otter, before the blackened steel and broken glass. Before stripping her beauty to save her hull. But even as she had struggled back to life, the Otter . . . Rik . . . had defiled her again, penetrating the great hull, lodging his submarine in her . . . defiling her again after destroying her with fire and water . . . *fire and water* . . . suddenly Gates thought he knew how to destroy the Otter . . .

'Grab that control wheel on the ceiling, Cordi. It aims the firefighting nozzle.' The *Queen Mary* was looming above them as if they were standing on a pier, watching her dock.

Steering with one hand, Gates leaned over and threw a lever that turned on *Hollandia*'s two-thousand-gallon-per-minute fire pump. A huge jet of water soared over her bow and crashed to the waves a hundred feet ahead of the tugboat.

Gates touched the round scar on his cheek – one of those water jets had tossed him eighteen feet across the burning *Normandie* and slammed him into a hot wall. It had been like being hit by a cannon.

Cordi stretched for the nozzle control wheel on the ceiling. The roof-mounted nozzle swivelled side to side and angled up and down. She turned the wheel. The powerful spout swept from side to side far ahead of the tugboat. She angled it lower to extend the range. The thick water jet sought the submarine and crashed a blaze of white spray onto its rear deck. Cordi angled the nozzle lower, and the thick water jet arced over and onto the Otter like a vengeful arm.

Gates saw tons of water crash onto Rik, driving him down into the cockpit. The boat weaved and twisted in the path of the *Queen Mary*.

The water crushed the Otter into the cockpit, blinding him, slamming his back and shoulders, hurling and pushing

549

him down into the *Seehund*. The sheer volume of water overwhelmed the electric cockpit bailing pump the Otter had turned on when Gates started his fire nozzle attack, and he was driven underwater, remembering as his hands slipped from the controls a truly violent attack his mother had launched at him when he was three . . . or was it four? . . . and she was enraged that Uncle Willy had cancelled at the last minute a long-awaited visit . . . She was a big woman and she had pummelled him beyond pain towards unconsciousness. He had fought back then, as he was trying to fight now, fought to survive, but then as now it had been a hopeless fight and he had survived only by squeezing his small body into a narrow cupboard which had protected him until his mother's inevitable collapse in tears and exhaustion . . .

The ferocious impact of the water jet was pounding the life out of him . . . if only he could lift his uninjured arm, raise it against the crushing water, if only he could reach the hatch cover and pull it shut he might escape death. Again. But as he struggled against the crushing weight and the roaring, noisy spray he felt the water jet begin to hit him harder than before, as if the tugboat had come closer . . . Gates was coming alongside and pounding him at point-blank range.

The *Seehund* stopped dead in the water directly in the path of the *Queen Mary*. 'Keep the water on him, don't let him get to the controls — '

The water spout thundered around the hatch, curtained the entire middle of the surfaced submarine in white spray. Gates nosed the tug into the low hull to push it, but he couldn't see over *Hollandia*'s high bow. Capped by the shaggy hemp bumper, the front of the tugboat stood eight feet above the water. Gates mistook the distance between the front of the tug and the submarine, and hit too hard.

The submarine sank and scraped under the pushing tug. Gates frantically reversed and backed away, *Hollandia* shuddering and flinching as if she were alive. The Otter's submarine scraped loose and bobbed up in front again.

Gates turned off the fire pump; the water jet stopped.

'Guide me, Cordi. I can't see over the bow.'

Cordi dropped down the wheelhouse ladder to the main deck and ran to the bow, where she pulled herself up onto the front bumper, which, draped over the bow and spilling onto the deck, provided hand- and footholds. It was soaked with seawater, the ropes stiff and slippery.

From the wheel Gates watched anxiously as she clawed her way up towards the crest of the bumper, afraid that the rolling, pitching tug would throw her off. He felt the bow connect with the submarine again and powered forward, gently, so as not to unbalance her. The forward motion and pressure of the bow against the submarine reduced the pitching and steadied the tug. And Cordi continued to the top of the bumper. She was already raising one arm to signal him, when she suddenly stopped, rigid like a statue.

The Otter jumped from the *Seehund* onto the bumper and clawed his way up *Hollandia*'s bow, face bloody and welted, purposeful as an animal bounding towards the kill. When his eyes met Cordi's — wide, pale but focusing into action — he lunged at her.

His big hand fastened around her arm. She jabbed at his eyes, wrenched free and leaped backwards to the deck. He came over the top of the bumper, and she heard Steven call out, '*Rik . . .*'

The Otter looked up at the wheelhouse and the fire pump roared again, the nozzle on the wheelhouse roof sending a water jet that hit the Otter a glancing blow on the shoulder. Cordi thought it had knocked him off the boat, but he'd dodged the rest of the torrent, managed to catch his balance, jumped to the deck and headed for the wheelhouse.

Cordi staggered after him but he was already climbing the wheelhouse ladder.

Gates watched him coming as he drove the tugboat forward. He still couldn't see the exact point of impact with the submarine, but his bow had seated squarely in the middle of its hull and *Hollandia* had started pushing – hard . . .

'Gates . . .'

He pulled a fire axe from the wall and met the Otter at the door.

'I'll kill you, Rik – '

Rik – the name Otter had no reality to Gates – was battered, bleeding, but his eyes gleamed with the spirit of hate that hardly belonged to Rik . . .

Rik gestured at the *Queen Mary*, which now seemed to fill the wheelhouse windows as she cleaved towards the tug stubbornly pushing the submarine. 'You're too late, you crazy meddler . . . get away from that wheel – '

He shoved into the wheelhouse.

Gates swung the axe. The Otter grabbed the handle while it was still in the air and jerked it out of his hands, sent it tumbling through the air until it vanished into the waves. Gates backed to the wheel, trying to guard it. The Otter followed, moving lightly on the balls of his feet. His power amazed Gates . . . Rik was, he knew, strong . . . but *this* Rik van Slough . . . this *Otter* . . . was awesome . . . he'd survived both rammings and the brutal pounding of the fire nozzle. Gates knew he was outweighed by a hundred pounds. It was a hopeless – but what was the matter with Rik's left arm? . . .

Cordi made it to the wheelhouse door behind the Otter, and hit the back of his head a glancing blow with her empty pistol. The Otter staggered, shook himself to get control, and turned on her. His left arm did seem to hang at his side. Hurt in the ramming? Broken? But Rik was right-handed, which made it a relatively small chink, *if* he was injured at all. Still, it was the only possible advantage Gates could see for himself as he balled his fist and hit the left arm with all the strength he had.

A sharp cry — cut off abruptly.

Gates punched again. Too late. The Otter was already back in action — a near-blur of motion that made the wheelhouse seem to explode. Gates went down, kicked and punched in the face, punched again even before he saw it coming, his head ringing, his vision blurred.

The Otter turned on Cordi. She grabbed the binoculars that were beside the wheel, swung them by their leather strap at the Otter's left arm.

The Otter clutched at his arm, felt the pain slowing him down. He gathered himself and glanced out the wheelhouse windows. The *Queen Mary* was nearly on top of them, minutes from collision, but *Hollandia* was still pushing the *Seehund*, beginning to move it now across the channel. Were they already slightly to one side of the *Queen Mary*? He lurched past Cordi, reaching for the controls —

Again she hit him with the binoculars, and for a moment the pain in his arm devoured his effort. Gates managed to get back to his feet, saw Rik trying to get to the wheel and Cordi hitting at him with the binoculars. She had turned dead-white, he could see the exhaustion sapping her strength. She swung again, and the Otter lashed back, slamming her against the wall. He put his hands on *Hollandia*'s wheel —

'*No.*' No more destruction, no more ships dying. No more death . . . Gates leaped at Rik's broad back, grabbed his injured arm with both hands and yanked with all the rage he'd stored since the war began.

Rik screamed, a shockingly satisfying sound to Gates, who kept pulling, tearing him across the wheelhouse, dragging him out the door onto the narrow deck and twisting his arm when Rik tried to hold onto the handrails.

As Gates got him to the ladder, Rik kicked his feet out from under him, but Gates hung onto his arm and they fell down the ladder, landing hard on the main deck. Gates got up first, still hanging on, heaving the Otter towards the bow.

The Otter fought to break free, pounding at Gates with his other hand. Gates dodged what he could, absorbed the rest while he continued to wrench at the wounded arm. He pulled the Otter to the bow, then halfway up the bumper. And the Otter abruptly changed tactics, stopped pulling away and leaped on him, crushing him against the shaggy, stiff wet ropes. Gates twisted on his arm, the Otter's right hand closed on Gates's throat. He saw the lights storming in front of his eyes . . . saw the peak of the *Queen Mary*'s sixty-foot stem knifing towards them . . . saw Cordi climb up the bumper and once more swing the binoculars.

Without a sound the Otter half-rose off of Gates. Cordi swung again. Gates got himself free of the Otter's grip and twisted his arm as he struggled to his knees, then his feet, pulling the Otter up to the crest of the bumper. Cordi shoved his legs over, and together they dropped the Otter off the tug's bow.

The Otter landed on his submarine beside the open hatch.

The *Queen Mary*'s bow wave roared – a thundering collapse of tons of water driven on water. Gates and Cordi ran for the wheelhouse, where Gates took the wheel. She directed him from outside. Realizing now that the tug had begun to veer from the submarine, Gates spun the wheel to keep *Hollandia*'s nose against the sub, and throttled full ahead.

The *Queen Mary* was on top of them. Her huge bow wave had a life and sound of its own, louder than the tugboat's engine.

The submarine went down again. Gates had pushed too hard . . . he felt the blood drain from his face, thinking he had sunk the torpedo-laden sub *right in the path of the Mary* – and then it bobbed up suddenly in front again, ahead of the tug, shedding water like a reptile, its watertight hatch somehow shut.

Hollandia thudded into it once again, trying to knock it out of that path.

Cordi backed into the wheelhouse, the *Queen Mary*'s shadow on her face. The liner's bow was thirty yards from the submarine. Gates could read her draught numbers. He put the throttle full open. The towering knife stem was slicing straight for the wheelhouse. Twenty yards. The tug started to move the submarine. The collision point slipped back to the tug's waist. Then to its stern . . . And then the liner's bow wave caught the tugboat, still shoving the Otter's submarine, lifted both, and flung them crazily from her flanks as the *Queen Mary* crashed past, seabound and free.

Gates sprawled with Cordi in his arms. They clung to the deck railing and through the pipework saw the submarine's stern stand up, then vanish beneath the waves, surely, he thought, mortally wounded, swamped with water, and a safe distance from the speeding *Queen Mary*.

'*We did it.*' Gates was clinging to Cordi, who was laughing and crying at the same time.

The *Queen Mary* was infinitely long and high, towering over the tugboat as it sped by. Gates heard shouting and looked up the lofty, rivet-studded hull, up the terraced stern decks. A thousand painfully young faces looked down on them, cheering what was gloriously sculpted by Cordi's wet blouse, giving joyful homage to her long bare legs.

Gates held her tight.

'Wave . . . they're not about to see the likes of you again for a very long, long time . . . '

EPILOGUE

The cover-up, which was engineered smoothly by the BSC operative Weatherburn and Commander – later Captain – Percy Ober, was typical of the improved Anglo-American cooperation in the later years of the war. The two men were able to suppress the story of the Otter's attack on the *Queen Mary*, a story both their wartime governments believed would harm the morale of the thousands and thousands of Allied soldiers being transported across the North Atlantic on the great liners.

The torpedo that the Otter had launched at Gates and Cordi in the *Hollandia* was noticed by a fair number of anchored merchantship sailors and early morning fishermen when it exploded underwater in the shallows off Sandy Hook, but the explosion was blamed on a drifting army mine – similar to the type the navy said had blown up the ammunition ship in Gravesend the month before, although an army investigation laid the blame for that incident on the obliterated navy crew, and the blame for the Sandy Hook explosion on a depth charge accidently dropped by a navy sub chaser.

The Otter's body was never found. Nor was his *Seehund*, though the navy searched the shoals and channel for weeks.

Rik van Slough disappeared the day of the attack but despite what . . . who . . . Gates and Cordi knew they had seen, the official assumption that van Slough was the Otter was short-lived . . . A week later a Manhattan grand jury deliberated over evidence presented by District Attorney Frank Hogan and handed down indictments against the Dutchman for black market profiteering; it was considered a strong possibility that van Slough had got wind of the indictments and fled.

In Germany, immediately after the war, when the victorious Allies had divided the defeated nation into four sectors, a man charged with a brutal but apparently motiveless murder claimed to have burned the *Normandie* at her pier in New York and escaped from New York in a submarine. He made other wild claims as well, even suggesting that he was the son of Admiral Wilhelm Canaris, the former head of the Abwehr who had been executed in 1945 on suspicion of complicity in a failed bomb attack on Hitler. By the time Weatherburn had arrived in Berlin, the accused man had disappeared, and Weatherburn, who had other reasons to visit the ravaged German city, slipped quietly behind Russian lines to prepare for a new war.

And so the *Normandie* fire — even in recent exhaustive accounts — remains an accident made worse by the over-zealous application of hose water. In order to suppress rumours of attacks on the *Queen Mary*, Ober and Weatherburn were obliged to suppress the existence of the Otter, which, of course, meant they had to continue to deny that an agent of Canaris had destroyed the *Normandie*.

Steven Gates was persuaded to make a last secret night dive into the *Normandie* before she was raised. Charlie Collins tended and the operation was cordoned off by senior ONI men so Gates could reweld a strut the Otter had removed to widen the underwater entrance to his lair. When Gates surfaced, no physical evidence remained of the Otter's *Seehund* attack on the liner *Queen Mary*.

On a sunny November morning, two and a half months after that attack, Steven Gates and Cordi Grey watched the French transatlantic express liner *Normandie* depart her super-pier for the last time. Raising her had taken many weeks longer than the salvors had expected when they started pumping in August, but she was up at last, listing a couple of degrees and mud-scarred with long, horizontal streaks that marked the stages of her slow climb. But the splendid, naked hull looked like a vessel again.

Eighteen tugs gentled her into the Hudson. Thousands of people watched from the shore and from office buildings. Seagulls flocked ahead of her and sentimental tugboat captains told their crews that she was behaving like the queen she had always been.

'She's beautiful,' Cordi said.

'The new look in liners,' Gates replied with a thin smile. 'No superstructure and no engines.'

'But she's floating.'

Gates tightened his hand around hers, looked directly into her pale eyes. 'I love you.' He was astonished by her existence, as he had been those first moments they had met in the grand salon.

'But she'll never sail again,' he told her.

'Of course she will. They're going – '

'No.' And then he told her how the Otter and his Italian frogman had opened seams in watertight compartment sixteen, afraid that the salvors would raise the *Normandie* before they could attack. The leaks had stalled pumping for five weeks, during which time the hull had seesawed on a knob of rock, twisting her keel beyond redemption. The navy was towing her to dry dock, going through the motions of starting a refit, but the great liner was doomed for scrap.

'They'll break her up after the war's over. They won't waste the manpower now. They'll wait until people have forgotten her.'

Cordi shook her head. 'They may wait, Steven. But no one will forget her. Not ever.'

AUTHOR'S NOTE

I thank the kind people who helped me with research, answered questions, told me stories, and pointed me in fruitful directions – Manhattan during the war: Louise H. Lent, James Frye, Captain Donald Clark, and particularly my mother Lily K. Scott. Things British: Hartney Arthur, George Moveshon, Martin Eddison and Antonia White, who wrote a great wartime pamphlet, 'The BBC Goes to War'. Things French: Miss Laura Patrick. The intricacies of World War II and its spies: James O'Shea Wade, Rik and Anna de Leeuw, and books by David Kahn, Ladislas Farago, William Stevenson, Robert T. Elson, B. H. Liddell-Hart, Robert Graves, Alan Hodges, Vera Brittain, and Lothar-Günther Buchheim. Ships, shipping and salvage: John Maxtone-Graham; Captains Clark, Peter Driver, Torbjorn Hauge, Hartuig von Harling; Captain C. E. Lundin, US Navy; historians Terry Hughes, John Costello, Barrie Pitt; and Frank Pachesa, long-time neighbour of the Brooklyn Navy Yard; and especially the anonymous authors of the US Navy's report on the salvage of the *Normandie*. Miniature submarines: Captain Alberto Allievi. Thanks too are owed the editors and writers of the WPA *New York City Guide*, and the photographers Andreas Feininger, Berenice Abbot and Lewis W. Hine for a vivid sense of New York in the early years of World War II.

Nearly twenty years after the *Normandie* burned, the French launched a grand successor, the *France*. She too had a sad and early end when they withdrew her from transatlantic express service, still young. Happily, she has since been refitted, renamed *Norway*. My wife and I sailed on her from Oslo to New York. It was a stately two-engine

559

fuel-conservative crossing at a moderate speed more reminiscent of the twenties than the *Normandie*'s dazzling thirties, but the music was swing, and more than one passenger, high on martinis or nostalgia, was heard to call her the *Normandie*; for that, as well as the new life given the *Normandie*'s successor, Mr Knut Kloster of Norwegian Caribbean Lines deserves the thanks of all of us who still desire to go down to the sea in very large and gracious ships. Perhaps someone will do the same for the *United States*, languishing so long in mothballs that people forget she was once the American glory.

– Justin Scott
Newtown, Connecticut, 1982